Praise for Len Joy's

American Past Time

"This darkly nostalgic story is a study of an American family through good times and bad, engagingly set against major events from the 1950s to the '70s as issues of race simmer in the background…an expertly written examination of the importance of dreams to the human psyche.

A well-crafted novel that will particularly appeal to sports and history aficionados."

Kirkus Reviews

"Len Joy has an eye for the humble, utterly convincing details of family life: the look, feel, taste, and smell of work and school, meals and sport. This is mid-twentieth-century America seen neither through the gauze of nostalgia nor with easy cynicism but rather with a clear-eyed tenderness. Readers will care deeply, as I did, about the Stonemasons's inextricable triumphs and failures."

Pamela Erens – author of *The Virgins*

"Here is a "baseball novel" that transcends sport and offers an in-depth portrait of a family and an era.

The novel begins in Dancer Stonemason's perspective but later moves to his wife's and son's perspectives and the effect allows their perceptions and understandings to bump against each other, complicating ideas of truth and love. The scenes are well-drawn and well-edited, filled with dialogue that reads like spoken word (a feat!) and characters who are as complex as real people, with the same complex desires, anger, sadness, and hope as real people as well.

Themes of race, family, father-son relationships are present… But for me the most poignant moment happens near the end when a scene related to the end of the Vietnam War echoes against our present moment. Len Joy does write about a Past Time in America's history, but everything he details feels prescient now."

Kristiana Kahakauwila – author of *This is Paradise*

"…Len Joy's bracing debut novel that cuts deeply into the American social fabric and lays bare many of its myths.

Like his protagonist, Mr. Joy throws a few curves for the reader, although not many and none that can't be forgiven in this true and honest and unflinching portrait of America that should not be ignored."

Gary D. Wilson - author of *Sing, Ronnie Blue*

"…in Len Joy's nostalgic and moving first novel American Past Time, we follow the Stonemason family through the better part of three decades, exploring the unpredictable influences that family, society, and responsibility exert on one's life choices. In this impressive debut, Joy deftly and emotionally explores the many ways in which our relationships, hopes, and dreams can alter the course of our lives."

Mary Akers – author of *Bones of an Inland Sea*

"American Past Time is not only a baseball lovers' novel but one that history buffs will enjoy as well. Through a narrative voice reminiscent of times gone by, it covers the changing social structure in 20th Century America including racial tensions, Vietnam, and parenthood. Men of all ages will love this book."

Eileen Cronin – author of *Mermaid: A Memoir of Resilence*

"An all-American story that goes beyond the scope of the domestic and into the realm of history. A very engaging read."

Chinelo Okparanta – author of *Happiness, Like Water*

"I finished this book some weeks ago and wanted to wait to review it, to see if the story stayed with me. So many books I initially love I don't remember much about weeks or even days later.

This book held up. I've been thinking about why. It's not a hurtling read, nor is the writing so innovative your mind shatters. It's got baseball in it, and I hate baseball. However, the story is so clearly and simply told--the book doesn't get in the way of itself at all, and what you're left with is a clean-lined beauty. There's nothing extraneous, nothing sentimental, even though there are emotional moments. This book follows a family through the 50s and into near-contemporary times. One review I saw said that it was a good book for "history buffs," but I disagree. Okay, it might be fine for history buffs, but really it's a clear and poignant portrait of a time not only in American life, but in the life of a certain class of people. Working class people, lower middle class people. Many people of my parents' generation, who grew up with relatively simple aspirations. Dancer Stonemason, the father in this family, is the most ambitious of anyone we see closely, in that he has long-shot career goals... to pitch in the major leagues. Otherwise, it's a matter of raising a family, paying a mortgage on a modest house, getting your kids through high school and maybe college. These are humble but dignified people living through a period of enormous social and economic change, including the Civil Rights movement. Even though my parents aren't midwesterners or southerners, I felt I gained a window into their pre-me lives and expectations of their futures. None of which went the way people of that generation expected. This is about regular people, living in a small town yet nonetheless immersed in a larger social context that causes challenges for their daily lives. They work through it, over the course of decades, and so the book has a nice resolution without the reader having to feel hit over the head with THIS IS A RESOLUTION."

Claudia Putnam – author of *Wild Thing in Our Known World*

"Len Joy's American Past Time is a wonderful debut. Its protagonist, Dancer Stonemason, is a lifelong Midwesterner trying to live out his dreams as a pitcher in the St. Louis Cardinals organization. But with a growing family and an arm that no longer cooperates, plans change.

Told against the backdrop of the "idyllic" 50's and "turbulent" 60's, Joy's compelling prose and exceptional characters take the reader through an intriguing period in American history."

Roland Goity – editor of *WIPs: Works in Progress*

"American Past Time is a good story well told. In one of his interviews, the author, Len Joy, speaks admiringly of the spare style of Ray Carver and Ernest Hemingway. One can see it in his writing too. The novel is set against a backdrop of the 1950s, 60s, and early 70s and many memorable events of that period figure into the plot, tangentially if not head-on. The story moves crisply forward and pulls the reader along with it, especially for someone who lived in those times. It's a very good read."

Jim Tilley – author of *Cruising at Sixty to Seventy: Poems and Essay*

"American Past Time tells a riveting story, one that draws readers "of a certain age" into sharp and ambivalent memories of the 1950s, 1960s, and 1970s. For those of us who passed through these decades in America, the book rings true to our memories. The past is neither romanticized nor reduced to a "simpler time" of relative innocence. The characters face the challenges of the day with courage and, at times, with the sardonic humor that lives on in my own memories – "Candy" throws a "Draft Lottery Party," while my own friends, in 1968, threw for our graduating senior men a party we called "Viet Nam À Go-Go." This is a compelling book, faithful to its subject and evocative of its time. For those who did not know the mid-twentieth century first-hand, this book provides insight not only on the struggles of their parents' generation, but also on the evolution of the world in which Americans live today."

Constance Groh

"Life is a series of choices, a series of dreams, each impacting the dynamics of relationships in complex ways.

Set in the 1950s--1970s, this historical novel about a complicated family impacted by the father's decisions and dreams is fast paced, clearly written and quite relevant. Bits of history are ambient reminders of what era the reader has been submerged into. The civil rights movement, memorable baseball names and moments, pop culture of the 1960s, Vietnam war. Len gets under the skin of his characters and succeeds in placing the reader right there-- in the small town world of high school games and minor league baseball, the heated drudgery of the foundry, the smokey filled bars, the blue collar culture. I felt that I was right there in the middle of it all.

Don't miss this book. Easy to buy, easy to read. You'll finish it fast because you won't want to leave these characters."

Debbie Ann Eis – author of *Lament for the Coons*

"The story was set against a backdrop of a number of major events in American history, such as the moon landing, the Vietnam war, the assassination of Kennedy, etc.

This was most definitely one of those books that I did not want to end. I found myself always wanting to know what happened next to the characters. I would have been happy had the book been double the length.

I would recommend this book to, well, just about anyone really. I enjoyed this immensely."

Julian Froment book review blog

"…a timeless classic."

Jersey Girl Book Reviews

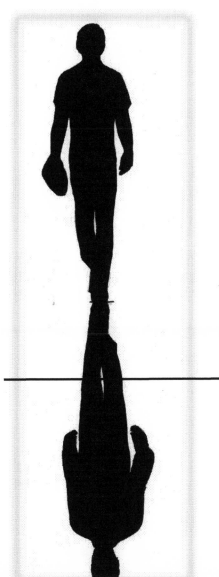

American Past Time

A Novel

By

Len Joy

Silhouette illustration by Nicole Joy

ISBN 978-0-9916659-0-7

First Edition: April 2014

10 9 8 7 6 5 4 3 2 1

Printed in the U.S.A

Hark!

Hark! New Era
Publishing, LLC

A version of Chapter 1 first appeared in the literary journal _The Writing Disorder_ www.thewritingdisorder.com
www.facebook.com/thewritingdisorder

AMERICAN PAST TIME
Copyright © 2014 by Len Joy

eBook and other digital content published by Hark! New Era Publishing, LLC. For digital permission requests, write to the publisher Hark! New Era Publishing at staff@harknewerapublishing.com
www.harknewerapublishing.com

Hark! New Era Publishing name and logo are trademark of Hark! New Era Publishing, LLC

Cover design and layout by Ellie Bockert Ausburger
www.creativedigitalstudios.com

For Suzanne

Dancer

1

September 5, 1953

Dancer Stonemason drove through Maple Springs headed for Rolla. His left hand rested gentle on the steering wheel, and in his pitching hand he held a baseball – loose and easy – like he was shooting craps. The ball took the edge off the queasy feeling he got on game days. His son, Clayton, sat beside him and made sputtering engine noises as he gripped an imaginary steering wheel, while Dede, Dancer's wife, stared out the window with other things on her mind.

They cruised down Main Street, past the Tastee-Freeze and Dabney's Esso Station and the Post Office and the First National Bank of Maple Springs and Crutchfield's General Store. At the town's only traffic light, he turned left toward the highway. At the edge of town they passed the colored Baptist Church with its neatly-tended grid of white crosses and gravestones under a gnarled willow. The graveyard reminded him of the cemetery up north, near Festus, where his mother was buried with the rest of the Dancer family. She'd been gone fifteen years now and some days Dancer had trouble remembering what she looked like.

Across from the Baptists, A-1 Auto Parts blanketed the landscape with acres of junked automobiles. His father's Buick was out there somewhere. Walt Stonemason had been a whisky-runner for Cecil Danforth. He knew every back road and trail in southern Missouri and there wasn't a revenue agent in the state who could catch him.

At his father's funeral Cecil told Dancer that Walt was the best damn whiskey runner he ever had. Dancer wanted to ask Cecil if his dad was so damn good how'd he manage to run that Roadmaster smack into a walnut tree with no one chasing him. But Dancer knew better than to ask Cecil those kinds of questions.

They turned north onto Highway 60, and the '39 Chevy coughed and bucked as he shifted into third. As he cruised north, Dancer's fingers glided over the smooth cowhide of the baseball as he read the seams and adjusted his grip from fastball, to curveball, to changeup. He had a hand built for pitching – a pancake-sized palm and long, tapered fingers that hid the ball from the batter for that extra heartbeat.

It was the Saturday before Labor Day, and Dancer's team, the Rolla Rebels, was hosting the Joplin Miners. Rolla was only an hour's drive from Maple Springs, but Dancer had his family on the road early. This was going to be a special game. Not for his team – the Rebels were in third place going nowhere – but because today would be Clayton's first baseball game. The first time he'd see his dad pitch.Dancer was eight when his mom got sick. He went to live with Cecil's brother Clem and his wife Ruthie. They had nine kids so one more didn't matter much. One day in late May his dad showed up at the schoolhouse and told Dancer they were going up to St. Louis to see the Cardinals play.

The Cardinals' stadium was packed with more people than Dancer had seen in his whole life. They sat in the upper deck behind home plate. Dizzy Dean pitched for the Cardinals and the crowd cheered madly every time he took the mound. In his last at bat he hit a foul ball that was headed straight for Dancer. He stood and cupped his hands to catch it, but at the last moment the man in front of him leaped up to catch the ball. It splatted against his palms and the man yelped as the baseball rolled into the aisle. The usher retrieved the ball and handed it to Dancer.

Dancer fell asleep on the ride home. He woke up when his father stopped the car in front of Grandpa Dancer's house. His father told him that his mom had passed, but Dancer already knew.

The hot-towel Missouri heat, which had suffocated them through July and August, had finally retreated to Arkansas. A few wispy clouds hung on the horizon, and the air was light and fresh. Dede's head lolled backwards, her eyes closed as she let the cool wind from the open window billow her white cotton dress. She only wore that dress to church and on special occasions. It didn't get much use.

Her short blonde hair, which wrapped around her ears and curled down the nape of her neck, was still damp from her morning shower. As Dancer had attempted to shave, she flung open the shower curtain and wiggled her ass, letting the hot water pelt her breasts. "Soap me, honey. Do my back," she said.

"You're getting water on the floor," Dancer said.

She glanced over her shoulder at him. "If I squint really hard, you look just like Gary Cooper."

3

"He's taller. Close the curtain."

Water was pooling on the floor. Dancer took the washcloth and soaped her back and her little butt. As he brought his hand up between her legs, she reached around and slipped her hand into his boxer shorts.

"Come on in, the water's fine," she said.

Dede knew he couldn't fool around on game day, but she didn't care. She could never get enough, and now they had a problem.

Traffic was light, and Dancer had the Chevy cruising along at close to sixty. Beside him, Clayton pressed his foot down on a phantom gas pedal, and his sputtering engine revved into a high-pitched whine. He drove hard, just like his whiskey-running grandfather. He reminded Dancer of his father. The wheat-colored hair, the dirt tan, and the need to race everywhere even when there was no place to go.

Dancer glanced over at Dede. She had a crooked mouth and a gap between her two front teeth that he hadn't noticed when they first met because of her eyes. Her eyes were big, wild, and crazy-blue. They had met when Dancer was a senior. Even though she was two years younger, she had been the one to make the first move. He'd never been with another girl, but Dede made it easy. She knew too much for a fifteen-year-old.

But now, with her face half-covered by her wind-tossed hair, she appeared so innocent. She didn't look like she was two months pregnant. Her belly was still flat, and her breasts hadn't swelled, not like they had when Clayton was on his way.

Maybe the doctor was wrong.

After Clayton was born, Dancer had found an offseason job at the Caterpillar plant – parts inspector – a dollar an hour and boring as hell. He wasn't cut out for factory work, but they needed the money. When he moved up to the Rolla Rebels, the pay was better, and he thought he'd be done with the factory, but Dede fell in love with the red brick house on the hill east of town. So they bought the house, and then he had a wife, a baby, a house, a mortgage, and another offseason back in the factory inspecting parts. And now with a new baby on the way, he'd have to work overtime just for them to survive.

"Hey Dad, is that the ballpark?" Clayton asked. He pointed at a well-groomed Little League field that was in a clearing surrounded by spruce and poplars.

"No. It's just over the hill, beyond the fairgrounds."

Mr. Seymour Crutchfield, the owner of the Rebels, was a merchant. His father had built a general store in downtown Maple Springs fifty years ago, and Seymour had taken the idea of that general store and built stores all over Missouri and Arkansas. When he expanded into Rolla, he bought the Rolla Rebels baseball team because their stadium was sitting on the land he wanted to develop. He built his store, renamed the stadium, and hired his son-in-law, Doc Evans, to manage the team.

Clayton creased the brim of the Cardinals cap Dancer had given him and leaned forward in his seat to get a better look. The hat was several sizes too big, so Dede had bobby-pinned the back so it would stay on.

5

"Are you going to strike them all out, Dad?"

"Your daddy can't strike everyone out. He's not Superman," Dede said. She winked at Dancer.

Dancer squeezed the ball into Clayton's small hands. "I'm going to try."

As they crossed into Phelps County and the outskirts of Rolla, the woods and small lakes that had lined the highway for the last twenty miles gave way to cheap motels, filling stations, and car dealerships. The Phelps County Fairgrounds, with its huge parking lot and grandstand, stretched along the east side of the highway for nearly half a mile. Beyond the fairgrounds and next to the brand new Crutchfield General Store was Crutchfield Stadium, home of the Rolla Rebels.

Dancer pulled the car up to the box office. "They'll have your tickets here. See you after the game."

"Not so fast, mister," Dede said. She leaned across Clayton and kissed Dancer hard on the lips.

"Mom, you're squishing me," Clayton said.

As they slid out of the car, Dede leaned back in the window. "Now don't wear yourself out," she said. And then she giggled and skipped away with Clayton to pick up their tickets.

2

Dancer parked close to the centerfield gate where all the players entered the ballpark. In centerfield, Mr. Seymour Crutchfield, looking like an undertaker in his black wool suit and bow-tie, was shouting directions to one of the Negro groundskeepers who was on a ladder applying a patch to the Crutchfield General Store sign that covered twenty yards of the center field wall.

"A little higher, boy. And move it to the right. A little more. That's it."

The sign had read, "Over 100 stores in Missouri, Kansas, and Arkansas." Now the "100" had been covered up and replaced with a "150." When Dancer had joined Rolla, the store count had been fifty.

Doc Evans stood beside his father-in-law, puffing on a cigar and looking impatiently at his watch while Crutchfield finished his instructions. When Doc spotted Dancer, he waved him over.

As Dancer approached, Mr. Crutchfield turned to him. "Look at that, Dancer. One hundred fifty stores. Next year there'll be over two hundred. Y'all be able to shop at Crutchfield's no matter where you live in Missouri."

Dancer was surprised Crutchfield knew his name. "That's really something, Mr. Crutchfield."

"Yes, it is, son. Yes, it is." He looked back at the sign again and frowned. "Hey, boy!" he said to the groundskeeper who had started to fold up the ladder. "Could you clean those bird droppings off the corner of the sign? Right there by the 'C'?" He pointed to the big "C" in Crutchfield, then turned and faced Dancer again. "Wilbur has some things to discuss with you, so I'll let you two get down to baseball." He extended his hand. "Good luck, son. It's been a pleasure." He shook hands like a preacher, holding on just long enough to make Dancer uncomfortable, and then he walked over to get a closer look at his sign.

Doc Evans stared at his father-in-law walking away and slowly shook his head. "Just stop in my office before you go out for warm-ups. We can talk then." As he walked off toward right field, still shaking his head, it sounded to Dancer like he muttered, "Bird shit."

3

Something was happening. In the three years he had been with the team, Mr. Crutchfield hadn't said ten words to Dancer. And Doc never wanted to talk to anyone before a game.

The Joplin Miners were taking batting practice and Billy Pardue, the Rebels' veteran catcher, was on the top step of the dugout studying them. The Rebels were either young hotshots on their way up, or old-timers on their way down. Billy was an old-timer, but he had had his day. Three years in the big leagues. He knew his baseball, and he shared everything with Dancer—even showed him how to throw a tobbacy-spit pitch. When thrown properly, the ball would squirt out of the pitcher's hand and waggle its way to the plate like a leaf in a windstorm. It was, in Billy's words, "a fucking unhittable pitch." But Dancer couldn't stomach tobacco-chewing, and he figured with his fastball, he didn't need to cheat. Not too much anyway.

Billy spit his tobacco juice in the direction of Dancer's feet. "Get your ass out here as soon as you change. We got work to do."

"Doc wants to see me first."

Billy grinned. "That ain't going to take long. Get a move on."

The locker room was a concrete bunker that even on the hottest days was cool and damp. It smelled of liniment, sweat, mildew, and Doc's cigars. The only player who had arrived before Dancer was Ron Bilko, who sat on the bench next to the row of banged-up metal lockers that lined the front wall. Bilko was in his underwear, eating a hot dog, and studying a crumpled issue of *The Sporting News* as if it were a foreclosure notice. Next to him on the bench was a cardboard tray with a half-dozen more hot dogs.

"What's the problem? Someone take away your homerun title?" Dancer asked as he opened the locker next to Bilko.

Bilko smacked the paper down on the bench. "Goddamn Enos Slaughter." He grabbed another hot dog.

Enos Slaughter was the right fielder for the St. Louis Cardinals. The one man standing between Bilko and the major leagues. The last few months a man couldn't have a conversation with Bilko without Goddamn Enos Slaughter joining them.

"Slaughter's still playing?" Dancer said, grinning. Dancer and Bilko were the top minor league prospects in the Cardinals organization. At the end of the season, most of the major league clubs brought up their promising young players to give the veterans a rest and check out the prospects. But the Cardinals' skipper, Eddy Stanky, didn't want a player if he didn't have a spot for him. The Cardinals had an all-star outfield led by Stan Musial, Slaughter, and a solid corps of pitchers that never seemed to get injured. There was no place for Dancer or Bilko.

Bilko showed Dancer the stat box for the Cardinals. "Look at that. Slaughter's batting .294. Thirty-seven goddamn years old. That son of a bitch ain't ever going to retire."

Dancer flipped the paper over to the minor league stats. "Siebern's got twenty-seven homeruns – only three behind you. He could hit that many today."

Norm Siebern was a power-hitting lefty for the Joplin Miners. Twice this year, Siebern had smashed Dancer's fastball out of the park.

Bilko picked up another hot dog. "I ain't worried. Norm Siebern's not going to hit three homeruns off Dancer Stonemason, because after the second homerun, I expect you to plant your fastball right between his numbers. Give that son of a bitch a decimal point."

"That's not a bad idea."

Bilko winked. "Have a hot dog, Dancer. Put some meat on those bones." Bilko pushed the tray toward Dancer.

Dancer shook his head and grabbed the uniform hanging from the door of his locker. "No thanks." He was always too nervous to eat before he pitched.

The rest of the team had arrived. Bilko set the hot dog tray on a table in the middle of the locker room floor and yelled, "Any of you yahoos want a dog?" A minute later the tray was empty.

Dancer tugged on the grey pullover jersey with the two rows of decorative buttons running down the front. It was supposed to look like a Confederate officer's longcoat. He sniffed the armpit. "Shit, these still haven't been washed."

Bilko grinned. "Season's almost over. Crutchfield probably figures he can hold out until we're done. Save a few bucks. Is Dede coming today?"

"Already here. We brought Clayton. He's never seen me pitch."

"You're a lucky man, Dancer. Got a good woman and a boy who looks up to you. Ain't nothing better than that."

"Dede says we're going to have another one."

"Holy shit, Dancer!" Bilko jumped up and thumped Dancer on the back. "That's great. When's she due?"

"March or April. Probably right in the middle of spring training." Dancer pulled on his gray Rebel cap. Ever since he'd got that GI-style crewcut last month, his hat didn't sit right. "Can't afford another kid right now. Hard to get by on meal-money and a hundred bucks a week."

Bilko put his hand on Dancer's shoulder. "I hear the Cardinals get ten dollars a day just for meals. When I play for the Cards, I'm going to have a T-bone every night."

Dancer readjusted his cap and checked himself in Bilko's mirror. The sun had turned his light brown hair almost blond.

"You making yourself look pretty for old Billy?"

"Doc wants to see me."

Bilko smiled.

12

"What's going on, Bilko?"

Bilko shook his head, but kept grinning. "Maybe he's tired of you always bitching about the laundry service."

4

Doc was in his office, feet propped on his desk, reading the *New York Times*. Before every game he studied that Yankee paper like it was the Bible or *The Sporting News*. Doc was from someplace back east. He knew his baseball, but he was skipper because he'd married Mr. Seymour Crutchfield's daughter, Melissa. He wasn't really a Doc either, but he wore wire-rim glasses, and his gray hair was always Brylcreemed. What with the glasses, the gray hair, the newspaper-reading, and the rich wife, he seemed a whole lot smarter than the rest of the boys, so they all called him Doc.

Doc had been a pretty fair shortstop before the war. He had an invitation to spring training with the Tigers back in '42, but enlisted instead. He was part of the 45th Infantry Division that landed in Sicily in July '43. Got his right arm shot to hell just outside Salerno. That was it for his baseball career. There wasn't much demand for left-handed shortstops.

Doc motioned for Dancer to take a seat and then kept reading the paper as though he'd forgotten about him. Dancer tried not to fidget. Billy would be pissed if he didn't get out there while the Miners were taking batting practice. Finally, Doc folded up the paper and placed it on his desk.

"I don't know what this world's coming to, son."

"Yes, sir."

"Eisenhower's a damn fool to settle for a tie in Korea. Truman would have never let that happen."

"No, sir."

"And look at this. Russians just exploded an H-bomb." He poked his finger at the headline.

"Yes, sir."

"That's serious business." He shook his head. "Do you have children, son?"

"Yes, sir. My boy Clayton just turned four, and we got another one on the way."

Doc took off his glasses and pinched the bridge of his nose. "You aren't Catholic, are you?"

"No, sir. My mama was a Baptist. Dad wasn't much of anything. They both passed, sir."

Doc gave a sympathy nod. "How you going to feed a family of four on what we're paying you?"

"Well, I was kind of hoping..." Dancer caught himself. Doc wouldn't think hoping was any kind of plan.

"You're planning to make it to the big leagues, right? Get that major league paycheck. That boy Mickey Mantle just signed a new contract – seventeen thousand five hundred dollars. That's a lot of beans."

"Goddamn Yankees."

"I had a call from Mr. Stanky this morning." Doc pulled out a cigar and sniffed it up and down. He acted as if the Cardinals manager called him every day. "Haddix has a sore arm. They're thinking about shutting him down. Cards ain't going nowhere."

Doc bit off the end of the cigar. Dancer crept to the edge of his chair. Doc could spend ten minutes farting around with his goddamn cigars.

"So?" Dancer asked, his voice breaking.

"So they might need you for the Labor Day doubleheader Monday."

Dancer jumped up. "Holy shit! The Cardinals!" His spikes almost slipped out from under him, and he had to grab Doc's desk to keep from falling.

"Try not to kill yourself before you get there, son."

Dancer sat back in his seat. "But I'm still pitching today, right? My boy's out there. He's counting on me."

Doc cocked his head to one side. "I can't send you up to St. Louis with your arm dragging around your ankles. Mr. Stanky would rip me a new asshole." He puffed harder on the cigar. "Tell you what. You can go three innings. That'll keep you fresh enough so you can still pitch in two days if Stanky needs you."

As Dancer ran back through the locker room, he almost collided with Bilko. "Doc like the way you looked?" Bilko asked, grinning.

16

"You asshole. You knew?"

"Eh, I hear things." He smiled. "Congratulations, Dancer. Make us hillbillies proud." He clasped Dancer on the shoulder. "But don't keep Billy waiting."

The Joplin Miners were still taking batting practice when Dancer joined Billy in the dugout.

Billy pointed to the umpire out by home plate. "That's Lester Froehlich. He's got a low strike zone. Froehlich will give you a pitch down by the ankles, but anything above the waist he's calling a ball. So keep the goddamn ball low."

After he finished on Froehlich, Billy ran through the lineup, reminding Dancer where he wanted him to pitch each batter. Dancer wasn't paying attention – he was far away, trying on his new uniform with those two red Cardinals perched on the baseball bat. The same uniform Dizzy Dean had worn.

Billy backhanded Dancer's hat off his head.

"Listen, boy. I know you got the call. You earned it, and you're going to be aces. But right now we got a game to play. You want to stay up in the Bigs, remember this – respect the goddamn game. Play every game like it's your last."

"I'll always respect the game, Billy."

Billy picked up Dancer's hat and put it back on his head. "I know you will, kid."

5

While they sang the national anthem, Dancer scanned the crowd and found Dede and Clayton in the third row behind first base. He got a warm feeling thinking about Dede's morning shower. He was half-sorry he'd passed up the opportunity. But tonight they'd have a good time, especially after he gave her the news. The St. Louis Cardinals. Next year he'd make eight grand, maybe more. Next year they could afford all those kids.

As Dancer trotted to the pitcher's mound, there was an easy buzz to the crowd, as though the fresh-scrubbed families from Maple Springs, the gang from Paddy's Lounge, the hillbillies from Cabool, and the Klansmen from Mountain View had all set aside their differences and were out to enjoy the last weekend of the summer. The afternoon sky was a great-to-be-alive blue, and the air had a trace of autumn crispness. It was warm enough to work up a sweat, but not so hot Dancer would be worn out after three innings.

Dancer nestled the baseball in his glove as Billy signaled for a fastball. He gripped the ball across the seams, torqued his body so he was almost facing second base, and whip-cracked his right arm toward the plate. The ball exploded into Billy's glove for a called strike.

Dancer walked off the mound to catch Billy's return toss. As he headed back to the mound, he rubbed the ball down and stole a glance over to the stands. Clayton waved at him, and Dancer could see him yelling something to his mother.

He struck out the first two batters on six pitches. The third batter was Norm Siebern. Billy made a target wide off the plate and gave him a thumbs up, meaning he wanted the ball high. The pitch was chin-level, and Siebern swung and missed. The next two pitches were even higher, and he missed those too. Nine pitches – three strikeouts.

In the bottom of the first, with two men on, Bilko hit his thirty-first homerun of the year giving Dancer and the Rebels a three run lead.

Dancer cruised through the second and third innings without a ball hit out of the infield. He was in a groove – his fastball overpowering, his curveball buckling the batters' knees. As he jogged toward the dugout at the end of the third inning, he spotted Clayton jumping up and down on his seat waving his cap. Dancer had thrown only forty pitches. A couple more innings wouldn't tire him out.

Doc greeted him as he returned to the dugout. "Nice work, son. Bullpen can take it from here."

"Don't take me out. I haven't even broke a sweat. I got plenty left."

Doc sighed. "What do you think, Billy?"

Billy was taking off his shin guards. Dancer sat down next to him. "Can't stop with a perfect game going. That's not respecting the game."

Billy wrinkled his nose. "You are a long fucking way from a perfect game."

"Still," Dancer said.

Billy shrugged and glanced over at Doc. "Not my call, Skip. That's why you get the captain's pay." He went back to unhitching his shin guards.

Doc stood up and pointed his finger at Dancer. "As soon as they get a hit, I'm pulling you out."

Bilko hit another homerun in the third to give the Rebels a five run lead. When Siebern came up again in the fourth inning, Dancer waved off Billy's sign for a curveball and Siebern smashed it over the right field fence, inches wide of the foul pole. Billy raced to the mound and told Dancer if he had any fondness for his teeth, he best not shake off any more signs. Dancer didn't think he was joking about the teeth. Billy called for a curveball, and Siebern popped it up for the third out.

By the fifth inning, his fastball had lost its pop, and there was a hot spot on his index finger that burned whenever he threw the breaking ball. But somehow Dancer kept getting them out. When he took a seat on the bench after the sixth inning, he was all alone. Nobody dared talk to him. Doc just stared at his feet, shaking his head and mumbling. Didn't even smoke his cigar. Doc couldn't take him out with a perfect game on the line. And Dancer would still be able to pitch on Monday. He was young and strong. Three days rest was for old men.

As he walked out to the mound for the seventh inning the crowd was eerily quiet, as if they were afraid that cheering might upset the baseball gods. The first two batters in the seventh worked full counts – Froehlich wasn't calling anything above the belt a strike – but Dancer got them both to fly out.

Norm Siebern was up again.

Billy Pardue called for a curveball, and Siebern hit it over the right field fence, but again, just to the right of the foul pole. There was a collective gasp of relief from the crowd as they settled back into their seats. Billy called for a changeup, and Siebern hit a bullet over the first basemen's head. Dancer scuffed the mound in disgust, but Froehlich signaled foul. Billy called time.

"You ain't fooling him, kid. Throw this the way I taught you, and let's go sit down." He handed Dancer the ball, a glob of tobacco spit nestled between the seams. Dancer wiped the sweat off his brow and gripped the ball with his fingers between the seams like Billy had shown him. The ball floated toward home, and Siebern smiled as he stepped into the pitch, but as it reached the plate, it dive-bombed into the turf. Siebern missed it by two feet.

In the eighth, the Miners batted as though they had somewhere else they wanted to be. Seven pitches and Dancer was out of the inning. Bilko walked over and sat down next to him on the bench. The first player in the last three innings, other than Billy, to even acknowledge his existence. "No one's going to think less of you if you stop right now. Shit man, it's the Cardinals. I'd give my left nut to get that call."

"This game is mine. I ain't quitting now."

Bilko squeezed Dancer's neck. "That's all I wanted to hear. Take 'em down, buddy."

Dancer massaged his arm as he walked to the mound for the ninth inning. It was sore, but it was a good sore. Froehlich stood at home plate, hands on hips, staring at him. Dancer offered a nod, sort of humble-like, as he reached the pitcher's mound. If Froehlich noticed, he didn't show it.

First batter, Wagner, had struck out twice on curveballs. Billy called for another curve. Dancer's pitch missed the plate by five feet. The hot spot on his finger had become a blister, and the blister had popped. Billy called time and walked slowly to the mound.

"I can't throw my curve," Dancer said, his voice tight.

Billy laughed and thumped Dancer on the back like he'd just told him a dirty joke. "Don't look at your hand. Smile. Work the corners – in out, high, low. It's the bottom of the lineup. Just three more outs. This is the game that counts, Dancer."

Billy walked back to the plate like he was on a Sunday stroll. Laughing and joking with Froehlich and Wagner about Dancer's wild pitch. He called for a fast ball inside and Wagner smashed it deep to right, but the wind kept it in the park and Bilko caught it at the wall.

Heinz, the Miners slick fielding shortstop, was the eighth batter. Heinz couldn't hit his weight, and he didn't weigh much. Billy signaled fastball and Heinz squared around and bunted the ball to the right of Dancer, toward the shortstop. Dancer dove headlong and speared the ball before it could get by him. He pivoted on his knees and flung the ball sidearm to first base. Heinz was out by a step.

Billy had run down the first base line to back up the play. As he trotted back to home, he glared at the Miners. "You're down five runs – swing the goddamn bats."

Dancer rubbed down the baseball and waited as the field announcer introduced the pinch hitter. "Now batting for the pitcher, number thirty-three, former slugger with the Cincinnati Redlegs, Mister Connie Ryan!"

Billy called time and sprinted to the mound. "I've played against Ryan. He's a dead pull hitter. Likes the low ball, so try to keep it up out of his wheelhouse." He pounded the ball into Dancer's glove. "This is the game, Dancer."

Billy gave him a target off the outside corner, and Dancer's pitch was knee-high, three inches wide of the plate. Ryan took the pitch for a ball. He stepped closer to the plate. Dancer's next pitch was in the same location, and Ryan drove it out of the park, foul by ten feet. He stood at home plate admiring the flight of the ball. Froehlich threw Dancer a new ball, and Ryan stepped back into the batter's box. He took a slow, deliberate swing and pointed his bat at Dancer's head. Ryan didn't respect him. Dizzy Dean would have never let a batter get away with that.

Dancer nodded at Billy and unleashed a fastball right at Ryan's chin. He hit the turf like he'd been shot, but as he was going down, the ball hit his bat and bounced harmlessly foul down the first base line.

Billy cackled, "Hey, Connie! I think the kid wants your ugly mug off the plate."

Ryan dug in, but this time a respectful six inches farther back. Dancer caught the outside corner with a waist-high fast ball, but Froehlich called it a ball.

Two balls, two strikes.

Dancer came back with a change-up, and Ryan started to swing, but at the last moment held up. Froehlich called the pitch high.

Full count.

Dancer stared in at the plate. Ryan wasn't smiling anymore. The crowd was so loud he couldn't hear himself breathe. Billy signaled for a fastball, Doc perched on the top of the dugout steps, unlit cigar clenched in his teeth, Dede stood with her hands in front of her face, and Clayton jumped up and down on his seat waving his cotton candy like it was a flag.

Dancer exhaled through his teeth and threw with everything he had left.

As soon as he released the ball, he knew it was a bad pitch. Right down the middle, but chest high. Billy came half out of his crouch to catch the ball, then pulled it down ever so slightly and held it there. Ryan dropped his bat and headed for first.

"Strike threeee!" Froehlich croaked as he punched the air with his left fist.

The next thing Dancer knew, Billy had him in a bear-hug and all the guys were grabbing him, pounding him on the back. A swarm of teammates carried him toward the first base seats. Dede was in the aisle with Clayton and he lifted them both over the rail. Dancer's throat ached as he kissed away Dede's tears. Her tousled hair tickled his face as she wrapped her arms around him. He wanted to tell her how much he loved her and how things were going to get better and better, but he could hardly breathe.

Together they hoisted Clayton on to Dancer's shoulders. Clayton clung to his dad's neck with cotton-candy sticky hands as the three of them paraded along the fence from first base to third base while the crowd chanted, "Dancer! Dancer! Dancer!"

6

The next day, Dancer was on his back porch soaking his hand in ice water when Doc pulled into the driveway in his navy blue Mercury cruiser. Doc smiled, an unnatural look for him, as he walked over to Dancer. "How's the hand?"

Dancer jumped up from his chair and wiped his hand dry with Dede's dishtowel. "It's great. Just soaking out some of the soreness."

Doc stepped on to the porch. "Let me see."

Dancer held out his hand. There was a nickel-sized open sore on the pitching side of his index finger. Doc frowned. "You pitched a great game, Dancer. You're going to remember that game for the rest of your life. Hell. We all are."

"What about the Cardinals?"

Doc shook his head. "You can't pitch with your hand like that."

"I can still throw my fastball."

"Son, it's the big leagues. You got a good fastball, but you ain't no goddamn Bob Feller. Without a curve they'll kill you. I can't do that to you."

Dancer hung his head and stared at his wounded finger. Doc patted him on the shoulder. "I'm telling the Cardinals you can't pitch on Labor Day. They'll probably bring up that kid from Columbus."

"Then what?"

"You'll get your shot. Next year. Take care of that hand."

It was a perfect game. No one could take that from him. Or from Clayton. No matter what else happened they would always have that game. That moment. And Doc was right. He was young. He'd get another chance.

7

July 1956 – three years later

The only good thing about the used '51 Bel Air Dancer bought the previous year was that he never had to change the oil. It burned a quart a week and leaked enough that he had stopped parking it in the garage. He just let the oil seep into the gravel driveway. Every Saturday morning, he would top off the crankcase and rake the driveway, mixing up the oily gravel with the clean. Today he had poured in his last can of oil, but was still down a quart. He figured he better make a trip to Crutchfield's for another case before he drove up to Rolla again.

The sun had been up for an hour, and the temperature was already pushing eighty. The air was so heavy with moisture that nothing evaporated. A layer of sweat coated Dancer's body like he'd been painted. He rubbed his brow with his T-shirt and wiped his oily hands on his denim workpants. He scanned the yard for the newspaper.

Every day during baseball season, he would check the newspaper to see how the Cardinals pitcher had performed, secretly hoping he had been shelled. The paper wasn't in the yard, or on the driveway, or buried in the smoke bush that guarded the entrance to the seldom-used front door. Dancer walked to the curb and peered down Hill Street. The paperboy was slowly pedaling his bike up the hill, flinging a newspaper into each driveway as he meandered leisurely from one side of the road to the other.

Dancer rubbed his shoulder. Ever since last week when Doc had called him into his office and said he was moving him to the bullpen, his arm had been pain free. He poked and prodded around the shoulder to see if he could find the sore spot. Nothing. He made a throwing motion, and there was not a hint of the soreness that had plagued him for the last three years. It was as though the demotion to the bullpen had miraculously cured him.

The paperboy had disappeared into one of the cul-de-sacs. He wouldn't make it to Dancer's driveway for another fifteen minutes. The Rolla Rebels were playing Des Moines tonight, and with Dancer's new status, he needed to be ready for every game. But fifteen minutes of throwing balls against his garage wall wouldn't tire him out. And if the pain were really gone for good, maybe Doc would put him back in the rotation.

The problem with his arm had developed the spring after the perfect game. That offseason before Jimmy was born, Dancer had gone back to the Caterpillar plant as a parts inspector. But when Percy Thacker, who ran the Caterpillar foundry, offered him a better paying job pouring steel, he jumped at the opportunity. There was a lot more physical labor in the foundry, and by the end of his five months, Dancer had built up his arm and back muscles. He was almost ten pounds heavier when he reported for spring training. Doc thought the extra muscle might have thrown off his mechanics.

He headed back up the driveway and grabbed the gunny sack of old baseballs he had stashed on the back porch. The porch had been built last year when Dancer was sidelined for two months with the mysterious sore arm. It was really just a deck, and now that Jimmy was walking, Dancer needed to add a railing to keep him from tumbling into the rosebushes Dede had planted around the perimeter.

Dancer had been pitching at the brick wall of the garage ever since they had moved into the house. There was something about throwing a baseball that made him feel good. It relaxed him – allowed him to escape the kids, and Dede, and their financial problems. When his arm first got sore, he had tried to stop. But after a couple weeks he was back in the yard pitching. His concession to the pain was to throw easy, like a batting practice pitcher. Dancer walked out to the bare spot, pretended he was facing Stan Musial, and went into his windup. The ball thudded against the bricks and rolled halfway back to Dancer. He hitched his shoulder and gave his bicep a quick massage. His arm felt loose and alive.

Last offseason, just to be safe, he decided not to return to the foundry. Instead, he went back to his old job as a parts inspector. The pay was a dollar less an hour, and with two growing boys, a mortgage, house repairs, and a car that always needed fixing, they were digging themselves a big financial hole.

And now, with the move to the bullpen, the financial pressure was even greater. Not many minor league relief pitchers made it to the majors. But Doc said that would be changing. He told Dancer that in the big leagues, relief pitchers were no longer just mediocre starters. He wanted Dancer to work on developing a knuckleball like Hoyt Wilhelm. Wilhelm was 29 when he made it to the majors in '52 and he won fifteen games as a reliever. No one could hit his knuckleball. It fluttered and dipped a lot like Billy Pardue's tobacco juice spitter. Dancer could have really used Billy's help with the knuckleball, but Billy Pardue got the cancer last spring and was gone before the World Series.

Dancer gathered up the balls and repeated the process, harder this time. Now the balls rolled back almost to his feet. Sweat dripped from his brow, and his T-shirt clung to his chest. He grabbed another ball out of the sack and clutched it the way Doc had shown him. He pressed his middle and index fingernails into the seams and braced the ball with his thumb. The idea was to throw with the same arm speed as the fastball. But because of the grip, if he released it correctly, the ball wouldn't have any spin, and that would make it flutter and dip.

He had been working on that pitch all week. When he got it right, it worked like a charm. But when he flubbed the release, the ball spun up to the plate with a big sign on it saying, "Hit me." He wound up and threw the knuckleball. It rotated so slowly Dancer could see the seams.   It dropped sharply and hit the dirt in front of the garage. Dancer tried three more pitches with the same result. He smiled.

The screen door to the kitchen snapped open, and Dede walked on to the porch wiping her hands on a dishtowel. "Maybe you should move closer," she said. She shaded her eyes with her hand, but Dancer could still see a mischievous twinkle. She had on her dingy white halter top and the faded khaki shorts that used to hang on her before she had kids. Now there was a pinch of flesh around her waistband. But just a pinch.

"No one could hit that ball," Dancer said

"Glad I'm not your catcher. Kelly Doyle called."

31

Dancer grabbed another ball and tried to adjust from the fastball to the knuckleball grip without looking at the ball. "What's he want?"

Dede shrugged. "I don't know. I told him you were walking Clayton over to their place. Tammy's going to take the boys to the cartoons. Kelly said he'd talk to you when you came over."

Clayton's best friend was Alex Doyle. The first year Dancer worked in the foundry, Alex's father, Kelly Doyle, had the workstation next to him. Kelly had shown Dancer all the tricks for making four hours of effort look like a full day's work.

Dancer dropped the ball back into the gunny sack and walked over to the garage to pick up the knuckleball pitches. "I guess I've had enough practice. My arm feels pretty good."

Dede smiled. It was her polite smile – the one she used when she thought he was fooling himself. "Do you want some coffee before you leave?"

Dancer followed her into the kitchen. Jimmy had been plopped in the middle of the linoleum floor in his diaper. He was surrounded by alphabet wood blocks, one of which he was chewing on. Dancer picked him up and buzzed his belly. "Hey Jimbo, don't eat that block. Your mom's cooking can't be that bad." Jimmy giggled and squirmed like a puppy. Dancer set him back down amidst his battlefield of blocks.

Dede flicked her dishtowel at him. "Doesn't look like you've had any trouble with my cooking."

Dancer poured a cup of coffee and sat down at the kitchen table, which was half-covered with sheets of S&H Green

Stamps. Dede sat down across from him with her shoebox of trading stamp books. She frowned as she studied the catalog. "Those sons-of-bitches."

"What's wrong?" Dancer asked. Dede had been saving stamps for the last six months to buy Clayton a baseball glove for his birthday.

"Now they want ten books instead of nine, and it's the Mickey Mantle model instead of the Stan Musial glove."

"Mickey's having a good year."

"It's not funny. I'm a book short, and his birthday is in six weeks."

"Why don't we just tell Clayton we're moving his birthday again."

Dede gave him a look. Clayton had been delivered at home by a midwife because Dede had waited too long for Dancer to return from a doubleheader in Joplin. When Dancer raced the mother and new baby to the hospital, they arrived just after midnight on August 31st. That's the day that got recorded for Clayton's birthday, and when Dede tried to correct the error, she discovered they would have to hire a lawyer to take depositions and petition the hospital. They couldn't afford the expense, so they let his birthday stand.

Dede licked a large rectangle of stamps and pressed it on to a page of the half-filled trading book. "When you go over to see Kelly, ask Tammy if we can borrow a book of stamps from her."

"I've got to pick up a case of oil over at Crutchfield's. Why don't I buy a glove while I'm there? Seymour will give us a good deal."

Dede fluttered her lips. "Look at the bill tray. We're behind with everyone but the bank. We can't afford twelve dollars for a damn baseball glove."

Dancer dumped the rest of his coffee into the sink. Dede was right. They were drowning. Dancer needed to make more money, and if the Cards stopped thinking of him as a prospect, the Rebels would cut his pay, not increase it. But maybe Doc was on to something. Every team was starting to look for someone like Hoyt Wilhelm. With a good relief pitcher, the starters didn't have to throw nine innings every game. They stayed fresher. The batters, having faced one kind of pitcher for seven or eight innings, had to adjust to a new pitcher. And that pitcher only had to fool them once.

Dancer walked to the back stairway. "Hey Clayton, let's get a move on it." He turned back to Dede. "I'll ask Tammy about the stamps."

8

Dancer and Clayton headed over to the Doyles' on what had been Clayton's secret trail that linked his house on Hill Street with Alex's house on Crandell Road. All last week, the boys watched as a construction crew destroyed the vacant lot that had was their playfield. New houses were being built, and the raspberry bushes and scrub pines were plowed under. Their secret trail had been bulldozed and was now wide enough for two big tractors to pass. The work stopped for the weekend, and the workmen left their equipment parked along the shoulder of the new road they had carved.

Clayton ran ahead of Dancer, zigzagging from dozer, to grader, to tractor, inspecting each piece. "Look, Dad, just like I told you. The new road's going all the way to Alex's house."

The foundry where Kelly worked was part of the Caterpillar Works. In the last three years, the Works had doubled in size, and there were jobs to be had. Good jobs. New families arrived in Maple Springs every week. When Dancer and Dede bought their house back in '51, there were only a few houses on the hill road east of town. Most of the surrounding land had been part of the Landis farm, but when Ted Landis came home from the war, his dreams for a better life didn't include trying to make a living on a piece of land that was mostly hills, rocks, and heartbreak. He stopped farming and began building houses for the returning veterans and new arrivals.

The hill road was now Hill Street. Landis had built houses all the way to the top of the hill, and when he ran out of highway, he built his own roads. Two months ago, he broke ground on the project he called Indian Village. It was a maze of streets that went nowhere with names like Tomahawk Trail and Apache Drive. The boys' secret trail was now Mohawk Lane.

"Slow down, Clay. You're wearing me out. I might have to pitch tonight."

"Can me and Alex go to your game?" Clayton asked. The workmen had plowed driveways off the new road about every hundred feet and left a huge pile of gravel in each one. Clayton scrambled to the top of one of the piles. He put his hands above his head and slid down the pile. "Can we, Dad?" He jumped to his feet and brushed the gravel dust off his dungarees and his red and blue-striped T-shirt. His buzzcut was gray from the powder.

Dancer shook his head. "Can we what?"

Clayton hopped on one foot as he pulled off his sneaker and shook out the gravel that slipped in through the hole where his big toe stuck out. He'd grown so fast they couldn't keep him in shoes that fit. And the dungarees they'd bought last September barely reached his ankles now. "Can we go to your game?" he said. "I want Alex to see you pitch."

Dancer wasn't ready to tell Clayton about his demotion to the bullpen. Clayton still expected him to walk out on the mound and be perfect. "I thought Mrs. Doyle was taking you and Alex to the picture show. Cartoon Saturday, remember? Come here. Let me tie those shoes."

Clayton ran over and pushed his holey sneaker forward. "We can watch the cartoons anytime. We want to go to your game."

Dancer kneeled down and tugged the laces so the sneaker was snug on Clayton's foot.

"Maybe later in the year when it cools off."

Mohawk Lane dead-ended thirty yards from the Doyles' backyard. Every one of those piles of gravel they passed would be the driveway to a new home. Families were pouring into Maple Springs to work at Caterpillar, or the new school, or in one of Seymour Crutchfield's new stores. "You're going to have a lot more kids to play with when school starts again," Dancer said.

Clayton put his hands over his ears. "Don't talk about school." He sprinted toward Alex's house.

Dancer hiked through the knee-high prairie grass at the end of the new road and stepped over the split-rail fence that enclosed Kelly's backyard. Clayton and Alex began to play in Alex's sandbox.

From the backdoor of the garage, Kelly Doyle emerged with two folding lawn chairs and a beer. Doyle was thirty-two, six years older than Dancer, but his cowlicky red hair and the freckles splashed across his nose and cheeks gave him a boyish, innocent look. It was just a look. He already had three kids with four different wives. Alex was the son of wife number two. He handed a chair to Dancer. "Want one?" he asked, holding up his beer.

"It's 9 o'clock," Dancer said. He eased himself into the rickety aluminum contraption.

"Trust me, you don't want Tammy's coffee."

"So what's the big news?"

"Goddamn, Dancer. Where you from? New York?" Kelly never said anything in one sentence if he could stretch it to three.

"Sorry. Nice weather we're having," Dancer said, mimicking Kelly's east Texas drawl. "How's Tammy?"

"Glad you asked," Kelly said. He took another gulp of his beer. "She's doing fine, cause her man just got promoted, and she's already figured out what to do with all the extra take-home pay."

"You're not pouring steel anymore?"

Kelly grinned. "Starting next week, I'm running the coke furnace. Five dollars an hour and I report to Engineering instead of Percy."

Percy Thacker, the man who had given Dancer his foundry job three years ago, was a powerful man in the county, but not because he ran the foundry. Thacker was the Grand Wizard of the Mountain View chapter of the Klan, and he and his brother controlled all the bars and roadhouses in Mountain View. Kelly got along with Percy, as he did with everyone, but he didn't like him.

Dancer glanced over at Clayton pushing a toy cement truck through Alex's sandbox. He did the arithmetic on Kelly's new job. "You'll be taking home more than two hundred a week if you get any overtime."

"And we got a new contract. Medical expenses for the family, sick leave, and a company savings account where they do the saving." He leaned forward and tapped Dancer on the knee. "Here's the deal. Percy will let me pick my replacement. With the new contract, the pourers make $3.50 an hour. You interested?"

With overtime, that would be over a $150 take home. Fifty bucks better than the Rebels were paying him, and it was all year around. He scratched the two-day stubble on his chin. "They pay for the kids' doctor bills?"

"And the hospital. So when Dede corrals you into another baby, you don't have to hock the goddamn silverware. Of course, you have to join the Klan." Kelly winked and drained the rest of his beer. "I'm just kidding, Dancer. You're too tall for the Klan. None of those sheets would fit you right."

Dancer rubbed his arm again. Probing for that sore spot, but there was nothing. He was supposed to ask Tammy for a Green Stamps book, but that could wait. If he got back in the rotation, there was still time to get called up this year. The Cardinals hadn't given up on him.

"It sounds great, Kelly, but I've got a job." He looked at his watch. "I gotta get some oil over at Crutchfield's before I drive up to Rolla." He glanced over at the boys playing in the sandbox. "Tammy's okay with taking them both to the cartoons?"

"Hell, it's the high point of her week," Kelly said. He stood up and clapped Dancer on the back. "Look. I got a few days before I have to tell Percy. Think it over. "

9

Crutchfield's had a special on Havoline motor oil: two cases for $6.99. Dancer hoisted the cases into his shopping cart and wheeled the cart back toward the checkout line at the front of the store. As he rolled through the sporting goods section, he stopped and checked out the baseball gloves. The "Crutchfield Value Special" was the Enos Slaughter model for $3.85. Dancer picked it up and tried to put it on his hand. The leather on the inside was rough and the stitching was loose, shoddy. According to the tag, it was made in Japan.

"I hope you're not buying that for yourself."

Seymour Crutchfield stood in the aisle, smiling, still wearing his undertaker suit. "Just looking for a glove for my boy," Dancer said. He put the glove back on the shelf and picked up the Bob Feller model. "This is more like it," he said. The glove was a smaller version of his own Rawlings fielder's special. It was made in America.

"That's the top of line," Crutchfield said. "Regular price is $14.95, but I'll let you have it for $12.95. Professional courtesy."

Dancer had nineteen dollars in his pocket and he would need a couple dollars for gas to make the trip to Rolla. He pounded his fist into the glove a couple times and set it back on the shelf. "I'll have to think about it. His birthday's not till the end of August."

Crutchfield repositioned the gloves Dancer had returned to the shelf so that they all lined up again. "How do you like being a relief pitcher?" he asked.

"Haven't actually been called for yet. Maybe tonight."

Crutchfield pursed his lips. "Have you ever thought about what you want to do after baseball?"

"I'm only 26."

Crutchfield re-hung a St. Louis Cardinals baseball cap which had fallen from its hook. "I'm just saying that when you do decide to leave the game, or it decides to leave you, remember that I'm always looking for a good team player. We might have an opportunity for you."

"I appreciate that Mr. Crutchfield." It seemed that everyone wanted to give him a job now. Dancer tried to imagine himself selling washing machines or working behind the Crutchfield candy counter. "Hope I don't have to make a decision for a few more years."

Crutchfield stood back and studied the baseball hat display, cocking his head to one side, then the other. He frowned. "You never know, son. You never know."

10

Dancer added the extra quart of oil to his car, and then walked up the backstairs to their bedroom. It was only one o'clock, and he didn't have to leave for Rolla for another three hours. Once Dede put Jimmy down for his nap, they would have the house to themselves. He could hear Dede singing softly to Jimmy in the boys' room. He stripped off his clothes and flounced down on their double bed. Jimmy made quiet gurgling sounds which faded as Dede finished her lullaby. As she skipped into the room, she'd already started to pull off her sack dress. She left the dress on the floor, slipped off her panties, and snuggled up next to Dancer, her head resting in the crook of his arm.

Dancer ran his hands over her body. He loved the feel of Dede's skin on his fingertips. Smooth, and supple, and soft, like fresh cream. In his whole life, he'd never felt anything that soft. They spooned and Dancer cupped her breasts. He slid his hand down her belly.

Dede pressed his hand on her stomach. "I can't get rid of this baby fat."

Dancer feathered her belly with his lips. Her skin smelled of talcum powder. "Nothing to get rid of," he said.

Dede laughed and rolled on top of him. She kissed him hard. "For a hillbilly, you're pretty smart."

When they were finished making love, Dancer slipped off of Dede and tried to catch his breath. His heart raced like he'd just stretched a double into a triple. As they rested hip-to-hip, their bodies slick and glistening, Dede squeezed his hand and elbowed him in the ribs. "Hey. Have you been practicing without me?"

Dancer laughed. He stretched and was about to get up and head to the bathroom, but she wrapped her arms around his waist. "What's your hurry? Snuggle with me."

Dancer dropped back on the bed and scootched his arm under her. "Yes, ma'am." He glanced at the clock on the nightstand. It was one thirty. He still had two hours.

From the boys' room, Jimmy cried out. They both froze. Jimmy babbled and cooed and then it was quiet again.

"He's dreaming," Dede said. "Did you ask Tammy for the Green Stamp book?"

Dancer stared up at the ceiling. "I forgot. Kelly was telling me about a factory job that is opening up, and it slipped my mind."

Dede propped her head up. "A job? What kind of job?"

"In the foundry. Back with Percy."

"How much does it pay?"

"$3.50 an hour."

Dede closed her eyes as she calculated. "That's not bad. Full time employees get medical, don't they?"

Dancer swung his feet over the edge of the bed and sat up. "I guess."

Dede wrapped her arms around him and rested her head on his shoulder, so he couldn't escape easily. "It sounds pretty good. Steady pay all year and help with all the doctor bills."

Dancer sighed. "Bob Feller made forty grand last year. There's nobody in the plant making money like that." He knew it was a foolish thing to say. Bob Feller was the best pitcher in baseball.

Dede nuzzled his neck. "I know, Dancer," she whispered. "But-"

"What?"

"It's not just the money. You'd be home every night. With the boys. And me." She squeezed tighter. "I miss you when you're gone."

"I miss you, too." Dancer sighed and rubbed his neck. "I know I'm no Bob Feller. But I'm a good baseball player. I could still make it, Dede."

She stroked his cheek and whispered in his ear, "I think you can be good at anything you put your mind to."

Dancer pushed Dede down on to the mattress and kissed her. "I'm not so good at taking orders," he said. "Except from you."

Dede wrapped her legs around him. "Will you think about it? That's a request, not an order."

Dancer molded himself to her body and squeezed her butt. "You have very persuasive requests."

11

Crutchfield Stadium didn't have a bullpen for its relief pitchers. The pitchers and other spare parts sat on a bench along the wall just beyond the dugout. That was no change for Dancer. On the days he wasn't starting, he sat out there, but never before with the expectation of pitching later in the game.

Doc Evans wanted Dancer's first relief appearance to be a mop up effort where the score was so lopsided there wouldn't be any pressure. But in the ninth inning with the Rebels leading by three, the first reliever gave up a leadoff homerun, and Doc pulled him for a lefty who topped that effort by giving up a homerun, a single, and two walks. With the score 3 to 2 and nobody out, Doc marched out to the mound and took the ball from the pitcher. He looked over at Dancer, who was warming up, and tapped his right arm, indicating he wanted the right-handed pitcher.

A disappointed murmur rippled through the crowd as Dancer made the short hike to the mound. Probably some of the fans had been there three years ago when Dancer was king of the hill. Now they saw him as just a journeyman trying to hold on.

Doc handed the ball to Dancer. "Okay, this wasn't the plan, but you know what to do. Just use your regular stuff. Don't mess with any of those trick pitches yet."

The catcher who had been brought up when Billy got sick was just a kid, a year out of high school. He stood beside Dancer on the mound as Doc walked back to the dugout. "Ain't no place to put'em, Dancer. Throw strikes."

Dancer checked the runners. The shortstop was batting, and he couldn't have weighed more than one forty, even after a big meal. But he was a good contact hitter, and a single was all they needed to win the game. Dancer took a slow, deliberate windup and whipped the ball home. His arm was fresh and the pitch had good velocity, but the ball tailed back over the heart of the plate. If the kid had been more patient, he could have won the game right there. But the crowd noise and the chance to be the hero made him just anxious enough that he pulled the trigger a heartbeat too soon. He got under the ball and popped it weakly to the first baseman.

Dancer recognized the next batter. He'd played for Des Moines for five years and, like Dancer, was just hanging on. But Dancer was hanging stronger. Three hard fastballs and three tardy swings and the hitter was gone. One out to go. The murmurs of discontent that had greeted Dancer's arrival on the mound died out. Now the crowd applauded, and there were some isolated pockets where folks began the once familiar chant of, "Dancer, Dancer, Dancer."

Up next was the Braves' stocky, gum-chewing third basemen – a country boy named Shepherd. He reminded Dancer of Bilko. Dancer whip-cracked a rocket right under Shepherd's hands. A nasty, almost unhittable pitch, but Shepherd pulled in his hands like a pro and hit a line shot just foul over the third basemen's head.

Shepherd crowded the plate, so Dancer busted him inside at chin-level. Shepherd didn't flinch. The next pitch was a curveball in the dirt, a good pitch, but he didn't bite on it. Dancer came back with a fastball off the plate outside, hoping to catch him looking inside, and Shepherd swung late, but with his powerful arms extended, he drove the ball into the right field bleachers, foul by ten feet.

The umpire threw Dancer a new ball. He caught it in front of the mound and started rubbing it down. He hitched his shoulder a couple of times. The soreness had returned.

Dancer signaled for the catcher to come out to the mound. The chanters had run out of energy, and there was a quiet, nervous buzz to the crowd. So different from that day when they'd all been on their feet exhorting Dancer on every pitch, confident he'd come through.

Three years. It seemed like a lifetime. The whole world had been out there waiting for him back then. Some folks believed that if he'd walked off that mound after three innings, he'd have gotten his chance, and he'd be in high cotton now. But he couldn't have done that. A ballplayer doesn't walk away from a perfect game.

Dancer rubbed his arm. The soreness was never going away. He loved baseball. Some days he couldn't hardly believe he was getting paid to do something he loved so much. If it had been possible, he'd have played for free. But he had a family to support. He could hang on, try to scratch out a living for a few more years, but that would just make things worse for Dede and the boys.

Dancer took a deep breath and let it out. It was time to let go.

"Knuckleball, kid," he said, as he took the ball from the catcher. "If he doesn't hit it out of the county, it's going to drop into the dirt. Make sure you catch it."

Dancer pounded the ball into his glove. He glanced at each of the runners as he ran his fingers over the ball like he was reading braille. He dug his nails into the seams and went into his windup. He torqued his body and whipped his arm forward. The ball floated toward the batter waist high, begging to be slammed. Dancer could see Shepherd's eyes get wide and the muscles in his forearm tighten as he stepped into the pitch.

But just as Shepherd's bat was about to make contact, the ball dropped sharply clipping the front of the plate and bouncing into the catcher's glove. Shepherd corkscrewed himself into the ground striking out to end the game.

As Dancer headed for the locker room, the crowd was on its feet cheering. He stopped at home plate and looked up at the crowd as the cheers blanketed him. He doffed his cap, not boastfully, but to show respect for the game. His heart ached.

12

There was a plate of dried-out meatloaf and cold mashed potatoes waiting for Dancer when he got home, just after nine. Dede had put Jimmy down for the night and snuck out to play euchre at Joyce Landis's place. Joyce was Dancer's age, ten years younger than her wealthy homebuilder husband. Joyce had been Dede's best friend since high school. They were the odd couple – free and easy Dede living in a trailer on the poor side of town with her alcoholic mother, and Joyce, honor student, cheerleader, and the daughter of Maple Spring's most popular doctor. Dancer dropped his gear bag on the kitchen floor, poured himself a glass of milk, and sat down at the table. He didn't care if the meatloaf and mashed potatoes were cold. As he attacked his food, Clayton crawled into the chair opposite him.

"Hey, sport. Jimmy give you any trouble?" Dancer asked.

Dancer didn't like Dede leaving the kids alone. She was a good mother. A natural. She always seemed to know the right way to comfort her boys, or soothe hurt feelings, and she loved to play. It wasn't a chore. She had as much fun as they did, but lately she was spending more and more time with Joyce. Who would have thought that popular, proper Joyce Landis could be a bad influence on Dede?

Clayton shook his head. "Jimmy didn't make a peep. Just did that thing with his lips like he's eating." Clayton made a fish face. "He's probably dreaming about food. He's a porker."

"Your mom makes a mean meatloaf. I was dreaming about it myself tonight."

"Did you pitch?"

"Just the last inning. But we won the game 3 to 2," Dancer said. "Hey, I got something for you." He got up from the table and walked over to his gear bag. "Here you go, son." He handed his baseball glove to Clayton. "It's a Rawlings pro model just like Stan Musial's."

Clayton stared at the glove, his eyes bugged. "Wow," he whispered. "Can I put it on?"

"You bet, partner. It's all yours, but you gotta take care of it. Olive oil every week. No leaving it out in the rain."

Clayton had to stretch his fingers to get them to fit in the finger holes. "Man oh man. My own glove. This is keen. Did you get a new glove?"

Dancer tried to swallow. This was harder than he thought. He cleared his throat. "I'll be getting one, one of these days, you better believe it. You and me gonna play lots of catch."

"But you'll need a glove when you pitch again."

Dancer got down on one knee to check how the glove fit on Clayton's hand. "Here's where you want to catch the ball." He pointed to the palm of the mitt. "This is the pocket. You catch it in there, and cover it up with your right hand. No one-handed catches. One-hand is for showboats."

Clayton pounded his fist into the pocket. "I'll let you have it back when you pitch if you haven't got your new glove yet," he said.

Dancer, still on his knees, put his hands on Clayton's shoulders. "I'm going to go work with Alex's dad at the plant, Clay."

"You mean after the season's over?" Clayton was staring down at his shoes.

Dancer squeezed Clayton's shoulders until he looked up at him. "I'm not going to play baseball anymore. I need to try something new."

Clayton tried to twist out of Dancer's grip. "You can't quit, Dad." His voice squeaked, as though he were being strangled.

Dancer let him go and stood up. He wanted to say something, but he couldn't find the words. He wished Dede were here. She always knew what to say to make them feel better. To make them laugh.

Clayton grabbed Dancer's arm and tried to push the glove on to his hand. "Take the glove, Daddy. Take it. You're the best pitcher they ever had. You were perfect. You can't quit."

Dancer refused to take the glove, and Clayton let it drop to the floor. He ran out of the kitchen and up the stairs to his room.

13

Dancer stood on the porch looking out at the lilac bushes that Dede had him plant to mark the edge of their property. The gunny sack of baseballs was on the deck where he had left them this morning. He picked up a ball. It was misshapen from being pounded against the garage bricks. He reached back and hurled the ball over the lilacs, deep into the vacant lot behind the house. He threw another and another and another. He had just hurled the last one into the brush when he heard the crunch of gravel.

Dede walked up the driveway cradling a small globe in her hands. Her cheeks were flushed as though she'd been running. "Look what Joyce gave me."

Dancer rubbed his shoulder and stared at the object Dede lifted up like it was some kind of offering. "What is it?"

"It's a crystal ball. Joyce collects them. See how it sparkles in the moonlight? I'm going to put it on the hutch." The hutch was reserved for special family things, like the picture of Dede's mama when she was young and the framed newspaper clipping about Dancer's perfect game.

Dancer followed her through the kitchen into the living room. The globe rested on one of her grandmother's satin souvenir pillows. Dede stood back from the hutch, her hands clasped together under her chin, her mouth open. "Isn't it pretty, Dancer?"

"Yeah, it's nice," he said, his voice flat.

Dede put her hand to her mouth. "Oh, shit. The game. How did it go tonight, hon?" She walked over and wrapped her arms around him.

"I quit."

Her eyes studied him to see if he was kidding. "Are you okay?" she asked.

Dancer buried his face in her neck. Her skin was damp and smelled like baby powder. "I told Clayton. Didn't go well."

Dede stroked his cheek. "We're going to be fine, Dancer. All of us."

14

Dede had percolated a whole pot of coffee as a special treat for this first day of the rest of Dancer's life. He stood at the kitchen window and tried to drink it as he read the newspaper and kept an eye out for Kelly Doyle's car. On the front page of the *Dispatch* there was a photo of Marilyn Monroe and Arthur Miller. The paper reported they were married by a justice of the peace – just like Dancer and Dede. No big splashy wedding like when Marilyn married DiMaggio. Dede had the same little-girl look as Marilyn. A look that made some guys think she was simple or easy. And neither of those women made good baseball wives. Dede didn't like to watch. She liked to play. Probably the same with Marilyn. DiMag must have figured that out quick. Their marriage didn't last a year.

Dancer glanced up from the paper. Kelly Doyle pulled into the driveway in his new egg-yolk-yellow convertible. It was a Ford Fairlane Sunliner with black trim, and Kelly was using his shirtsleeve to wipe an imagined blemish from the shiny hood.

Upstairs, Dede was getting Jimmy dressed. Dancer could hear her gentle murmurs as she changed his diaper, punctuated by the sound of Clayton's growling, erector-set bulldozer, which he was using to plow a road through the middle of the boys' bedroom. Dancer's glove had remained on Clayton's toy shelf, untouched.

Dancer yelled up the back stairs, "Kelly's here."

"I'm coming down," Dede said. She skipped down the stairs in her washed-out blue housedress with a naked Jimmy nestled against her chest. "Don't forget your lunch."

Dancer held up the black metal lunch pail. "Got it," he said.

"You look nice." He was wearing one of the new white T-shirts Dede had bought him last week at Crutchfields. She kissed him quickly on the lips. "Say good-bye to your daddy, Jimmy."

Jimmy squealed as Dancer raised him high above his head. "Okay, Jimbo. Be good to your mama, and don't take any crap from that big brother of yours." Dancer yelled up the stairs, "Hey Clayton, I'm taking off."

The bulldozer sounds stopped. "Bye, Dad." Clayton's voice was flat.

Dede squeezed Dancer's hand and whispered, "He'll get over it."

Kelly stood by the Sunliner, grinning like a used-car salesmen, as Dancer stepped off the porch. "Where's my girl, Dede?" Kelly asked.

Dancer winced. Dede didn't like Kelly. She thought he was way too impressed with himself.

Dede walked out on to the deck with Jimmy. "I ain't your girl, Kelly Doyle."

"How do you like my new wheels?" Kelly asked her.

"Take more than a fancy car to get me interested. I need something under the hood."

Dancer shook his head as he opened the passenger car door. "Dede."

"Don't fret, darling. I just like to have my fun with God's gift to women."

Kelly laughed. "Harsh, Dede. Very harsh." Kelly started up the engine and revved the V-8 until it whined. "That gal of yours is a real ball-buster."

"You working today, or you got a date?"

Kelly was wearing his usual wranglers, but instead of the company-issued industrial-green, he had on a fitted white denim work-shirt, and his unruly red hair was wet-combed as though he were headed to church or one of those fancy bars in Springfield.

"New job, new threads. How do you like these boots?" He slid his foot off the gas pedal so Dancer could check out the cowboy boots he was wearing instead of the steel-toed work boots the pourers had to wear.

"I'll try not to pour any hot juice on them," Dancer said.

Kelly backed out of the driveway and headed down Hill Street to the highway. The foundry was one of seven operations of the Caterpillar Works, which covered twenty acres on the south side of the highway, two miles east of Maple Springs. The foundry produced steel castings for the Cat tractors and combines.

"You don't want to be spillin' any of that precious iron. That's a surefire way to get Percy upset with you."

"I've never had any problem with Percy. He always treated me good."

"That's because you were just a part-timer. And a celebrity." Kelly floored it as he pulled onto US 60.

A celebrity. The thought gave Dancer a sour taste in his mouth. He folded his arms and stared out the window.

Kelly peered over at Dancer. "You'll do fine with Percy. He's pretty low key. It's his dipshit son Brandon who's a pain in the ass. Always talking up his Klan shit and trying to get people to join."

"Brandon? That goofy kid who followed his old man around with a clipboard?"

"Yep. Goddamn Percy put him in charge of the Pattern shop." Kelly shook his head. "Look at this traffic. When I started this was a five minute drive."

Cars were streaming into the employee parking lot from east and west. A highway patrol officer was directing traffic. Each of the seven operations had their own building. The structures ran perpendicular to the highway with Assembly and Distribution closest to the road and the foundry, where it all began, at the far end. It took Kelly another five minutes to reach the foundry parking area.

The Caterpillar foundry had been built in 1921, and from the outside, it still looked new. But inside, the decades of carbon

59

that had belched from the coke furnace had covered the red-brick walls with a crusty black coating. The windows were caked with soot, and the lighting was dim. Once the furnace was fired up and the men started building molds, the air would be filled with carbon ash and fine black molding sand. The junk hung in the air and made everything look blurry, like a bad dream.

15

Dancer worked five offseasons for Caterpillar. The first two years he had been a parts inspector. Didn't pay much, but it was easy, sit-down work. He moved to the foundry when Dede got pregnant. Kelly had shown him the ropes. As a part-timer, he wasn't expected to produce big numbers. They just needed a body that could fill in while the men rotated on to vacation.

The work was hard – six hours of shoveling sand into molds and then an hour or more pouring sixty pound buckets of steel – but it was the suffocating closeness, not the wear and tear, that made Dancer so anxious to escape the foundry each spring. He wanted to feel the sun on his face. Even playing baseball on those insufferably hot summer days, he loved that feeling. The foundry was dark, steamy, and smelled like rotten eggs. The molding sand hung in the air like a fog in hell, making it hard to see and even harder to breathe. By December, he was counting the days until he could leave for spring training. The countdown had been in weeks, but now as he sat in the Admin office waiting for Percy Thacker to officially welcome him, he realized this was going to be his life. Now the countdown wasn't even years. It was decades.

Percy burst into the room – a dapper bundle of khaki from head to toe. Dancer thought he ought to have one of those safari helmets and maybe a monocle. He wasn't more than five foot four, a little man with a pug nose, pinkish skin, and tiny hands. "Dancer, welcome back," Percy said.

Dancer stood up when he entered, prepared to shake hands, but Percy scooted quickly behind his large desk. He motioned for Dancer to sit back down on the bench in front of his desk. He flipped through a file folder, frowning and nodding. "The baseball thing didn't work, huh?" he said, as he glanced up from the file.

Dancer shrugged. "Time for a change."

Percy leaned back in his chair and swiveled so he was staring off to the side, his hands laced behind his head. "Well, son, this is foundry work. It's tough. Dangerous. It ain't for the faint of heart."

"I've worked the foundry before."

"Shit, boy, you weren't working. That was just public relations. I let you get by with twenty molds a day. Figured I was helping out a future major league ballplayer. But if you're expecting this to be your new career, I'll tell you right now, I expect fifty molds from all my men. Every day."

Dancer rubbed the back of his neck and shifted on the low bench that enabled Percy to look down on whoever sat there. "I can do that."

Percy swiveled so he was facing Dancer again. He rubbed his jaw. "I suspect you can, son. You're a big strapping boy. No reason you can't give me fifty molds. Okay, now. Go see Brandon. He'll get you squared away."

Percy's fifty mold rule didn't make much sense. There were cake jobs – camshaft and crankshaft gears that were easy to build and easy to pour. Then there were the backbreakers – housings and manifolds that sucked up twenty, even thirty pounds of sand, and took four times as long to pour. A man could do fifty cam gears in his sleep, but fifty radiator housings, that were near impossible.

Brandon Thacker had been the Pattern Shop superintendent for three months. Every morning, the pourers reported to him to get the casting mold they worked for the day. Brandon was a skinny kid with close-set eyes and thinning brown hair. His "shop" was just a big closet with a Dutch door, which Brandon stood behind and assigned molds.

When he spotted Dancer he smiled broadly, but there was something about that smile that wasn't right. Reminded Dancer of how some batters used to have a big grin on their face when they stepped into the batter's box. Did it to boost their confidence, but after Dancer buzzed them with a fastball under their chin, the smile and their confidence disappeared. He wished he could do that to Brandon.

"Dancer, welcome. It's an honor." Brandon shook Dancer's hand like he was pumping water.

"Congratulations on your new job, Brandon. Got a mold for me?"

"Well, I guess I do, yes, sir." He grabbed a small mold off the shelf behind him and set it on the counter. He studied his chart as he rubbed his chin. "We don't need a ton of these, but what the heck, it's your first day. Do this little cam gear. A welcome gift from Brandon Thacker."

Kelly had already fired up the furnace, and the acrid sulfur fumes stung Dancer's sinuses as he walked on to the pouring floor. At the end of the day, Kelly would fill a vat with molten steel and guide it to each pouring station. The vat hung from a twenty foot conveyor. The conveyor track bisected the foundry, like a big zipper in the ceiling. Operating the furnace wasn't as easy a job as Kelly liked to pretend, but it reported to Engineering instead of Percy Thacker, which made it better than any other foundry job.

The foundry was nearly half a football field in length, and every ten yards there was a pouring station, five on each side. Behind each pouring station was a pile of black sand, which the men would shovel into the molds. A radiator housing mold took close to thirty pounds of sand, but the cam gear that Brandon had given Dancer used less than ten pounds.

The foundry shift commenced at eight a.m., and the men got half hour breaks at ten and at noon. They built molds until two p.m., and then poured steel until they were done. It was supposed to take around an hour, and they got paid for two hours to make up for the short lunch break. As soon as they poured their molds they could go home, drive over to one of the Thacker roadhouses in Mountain View, or stop off at Jake's Bar, which had just opened up outside Maple Springs.

Dancer was assigned the first pouring station, only twenty yards from the furnace. In that first position, the combustion produced a constant dull roar, and the temperature never dipped below eighty. Dancer's shirt was soaked with sweat before he even finished clamping the cam gear into the center of the box-shaped wood mold. The mold rested on the waist-high vibration table.

Dancer was a rookie again, just like back in'49 when he played for Hannibal in the Missouri-Kansas league. It had taken him less than three years to move up from Hannibal to Rolla. But in this league, all he would have to look forward to was moving out to the second pouring station. It would take him years to get to a position where he could actually hear himself think, and by then he wondered if he'd have anything to think about.

He hoisted a shovel of sand and dumped it into the mold. Two more shovels and then he stepped on the vibration pedal to hard pack the sand. He set the bottom half-mold in the first pouring spot and filled the top side of the mold. When he was done, he carried it over and matched it up with the bottom half. One down. A lifetime to go.

16

He finished his fiftieth mold at ten minutes to two. As he set it on the floor, Brandon, with that same cocky smile, walked over to him. "You did right fine for your first day, Dancer. Good work."

Dancer wiped his brow with the edge of his tee-shirt, which was now smudged with black sand residue. "Thanks, Brandon."

"Now that you're part of our team, I sure would love to see you join us boys at our regular meeting. We get together twice a month over at the VFW in Mountain View. It's a good time. Swap a bunch of lies, have a few beers, discuss the issues of the day."

For the Klan, the issue of the day was those Negroes down in Montgomery who had been boycotting the bus line all year. It didn't make sense to Dancer. Montgomery was over five hundred miles from Maple Springs. That was Alabama business – it didn't have anything to do with Missouri--but folks around Maple Springs didn't seem to have anything better to talk about some days. Most of his neighbors would say they didn't have anything against the Negroes, they just didn't like a bunch of Northerners sticking their noses into something that was none of their business. But that was bullshit.

Dancer knew what it was like to be an outcast. After his father died he lived with Clem Danforth and his brood. He was considered part of the family. The righteous, God-fearing folks of Maple Springs hadn't wanted their children associating with hillbilly moonshiners like the Danforths. Of course, after Dancer struck out twenty batters in one game, they stopped caring where he came from. But as far as Dancer was concerned, the merchants up on Main Street, the good old boys down at the Elks Lodge, and the losers in the white sheets were all the same, and he didn't want anything to do with any of them.

"I'm pretty busy, Brandon. Couple of kids," he said.

"Oh, I hear ya. We got a lot of good family men. That's why we only meet every other week. Next Tuesday at seven."

17

Kelly had insisted they go to Jake's Bar to celebrate Dancer surviving his first day of work. Dancer had never been there, even though it was only a mile from his house. Jake McMurray worked for his father at McMurray's Hardware for fifteen years, but last year when the Maple Springs city council voted to make the town dry, he quit his job and opened Jake's just outside of town. Jake's was an oasis for Maple Springers who otherwise would have had to drive the ten miles over to Mountain View to one of the four roadhouses there that were all controlled by Percy Thacker and his brother, Lowell.

Dancer braced himself as Kelly steered into the parking lot, trying to avoid the huge potholes and tree stumps Jake hadn't had time to clear out yet. There were vehicles parked on all sides of the shack. Kelly parked his dreamboat a good fifty yards from the bar, next to a souped-up, black hot rod with red flames painted on the fenders, a safe distance away from the two Landis Construction Cement Trucks that took up a huge chunk of the parking lot.

"Jake's making a fortune with all these construction workers," Kelly said as he stepped out of his car. "You'd think the cheap son of a bitch could spend a few bucks and get his goddamn parking lot paved."

Dancer surveyed the scene; pickups, motorcycles, flatbeds, street rods, delivery trucks were scattered around the lot. Most of them perched on the edge of a pothole or between tree stumps. "One beer. I gotta get home."

"Why? Can't you go a day without banging that garage wall with a baseball? Or does Dede have you on a short rope?"

Dancer gave him a look. "One beer, Kelly."

There were no windows in the bar, and the only lighting came from the Budweiser and Hamm's signs provided by Jake's beer distributors. It took a moment for Dancer's eyes to adjust. Jake had installed a U-shaped bar in the back of the room. Scattered around the dance floor in front of the bar were a bunch of mismatched tables and chairs. The back wall was lined with mirrored tiles so Jake's patrons could sit at the bar and keep an eye on the entrance without having to turn around. The sidewall was partially covered with photographs of local celebrities.

As Dancer and Kelly settled on to their barstools, Kelly nudged Dancer. "Lookie there, Dancer. You ain't never set foot in this place, and you're already famous."

Dancer looked up at the photographs. In the far left corner at the very top was a picture of Dancer waving to the crowd with Clayton clinging to his neck. Dancer stared at the photo even though he'd seen it a thousand times. The man in the picture didn't know it was all over. That he had peaked. A perfect game. And from the look in Clayton's eyes, maybe a perfect father, too. How would he ever be able to compete with that man?

Jake McMurray had drawn two beers and placed them in front of Kelly and Dancer. He held out his hand. "How you been, Dancer? I was at that game." He nodded at Kelly. "You should have seen it. A goddamn perfect game. When Dancer struck out the last batter that crowd went crazy. Everyone on their feet whooping, and hollering, and shouting his name. I get chills just thinking about it."

Jake was short, barrel-chested, with a tangle of wavy black hair that had gone mostly gray. "Looks like business is good," Dancer said. "How much for the beers?"

Jake held up his hand. "On the house. Even though I can't say much for the company you're keeping."

"You're always generous with the guys who don't drink," Kelly said. He picked up his glass and chugged down half his beer. "Come on, Dancer. Drink up before he changes his mind. We'll bowl for the next round."

In the opposite corner from the Wall of Fame, Jake had installed a bowling arcade game. The alley was ten feet long, and the pins were suspended from a panel that stuck out of the scoreboard. The bowling ball was really a puck that was slid down the waxed surface of the lane. It hit triggers positioned on the alley surface that determined how many pins were knocked down.

"One beer, remember?"

"Yeah, yeah – one round each. I'll go play that farm boy and then we'll play. This should be a snap for a superior athlete like you." Kelly jumped up from the bar and walked over to the two men who were playing on the machine – a rangy, scruff-bearded boy in overalls and a denim shirt, and a big bear of a man who was wearing a John Deere hat. Kelly talked to the two like they were old friends. He clasped the big man on the back and looked back at the bar. "Hey, Dancer, come over here. Bring the beers. We got a match."

Bernie, the big man in the Deere hat, sprinkled the alley with wax crystals. With his belly resting on the edge of the machine, he practiced his bowling stroke a half-dozen times before finally sliding the puck up the lane. He managed to make a spare and Kelly matched him.

The kid, Mickey, stepped up to the machine. "Y'all makin' this too difficult," he said, as his cigarette bobbed up and down out of the corner of his mouth. He took the puck between his thumb and forefinger, and winked at Dancer as he casually glided the puck down the lane for a no-look strike. "Your turn, Danceman,"

Dancer took the puck. The metal felt cold and slippery. Different from a baseball. He focused on the target like it was the catcher's mitt and copied the kid's backhand stroke. But the puck slid across the waxed surface much faster than Dancer anticipated. His shot hit the right side rail, flipped onto its side, bounced off the machine, and rolled to the back wall of the bar like a runaway tire.

The barroom exploded with laughter. Dancer laughed too, but his face burned.

Mickey chased down the puck and handed it back to Dancer. "Ain't never seen that before," he said, grinning.

Kelly came up behind Dancer. "Go a little easier, big fella."

Dancer slowed his motion, but the puck still slid across the lane into the right side rail. This time it bounced back across the lane to the other rail and stopped just short of the pins.

Kelly slid the puck back to Dancer. "How about a mulligan, boys?"

Dancer managed a 78 in his first game. His inept performance had drawn a crowd. Men who had marveled at his mastery on the mound enjoyed watching him struggle and didn't hesitate to offer him advice. "Ya gotta breathe easy on the release. It's like hunting, man," said one. "Bend at the knees. Keep your head steady," said another. "More whiskey, less beer," said their friend, who brought Dancer a shot.

Dancer was angry at himself, but he smiled and downed the shot. It was smooth and went down easier than he had expected. The Hamm's Bear clock over the bar showed that it was already after eight. Dede would be wondering what happened to him. She didn't trust Kelly, but she had wanted him to take that factory job so she'd have to get used to it. The whiskey gave him a warm, good-time feeling.

Kelly handed him another beer. "I think we've built their confidence enough, Dancer. Let's take it to them this game."

Dancer settled over the machine and focused on the spot Kelly called the pocket. He could hit a catcher's mitt from sixty feet, so pushing a metal disk eight feet should be nothing. He exhaled slowly and guided the puck down the lane for a strike. They lost the second game, but it was closer. Dancer, with a score of 143, had improved from abysmal to mediocre, and that sent the hecklers back to their barstools.

By the third game, Dancer had it figured out. He rolled a 185 with three strikes in the tenth frame. They won the game by nine pins. In the fourth game he broke 200 for an easy win. As he downed his victory shot, he glanced at the clock. It was past nine and he knew he should leave, but he couldn't quit with the match tied.

He had at least four shots and more beers than he could count. His face had gone numb, and as he approached the machine, he stepped deliberately like one of those zombies from the late night movies. But once he braced over the machine he felt in charge again. Strike. Strike. Strike. By the fifth frame, the crowd had returned and after his eighth straight strike, they were three and four deep around the machine, cheering him on. When he pitched, he had never been really conscious of the crowd. Here with the booze making everything more alive and the crowd so close, he could feel his heart racing with excitement.

As Mickey slid the puck over to him for the ninth frame he said, "Goddamn, Dancer. You're two frames from a perfect game."

Bernie cuffed Mickey upside the head. "Don't jinx him, asshole."

Dancer laughed and glided the puck up the lane for his ninth strike. As the game moved into the tenth frame, the crowd took up the chant, "Dancer, Dancer, Dancer," just like years before. He rolled another strike, but on his second roll of the tenth frame, the seven pin refused to fall.

The gang around the machine all groaned with disappointment. Dancer stared at the surviving pin, waiting for it to get the message, but it hung there defiantly. "Shit," he said and forced a smile because he knew, even though he was drunk, that this wasn't supposed to be a big deal. This was just a barroom game played by men who wanted to escape from their real lives for a few hours.

Kelly slapped him on the back. "Great game, Dancer. With your talent and my charm, we'll be drinking for free from now on. Come on, let's have another shot."

"No shots. I need to get home."

This time Kelly didn't try to talk him out of it. They stumbled through the parking lot, which was still packed, and Kelly made it to Dancer's house in five minutes. Dancer could see Dede reading her magazine in the living room where she could keep an eye on the road.

He stepped carefully down the driveway practicing his walk. By the time he climbed the porch steps, he was convinced that his gait resembled that of a sober man.

Dede was waiting for him in the kitchen. She looked him up and down and giggled.

"What's so funny?"

"You look like a little breeze could knock you over. How many beers did you have with Mr. Ladies' Man?" She walked up to him and then stepped back. "Pheweee. You stink." She waved away imaginary fumes. "I guess I didn't need to worry. I don't reckon any decent gal would get within ten feet of you. I thought that T-shirt was white when you left the house."

Dancer relaxed, relieved that she wasn't angry. "Too much to drink," he said, "but at least the drinks were free. And my uniform rentals begin Monday, so next time I go to the bar you can start worrying." He pulled off the T-shirt and tossed it at her.

She skipped over and wrapped her arms around him. "You look pretty good without that shirt. I better not let you out of my sight." She feathered kisses on his cheeks and lips.

Dancer had slipped his hands under her blouse and begun to unhook her bra when Jimmy began to wail. Dede pushed him away. "Go take a shower," she said.

18

The first week of work was hell. Standing all day on the unforgiving concrete floor made Dancer's feet and knees ache. By the end of the day, the dull pain had worked its way up to the base of his spine so that it even hurt to sit down. The mental strain was even worse. He didn't have a dream any longer – there was nothing to take his mind off the numbing reality of the work. When he crawled home Friday night, he skipped supper and collapsed on the bed without even taking a shower. He closed his eyes and wished he could sleep forever. He didn't want to go back.

Then it started to get better. His body recovered quickly. By Sunday the aches and pains had vanished. And on Tuesday when Kelly dropped him after work, Dancer spotted Clayton in the backyard throwing a rubber ball against the garage wall. He was using Dancer's baseball glove.

Dancer jumped out of Kelly's car and slammed the door. "Want to try some pitching, Clay?" he asked. "With real baseballs?"

Clayton frowned. "You don't have a glove anymore."

"You forget about my catcher's mitt? Stay there." Dancer jogged over to the garage at the end of the driveway. Just inside the door on the top shelf next to the turpentine was the mitt he kept handy so when Ronny Bilko visited he could pitch to him.

The glove was wrapped in twine with two baseballs nestled in the pocket.

He squatted down next to the clothesline and flipped one of the balls to Clayton, who trapped the ball between his glove and hand.

"Let the ball settle into your pocket, then bring up your hand. Don't catch with your bare hand, just use it to make sure the ball stays put." He pounded the mitt and held it up as a target. "Show me what you got."

Clayton pumped his arms up and back, twisted his body and flung the baseball. The ball hit the brown grass in front of Dancer and bounced into his mitt like a skipping-stone on the water.

"Don't overthrow. Let your body do the work. Your arm just goes along for the ride." He stood up and demonstrated his simple windup. He let up on the follow through, but the ball still made a loud pop when it smacked into Clayton's glove. He made another target with his mitt. "Try again."

This time Clayton backed off on the furious arm pumping and just tried to imitate his dad's windup. The ball was on target and Dancer opened the mitt so it made a nice pop when he caught it. "Now you're cooking. They ought to let you pitch."

"They only let the dads be pitchers. I can't pitch until next year when I'm in Little League."

Clayton made a few more tosses and when Dancer sensed he was getting tired, he flung the ball high in the air. "Pop fly – go get it."

Clayton looked up and with his glove outstretched ran around in a circle trying to get under the ball. It landed with a plop two feet behind him. "Ah jeez. You threw it too high," he said. "Hey, Dad, can you come to our game tomorrow? We're playing the Yankees again. They beat us 25 to 21 last time."

"Like I said, they ought to let you pitch." Dancer flung another ball into the air, not as high. Clayton staggered back a few steps and caught the ball just before it hit the ground. "Nice grab!" Dancer said.

Clayton grinned. "Can you come?"

"Soon as I get off work. Can't miss a chance to see you beat those damn Yankees."

Clayton whipped the ball back to him. "They're not the damn Yankees. They're the Landis Construction Yankees. Throw it again, Dad."

Dancer shook his head. Landis. That guy was everywhere. "Not much better," he said as he flung the ball into the sky.

19

The next day when Dancer presented himself at Brandon's door for his mold assignment, Brandon's goofy grin had vanished.

"We missed you last night, Dancer."

"How's that?"

"Our meeting at the VFW. Remember?"

"I'm not much on meetings, Brandon."

Brandon's face flushed. "I told my dad you were coming." He appeared more hurt than angry. "Not a meeting guy, huh?" He bent down below the Dutch door. "Here. You'll have fun with this one." He hoisted up a mold ten times larger than the cam gear mold.

"What the hell is that?"

"742 radiator housing. Goes in those big combines."

The cam gear mold had only taken three shovelfuls to fill. The radiator housing needed six. It took Dancer over five minutes to fill both sides of the mold and vibrate the sand into place. The completed mold was heavy, and he almost dropped it as he carried it over to the first spot on the floor. When he positioned the mold on the floor, it fell apart. On his second attempt he vibrated the sand for an extra thirty seconds so it would be harder packed. His arms tingled from the rat-a-tat-tat of the table, and his teeth were on edge. He lifted the mold off the table and tiptoed over to the spot where he gently set it down. It crumbled. After the third failure the veteran pourer at the station next to him yelled over that he needed to add more water to his sand pile.

It took him another fifteen minutes to get the whole sandpile sticky. By noon he'd only finished twenty molds. He worked through the break, but when the two o'clock whistle blew he'd only finished thirty-five.

Kelly maneuvered the vat of molten steel down the track to where Dancer waited with his pouring bucket. Doyle cranked the tilt wheel on the vat hard to the left and slowly, the vat of steel tipped toward Dancer. The pourer's bucket held sixty pounds and was fastened to a steel rod four feet long with a loop handle at the end like a snow shovel. Dancer braced the rod on his right thigh as the steel bubbled over the vat rim and streamed into his bucket like a molten waterfall.

Percy Thacker had told him he'd get used to the heat, but Dancer had his doubts. Every time Kelly tilted the vat, it felt as though Dancer's face were going to melt. The steel popped and hissed and hot embers hit his face, arms, hands. The men weren't allowed to wear gloves because an ember could get trapped inside and that would burn worse than if the steel hit the bare skin and bounced off. None of the old-timers had any hair left on their hands.

Dancer could only fill three molds with each pour. Kelly returned twelve times to fill Dancer's bucket. It was four fifteen by the time he poured his last mold. He hung up his pouring bucket. As he wiped his sweaty brow with the sleeve of his work-shirt, he noticed Percy Thacker, clipboard in hand, staring at him, a frown creasing his pink little face.

"What the hell is this, Stonemason?" He waved his clipboard at Dancer's molds.

"Radiator housing."

Percy's lips were pressed tight as he counted the molds. He shook his head. "Goddamn it. This ain't even forty. What's wrong with you?" He jabbed his dainty finger into Dancer's chest.

Dancer stared down at him. There was an ache in his jaw. "I'll do better tomorrow."

"If'n you don't, you'll be out of here. This here's man's work. It ain't some goddamn baseball game, boy. Now get back to that pile. I want ten more molds before you leave."

Kelly had closed down the coke oven, and was waiting to drive them over to the Grasshopper game. "There's no juice to pour," Dancer said.

Thacker kept on walking back toward his office. "You ain't going to pour 'em. Just build 'em. Maybe next time you'll remember."

Dancer told Kelly to go on to the game. He attacked the sand pile like it was Percy Thacker. Sweat stung his eyes and his arm muscles screamed, but he was blind to everything but finishing those molds. He was done in less than thirty minutes, and he sprinted through the Caterpillar parking lot back to the highway. He slowed to a jog as he headed west along the shoulder of the road the half mile back to Landis Park.

His toes were rubbed raw – the steel-toed boots weren't designed for running – but Dancer felt like he had escaped from prison. It was great to be outside. And even though it was hot, it was a good heat – from the sun, not that damn furnace.

As he approached the ball field, he could hear a crescendo of squeals coming from the baseball diamond. By the time he reached the backstop, there was a clump of boys jumping up and down at home plate. In the center of the clump was Clayton.

"Hey Dad, we beat the Yankees!" Clayton pushed his way through the throng and ran up to Dancer. "I hit a homerun and we won 14 to 12."

There was a catch in Dancer's throat when he tried to speak. He covered it with a cough and squeezed his son's shoulder. "Only one homerun?" he asked with a wink.

"Two. And a double. And Alex had three hits, too," Clayton said, as Alex ran over to them followed by his father.

Kelly grinned at Dancer. "Your boy saved the day."

"Where were you, Dad?" Clayton asked.

Dancer tried to swallow away the angry bitter taste in his mouth.

"Your old man had to do some overtime for the boss," Kelly said. "Come on gang. Let's take a cruise over to the Tastee-Freeze."

Clayton and Alex jumped up and down and clapped their hands. "With the top down, Mr. Doyle?" Clayton asked.

Kelly laughed. "That's the only way we ride, son."

As Clayton recapped the game for his father, Dancer's pride became a hollow aching disappointment. But by the time he had slurped up the last of his root beer float, his disappointment was almost forgotten. As Kelly drove them home, all Dancer felt was rage.

20

Dancer expected Brandon to give him the radiator housing again, but he was wrong. The next morning Brandon pulled a crank gear out of the pile – a cake job. "Sorry about the old man, Dancer. He gets all bent out of shape about his goddamn rules. Always been that way." He had a thin, apologetic smile.

Dancer hitched his shoulders. He wasn't in a talking mood. The men usually had a cup of coffee in the break room before their shift began, but Dancer took the mold and marched straight to his pouring station. Fuck Percy Thacker and his stupid rules. Dancer locked in the mold and started shoveling.

He had fifty molds finished by noon, but he skipped the break and kept on building. When he placed his eightieth on the floor at one thirty, Kelly ambled over and placed his hand on Dancer's back. Dancer continued to shovel furiously.

"You don't want to do this, Dancer."

"His rules are bullshit. Watch out." Dancer hoisted a shovelful, and Kelly had to shift quickly to avoid getting the sand dumped on him.

"Everyone knows that. What are you trying to prove?"

"I'm going to prove I can do this work. Get out of my way, Kelly. This isn't your problem."

By the time Percy came out for his pre-pour inspection at two forty-five, Dancer had a ten by ten grid of a hundred molds. When he came to Dancer's floor he stopped. He stared up and down the rows, and his face flushed like he'd been running. He stared hard at Dancer, and Dancer stared back. Finally, Percy spun on his heels and walked off the floor without checking the other stations.

Dancer raised his shovel and smashed the last mold he had built. The sand splattered pleasingly. Fuck Percy and fuck the Klan and fuck that little shit Brandon. He crushed the next mold and then another and another and another. He moved down the line and in less than a minute he had destroyed half his molds.

Kelly stood at the edge of Dancer's pouring station as he flattened the fifth row. "Jesus Christ, Dancer. What are you doing?"

"The man wants fifty molds, he'll get fifty molds. I don't want him calling me a showboat."

Kelly shook his head. "Don't worry, pardner. Showboat ain't the word that's coming to mind for old Percy right now."

Two hours later, Dancer and Kelly were parked at their favorite barstools at Jake's. Kelly slammed his empty mug down on the bar as Jake brought him another draft. He wiped the foam from his mouth and finished his story, "...and then this son of a bitch goes and smashes half his molds." He jerked his thumb in Dancer's direction.

Jake studied Dancer who was nursing his second beer. "You are an ornery son of a bitch aren't you, Dancer?"

Dancer slid off his barstool. He knew it was stupid to antagonize Percy Thacker, but he wasn't sorry. "Come on, Kelly. Let's bowl."

"Wait a minute," Jake said. He reached under the bar and pulled out his bottle of Jack Daniels. "Making Percy Thacker eat shit, that calls for a special celebration." He grabbed three shot glasses and poured them to the rim. "To Dancer Stonemason, greatest ballplayer to ever come out of Howell County. He ain't too bright, but he's got balls."

Dancer threw down the shot like he'd been doing it for years. It burned, but it brought back that warm feeling. "Do it again, Jake. I'll buy."

21

October 1956 –three months later

Kelly parked his Sunliner near Assembly, a good three hundred yards from the foundry entrance.

"You need some exercise?" Dancer asked, breathing hard. He had gained weight since starting work in the foundry. It wasn't all muscle, either.

"Too many of your foundry buddies putting their goddamn fingerprints on the hood. At least the assembly guys have clean hands."

"Clean hands, huh? Nothing to do with those McCauley twins that just got hired in small parts?" Dancer looked back at the two young brunettes who had stopped to admire Kelly's convertible.

Kelly slow-smiled him. "Twins, you say? I better go see if I can help those ladies. Don't want to interfere with Brandon's recruitment speech." He tipped his head in the direction of Brandon Thacker, who was double-timing it toward them, a rolled up newspaper clutched in one hand.

"Ah geez," Dancer said, "I thought he'd given up." Brandon had been decent to him since the incident back in July.

Had given him a good mix of molds and hadn't once brought up the Klan meetings.

"Percy ain't giving up that easy. You're a goddamn celebrity. He wants you on the team." Kelly hand-combed his hair and tugged on his jeans as he cowboy-walked back toward the Sunliner and the McCauley twins.

"Make sure you tell them not to touch your car," Dancer said.

Kelly glanced back and winked. "And you make sure to get the extra-long bed sheet from Brandon, pardner."

He was two hundred yards from the entrance when Brandon intercepted him. That was about a hundred ninety yards more walking-together-time than Dancer wanted, but there was no escape.

Brandon waved his newspaper at Dancer. "Did you read about Don Larsen?"

Larsen was a pitcher for the New York Yankees, who were playing the Brooklyn Dodgers in the World Series. Three days ago, the Dodgers had pounded Larsen for eleven runs in a lopsided victory. "I didn't read the paper this morning," Dancer said. "Did the Dodgers clobber him again?"

"Clobber?" Brandon practically sputtered as he stopped and unrolled the paper. "He pitched a perfect game. Just like you."

Dancer was surprised Brandon followed baseball. And even more surprised he knew about Dancer's perfect game. "Can I see?" he asked.

Brandon handed him the paper and pointed to the photo in the center of the front page. "Look at those guys!"

Below a headline that simply said, "PERFECT!" there was a picture of Yogi Berra hugging Don Larsen as the Yankees celebrated Larsen's perfect game. It didn't make any sense, but the picture saddened Dancer. Made him wistful for a life he would never have. He handed the paper back to Brandon. "Incredible. To do that in the World Series, that is really special."

"Your game was special, too," Brandon said, as he tucked the paper under his arm. "People were talking about it for weeks. You made us all proud."

Dancer didn't want to talk to Brandon about baseball, his perfect game, or anything else. He picked up his pace. Short-legged Brandon had to take three steps for every two of Dancer's.

"I need a favor," Brandon said. He grabbed hold of Dancer's sleeve, and Dancer stopped walking. Brandon's smile had faded, and he licked his lips as though he were preparing to deliver a speech. "Look. I'm sorry I gave you that radiator housing. Got you in all that hot water with my dad. But God's honest truth, once he cooled off, Percy thought it was goddamn funny – you building all those molds and then busting them."

"He doesn't act like he thought it was funny." Percy hadn't said a word to him since the incident.

Brandon snorted. "He's a hard ass. I know that better than anyone." He looked around the parking lot as though he thought someone might be watching him. "Here's the thing. I'm supposed to be in charge of recruitment for, you know, our group over in Mountain View. My dad doesn't think I'm up to the job. I need to show him he's wrong."

Dancer almost felt sorry for Brandon. Growing up under the thumb of Percy Thacker would have been hell.

"We've got this special guest tonight. Duane Wolcott. He's in charge of the Birmingham chapter, and he's going to report on all the problems down there. Percy wants a big turnout. I know you're never going to join us, but if you just go to this one meeting it would really help me out with the old man. Get him off my back."

Dancer was almost tempted to help the kid out, but he knew it wouldn't stop there. Percy preyed on weakness. Too bad Brandon couldn't see that. "Sorry, Brandon, but this race thing, I'm just not interested." They'd reached the entrance to the foundry. The men were queued up to file into the locker room, stow their lunch-pails, and punch the time-clock. Dancer took his place at the end of the line.

"It's not all about race. We need to do something about all these outside agitators coming in here, trying to tell us how to live." Brandon stepped closer and with a voice tight with desperation he whispered, "Come on, Dancer. Just one meeting. Will you do that for me? Please?"

"No," Dancer said.

Brandon's face clouded, and it almost appeared like he was going to cry. "You'll be sorry, Stonemason." He pushed his way to the front of the line and disappeared into the building.

22

The mirror in the bathroom was still foggy from Dede's morning shower so Dancer didn't have to face how bad he looked. For the last two days, Brandon had given him the radiator mold. He'd managed to pour fifty both days, but last night he and Kelly had gone to Jake's for a quick one – that had become their routine – and one thing had led to another and he didn't get home until after one. When he slipped into bed, Dede was wearing her don't-touch-me pajamas. When she was horny, she'd wear her shorty nightgown or nothing at all. Even though she hung out more and more with Joyce, playing those stupid card games or watching the Landis' new twenty-four inch television, Dede didn't like it when Dancer stayed out late. Not with Kelly Doyle. Dede liked most guys, but not Kelly. She'd been wearing those goddamn pajamas most every night to make sure Dancer got the message.

He splashed his face with cold water and rubbed his hand over his two-day beard. Shaving could wait for a better day. Even after he brushed his teeth he had a puke taste in his mouth. He took a gulp of Lavoris. It burned his throat when he swallowed, but not like the cheap whiskey Jake had been pouring. He held his hand up to his mouth. His breath smelled like sour milk, but now it had a trace of cinnamon. He retrieved his workpants from the hallway and grabbed a fresh shirt from the closet. As he bent over to pull on his work boots, the floor started to spin again.

Dancer's hands shook as he poured himself a cup of coffee. It scalded the tip of his tongue. He blew on the rim and sat down next to Clayton who was studying the pictures on the sports page.

"Hey, Dad. Who's this?" He pointed to the photo in the center of the page.

"Warren Spahn. It says, 'Will Spahn be first to win Cy Young award?'" The award, named for the Hall of Fame pitcher, had just been established by the Major League to recognize the best pitcher in baseball.

"Spahn looks funny. His foot's above his head. You didn't pitch that way."

"I'd have fallen off the mound if I'd kicked my leg that high. But he's a lefty. They do everything different."

"Do you think he'll win?"

"He's a good one, no doubt about it. But the best pitcher this year was Don Newcombe. Man won twenty-seven games. No one came close to that."

"So why don't they put his picture in the paper?"

"Some folks don't think a colored boy should win the prize."

Clayton wrinkled up his face. "That's stupid." He picked up his bowl and slurped his cereal-milk. "Don't forget our game tonight."

"Game? I thought your season was over," Dancer said. He tried to furrow up his brow and look extra serious.

"The father and son game. Remember?" Clayton said. He squinted at his dad.

Dancer scratched his beard. "Now that you mention it, I seem to recall something about a game."

"What game?" Dede asked as she walked into the kitchen with Jimmy.

She set Jimmy down, and he toddled over to Dancer clutching his storybook. "Read, Daddy." He held the book up over his head and Clayton snatched it from him.

"Not *Ten Little Indians* again. I'm sick of hearing that," Clayton said.

Before Jimmy could start to wail, Dancer scooped him up and lifted him high, so that his head brushed the ceiling. "I'll read tonight, sport. Daddy's got to get to work now."

"Dad's going to play in the father and son game," Clayton said.

Dede looked at Dancer and smiled. If she were still angry about his late night out, she was hiding it well. She whisked the book away from Clayton and put it on the counter. "Go brush your teeth, hon. The bus will be here soon."

The crunch of tires on gravel drew their attention to the kitchen window. Kelly Doyle had just pulled in. "Looks like my bus has arrived," Dancer said. He handed Jimmy to Dede. "See you tonight."

She kissed him lightly on the cheek. "Come on, Jimmy, let's say hello to Mr. Doyle."

When Kelly spotted Dede coming down the walk, he jumped out of the car and flashed the smile he usually saved for the girls who liked him. "You're looking exceptionally pretty this morning, Mrs. Stonemason."

Dancer slipped into his seat hoping Kelly would get back in the car before he got Dede all riled up. But Dede gave Kelly a smile to match his own. "Thank you, Kelly." She walked around him, and shifting Jimmy on her hip, she leaned over the back door of the convertible as though she were checking out the backseat upholstery. "Don't look like the backseat gets much use."

Kelly opened the driver's door and settled into his seat. "No ma'am. Just little Alex when we go out for Sunday dinner."

Dede stepped back. "That's good." She smiled at Dancer, but she didn't look happy. "Those family things are important. Now y'all have a nice day. And Kelly, you get my man home safe. Okay?"

23

As they headed down Hill Street, Kelly looked over at Dancer. "That woman of yours is something else."

Dancer shook his head. "No Jake's tonight. You're killing my sex life, you know."

"How come Dede can spend all that time watching television with big Ted Landis, and you can't go out for a few beers after work?"

"She's friends with Joyce, not Ted."

Kelly smiled. "Whatever you say, pardner."

"Dede doesn't like fat men," Dancer said. He looked down at Kelly's lizard-skin boots. "Or cowboys."

Kelly gave him a sideways glance. "I'm just saying. I'd watch her close if old Teddy brings home one of them color TVs."

"I've got bigger things to worry about," Dancer said. "Goddamn Brandon needs to give me something easy today. Son of a bitch is killing me."

Kelly pulled on to the highway and gunned it. "Little Brandon ain't giving you a cake job till you make him look better to his old man. You need to get yourself to one of his Klan meetings," Kelly said.

Dancer cracked his knuckles and stared out the window. "One is never enough."

Dancer dropped his lunch pail off in the locker room and walked over to the pattern shop. "I'll take that 243 gear there." Dancer pointed to the cam gear that was on the top of the pile of molds Thacker was doling out.

Brandon picked up the gear before Dancer could grab it. "What? This little thing? For a big man like you? That'd be an insult." He picked up the 792 radiator housing he'd given Dancer the last two days and held it up like a pawnbroker inspecting a diamond ring. "Don't need any more any of these, though." He returned it to the shelf and pulled out a curved, tubed contraption. "Here we are – the DD920 exhaust manifold. This'll keep you busy."

It took Dancer twenty minutes to finish his first mold. Sour hangover sweat coated his body, and his face, hands and arms were caked with black grit. He needed to build eight molds an hour, but by 10 a.m., he'd only finished twelve, so he worked through the break. Didn't help that he had a pounding headache and the runs. By noon he'd only filled thirty spaces on the pouring floor so he worked through that break too. With an hour to go, he was still twelve short.

Kelly brought him a jar of ice tea. "Here, pardner. It ain't Jake's whiskey, but it might help."

97

Dancer drank it down in one long swallow and handed the jar back to Kelly.

"Steel's not cooperating today," Kelly said. He winked at Dancer. "Don't think I'm going to be able to start the pour until quarter after." He patted Dancer on the back and moved on down the line, like a politician at a county fair. He'd just given Dancer an extra ten minutes.

Dancer finished his fiftieth mold at five after two. The exhaust manifold wasn't larger than the radiator housing, but because of its odd shape, it took longer to pour. It was nearly four when Dancer finally finished his pour and made it back to the locker room. The room was damp and close. It smelled of Lysol, sulfur, sweat, and piss. There were no showers, just an open space with lockers in the back, a long urinal trough along one wall, and a row of toilets along the opposite wall. In the middle of the floor was a large circular steel sink with a foot pedal to turn on the water.

The floor was slimy with black, ashy slop. Brandon Thacker huddled in front of the sink talking with a couple of his Klan buddies. Dancer stepped around them, leaned into the sink, and stuck his head under the ring of water.

"Ah, Stonemason, don't wash it off. You look just like one of those bug-eyed nigra children down there in Alabam."

Dancer shook the water out of his eyes. He was tired. Tired of the job. Tired of all the Klan bullshit. Tired of Brandon Thacker. With rattlesnake-quickness he grabbed Brandon by the throat and pulled his face under the ring of water. Brandon sputtered and flailed, but Dancer had a steel grip. The men laughed at first, but when he didn't let him go, the laughter faded. The locker room became silent, except for Thacker's frantic gasps. No one made a move to stop him.

Dancer felt strong. He was in charge again. He tightened his grip on Thacker's throat. It would be so easy with just a little more pressure to crush his windpipe. Thacker's face turned purple as he ineffectually clawed at Dancer's hands.

Kelly came up next to Dancer and squeezed his shoulder. "Hey, pardner. The boss-man ain't going to like you drowning his boy."

"He doesn't like me anyway," Dancer said. He stared down at Thacker and jerked him out of the sink and set him back on his feet. Brandon wobbled, but stayed upright.

"You're looking a little bug-eyed, too, Brandon. And I think you pissed yourself."

24

Being in charge had consequences.

Dancer and Kelly sat at Jake's, nursing their first beer. "You are goddamn lucky Percy didn't fire your ass," Kelly said.

Jake pulled a bottle of Jack Daniels from the top shelf of his bar. "I wish I could have been there to see that little shithead getting drowned. I'd pay money for that." Jake's cheeks were even redder than usual as he reached down below the bar and came up with three over-sized shot glasses. He held up each glass to the dim bar light and polished them with his bar towel.

"Them glasses are clean enough, Jake," Kelly said.

Jake poured them to the rim with the amber whiskey and raised his glass. "To Dancer Stonemason – the best ballplayer in the county, and Percy Thacker's worst nightmare."

Kelly downed his shot along with Jake, but Dancer held on to his beer with both hands, staring down at it like there was some answer waiting for him at the bottom of the glass.

"Come on Dancer, drink up. You don't have to work tomorrow," Kelly said.

Dancer had expected Percy to fire him. Maybe, if he was honest with himself, he'd even hoped for that. But Percy didn't fire him, just suspended him for a week. Maybe Percy kept him on just to torment his son. Or maybe he didn't want the attention from the home office. Didn't want the corporate snoops coming down sticking their noses in Percy's little kingdom. Hard to tell with Percy. The man could be a prick ten different ways.

Dancer cracked his knuckles and twisted his neck from side to side. "I feel sorry for Brandon. I should have drowned Percy." He studied his picture on Jake's "Wall of Fame." "Ah, fuck it." He drained his beer, threw the shot down and slammed the glass on the bar.

Kelly reached for the bottle and poured three fresh shots. "Hey, Jake? Who's that mope hanging between Dancer and Charlie Pendergast?"

Jake squinted at the wall. "That's Homer Judson."

Dancer's head jerked around. "You mean Homer Judson is for real?"

From the first day he had worked at the plant, back when he was a part-timer, Dancer had heard stories about Homer. Fresh off the farm, barely eighteen, strong as an ox, he'd been hired as an extra pourer. Half-hour into his first pour the guys noticed Homer's boot was melting. He had worn waders and somehow managed to pour the steel into his boot instead of the mold. It was his first day and everything must have felt hot to him, so somehow he didn't realize his foot was burning. By the time they got the boot off, there wasn't much foot left.

Jake slammed his fist on the bar. "You bet your ass Homer Judson's for real. Living the good life down in Florida. Full disability pension."

Kelly shook his head. "I heard he lives in Arizona all winter and when summer comes, he drives up into the Rockies, fishes all day. Lucky SOB."

"He's fishing alright," Jake said, his voice rising. "Deep-sea fishing. Marlin and barracuda and big-ass fish like that. He ain't fishing in some pissy little mountain stream."

Dancer stared at Homer Judson. Crew-cut, broad flat-face. "Can he walk?" Dancer asked.

"Hell yes. He ain't going to win no Olympic medals, but he gets around," Jake said.

"Then that's a sweet deal." Dancer grabbed the bottle of Jack Daniels and poured another round of shots. "To Homer."

It was almost two in the morning when Kelly dropped Dancer off in front of his house. He tugged off his work boots on the back porch and carefully opened the door trying not to make a sound. With his sock feet, the footing was treacherous on the hard-wood stairs. He slipped halfway up, banged his knee, and almost fell back down to the first floor landing. There was no sound from upstairs.

When he reached the top of the stairs, he looked in on the boys. Jimmy was asleep in his crib, and Clayton was sprawled facedown with his feet sticking out of the untucked bed sheet. His baseball uniform was wadded up on the floor next to his ball and glove.

Dancer had forgotten about the father and son game. After the scene with Brandon and getting chewed out by Percy, Dancer hadn't thought of anything but going to Jake's and drowning the memory of the Thackers and that whole goddamn foundry. His good-time buzz vanished. Now his gut ached, but it wasn't because of the Thackers, the foundry, or the booze.

He tucked in the covers and pulled the sheet up around Clayton's shoulders. He stroked his son's hair, then picked up the baseball and the glove. His hand slid easily into his old mitt. The leather was still smooth, and he could smell the olive oil. Clayton must have given it a treatment before the big game. He gripped the baseball. It was scuffed, and the stitching was loose, but it still felt right.

Dancer could see the umpire raise his fist, giving him that final perfect out. He could hear the crowd screaming his name and feel Clayton's sticky hands on his neck as they paraded triumphantly around the field.

"The game's over, Dancer."

Dede stood in the doorway wrapped up tight in her terrycloth bathrobe.

"I know."

"If you keep this up, you're going to lose us."

"I hate that place."

"You don't have to work there. Call Mr. Crutchfield. He practically offered you a job last time you saw him." She took a step into the room. Her face was tight, her eyes hooded.

"He won't pay enough." Dancer waved his arms around the room. "These guys aren't cheap."

"I could get a job. Joyce needs help showing folks through the model home at Indian Village." She took a couple more steps into the room.

Dancer tossed the glove back on Clayton's bed. "You want to work for Landis?"

Dede smirked. "Are you jealous of Ted Landis?"

"Maybe."

"Darling, I'd bang Kelly Doyle before I'd go to bed with Teddy, and you know how I feel about Kelly."

"I'm sure Kelly will be happy to know he's moving up the ladder."

Dede unbelted her bathrobe. She wasn't wearing her pajamas. "There's only one man I want, Dancer." She wrapped her arms around him. "Tomorrow you call Mr. Crutchfield. Okay? You might be worth more than you realize."

25

Dancer was starting to sweat. He had an interview with Seymour Crutchfield in one hour, and he couldn't make his necktie come out right. The tail was too long, and the knot was all bumpy.

"Can you help me?" he yelled out the open bedroom door. Dede was in the boys' bedroom stripping their beds. It was almost nine, and his appointment with Mr. Seymour Crutchfield was at ten.

Dede, her arms loaded with sheets from the boys' room, walked into their bedroom and dropped everything on the floor. She looked at Dancer and laughed. "Are you trying to hang yourself? Come here." She undid the mess he'd created and arranged the business-end of the tie so it hung below his belt buckle. Her tongue peeked out of her lips like it always did when she concentrated. Dancer stole a quick kiss.

"Hey. You want this done right, or not?"

She cinched up the knot and stepped back to appraise her work. "Well, if I were Mr. Crutchfield, I'd hire you on the spot."

The original Crutchfield General Store, where Mr. Seymour Crutchfield maintained his office, was on the corner of West Main and Harris, across from the Post Office. The front part of the store appeared much the same as when Seymour's grandfather opened for business back in 1884. A rough-hewn wood plank floor with a pot-bellied stove in one corner and a counter with jar of colorful hard candy in the opposite corner. On top of the counter was an old-fashioned cash register operated by a clerk with a handlebar mustache and a long-sleeve shirt, cinched up with garters. Next to the counter were two coin-operated horses the boys and girls could ride for a nickel.

Kids amused themselves in the front of the store while their parents shopped. The store had lumber, building products, and tools in the back, fishing and hunting gear in the middle section, and in the front, so you had to walk by them even if all you wanted was a two-by-four, were all the appliances: refrigerators, ovens, washing machines, and in the last year, clothes dryers and a line of Admiral television sets.

Seymour Crutchfield's office was on the mezzanine level. There was a walkway around the perimeter of the store, and the door to Mr. Crutchfield's office was in the center of the mezzanine. Next to his door he had a large picture window. As Dancer walked to the rear of the store, he could see Mr. Crutchfield, dressed in black, standing in the window looking down at the shoppers, like a preacher ready to deliver a heavy dose of fire and brimstone.

Dancer made his way up the stairs, and Crutchfield stepped out on to the walkway. "Ah, Dancer, right this way. Come on in."

The office was small and spartanly furnished. Dancer took a seat opposite Crutchfield's battleship-gray metal desk. From his desk, Crutchfield could keep an eye on most of the store aisles.

"Wilbur tells me you might be looking to make a change in your career path."

Mr. Crutchfield was not one to waste time with idle small talk. It took Dancer a moment to remember that Doc's real name was Wilbur. "I'm working at the foundry."

"Mr. Percy Thacker's operation," Crutchfield said. He nodded as though that meant something special. "When you called you mentioned something about an altercation with Mr. Thacker's son."

"I got suspended for a week," Dancer hesitated. "For fighting with Brandon." It wasn't really a fight, but Dancer figured calling it a fight didn't sound as bad as saying he half-drowned the kid.

Crutchfield pursed his lips. "That is unfortunate."

Dancer wanted to ask him if he meant unfortunate that he had to work for the Thackers, or unfortunate that he picked a fight with the boss's son.

"I don't know young Brandon, but I've known Percy for many, many years. He wants to live in the past. The man doesn't understand the modern world. What he's doing is counter-productive."

Dancer licked his lips and tried not to tug on the scratchy shirt collar. It was hot in Seymour's office, and he could feel a drop of sweat start to trickle down his back. Crutchfield was a tough read. It was like facing someone he never pitched against for the first time. Best in those situations to just play it straight. "Yes, sir," he said.

"I don't want the government telling me I have to let the Negroes shop in my store. Fact is, most law-abiding Negroes don't want to shop with white folks. They want their own stores. But a man like Percy gets folks all stirred up and next thing you know, we have the government poking their nose into private matters. I've told Percy as much, but he's hardheaded."

Dancer shifted in his chair and tried to get comfortable. Why did everyone want to talk about the Negroes? He wanted to stand up. When he was on his feet he could think better. "I just want to do something different, Mr. Crutchfield. When we talked last summer, you said you might have an opportunity for me."

Crutchfield frowned as he stared at the section of the store where the television sets were displayed. He pressed a button on his desk. "Sorry. Unattended customer." He paused. "We always have a need for a good team player. Someone willing to work hard. Family man with good values." He opened a file folder that he had on his desk. It looked just like the folder that Percy had when he welcomed him to the foundry. "You have children?" Crutchfield asked.

"Yes, sir. My son Clayton just turned seven, and Jimmy was two this spring."

Crutchfield licked the tip of his pencil and scratched a note in the file. "And your wife?"

"Dede."

Crutchfield peered at Dancer like he was waiting for him to say something more. Dancer could play that game. Whenever a batter appeared too comfortable, Dancer would just hold the ball and make him wait. The man would get tired of trying to hold his bat ready, and he would have to call time out. Dancer waited him out. Finally, Crutchfield coughed and looked down at the file. "I understand your parents are both deceased?"

"Yes."

"What was your father's occupation?"

Crutchfield only asked questions he knew the answers to. That much Dancer had figured out. "My father was a farmer. After his farm burned down, he ran whiskey for the Danforths."

Seymour raised his eyebrows. An answer he hadn't expected. He put the file down and sat back in his chair. "Why did you stay in that game?" he asked.

"You mean?"

"The perfect game. If you'd come out of that game like you were supposed to, today you might be a starting pitcher for the St. Louis Cardinals. Why didn't you let Wilbur take you out like he had planned?"

Why? For men like Crutchfield and Percy Thacker, everything was a calculation. Baseball was just a game to them. They would never understand. The game was what counted. You played by the rules, you stood up for your teammates, and you played to win the game. "I wasn't thinking about the next game," he said.

"You wanted the glory," Crutchfield said. It was an accusation.

Dancer tugged his necktie loose so he could breathe. "A ballplayer can't give up on a perfect game. Sure, I wanted the glory. On that day, I was perfect. Not many men can say that.."

Crutchfield leaned forward and tapped the desk with his finger. "But it doesn't pay many bills, does it?"

Crutchfield sat back with his hands folded, confident he had made his point. "It doesn't pay anything," Dancer said.

Crutchfield smiled, comfortable again. He leaned forward. "We're going to add sports equipment to our stores. Not just baseball gear. We'll have football, basketball, maybe even golf. What do you think, Dancer? Could we sell golf clubs?"

Golf had always been a country club sport, but in the last few years, developers like Ted Landis had built public golf courses alongside their housing projects. "I think so," Dancer said. "They're starting a golf league at work. Going to play out at the new course on Burnham Hill Road. I doubt if any of those men will buy their equipment at the country club."

"Precisely," Crutchfield said. He rubbed his hands together and pushed forward in his chair. "I'm looking for a man who understands sports and the men and boys who play them. Someone who can help me build a sports department. Are you interested?"

"What would I do?"

"Everything. Anything. Meet with the suppliers – you know who they are – Rawlings, Wilson, Spalding. Check out the competition, the sports equipment stores, the country clubs, the department stores. We sell to working men and women. What kind of sports gear do those folks want? How much floor space do we need? I need a man who can decide what needs to be done and can work without me looking over his shoulder all the time. What do you think?"

It sounded a whole lot better than working for Percy Thacker. But would it pay enough to support his family? Could he make enough so Dede didn't have to work for Landis? "That's very interesting, Mr. Crutchfield, but I got two kids now and--"

"You need to know how much it pays, right? Good question. Family comes first." He scribbled a few figures on his pad and put the pencil down. "How's two hundred dollars a week sound? And some bonus opportunities if we have a good year."

Now Dancer moved forward in his chair. He was ready to start tomorrow "Sounds great, sir."

Crutchfield sat back in his chair. "I thought it would. It should. Now just for a moment, let's revisit that perfect game, okay?"

Dancer eased back in his chair. There was always something more with men like Crutchfield. Some catch.

"If you had it to do all over again, if you had known that was your only shot at the major leagues, would you have made a different decision? One that was perhaps better for your family?"

Dancer knew what he should say. It was foolish to insist that staying in the game was such a big deal. But it was *his* perfect game. And Clayton's. "No, sir. Doc would have had to shoot me to get me out of that game."

Crutchfield frowned. "That's the reaction of the boy with stars in his eyes. Now that you're older, don't you see that what you did lacked prudence? That it was a bad management decision?"

"It was a perfect game." There was no point in explaining it to Crutchfield. There was no more chance of him understanding what Dancer had done than there was of Dancer understanding how Crutchfield ran his store empire.

Crutchfield closed the file. "And that's your answer? That it was a perfect game? Do you think because I'm not an athlete, I don't understand that temptation? The desire to be the hero?"

Dancer pushed his chair back from the desk and stood up. "It has nothing to do with being a hero, Mr. Crutchfield. Heroes are a dime a dozen in baseball. That game was the only thing I ever accomplished that was all mine. And even you can't take that away from me."

Dancer wound his way past the fresh-cut lumber, through the aisle lined with fishing tackle, and past the new display of Maytag clothes dryers until he emerged from Crutchfield's store onto a sun-drenched Main Street. As he walked toward his car, he was more relieved than disappointed. The Thackers, with all their Klan bullshit made his life miserable, but Crutchfield wanted so much more. The foundry was hell, but Mr. Seymour Crutchfield was the devil.

26

When Dancer told Dede about the meeting with Crutchfield, he thought she might be angry that he had blown such a great opportunity. But Dede was always surprising him.

"You did the right thing, hon. You would never be happy working for him. Something else will come up. I'm going to call Joyce and see about that job. It will give us a little cushion."

She had been so understanding about Crutchfield that Dancer found himself unable to object. And even though the whole idea grated on him, when Dede described the job that Ted had hired her for, he had to admit it was a sweet deal.

Landis wanted Dede to open up the model home at Indian Hills at 9 a.m. each morning, Monday through Friday, and stay there until noon when Joyce would take over. The model was a fifteen minute walk up Hill Street so after she got Dancer off to work and Clayton on the bus, all Dede had to do was put Jimmy in the baby carriage and walk up the hill. And for that he was going to pay her fifteen dollars a day. Seventy-five dollars for the week just to dress nice and act friendly.

Dancer, who was feeding Jimmy, did a double take when Dede came down the stairs for her first day of work in a prim white blouse and pleated navy skirt. "You look like one of the girls from St. Mary's," he said.

"Shut up, Dancer."

"And," he paused for effect and moved closer studying her face. "Is that lipstick?"

Dede wrinkled up her face and pushed him away. She stared at herself in the hall mirror. "I look like goddamn Snow White. Come here, Jimmy." She grabbed Jimmy out of Dancer's arms and plunked him into the baby carriage. He squealed happily.

"I can drive you," Dancer said. He wouldn't be going back to work until next Monday.

"No. I want to work out the routine. You can mow the lawn, like you've been planning to do for the last two weeks." She pushed the carriage toward the door.

"You look right nice, Dede," Dancer said with an exaggerated drawl. "How about a kiss for the old man?"

She blew him a kiss. "Can't mess up the mouth. Bye, darling." She continued out the front door, headed for her new job.

Fifteen dollars a day, just for being Dede.

27

Dancer stood in the open doorway and waited for Percy to get off the phone. He motioned for Dancer to come in and gestured toward the bench, but it was covered with papers so Dancer stood to the side of Percy's desk and waited. He must have been on the phone with one of the home office bosses because he didn't say much. A few grunts, a couple of yessirs, and then he hung up. He peered at Dancer quizzically, as though he couldn't remember why he was standing in his office.

"You told me to check in with you before—"

"Yeah, yeah. Hold on a minute." Percy shuffled through a pile of papers on his desk. He pulled out a pink telephone call slip. "Take the specialty fab duty this week."

Percy Thacker had some kind of deal with Crenshaw, the supervisor of Specialty Fabrication. Whenever he needed help, Percy would loan him someone from the foundry. It was their special arrangement. The suits didn't know anything about it, but the foundry men didn't complain. It was easy duty, usually just carting sheets of steel to the fabricating stations so the operators could slice and dice it.

"You want me to report to the distribution center?"

"No. Tommy Harter threw his back out fishing. You need to go to Building 7. Johnny Gardner will get you squared away."

Gardner ran the machining operation. "Fishing?" Dancer asked.

Percy snorted. "Yeah. Must have been a hell of a cast."

"Isn't Harter the Pexto operator?" The Pexto was a hydraulic plate shearer. Dancer didn't even like to get close to it when he delivered the steel.

"They got a bunch of sheets need to be cut down for some prototype they're working on. It's an easy job, but it can't wait. Probably take you a couple of days."

"I don't know how to run that machine."

Thacker shuffled through the papers on his desk. "That's why you're reporting to Gardner. He'll get you trained on it today, and tomorrow, you'll be aces." He glanced at his watch. "You better get over there. Johnny's waiting on you."

Building 7 was on the opposite side of the complex, and it took Dancer almost a half hour to get there. He found Johnny Gardner in the crank-grinding department trying to settle a dispute between two operators. He was surprised to see Dancer.

"I thought Brandon said they were going to send over McGrady. That old boy ran the Pexto for five years."

Dancer gave him a palms-up gesture. "I guess Percy changed the play."

Gardner's face wrinkled up like he had gas. "Don't make any goddamn sense. But what else is new? We don't ever do things the easy way around here." He studied his clipboard.

"You're going to be working on the BX-47. Job's a total fubar. Go over to the DC, and start hauling the sheet stock for that job. When you get done, help out the lift drivers for the rest of the day. Tomorrow, when I'm not up to my ass in alligators, I'll train you on the Pexto. It ain't hard – you just got to be careful."

28

One of the valve-testers in small parts was leaving, so all the women in that department were having a going away party at Jake's. The tables and dance floor were filled with gals of all ages. Dancer watched from the bar as Kelly jumped from table to table, spreading his gospel, and buying drinks. Despite his heroic efforts to stoke the party fires, by eight o'clock the ladies had all gone home and Kelly joined Dancer at the bar.

Jake walked over and grabbed the bottle of Wild Turkey from the whiskey shelf. "How about a shot of the good stuff, Dancer?"

Dancer shook his head. "Gotta keep a clear head. Don't want to screw up with that Pexto tomorrow."

Kelly held out his glass. "Hey, I could use some of that Turkey."

Jake poured him a shot and put the bottle back on the shelf. "What's the Pexto?"

Kelly downed the shot with a flourish and slammed the glass on the bar. "Old Dancer's going to run the sheet shearer tomorrow. Fucker's like a giant paper-cutter for steel." He raised his arm and made a scrunching sound as he slammed it down on the bar like he was operating the machine. "This could be your big opportunity, Danceman."

Kelly's eyes were red. The Wild Turkey hadn't been his first shot. "I better drive you home," Dancer said. "I think those girls wore you out."

"I'm serious. Look." He held up his hand and pointed to the tip of his little finger. "You just stick the tip under that blade and whoosh, you've got it made."

"Why are you operating that machine?" Jake asked.

Dancer explained the Percy arrangement. Jake drew a fresh draft. "That's totally fucked up," he said as he took away Dancer's half-finished beer. "The company ever found out about that, they'd have Percy's ass. And if you ever got injured you could sue them. Do a damn sight better than old Homer did."

Dancer took a swallow of beer and set the glass back on the bar. "You're crazy."

"No, I'm not," Jake said. He leaned across the bar and lowered his voice. "Did you read about that guinea kid at the pipe plant over in Cabool?"

"Hey, I could use a beer, too," Kelly said.

Jake gave him a look, then poured him a short glass. "An office clerk. They were shorthanded so they sent him out in the yard to help load pipe. Damn kid pulled out a chock and was buried by a bunch of runaway culverts. Concussion. Busted up his arm real good and scared the piss out of him. The company paid him two hundred fifty thousand dollars to go away. God's honest truth."

Dancer squinted at Jake. "How do you know that?"

"My wife's cousin, Mavis, lives in Cabool. Everyone knows about it over there."

Kelly draped his arm over Dancer's back. His breath smelled like nail polish. "Shit, Dancer. Give yourself a little Pexto-manicure and you ought to be able to pull a half mil out of the company." He stuck out his little finger again and grabbed hold of the tip. "Come on. How bad do you need this?"

Dancer elbowed him in the ribs. "You're an idiot." He looked at his pitching hand and flexed it. "But I bet I could come up with a pretty neat knuckleball." He pointed to the whiskey shelf. "Okay, Jake. Let's have one shot for Homer, and then I need to get this shitfaced asshole home."

29

The Pexto was a hydraulic plate shearer with a six foot long guillotine. They called it the green monster, and it could slice through 16 gauge steel like it was hot butter. Johnny Gardner had tucked it away in the far corner of Building 7, away from the other machines so that the unexpected high-pitched screech didn't disturb the men grinding cranks and cams.

Dancer's job was to slice twelve inches off the end of a three by three sheet. Gardner had been right – the Pexto was easy to operate. The steel sheet was locked into the cutting frame, and the operator stepped on the activation pedal. The guillotine, poised twelve inches above the cutting frame, responded so quickly it was as though it anticipated Dancer's actions. *Kachunk. Screech.*

At first it was terrifying. But after a few dozen sheets the process became just another routine, like building a mold or pouring steel. By eleven-thirty when he stopped for lunch, he had sheared three of the seven stacks.

Dancer had driven his own car to work, instead of riding with Kelly, because he had to work until four in specialty fab. But, unlike the foundry, the men in specialty fab got a whole hour for lunch. Dancer reckoned he could drive over to Indian Village before noon, pick up Dede, and bring her back to the house. Shower-sex and a home-cooked meal would make the day go even faster. He stepped on the gas and made it back to Hill Street in five minutes.

Maybe he would ask Johnny Gardner if he could transfer to his group. The Pexto was scary, but he'd get used to it. And he liked the yard work, driving the forklift, hauling the materials. It gave him a chance to be out in the sun, a chance to breathe fresh air. He could come home for lunch once or twice a week to break up the monotony of work. Of course, Dede would want him to come home every day.

He pulled into the model home driveway. The front door was locked, and there was a clock sign hanging from the doorknob, which read "Back at" with the hands on the clock face pointed toward one o'clock. Dancer peered into the living room window. Jimmy's baby carriage was in the kitchen, but no sign of Dede. He walked around to the back and tried the door next to the garage. It was unlocked, and he walked into the kitchen. Jimmy was asleep in the carriage, sucking on his thumb.

Dancer could hear music coming from one of the bedrooms. He walked down the hall and opened the door. Joyce Landis was kneeling on the bed, naked, her pendulous breasts hovering over the face-down body she straddled. Everything happened in an instant, but it felt like slow-motion. Joyce saw Dancer and screamed, then tried to cover her breasts as she ran for the bathroom. In that first confused moment, Dancer thought he had walked in on Joyce and Ted.

His eyes had focused on Joyce's swinging boobs but that smooth slender back she was tending to couldn't belong to Ted Landis. Reflexively, Dancer backed out of the room and slammed the door. But in the fraction of a second before it closed, he looked into the sleepy blue eyes of Dede as she raised her head to see why Joyce had run off.

The next thing Dancer remembered, he was in his car backing out of the driveway. Dede, in her un-cinched bathrobe, was running after him.

"Dancer, honey. That was nothing. Just girls having fun. Come back!"

As he drove away he could see her in the rearview standing in the middle of the road, her bathrobe hanging open, with one hand on her hip, and the other shading her eyes.

Dede and Joyce? How could she do that to him? To her boys? And what made her ever think she could get away with something like that in Maple Springs? He pounded the steering wheel and raced down Hill Street headed toward US 60.

He pushed the accelerator to the floor. Sixty, seventy, eighty. He wanted to get away from Dede, Crutchfield and the Thackers, and his whole goddamn life, but he had no place to go. When he saw the entrance to the plant, he steered into the parking lot. There were still four stacks of steel to cut.

30

The steel sheets had been delivered earlier in the week, and there was a thin bead of lubricant on each sheet from the master slitter. Dancer's hand slid easily across the surface as he placed the first sheet in the Pexto.

A half million dollars for the tip of his finger. Why not do it? The thought gave Dancer a bad feeling in his gut. How could he consider such a thing? But why not? Why should the guys like Crutchfield and Thacker get all the breaks? Those men had no honor. No code. They took care of themselves and to hell with everyone else.

The tip of his little finger. On his left hand. He'd never miss it. He could give half the money to Dede, and she could run away with Joyce if that's what she really wanted. Dancer would take Clayton and Jimmy and start fresh. Someplace where no one had ever heard of Dancer Stonemason.

Dancer inched his finger toward the cutting line. With each sheet, he pushed closer and closer to the knife. But each time he got to the cutting line, he'd lose his nerve and pull his finger back.

Through the fourth, fifth, and sixth stacks he played that game. There were only two sheets left when the image of Joyce rubbing her tits all over Dede's body forced its way back into his head. He squeezed his eyes shut. That wasn't just "girls having fun." Dede had betrayed him. Betrayed her family.

As he sheared the next to last sheet, he could feel the force as the guillotine ripped through the steel. His finger was less than a quarter inch from the line. His heart pounded like it was the ninth inning, and the bases were loaded.

There was one sheet left. Now or never. He locked it in the frame.

And then, as Dancer was ready to push his finger across the cutting line, he felt Clayton's cotton-candy sticky fingers clinging to his neck. Clayton loved the man who was a hometown hero, not some lowlife cheater. And with Clayton in his corner, Dancer knew he could endure anything: the soul-killing monotony of the foundry, the harassment of the Thackers, even the unfaithfulness of Dede. He took a deep breath and relaxed.

"Dancer!"

Dancer tensed, and his left hand slipped forward on the oily surface at the same instant his foot pressed down on the activation pedal. He wondered why Brandon was over in Specialty Fab. Had there been an accident at his home? Blood splattered his goggles, and he collapsed to the floor.

31

When Dancer opened his eyes, Dede and some doctor were standing over his bed whispering. The doctor leaned in close enough for Dancer to smell his minty breath. "Welcome back to the world, Dancer."

He was in a hospital. It wasn't just a nightmare. What had he done? He tried to lift his arm, but he couldn't. A dull ache started at the tip of his left hand and flowed all the way to his shoulder. He moaned.

Dede dabbed a washcloth on his lips and forehead. "It's okay, Dancer."

The doctor put his hand on Dancer's shoulder. "I'm Doctor Langer. I operated on you yesterday."

Dancer remembered the cool dampness of the concrete floor on his cheek. It had smelled oily. His eyes had stung, and he had been afraid to open them. Far above he could hear Brandon wailing. Something terrible had happened, and Dancer didn't want to see. He wanted to stay right where he was on the cool, damp floor. Dancer blinked his eyes trying to bring the doctor into better focus. "What happened to Thacker?"

The doctor frowned and looked at Dede.

"That's his boss," Dede said.

"No." Dancer shook his head. "Not Percy. Brandon. What happened to him?"

"Nothing. You had an accident."

Three fingers. The doctor had said he was lucky. Lucky he didn't bleed to death. Lucky the machine had sliced so cleanly. Lucky he still had his thumb and index finger. So much fucking luck. Three fingers. It couldn't be. But when the doctor changed his bandages, he saw for himself. An inch long purple stub where his middle finger had been, a half-inch long ring finger, and no little finger. He looked away, anxious for the doctor to cover up the hand again with clean white gauze. His fingers throbbed, yet they weren't there.

"Phantom pains," the doctor said. "Your brain is confused."

Dede had told him everything would be okay, but that's what she wanted, not what she believed. She might be a good liar, but not that good. She kissed him goodbye, and Dancer watched her follow the doctor out of the room, like a lost child. Three fingers.

After they left, Dancer lay back in his bed and stared at the ceiling. What were they going to do now? How would he ever explain this to Clayton? A nurse bustled into the room. She gave him a shot of morphine, and within seconds the painkiller had pulsed through his body, leaving him with a warm, mellow feeling. Baseball. He could still play ball. Somehow he'd find a way. Hell, during the war, the Cardinals had a one-armed outfielder.

His body sank into the mattress. He felt warm and safe, and it was too much effort to keep his eyes opened. Three fingers. That was nothing.

There were heavy familiar steps on the stairs, and the door to his bedroom creaked open. His father, bare-chested under his farm overalls, stood over Dancer's bed, frowning. A whiff of manure and sweet molasses radiated from him. His hair was damp with sweat. He pulled a red bandana from his side pocket and wiped his brow. He reached over and grabbed Dancer's bandaged hand.

Dancer closed his eyes and willed himself to wake up.

"Look at me," his father said, his voice low and guttural. "Look at me, you son-of-a-bitch." He squeezed Dancer's hand.

Dancer's arm felt like it was on fire. He tried to pull his hand away, but his father was too strong. He opened his eyes, and Walter pinned Dancer's hand to his chest. "You're a fool," he said, his upper lip curled grotesquely. Dancer had to look away.

This was a dream, and he needed to wake up. When he opened his eyes again, Dede was next to him in the bed. He could feel the warmth of her naked body under the covers. She was rubbing herself, and her smile seemed indifferent, as though he weren't even lying there next to her. Then she giggled and rolled away. The bed had been stripped, and Joyce was sprawled in the middle of a bare mattress, her legs spread obscenely. Dede buried her head in Joyce's crotch while Joyce leered at Dancer. As Joyce began to whimper, Dede smiled at Dancer and slowly circled her lips with her little pink tongue.

When he woke again, Kelly was sitting in a chair by his bed reading the newspaper. Dancer was back in the hospital room. His fingers throbbed. According to the clock on the wall, it was 2:30. He'd slept through lunch.

"The world still out there?" Dancer said. His words were muffled like there was a towel over his mouth. His throat felt like sandpaper.

Kelly jumped up from his chair. "Hey, Dancer!" His smile was almost as good as the morphine. "How you doing, pardner?"

Dancer took a sip from his water cup. "I've had better days," he said, his voice still distant and fuzzy.

Kelly glanced at Dancer's bandaged left hand, and his smile faded. "I'm sorry..."

The buzz of good feeling that Dancer had felt when he spotted Kelly vanished. He didn't need Kelly's pity. "It was an accident," he said.

Kelly stuck his hands in his front pockets and cocked his head to the side. "What happened?"

Dede and Joyce had happened. Dede had betrayed him. Dancer remembered his hand sliding over the oily surface of the sheet metal like Joyce's hands had slipped along the curve of Dede's smooth, glistening back. He had been angry. Confused. He was willing to cut off his little finger to get back at Dede and start a new life. Someplace. But that's not what happened. Clayton had saved him. The feel of his hands clinging to Dancer's neck had stopped him. It *was* an accident.

"I don't know what happened. Brandon came over--"

"What the hell was Brandon doing there?"

Dancer shrugged. "I thought maybe something happened at home. Then I'm on the ground, Brandon's screaming, and the next thing I remember I wake up here. Without my goddamn hand." He stared hard at Kelly.

"Fucking Percy had no business putting you on that machine."

"Knock, knock." A man in a blue blazer, sporting a flattop crew-cut stood in the doorway gripping a shiny leather briefcase in one hand while he pretended to knock with the other. He was one of the suits from the plant. "Excuse me, Mr. Stonemason?" He marched to the foot of Dancer's bed, stiff and officious, like a shave-tail lieutenant. "I'm your personnel manager. Sam Kellerman."

Kelly's smile disappeared as he stepped back from the bed to face the man. The muscles in his jaw were working overtime. "Kellerman," he said, his voice flat.

"Ah, Mr. Doyle. We meet again."

Kelly looked back at Dancer, and his eyes rolled toward the ceiling. "I'll see you tomorrow, pardner." He walked past Kellerman to the door, but Kellerman put his hand on his sleeve. "Could we visit once more after work tomorrow? I have a few follow-up questions."

Kelly jerked his arm out of Kellerman's grip and kept walking to the door. "You're the boss."

Kellerman waited until Doyle was out of the room, then moved around to the side of the bed where Kelly had been standing. He attempted a smile. "How are you feeling, Mr. Stonemason?"

Dancer shrugged. "Not great." His throat was dry, and his voice raspy. He reached for his water cup. He sucked on the plastic flex-straw they had provided him so he wouldn't spill. Kellerman was one of those eager young managers who passed through the Maple Springs operation on their way up the corporate ladder. That was probably why Kelly couldn't stand him.

"Sorry we have to meet under these circumstances. Our kids are on the same baseball team. I was at that game when your boy hit two homeruns."

Dancer made a slurping sound as he sucked the cup dry. The tepid water soothed his vocal chords. "Missed that one. Percy gave me a special project." When he mentioned Percy's name, Kellerman's face brightened.

"Well, I have something that will make you feel a little better." He set his briefcase down and pulled an envelope from his blazer pocket. He smiled as he held up the envelope. "A check for two weeks' pay. The company doesn't want you fretting about your income at a time like this." He held out the check for Dancer.

"Just put it under the water pitcher," Dancer said, still holding on to his empty water cup. "My wife will be here later." Kellerman showed a twinge of disappointment that he couldn't make the handoff. He acted as if it were a special gift he had arranged, but Dancer knew the short-term disability payment was required by the union contract.

Dancer hoped the check delivery was the only reason for Kellerman's visit, but after he had secured the envelope under the water pitcher, he pulled a chair up to the side of Dancer's bed, like he was planning to stay for a while. From his briefcase he retrieved a manila folder full of papers.

He told Dancer the company took workplace accidents very seriously. They wanted to make sure not only Dancer was taken care of, but that this kind of thing didn't happen again.

He asked why Dancer was operating the Pexto. Dancer didn't reckon Kellerman knew anything about Thacker's special arrangement with Crenshaw in Specialty Fabrication.

"They needed someone to fill in for Tommy Harter," Dancer said.

"Did John Gardner select you for that assignment?" Kellerman asked.

"Percy sent me."

Kellerman smiled the same way that Crutchfield had smiled every time Dancer answered the question the way he expected.

"I know Thacker sometimes made his people available to Crenshaw. That's against company policy, but that's a matter for another day. What I don't understand is why he would send you over there to operate the Pexto when he had Bob McGrady available. McGrady has experience operating that machine."

"I just do what they tell me."

Kellerman frowned. "Come on, Dancer. Isn't it true that Percy Thacker had tried to recruit you for that little club he runs over in Mountain View?"

"Percy never asked me to join anything."

Kellerman shook his head. "You don't have to worry about Percy. I'll take care of him."

Dancer closed his eyes. This cautious young man intent on making it up the next rung of the corporate ladder would be no match for Percy Thacker. "Could we do this another time? I'm feeling like shit."

"Of course." Kellerman tried to smile, but at the corners of his mouth there was a twitchiness he couldn't conceal. He flipped through the file folder. "Just one last question. What was Brandon Thacker doing over in Fabrication?"

"I don't know. Maybe he missed me." Turning away from Kellerman, Dancer set his cup on the nightstand and reached for the call button. He needed another shot.

Kellerman had leaned forward in his chair. "Did you have words with Brandon? Did he get you agitated? Distracted?"

Dancer closed his eyes, willing Kellerman to leave. "I don't know why he was there," he said as he squeezed the button.

Kellerman patted the edge of Dancer's bed. "No worries. The company's going to take care of you, Dancer. We'll work it out – just you and me – we don't need to get a bunch of outsiders involved. After you get out of here, we'll get together and figure out how to get you back on your feet."

After Kellerman had stowed all his corporate documents and marched out of the room, Dancer held up his bandaged hand, which now throbbed with every beat of his heart. In one week his whole life had gone to hell. Getting back on his feet. That wasn't going to be easy.

32

Dancer wasn't ready to go home. As he sat in his wheelchair outside the entrance of Lutheran General, he shivered. Dede had gone to fetch the Chevy from the hospital parking lot and left Dancer with Roy, the Negro attendant who had carted Dancer everywhere for the last five days.

"Do you need a blanket, Mr. Stonemason?" Roy asked.

Dancer shook his head. "I could use one of those 'feel-good' shots." They stopped giving him morphine the previous day. Doctor Langer had prescribed painkillers – fancy aspirin that just dulled the pain, but didn't help his mood.

Roy patted his shoulder. "I hear ya," he said. "Here's your missus." Roy pushed the wheelchair to the curb. Dede jumped out of the car and started to walk around to open the door.

Dancer waved her off. "I can manage," he said.

Dede drove north toward Maple Springs. In thirty minutes they would be home. Dancer was desperate to see his boys and dreading it at the same time. Jimmy would be fine – he'd grow up never knowing anything but the defective version of Dancer. But Clayton. It was going to be hard to face Clayton. That boy thought his father could do anything, and now Dancer could hardly take a piss without help. Shaving, getting dressed, driving the car – he'd have to relearn everything, and he would never be as good as before. Neither would his marriage.

He had spent hours in that hospital bed trying to sort out his options. He could leave Dede and Maple Springs, start over someplace new. But what would he do with his boys? Without a job or even any prospects, he couldn't take them with him. He went round and round until he wanted to knock himself unconscious just so he could stop thinking about it. He craved the morphine, not because it dulled the pain in his hand, but because it let him stop thinking about the hopelessness of his life. It was sweet oblivion, and he needed that.

He wasn't ready to go home.

Dede turned onto US63, and the transmission screeched as she tried to shift the old Chevy into third.

"Use the goddamn clutch," Dancer said.

Dede's cheeks colored, but she didn't yell back at him like she would have if he hadn't been damaged. That made him even more angry. "We can't afford a new car," he said.

Dede stared straight ahead. "I'm trying," she said.

They passed through the Pomona four corners, and the engine labored as the Chevy climbed Walnut Hill. Dede had a death grip on the steering wheel. She was not going to shift out of third. Dancer swallowed his advice. He watched the scenery roll by. They sliced through a wooded area, and deep in the forest, Dancer thought he saw a cabin. It resembled the shack they had moved to after their farmhouse had burned down. He pushed closer to the window trying to get a better look.

They crested the hill and spread out below was a patchwork quilt of farmland. A dozen cows stared disinterestedly at the graveyard of rusted automobiles that bordered their pasture. On the horizon, a gleaming white farmhouse beckoned. As they neared the farmhouse it became grey and weathered. A small boy dribbled a basketball on the dirt-packed driveway, hoisted a shot toward the hoop fastened above the garage door. The ball rimmed around and fell through. The boy raised his arms in celebration.

"Does your hand hurt?" Dede asked. Her eyebrows were peaked as she glanced at Dancer, who was rubbing his hands together.

"No," Dancer said. He let go of his hands and tucked them under his armpits.

Dancer eased himself out of the car and stepped onto the gravel driveway. His body was stiff as though they had been riding for hours. The kitchen door snapped open, and Clayton raced down the porch steps followed closely by Jimmy.

"Daddy!" he cried. Clayton hugged Dancer around the waist and buried his face in his chest. Jimmy grabbed hold of Dancer's leg.

"Now this is what I call a welcome committee," Dancer said. The knot in his stomach relaxed. It was like when the morphine kicked in, and everything seemed right with the world. He knelt down and rubbed Clayton's back. He picked up Jimmy and held him high with both hands as Jimmy squealed.

"Does that hurt your hand?" Clayton asked.

Dancer set Jimmy down and smiled at Clayton. His first smile in a week. "No, it doesn't hurt. I just got to be careful that I get a good grip." He showed his hand to Clayton.

"What are those prickly things?" Clayton asked pointing at the sutures that sealed the ends of the three stubs.

"Stitches. They'll be taking them out next week." Dancer stood up and looked over his backyard. "Need to get these leaves raked. We better get on that tomorrow. Right, Clayton?" He winked at Dede. She smiled warily.

"Tomorrow's Halloween!" Clayton said.

Dancer rubbed his hand over Clayton's bristly crew-cut. "Is that why there's an angry pumpkin sitting on our front porch?"

"Can you take us trick-or-treating, Dad? I'm going to be Davy Crockett and Jimmy's going to be an Indian. Show Dad, Jimmy."

Jimmy jumped up and down and smacked his mouth with his hand. "Woo hoo woo hoo!"

"Go wash your hands, boys," Dede said. "We're having a special dinner. All of daddy's favorites."

Dancer took Jimmy and Clayton by the hand, and together they climbed up the deck stairs and into the kitchen. His boys loved him. They didn't care that he was damaged. There was a tightness in his chest as he watched them run up the backstairs to their room. It would break his heart to lose them.

The kitchen door snapped shut as Dede followed him into the kitchen. The mellow good feeling that seeing his boys had generated evaporated instantly. All the hours he spent in the hospital thinking about Dede and their situation, and he was still paralyzed. He didn't know what road he could take to get past, through, or around the problem.

Dede opened the refrigerator and pulled out the steaks she had been marinating. She turned on the oven broiler and looked over her shoulder at Dancer. "Dinner will be ready in a half hour." Her smile was cautious. He could see she was struggling to find a way out, too.

"I'm beat. I'm going to lie down for a while." He wasn't that tired, but he didn't want to be alone in the kitchen with Dede.

Dancer lay on his bed and listened to his boys playing in their bedroom. His hand ached. It seemed like every time he started to feel better, or at least a little less hopeless, the hand would start to throb as if to remind him that his life was a mess. In the next days and weeks, there would be countless physical challenges. It wasn't fair that on top of it all, he had to figure out his marriage and what to do about the woman he thought he loved. The woman he had been so certain of.

Dede called for the boys, and they rumbled down the stairs. Dancer walked into the bathroom and splashed water on his face. He looked gaunt and hospital pale. A good meal or two would help. He went down the front stairs and walked through the dining room, headed to the kitchen. The crystal globe that Joyce had given Dede was still on the hutch on its satin pillow, next to the framed picture of Dancer and Clayton celebrating the perfect game. His hand ached again.

The steaks sizzled as Dede pulled them out of the broiler. After a week of bland, easy-to-eat hospital mush, the aroma of the steaks made Dancer's stomach rumble with anticipation. But as he watched Dede carve the boys' meat into bite-sized pieces, his mouth turned dry. How would he cut his steak?

Dede finished cutting up the first steak and split up the pieces between Jimmy and Clayton. She began to cut up the second steak.

"You don't have to do that," Dancer said.

Dede gave him that same uncertain smile. "I don't mind," she said.

"I can cut my own meat," Dancer said. He held out his plate and Dede cut the steak in half. She kept the bone and gave him the easier-to-cut piece.

Dancer picked up the fork with his thumb and forefinger and stabbed the steak to keep it from sliding. With the steak knife in his right hand he sawed off a small piece of fat. He hadn't used his left hand for much of anything since the accident, and the muscles throbbed as he pressed down with the fork. Jimmy continued to shovel mashed potatoes into his mouth, but Clayton, fork frozen in mid-air, stared silently at his father.

Dancer carved off another piece. "Don't wait for me, Clayton. This might take a while," he said. He forced a smile.

He developed a rhythm. Stab. Saw. Stab. Saw. Stab. Saw. It only took him a couple minutes to reduce the steak to a small stub. He jabbed at the last piece and struck gristle. A jolt of pain surged up from his phantom fingers all the way to his shoulder. "Fuck!" he yelled as the fork torqued out of his hand and clattered onto the plate.

Dancer could feel his face burning as the boys stared at him. They finished the meal quickly and retreated to their rooms to play. As Dede cleared the table, Dancer took the bottle of Jack Daniels Kelly left him as a coming home gift and went out to the porch. Dede had bought two redwood stained picnic chairs with wide flat armrests and padded vinyl cushions at Crutchfields' end-of-season sale. Dancer poured a glass of whiskey and placed it on the armrest. He settled into the comfy chair and stared up at the star-studded sky. The moon was nearly full. Only a small sliver was missing.

There was a chill in the air, but as Dancer sipped the whiskey it warmed him from the inside. He hoped it would flip the switch that made everything seem a little less hopeless. He was on his third tumbler when he heard the swish of Clayton's foot pajamas behind him.

"Are you going to come up and read to us, Dad?"

"Not tonight, Clayton. Sort of beat right now." He put down his drink and gestured with his right arm. "Come here, buddy." Clayton scooted across the floor, and Dancer wrapped his arm around him. The sweaty boy smell and the nubby softness of Clayton's flannel PJs stirred a hazy memory of curling up in a musty blanket on his cot in Clem Danforth's cabin.

141

Clayton hugged him and with a muffled voice he said, "Goodnight, Daddy."

33

The next afternoon, Kelly dropped in after his shift was over with news from the plant.

"Let's go out on the porch," Dancer said. He grabbed the now half-empty bottle of Jack Daniels, ignoring the look from Dede.

Kelly pulled up his chair next to Dancer's and held his tumbler while Dancer poured. "Hold on to your hat, pardner. Your buddy Brandon up and quit."

Dancer stopped pouring. "You're kidding. What happened?"

"Don't know. Has to be something to do with your accident. Percy stayed in his office all day with the door closed. And there are fucking suits from corporate crawling all over the place."

Dancer filled his own glass and took a generous sip. The whiskey warmed the back of his throat as it went down. Brandon. He remembered lying on the damp floor and hearing Brandon wail. It hadn't sounded human. It was as if it had been his fingers amputated. "Damn. I always figured Brandon to be a lifer," Dancer said.

"I'll bet my car that they're going to settle with you. They ain't going to want all the bad publicity. You're going to make out alright, Danceman."

The kitchen door swung open, and Dede stuck her head out. "I've got to finish sewing Clayton's coonskin cap, so could you and Kelly swing over to the store and get us some more Halloween candy? I think there's going to be a lot more kids this year."

Kelly jumped up. "You bet, Dede. We got you covered."

Dancer shook his head. "I don't need Kelly's help. When we're done here I'll drive over to the store."

"It's no problem," Kelly said. He squeezed Dancer's shoulder.

"No," Dancer said. He said it hard, not wanting any more discussion. Dede wasn't going to dictate what he could do and not do. And he didn't want Kelly's pity.

He took a long sip of his whiskey. He got up, walked to the edge of the deck, and gazed at his yard where he had probably thrown ten thousand pitches. He made a fist with his good hand and pounded the palm of his bad hand. Pain surged from his missing fingers all the way up to his neck. But it wasn't as bad as it had been yesterday. Someday, he'd probably be able to use his bad hand and not feel anything. He reckoned not feeling anything was the best he could hope for.

Kelly stood in the middle of the porch, his hands jammed into his wranglers. "Guess I'll be going."

"Thanks for stopping by," Dancer said. His tone was flat; he didn't mean it. There was no reason to do that to Kelly, but he didn't want Kelly trying to do him favors. It made him angry. He flopped back into his chair and took another sip. Waiting for that switch to click on.

Driving the car was easy. He didn't need a left hand. He picked up a couple bags of candy bars at the Foodliner and was on his way home when he decided to take the long way back, past Maple Springs High School. He pulled into the school parking lot and drove around the tennis courts and the outdoor basketball courts to the baseball diamond. He pulled up in front of the chain-link fence behind home plate.

They still had the same plank bleachers along the first base line behind the bench where the players sat. The day he struck out twenty batters from Cabool, freshman Dede Holmes had sat in the far corner of the top row cheering her lungs out with her best friend, Joyce Reynolds. Dede and her alcoholic mom had moved in from the boondocks to a trailer on the west side of town a few months before Dede entered high school. Dede and Joyce. Even back then. Had she ever loved him? Had their whole marriage been a lie?

The sun was setting behind him, and it cast long shadows over the field. The moon was full – the sliver missing yesterday had been restored. It loomed, unnaturally large, over the centerfield fence, shining like a spotlight on the pitcher's mound.

Dancer closed his eyes and tried to remember that day. He had been invincible. Batter after batter had gone down. No one could touch him. No one.

There was a tap on his window, and he jolted awake. "Mister, are you okay?" A teenage boy dressed like a pirate and his girlfriend, wearing a witch's hat, had parked next to him. Dancer looked at his watch. Ten p.m. Shit.

He shook his head trying to wake himself up. "Yeah, I'm fine."

As the teenagers headed back to their car, he started the engine. He had let his boys down. Again. He drove the streets of Maple Springs for a half hour not wanting to stay out, but not wanting to go home either.

When he finally pulled into his driveway, he could see Dede looking out from the living room window. She met him at the kitchen door.

"Where have you been?" Her eyes were red and rimmed with tears.

"The boys still up?" he asked. He hoped he would hear them scramble down the stairs, but they had long ago gone to bed. He sighed and hitched his shoulders. "I drove over to the ballpark and must have fallen asleep."

Dede looked into his eyes. "Asleep? Are you drunk? Goddammit, Dancer. I was worried to death about you. You were supposed to take the boys trick-or-treating."

He walked past her into the dining room and tossed the bags of candy onto the table. "The boys can divide this up tomorrow. I'm going to bed." He stepped for the stairway, but Dede grabbed his sleeve.

"Jesus Christ, Dancer! It's one thing to treat me like shit, but those boys don't deserve it. You promised them."

Dancer ripped his arm out of her grip. His head pounded, and he wasn't in the mood to listen to Dede harping at him. "I treat you like shit? That's almost funny. Don't lecture me about keeping promises."

"Mommy, what's wrong?" Clayton peered down from the upstairs landing. "Daddy, where'd you go?"

Dancer reached back for the bag of candy he had dropped on the table. He would explain to Clayton about getting lost in his dreams and losing track of the time. A boy could understand that. But before he had a chance, Dede pushed past him and ran up the stairs.

"Come on, hon. You go back to bed now." She took Clayton's hand and led him back into his bedroom.

Dancer stood at the foot of the empty staircase. Dede was murmuring to Clayton as she tucked him into bed, but he couldn't hear what she was saying.

34

When Dancer awoke the next morning, Dede's side of the bed was empty. His hand throbbed, and his body ached from lack of use. He dressed, and as he headed down to the kitchen, he spotted Dede asleep on top of the bed in the guestroom. He hadn't slept well, and the lack of sleep made him edgy. Maybe a drink would help to smooth things out. He opened the cabinet next to the kitchen sink, but his whiskey was gone. He flung open the other cabinets. Nothing. He was about to check in the refrigerator, when he caught himself. What was he doing acting desperate for a drink like some kind of alcoholic? He took his hand off the handle to the refrigerator.

"What you looking for, Dad?" Clayton stood in the kitchen doorway, his head cocked like he was trying to find a better angle to view his father.

Dancer opened the refrigerator door and grabbed a bottle of milk. "Hey, you want to play a little catch before your bus comes?"

Clayton squinted at him. "Can you do that?"

Dancer flexed his finger and thumb. It didn't hurt much to do that. "Yeah, why not? As long as you go easy on me. Take a little off your fastball for now."

With the padded catcher's mitt, Dancer discovered he had no difficulty catching the ball and the discomfort was minor. In fact, it was a good pain. Something he could work through, like a tired muscle. And when he threw the baseball his whole attitude changed. His right arm was still strong, undamaged. His pitching motion was smooth and natural – not something he had to spend hours relearning. He had Clayton running all over the yard chasing down grounders and pop flies. Before either of them knew it, an hour had passed.

Dede stepped out on to the porch with Jimmy on her hip. She watched for a couple minutes, not smiling, not frowning. Just observing. Finally, she said, "You need some breakfast, Clayton."

Clayton scurried for a groundball headed for the driveway. With a smooth sidearm motion, he hurled it toward Dancer. "I'm not hungry," he said.

Dancer started walking toward the porch. "That's enough for today. You need your breakfast, boy. Keep up your strength."

Dede's face remained expressionless. "Do you want some coffee?"

Dancer shook his head. "I'm going to rake up these leaves." Until that moment he hadn't known that was what he was going to do. But playing ball with Clayton had given him an idea.

Dede looked at him with that same who-is-this-man tilt to her head as Clayton had. She shrugged and walked back into the kitchen.

The physical labor had the effect Dancer had hoped for. It was just hard enough that he didn't think about having a drink. It felt good to sweat. When he was sweating he didn't think about

Dede or his messed up hand or what he was going to do with the rest of his life. He had been at it for several hours before he noticed his hand no longer ached. No more phantom finger pains. Maybe his brain was no longer confused.

By the time Clayton came home from school, he had cleared the front and back yards and made a huge bonfire in the vacant lot behind their house. The leaves crackled and made a heavy white smoke that stung his eyes whenever the wind shifted. It reminded him of the fires the Danforths used to build when they percolated their moonshine.

"Hey, you burned my leaf fort," Clayton said.

"Don't get too close," Dancer said as he raked dirt over the dying embers. "How was school?"

Clayton made a face. "Do you want to play some more catch?"

Dancer smiled at him. "Can't today. Working on a special project. Do you want to help?"

Clayton's brow furrowed. "What is it?" he asked.

Dancer laughed. "I thought I'd make a mound and put in a home plate so we can work on our pitching."

By the time Dede called them for dinner, they had groomed a respectable looking pitcher's mound and had buried a flagstone in the ground in front of the wall of the garage that would have do for home plate until they found something better.

At dinner Dede acted like yesterday had never happened. Dancer tried to do the same, but he was not as good at pretending as Dede. He figured she'd had a lot more practice. He hadn't wanted a drink all day, the work had kept his mind off everything including the booze, but now with Dede being so normal-acting, he really wanted to get away and have a drink. But the whiskey was gone and he was tired from the long day's work, so while Dede did the dishes, he took the boys up to bed and read them a story.

After he put the boys down, he got ready for bed. The leaf raking had been a good idea. It kept him occupied and tired him enough that he reckoned he would fall asleep before he began stewing about Dede and everything else. He had just turned out the lights and was thinking of what project he should tackle next, when the bedroom door creaked open. Dede slipped into the room. She sat on the edge of the bed and undressed.

"Mind if I join you?" she asked.

"Okay," he said. He rolled onto his side and watched as she unclasped her bra and slipped off her panties. Dancer hoped she would just slip under the covers, and they could have sex without talking about any of the stuff they had been avoiding. But Dede jumped up and grabbed her nightgown from the chair next to her dresser. She gathered it up as if to put it on over her head and smiled at Dancer, with the flirty look he knew so well.

"Come on," he said, throwing back the covers.

She dropped the nightgown and skipped over to the bed. The sway of her breasts reminded him that the last time he had seen her naked she was in bed with Joyce. Dancer was aroused and angry. Dede slipped into the bed and snuggled up next to him. She ran her hand over his chest and stroked his cock. Dancer pushed her on to her back and rolled on top. He spread her legs, and she gasped as he entered her in one quick push. She wrapped her legs around him and dug her fingernails into his shoulders. With each thrust he grunted like some kind of animal. And as he came, an anguished sob escaped from deep in his chest. He pushed his fist into his mouth, as if stopping the sound would stop what he was feeling. His breath was ragged, and his chest heaved as he tried to fill his lungs with air.

Dede lightly patted his back. A tentative touch, as though fearful he might attack.

Slowly, his breathing returned to normal. He lay on his back and stared up at the ceiling, his good hand kneading the bad one.

"We need to talk." Dede was sitting up, her arms wrapped around her knees. "Well, I need to talk. You need to listen."

Dancer rolled his head back on the pillow and closed his eyes. "Okay," he said.

"I love you, Dancer. You have to know that. I'm sorry about Joyce." She took a deep breath and rubbed her hands over her face. "I was 14 when my mother lost her house and we had to move to that trailer. I had to go to a school where I had no friends, and everyone thought they were better than me. I thought so too. I gave the boys blowjobs just so they would like me." She laughed bitterly. "Who knows what would have happened to me if Joyce hadn't decided one day to sit down at my table in the cafeteria? Even then I knew she was different.

She just pretended to like boys. I'd stay over at her place, and we'd sleep together in her big, double bed. I let her do things to me. It made her happy."

Dancer winced. He'd been rubbing his hands again, and he had squeezed too hard on the damaged tendons.

Dede rolled on to her side and stared intently at Dancer. "I'm not like her. I know it seems perverted to you, but I let Joyce love me because I care for her." She stroked Dancer's cheek. "It's you I love, Dancer. I don't want to lose you."

Dancer lifted his mangled hand. "Are you sure about that?" he said.

"Yes, I'm sure. But this town is bad for us. Too much history to live up to. If the company comes through like that Kellerman guy was promising, maybe we could move away. Start over."

Dancer took a deep breath and slowly exhaled. Start over? What reasons did he have to stay in Maple Springs? So he could be reminded of his glory days? Kelly was convinced the company would be anxious to put the incident behind them. Maybe they would offer him a settlement. But would moving fix anything? What was he supposed to do when Dede found another special friend?

"What do you think?" she asked.

"Let's see how it works out with Kellerman." He rolled on to his side and pulled the sheet up around his neck.

35

Kellerman called on Monday and wanted to meet with Dancer the next day. He suggested that Dancer might want to bring Dede along. He didn't say why, but Dancer figured it had to involve offering him some kind of settlement. In the hospital, Kellerman had boasted that he would "take care" of Percy Thacker. That still seemed unlikely, but Kelly told him that the word in the foundry was that Brandon had a big fight with Percy just before he quit.

Whatever Brandon's reasons, Dancer figured the kid was better off out from under his father's thumb. He had a chance for a fresh start. A fresh start sounded like a good idea. Maybe Dede was right. With a decent settlement they could start over someplace new – California, or Florida, or even Arizona. It didn't matter. He would not miss Maple Springs, Missouri.

The receptionist ushered them into a small meeting room. It was windowless and smelled of over-brewed coffee and stale cigarettes. The walls were lined with black and white aerial photos of Caterpillar plants. Seated at the conference table were Sam Kellerman and Dickie Smith, the union rep for local 235.

Kellerman looked up from the yellow legal pad he had been studying and frowned as though he weren't expecting them. He stood tentatively and forced a smile. "Hello, Mrs. Stonemason." He extended his hand. "Sam Kellerman. Please sit down." He motioned to the two chairs on the opposite side of the table.

As they were taking their seats, the door flew open, and Percy Thacker burst in the room. "Sorry, I'm late." He came up behind Dancer and put his hand on Dancer's neck. "Don't get up." He smiled at Dede. "Welcome, Mrs. Stonemason. My name's Percy Thacker." He grabbed a folding chair that was propped up against the wall and placed it at the end of the table so that he was between the two groups. He nodded to Kellerman. "Go ahead, Samuel."

A look of annoyance flashed across Kellerman's face. There was no cocky smile as there had been in the hospital. It was obvious to Dancer that Kellerman had learned the lesson most of the eager do-gooder managers that preceded him had learned: it doesn't pay to fuck with Percy Thacker. He cleared his throat and began his speech.

"Mr. Stonemason, my department has conducted a thorough investigation of the incident of October 26th, 1956." He spoke formally like this was a speech he had memorized. He paused to make eye contact with Dancer and seemed to lose his focus. He picked up the notepad and began to read. "We have determined you caused the accident with the intent to extort a disability settlement from the company. We have credible evidence that you chose the venue for the accident so as to create an embarrassing situation for your supervisor, Mr. Thacker." Kellerman stopped and nodded at Percy who sat back in his chair with his arms folded across his chest, looking almost bored as Kellerman continued. "And that you did so because of some personal animosity you harbor toward him and his son."

Dancer's face tingled, and his chest felt hollowed out. All his stupid toasts to Homer Judson. His drunken fantasizing about million dollar accidents. In that euphoric, intoxicating bubble he never bothered to think about consequences. He could see Dede out of the corner of his eye, twisting her hands together. When Kellerman read the part about Thacker, she turned and stared at him. She wanted him to jump up and deny the accusation, but he couldn't do that. Even though in the end, he hadn't meant to push his hand across the line, he was still guilty as charged.

Kellerman continued. "We've discussed this with your union representative, Mr. Smith. The union does not in any way condone your actions. Having said that, the company is not without compassion. This is a small town, and we're all neighbors here. We are prepared to offer you a severance payment of one thousand dollars to help you transition to a new life. All we require is that you sign this release, absolving the company and Mr. Thacker of any culpability in this incident. This will be a confidential matter between you and the company so you will be able to get on with your life, without the stigma that would attach if you chose a more contentious route."

Kellerman took another deep breath as though reading the speech had exhausted him. He opened his briefcase and retrieved another document which he handed to Dancer. It was a single page of legal looking text, with a cashier's check for one thousand dollars stapled to it.

All Dancer wanted was to get out of that room. He needed a drink. He needed to get drunk. He shouldn't have brought Dede. As Dancer reached for a pen, Dede grabbed his arm.

"Tell them to go to hell. They're just protecting him." She spit the words at Thacker. "We don't need their goddamn money." She shoved the paper back across the table.

Kellerman blanched as he caught the check before it slipped off the edge.

Percy Thacker leaned forward and took the check from Kellerman. He smiled smugly and with more of a country twang than Dancer had ever heard from him, he said, "Mrs. Stonemason. I know you're upset. I don't blame, you. But now is not the time for fighting. This is the time for healing. Picking up the pieces. Making the best of a sorry situation."

"We don't—"

Percy held up his hand. "Please, let me finish." He nodded in Kellerman's direction. "Mr. Kellerman should have explained the most important thing that we're offering."

Kellerman flushed, but didn't say anything.

"Workmen's comp. Sign that paper, and we're not going to contest Dancer's claim. I suspect your hospital bills are sizeable." He paused. "Of course, if you don't want to accept this settlement, then we're going to have to dispute that this was an accident." He looked around the table. "Now I know I don't want to do that and I don't think Dancer wants that fight either. Do you, Dancer?"

Dancer reached over and tugged the paper out of Percy's hand. He scrawled his name on the signature line and shoved it back to him. "Fuck you, Percy."

36

Dancer walked quickly from the admin office to the parking lot and was ten paces ahead of Dede when he got to the car. She slipped into the car and slammed the door without saying anything. Dancer stuffed the cashier's check in his pants pocket and started the engine. Dede stared at the floor.

As they pulled on to the highway, she frowned at Dancer. "So that's why you were so intent on telling me this was an accident? I thought it was my fault, but you planned this?" she said, her voice rising. "Jesus, Dancer."

Dancer's hand shook and he had to bring his bad hand up to steady the steering wheel. "That was all just barroom talk. Bullshit. It was an accident." His voice cracked. The look on Dede's face made him feel dirty. Like a pervert. He needed a drink.

When they got home, Dede practically sprinted to the house. She paid the babysitter and put Jimmy in his baby carriage and hiked up the hill like she was still going to work at the Landis development. Dancer was relieved to see her go. He retrieved their checkbook and collected all the past due bills. He wrote checks to the hospital, the dentist, the electric company, McMurray's Hardware, and the bank for the December mortgage payment. With all those payments, after he deposited the company's cashier's check, they would have two hundred fifty seven dollars left. Not enough for anyone to escape.

When he presented the check for deposit, the teller called over the bank manager for his approval. The manager, who usually offered Dancer an ingratiating smile and a few baseball comments, glanced disinterestedly at the check, scribbled something on the back and said to the teller, "It's okay." Without a word to Dancer he turned and walked away.

The teller smiled nervously. "Would you like any cash back from the deposit?"

Dancer stared at the back of the bank manager as he lumbered back to his desk. The manager knew. In a few days, everyone in town would know about Dancer's "confidential" agreement. "Forty dollars," he told the teller.

After he mailed the bills at the drop box in front of the Post Office, he stopped at Main Street Liquor and bought a bottle of Three Feathers Whiskey for five dollars. It wasn't Jack Daniels, but it would work the same.

Dede hadn't yet returned to the house with Jimmy, and Clayton was still at school. Whenever he thought about a life without his boys, he got a cold feeling that began in his stomach and coursed through his body, as though he were dying from the inside out. The whiskey helped him get rid of that cold feeling but he knew it wouldn't solve his problem.

He set the bottle of whiskey on the deck and walked into the garage to find some baseballs. He had hurled most of them into the vacant lot the night he quit baseball, but in the bottom of the toy barrel he found four old ones that he had stowed long ago when Clayton was just a toddler. He walked out to the new mound they had built last week. Pitching always helped him think things through, and if he was going to escape from this mess, he needed a clear head.

He went into his windup and hurled an easy fast ball at the brick wall. It made a satisfying *plunk* sound and rolled about halfway back. He needed to get away. That was obvious. With Dede, the Thackers, and all the town gossips, there was no place for him in Maple Springs. He just had to figure out how he would take care of his boys.

The next pitch hit higher on the wall, but still in the strike zone. It rolled almost back to his feet. The key was to get out of Maple Springs. Out of Missouri. Out of the south. Maybe California. That was a land of opportunity. A place a man could start over. He'd get a good job, and then he'd bring the boys out.

He grabbed another ball. He was feeling okay now. He reared back to put a little extra on the pitch, but when he planted his right foot for the follow-through, a chunk of the new mound dislodged, and his foot slipped out from under him. He tumbled off the mound and instinctively stuck out his left hand to break the fall. The pain was almost as bad as when the Pexto had sheared his fingers off. He curled into a ball and rocked back and forth like a little boy.

When the pain finally subsided, he got to his feet. He picked up the last baseball and flung it deep into the vacant lot. Pitching therapy wasn't going to work anymore. He trudged back to the porch and flopped into the deck chair.

As he sipped his first drink of the day, he heard the front door slam and Jimmy squeal as Dede took him upstairs for his afternoon nap. After a while, he heard Dede's soft footsteps on the back stairs. They stopped at the door to the porch, and he knew that Dede was watching him. She didn't say anything, and he didn't turn around. He drained his tumbler and poured himself another drink. Maybe the booze wouldn't solve his problems, but at least it killed the pain so he could think about his escape plan.

He had just poured his third tumbler when Kelly Doyle's yellow Sunliner rolled into the driveway.

"You're looking mighty comfortable there, pardner," Kelly said. He was all dressed up in his good khakis and a button down white shirt like he was headed someplace important.

It felt great to see Kelly again. They had hardly talked since Halloween. He realized how much he had missed Kelly's company. "Want a drink?" Dancer asked as he stood up and clasped Kelly on the shoulder.

Kelly shook his head. "I got some errands to run, but I want to talk to you. Can you meet me at Jake's tonight? About 7? It's important." Kelly smiled, but it wasn't his charm smile. It was more real, more close to the bone.

Dancer set his drink down. "I'll be there."

A half hour later, Dancer had just poured his fourth drink when he spotted Clayton running up the sidewalk from the bus stop, his face flushed and contorted as though he were crying. Dancer heard Clayton yell for his mother before the door slammed. He set down his drink and pushed himself out of the chair. He hadn't eaten all day, and he felt lightheaded. It took a moment for him to gather himself.

When he walked into the kitchen, Dede was dabbing Clayton's face with a washcloth. There was a split in Clayton's lower lip, and his right cheek was turning an ugly yellowish purple.

"What happened?" Dancer asked.

Clayton stared at him like he was the one who had beaten him. Dede gave him the same impatient look as the bank manager. Like he wasn't worth her time. Her mouth twisted sourly. "He was in a fight."

"I can see that. What happened, Clayton?"

"Let it go, Dancer," Dede said. It was more of a plea than an order.

But Dancer couldn't let it go. "Who were you fighting with?"

"Sammy Kellerman." Clayton looked up at his father. His soft brown eyes flooded with tears. "He said you chopped off your fingers on purpose."

Dancer felt like someone had sucker punched him. He couldn't breathe. The look on Clayton's face was worse than losing his mother, his father, or his fingers. At that moment he knew he could never make things right with Clayton. He stared at the floor, wishing it would just open up and let him disappear forever.

Clayton ran out of the kitchen, through the dining room and up the stairs to his bedroom.

Dede ran after him. She yelled from the foot of the stairs, "Let me get you some ice for your lip, honey."

Dancer couldn't leave it like that. He had to say something to Clayton. He pushed open the kitchen door and found Dede standing in front of the hutch holding the framed photograph of the perfect game. "What are you doing?" he asked.

Dede's lip curled with disgust. "The perfect game. What a fucking joke. That game destroyed you. I hate it." She raised the frame over her head like she was going to throw it on the ground, but Dancer grabbed it from her.

"It's you and your girlfriend that fucked everything up." Dancer put the photo back and grabbed the crystal ball. "You want to break something, break this." He flung the ball at Dede like it was a basketball. She caught it against her chest, but it slipped out of her hands and crashed to the floor, shattering like a glass grenade – shards flying to all corners of the dining room.

Dede screamed. She knelt down to pick up one of the pieces and sliced open her finger. "Goddammit." She jumped up and shook her hand. Blood droplets splashed on the floor.

Upstairs, Jimmy wailed.

Dancer reflexively reached out toward her.

"Don't touch me," she screamed. "Get out of here! And don't come back."

"Mom!" Clayton had come back down the stairs. His eyes were wild.

"*You,* want *me* to leave?" Dancer said, angry again. He wanted to go, but not because Dede told him to. He reached out as though to grab her, but he didn't really know what he wanted to do.

"Don't touch her!" Clayton sobbed and ran at his father, his fists flailing. "Go away," he said. His tiny fists stung more than they should have.

Dancer turned away from his first born son, his unfaithful wife, and his wailing baby boy and walked out the back door. He jumped in the Chevy, but in his haste to escape he flooded the engine. He pumped the gas pedal and ground the starter until it gave up. He left the keys in the ignition and started walking to Jake's. He wasn't going to let Kelly down.

37

Dancer had finished his second beer by the time Kelly arrived.

"I see you got a head start," Kelly said as he settled on to the barstool next to Dancer. Jake brought them fresh drafts and shook hands with Kelly. "You take care, Kelly."

Dancer felt a twinge in his guts. Kelly smiled at him, but his trademark grin had lost its sparkle. "I'm starting a new job next week. Selling Cadillacs in K.C. with my ex-brother-in-law."

"You're leaving Maple Springs?"

Kelly swallowed hard and licked his lips. "Kellerman fired me."

Dancer's mouth had gone dry, but his throat was so tight he could barely swallow his beer. "I'm sorry," he said. His voice sounded brittle. Weak and inadequate.

Kelly tapped Dancer's forearm. "It's a good opportunity. You know me. I'm very persuasive." The old Kelly smile returned for an instant as he signaled for Jake. "How about a shot of the good stuff for old time's sake?"

They had a shot, but when Dancer suggested another round, Kelly begged off. He had to leave early in the morning. "You take care. I'll be back in a few weeks to check on you. Probably driving a fancy new Cadillac," he said, playing the Texas cowboy for Dancer one last time.

Dancer stayed at the bar and had a few more shots of Jake's cheap stuff. It was weak booze, and the feel-better switch hadn't clicked on yet. Across the bar at the bowling machine, he heard someone call his name.

"Hey, Danceman. Wanna play?" It was Mickey, his bowling opponent from that day he had rolled the near perfect game. He was with a bunch of his buddies, and they all laughed as though the invitation was some kind of joke. Dancer picked up his shot glass and drained the last remaining drops.

"Guess he's too busy, boys," Mickey said. "Thought you'd have plenty of time, Danceman. Now that your old lady's got her own girlfriend." Their laughter was an explosion that filled the bar for an instant and then vanished. They returned to their game like he was already gone.

Dancer held up his shot glass, but Jake shook his head. "You've had enough. I'm calling you a cab."

"Fuck you, Jake." Dancer slipped off the stool and pulled a ten dollar bill from his pocket. He slapped it on the bar and walked out the door. He wove his way through the cars, trucks, and motorcycles to the entrance of the parking lot, but instead of heading west on Burnham Hill Road toward his home, he stumbled down the hill to Highway 60 and walked east. Away from Maple Springs. Fuck Jake and his cab. Fuck them all.

38

If it's always darkest before the dawn, Dancer reckoned dawn ought to be arriving very soon. Highway 60 had tapered down so it wasn't much more than a strip of asphalt wide enough for two cars to pass. He could barely see the surface of the road as he shuffled along. He walked by feel – his right foot squishing into the soft crumble of the shoulder, his left foot scraping along on the asphalt.

A tractor trailer crested the hill and blinded Dancer with its high-beams as it roared past, headed west toward Springfield. He tripped as he pivoted away from the bright lights. As he fell, he twisted so he didn't land on his bad hand again. His shoulder hit first, and his chin scraped the road surface. He lay there just as he had in those moments after the accident, remembering the smell of the damp concrete floor, and how he couldn't see through his goggles. Far above him he could hear Brandon screaming.

Dancer had dinged his right knee, and now the knee and his phantom fingers throbbed with every step he took. The pain didn't distract him from his thirst. He was desperate for a drink of water. He had hoped that when he made it to the top of the hill, the lights of Holtville would speckle the valley below, but there was nothing but darkness. No farmhouse lights, no roadhouse, no stars, no moon. Nothing. It was as though the whole world had gone away. He marched down the hill. His pace was faster now, less cautious. Whereever he was headed, he needed to get there soon.

It was nearly dawn. The darkness had given way to gray. A milk truck pulled up next to him, the first vehicle to come down the road in the last hour. The driver, a husky black man with splashes of gray in his close-cropped haircut, stopped the truck and yelled to Dancer through the door opening. "Want a ride, sir?" the man asked.

"Do you have any water?"

The man grinned, his teeth brighter than anything Dancer had seen since he left the bar. He reached behind his seat and grabbed a bottle. "Got some nice cold milk, fresh from the cow. Come on up."

Dancer stepped up into the truck, and the man handed him the glass bottle. "Help yourself. The dairy won't miss it."

Dancer chugged from the bottle. "Thanks," he said. A trickle of the milk dribbled down his neck. He didn't bother to wipe it off.

The man grabbed an empty milk crate. "Sit here," he said. "Where you bound, sir?"

Dancer scratched his head. "I don't know."

"All the more reason to come with me. I can get you there, quicker." He chuckled and held out his hand. "Roland P. Savoy, but my friends call me Rollie."

"Dancer Stonemason."

"You got a strong grip, Dancer. Must be a working man."

He rubbed his sore knee. "Sort of between jobs right now."

"There's a lot of that going around. Don't let it get you down. The Lord will provide."

Dancer's bad hand trembled. He pressed his palms together.

Rollie studied him as he steered the milk truck off the highway onto Holtville Road. "You can't squeeze those shakes out. I been there, son."

"Been where?"

"Sober five years, now. AA saved my life. I can get you to a meeting."

Dancer looked at him to see if he was joking. "I'm not a goddamn alcoholic."

Rollie smiled. "That's what I said, too, the first time someone invited me."

"I'm not interested."

They rode in silence for the next mile.

Rollie downshifted as the truck climbed the last hill outside of Holtville. "You got some place to stay?"

"Just let me off in town, I'll find a place," he said. He hadn't realized how tired he was until he sat down. He could barely keep his eyes open. He needed to sleep. Get his head clear. A little rest and he'd come up with a plan. Right now he couldn't think straight.

"I got a trailer out behind my place. We got it for Matilda's good-for-nothing brother – Matilda's my wife – but that boy's long gone, and he ain't coming back. It's nothing special, but you're welcome to stay there," he said.

Dancer yawned. "Isn't there a motel just outside of town? The Hill something?"

Rollie's face crinkled. "You mean the Hilltop? You don't want to be staying there. They rent those rooms by the hour. And they don't cotton to white folks. Hold on, we're in the homestretch."

Dancer braced himself as they raced down the hill into Holtville. The sun had risen and the greyness had given way to a clear blue-sky morning. A few hours sleep, and then he'd come up with a plan. "Thanks," Dancer said. "The trailer sounds great."

Dede

39

January 1957

It snowed in the night and the sidewalks on Hill Street hadn't been shoveled, so the man walked in the street. From her living room window, Dede could see that he had parked his truck near the bottom of the hill. The early morning sun and the rush of cars headed toward work at the Caterpillar plant had melted the fresh snow, so the man stepped cautiously around slushy puddles as he made his way up the hill.

He stopped for a moment in front of Dede's house. He blew into his hands and rubbed them together – his breath visible in the chill of the morning – then continued walking up the hill. He was trying not to look suspicious, but he would know that a black man, even one in a milkman's uniform, was going to be noticed.

He crossed over and headed back down the street less carefully than he had walked up. Dede slipped on her coat and opened the front door. She marched down the driveway to intercept him.

"You must be Mr. Savoy. Dancer told me you would be stopping by," she said.

The man stopped walking when she addressed him. He smiled nervously. "Hello, Mrs. Stonemason." He fumbled in his corduroy dairy jacket and pulled out an envelope. "Dancer asked me to give you this, ma'am."

Dede - $56 was written on the front of the envelope. The script was shaky, like an old person's, but she recognized it immediately as Dancer's handwriting. "He's staying with you?"

The man nodded. "In our trailer. Just until he gets on his feet. Matilda's been cooking some meals for him. He's getting stronger."

On his feet. That's what that son-of-a-bitch from Caterpillar had said too. Everyone wanted to help Dancer get back on his feet. His feet weren't the problem. Right now the problem was how to put food on the table. After he left, Dede went back to work at the Camelot Square model home. But last week, Landis sold the last of the units, and she was out of a job. "That's very kind of your wife, "Dede said.

"Mattie's a good Christian woman. She figures she doing the Lord's work."

"Dancer said you got him work."

He blew on his hands again. "He helps load the milk. And when we come back from our routes, he washes the trucks. It's just part time, but it might lead to something. Meantime, I'll bring the envelope by each week. I can just leave it in the milk box. Don't have to be bothering you."

Loading dairy trucks. That's the kind of work a man takes when he can't get a real job. Working while the rest of the world slept suited Dancer. He wanted to be invisible. "Why doesn't he bring it himself?"

The man's face tightened. "He doesn't have a car." He stared down at his shoes. "He's got a lot of anger. I guess losing his fingers. That's a hard thing."

"He's not the only one who's angry," Dede stuffed the envelope in her coat pocket.

The man studied her. His face revealed his kindness. He had dropped the mask he wore whenever he talked to white people. "It's the liquor that's killing him. He's got to beat that, or he ain't going to be worth nothing. I been there. I'll help him anyway I can, but he's going to have to want to help himself."

Dede didn't believe Dancer had the "want to" anymore. The boy she had fallen in love with – that boy had a dream – a purpose in life. She shouldn't have encouraged him to give up baseball, even though he had no chance of making it to the majors. It was that dream he lived for, not her or even the boys. She still loved him. She reckoned she would always love him, but he was drowning, and she wasn't going down with him.

She had her boys to take care of. She wouldn't let everything go to hell like her own mother had when her father left. Family was all Dede had, and if she had to let Dancer go to save her family, that's what she would do. She would find another job and not wait for him to get on his feet.

Dancer hadn't caught many breaks lately, but it appeared that Rollie was a good man. Maybe his luck was changing.

She held out her hand. "I'm glad he found you. Or you found him. Thank you, Mr. Savoy."

The man hesitated for a moment and gently clasped her hand like he was afraid he might break it. "Call me Rollie."

40

Dede stood on her front stoop and watched the taillights of Rollie's truck disappear as he headed down the hill. She had just missed him. It was a gray rainy morning – winter was about done, but spring was still just a promise. The front yard, no longer covered by a cosmetic layer of snow, was ungroomed, scraggly-looking. Dede tugged her bathrobe a little tighter.

She didn't want to open the milk box. She still hadn't found a job, and last week there had only been nineteen dollars in the envelope. The bills had been damp and smelled like stale beer. Dede imagined Dancer sitting in some dive bar all alone, drinking himself into oblivion so he might, for a few hours, forget what he had lost.

Thinking that way made her sad, but angry, too. She only had enough money left to buy Clayton's school lunch for the rest of the week. The day before, Clayton had poured the last of their milk on Jimmy's oatmeal, not saving any for himself. He had eaten his frosted flakes dry, without complaining. He was trying so hard to be the man of the house.

She sighed and flipped open the milk box. Inside were two bottles of milk and a note from Rollie. The note said that Dancer had "some problems" at the dairy, but they had been worked out, and Dancer was getting regular hours again. Next week there would be money. This week all Rollie could do was leave those two bottles of milk, to soften the blow. Yesterday, when Joyce called, she warned that Dede wouldn't be able to depend on Dancer's milk money. Joyce wanted to talk about "their plans," but Dede had hung up on her – angry with Joyce's smug certainty that Dancer would fail.

She brought the milk into the kitchen and heated the water for her instant coffee and Jimmy's oatmeal. If it weren't for the boys, maybe she would have just curled up in a ball on her bed and waited for a better day. That's what her mama had done. Hunkered down under the covers of her daybed with her bottle of whiskey, praying for her luck to change. But their trailer was way back in the hollow, and the good days never found them.

Dede wouldn't wait for a better day or for her luck to change. She would go see Crutchfield. He was always hiring. And if Crutchfield didn't work out, she'd try McMurray's Hardware or the diner. She'd hike up and down Main Street and she'd find a job someplace.

Footsteps rattled the back stairs. The door flew open, and Clayton and Jimmy burst into the kitchen. "I got Jimmy dressed, Mom," Clayton said.

Jimmy was wearing the same elastic waistband corduroys he had worn the last two days and the same red T-shirt, but it was inside-out. "Thank you, Clayton. Come here, Jimmy. Let me fix your shirt."

"I flipped it over to hide the drool stains," Clayton said. "Hey! We got milk!"

Jimmy shuffled over and held his hands up over his head. "Clayton dressed me," he said, grinning.

Dede looked at the crusty food splotch and decided to leave the shirt inside out. "I think Clayton had a good idea. Get in your chair, Jimmy."

Jimmy crawled up into his high chair, and Dede set the steaming bowl of oatmeal in front of him.

"I'll get the milk," Clayton said. He grabbed the bottle off the counter and expertly pried the cardboard seal off with a fork. Clutching the bottle with both hands, he walked carefully over to Jimmy's chair. He stood on his tiptoes and tilted the bottle over the cereal bowl. "Yikes!" he yelled as a gusher of milk drowned the oatmeal. He jerked the bottle upright, and the bottle slipped out of his hands.

Dede watched it all unfold, sensing disaster, but frozen like a spectator to a train wreck. As the bottle crashed to the floor, Dede's brain flooded with the images of Joyce's glass globe shattering as her life with Dancer exploded. But the milk bottle didn't break. It hit like a brick and bounced. A puddle of milk quickly spread around Jimmy's chair.

Clayton stared at her, mouth agape, chin trembling. Trying so hard not to cry. "I'm sorry, Mom. I'll clean it up."

"It's okay, hon. Go sit at the table. I'll mop up later. We've got another bottle of milk. You can have the cream off the top for your cereal." She opened the kitchen cabinet and stared at the empty shelf. "Let's see. Would you like frosted flakes or... frosted flakes?" Clayton laughed, and his face lost its scrunched up, worried look.

Dede drained Jimmy's oatmeal of the excess milk and was about to sit down with her boys when the phone rang. It was Joyce calling to apologize. She tried to stop her, tell her it wasn't necessary, but once Joyce set her mind to saying something, she didn't stop for anyone.

She loved hearing Joyce's voice. Even when what she was saying made no sense, the warm seductive tone brightened Dede's outlook. Gave her hope that somehow things would work out.

When Joyce finally stopped talking Dede said, "Come on over for coffee. You can tell me all about your grand plans."

She refilled Joyce's coffee cup and set the pot down next to the glossy real estate brochure Joyce had spread out on the coffee table. Joyce raked her hand through her long, dark hair. It shimmered. So did her white silk blouse which draped her breasts in a way that was sexy and refined. She had been talking non-stop for at least ten minutes. She was desperate to leave her husband, and the town where it seemed that everywhere she turned he had some new project underway. Joyce wanted a new life a world away from the "hillbillies and cretins" of Maple Springs, Missouri. And she wanted Dede to be a part of that life.

The brochure promoted Rancho Grande, a desert paradise with year round golf and tennis and even a man-made lake for sailing. There were photos of a typical unit: a split-level adobe with a red tile roof and a sentry-like cactus planted beside the entry alcove. Instead of grass, the front yard was carefully groomed rust-colored pebbles, and in the fence-enclosed backyard, a kidney-shaped swimming pool with unnaturally blue water. Next to the pool, a hot tub.

She handed the brochure to Dede. "After I get my settlement from Ted, I can buy one of these units. Wouldn't it be fun, soaking in that hot tub, watching the sun come up over the mountains?"

"It looks like it's in the middle of nowhere," Dede said.

Joyce pushed herself to the edge of Dede's sofa. "The town's called Paradise Valley."

Her eyes were sparkly and full of hope. Nothing good would ever come from such high expectations.

"It's only five miles from Phoenix. They call it 'The Valley of the Sun.' There's sunshine every day. Not like this dreary place."

"It's so far away," Dede said. She put the brochure back on the table and tucked her legs under her butt. She had settled into Dancer's armchair, opposite Joyce instead of next to her on the sofa.

Joyce rolled her eyes. "It's Maple Springs that's far away. Paradise Valley is in the twentieth century. It's not populated with hillbillies and Klansmen and cousin-marrying hicks from the boondocks. We can make a new life there."

In some ways Joyce was just like Dancer. They both wanted the world to be better than it was. The difference was that Dancer had given up. Joyce would never give up. She would always believe, despite everything, that people were changing for the better. Joyce truly believed that she and Dede could live together like a married couple in this Paradise place. But Paradise was just a name. There would be snobs and bigots and gossips in Paradise, Dede was quite certain. "What about Candy?" Dede asked. Candy was Joyce's daughter. She was the same age as Clayton.

"I'm going to get custody. Ted's too busy becoming an important man. He doesn't want to deal with a seven year old girl." She reached out to touch Dede but couldn't with the table between them. "The house has four bedrooms. Clayton and Jimmy can each have their own room."

"When will your divorce be final?" Dede asked.

"My lawyer says six months. But that's just so he can look good and justify his big fee. Ted's not fighting this. It'll be done in three months. The kids can finish their school year, and then we can pack up and leave this place forever."

Joyce was so unrealistic. Even if they could overcome all the obvious problems, three months was a lifetime away. Dede had bills to pay, and she had to admit that Joyce was right about one thing – Dancer's weekly envelopes would never be enough.

"Could you watch Jimmy this afternoon? I'm going apply for a job at Crutchfield's."

Joyce frowned. Tiny worry lines creased the edges of her mouth. "Crutchfield's? Why would you want to work there? Seymour is creepy."

"I have to feed my kids. Keep the lights on. Like you said, I can't depend on Dancer."

Joyce held up the brochure. "You can depend on me. This is our future. We can have a great life together." She set down the brochure and plucked her wallet from her purse. "I'll take care of you."

Dede put her hand out like a stop sign. "I don't want your money. If you really want to help, watch Jimmy so I can look for a job."

Joyce bit down on her lip and her eyes scanned the ceiling as though there were an answer written there. "Okay," she said. She pulled out her address book and thumbed through it. "Remember Matt Gillespie? He was in Dancer's class. He had a huge crush on you."

"A crush on me? I don't think so. Who is he?"

"You are so blind to the effect you have on men. And women. He's a lawyer. The surviving half of Gillespie & Gillespie. I know you remember his wife. Carol Jenkins? She was one of those do-gooders in high school – National Honor Society, Y Club, that kind of stuff." She started to write something in the address book.

Dede shrugged. "I didn't really travel in those circles."

Joyce ripped out the page and handed it to Dede. "Carol's been his office manager since Matty's father died last winter, but she's about twelve months pregnant so he needs to replace her. He'll hire you in a heartbeat. Call him."

Joyce stood up and came around the table. "I'll watch Jimmy, but talk to Matty before you bother with that old fart, Seymour." She put her hands on Dede's shoulders and held her at arm's length. "I love you, Dede. You don't think you love me, and maybe you don't. But you will. It just takes time. I'm very lovable."

Joyce's eyes were so bright. So shiny. So hopeful. It hurt too much to look at her. Dede let Joyce embrace her, pressing Dede's face into the cool silk of her blouse.

41

Gillespie & Gillespie was the only law firm in Maple Springs, and they did everything from house closings to wills and divorce. Their office was on Main Street, on the second floor, above Scribner Stationary, two buildings down from the original Crutchfield General Store.

The door with *Gillespie & Gillespie – Attorneys at Law* painted on the opaque nubby glass door panel was opened. A receptionist desk, a tired sofa, and a couple of lumpy armchairs formed the office waiting area. Behind the receptionist station, two larger desks guarded doors, which Dede guessed were the offices for the Gillespies.

A stern-looking middle-aged woman, her unnaturally dark hair wrapped tightly in a bun, sat at one of those desks filing her nails. There was no one else in sight, and it appeared that Gillespie & Gillespie must be moving. There were stacks of legal books everywhere, and banks of file cabinets with half the drawers left opened.

The woman glanced up from her manicuring. "Can I help you?"

Dede stood in front of the empty desk, not certain whether she should walk over to the woman or state her business from where she stood. The woman's lips were pursed like she wanted to get back to her grooming so Dede decided to stay where she was. "I have an appointment with Mr. Gillespie."

The woman sighed. "He's not here yet. Have a seat." She nodded toward the armchairs.

Joyce had been right that Matt Gillespie would remember her. When Dede called, he acted like she was a long lost friend. He told her he would be delighted to talk, but explained that his secretary was assuming most of the office management tasks his wife had been responsible for. However, he thought she probably could use some help. From the appearance of the office, it looked like she needed more than a little help.

As Dede turned, she almost collided with a man racing into the office. It had to be Matt Gillespie. He was a taller, more filled-out version of someone she might have seen in high school. Gillespie's dark hair was carelessly combed, and his tie was draped around his neck. He was cute in a boyish sort of a way.

"Dede!" he said, grinning as he extended his hand. "You look great. What's it been? Ten years?"

The woman, who had put away her nail file and started to type, said, "You made another appointment." It was a question masquerading as a statement. The woman did nothing to conceal her disapproval.

Gillespie's brow tightened. "Mrs. Pritchard, this is Dede Holmes, I'm sorry. Stonemason. Dede Stonemason."

Mrs. Pritchard offered a tight-lipped nod.

"Come on back, Dede. Let's hear what you've been up to."

Mrs. Pritchard huffed, and as Gillespie walked Dede back to his office, she flung the carriage return so aggressively Dede was surprised the typewriter didn't go flying off the desk.

"She's a little set in her ways," Gillespie whispered as he motioned for her to take a seat at the chair in front of his desk. "She was my father's secretary for twenty years. I'm not sure she thinks I measure up. Actually, I am sure." He laughed.

Dede looked at the files scattered around the office. "Are you moving?"

He shook his head. "Carol had begun reorganizing the files, but she didn't finish. And now the doc tells her bed rest until the baby is born. You got kids?"

"I, uh, we have two boys." She could feel her face start to flush. "Clayton's seven and Jimmy will be three next month."

"I heard you and Dancer split up. I'm sorry."

Dede nodded. She was never sure whether she was supposed to thank someone for being sorry for her bad news.

"You got family to help you out with the kids?"

Whenever folks asked those prying questions, Dede wondered what they really knew. Matt seemed sincere, but did he know that Dancer was gone, her mother had drunk herself to death, and that her girlfriend was right now watching her baby boy? "My neighbor is going to babysit. I can start right away," Dede said. That wasn't really a lie. Tammy Doyle had told her she would watch the boys anytime. There was no need to mention Joyce.

"The job is probably temporary, but we need to get these files organized, and Mrs. Pritchard will never do it on her own. I can pay you a dollar an hour. Are you interested?"

Forty dollars a week. They couldn't live on that. But they couldn't live on nothing either. "When do you want me to start?" she said.

Gillespie smiled and picked up his phone. "Mrs. Pritchard, can you come in here please?"

42

It took Dede a month to get Gillespie's files organized. Yesterday, Matt told her to return on Monday as he had another project for her to tackle. She had been so relieved he wasn't cutting her loose that when Joyce called and made her weekly invitation to take Dede and the boys out for Saturday dinner with her daughter, she finally said yes.

But now, as she sat in the front seat of Joyce's car, she was starting to have second thoughts. They were headed to Mel's Drive-In, which was just a two minute drive down the hill at the junction of Hill Street and Highway 60. Joyce was driving Ted's powder-blue Cadillac convertible. With the three kids jammed in the back seat – Jimmy squeezed between Clayton and Candy – Dede felt like they were all on display. She imagined her neighbors on Hill Street staring at them as they cruised toward the drive-in.

"Candy, sit down," Joyce said.

Candy had raised herself as though she were going to sit on the top of the seat, like a parade beauty queen. She made a face at the back of her mom's head as she slid back into her seat. She adjusted the black-frame sunglasses her mother had bought her at Newbery's Five and Dime. "How do you like my sunglasses, Clayton?" she asked.

"Okay, I guess," he said, glancing at her and then turning away quickly as though something bad would happen to him if he stared at her too long.

Dede reached over from the front seat and patted Candy on the knee. "You look just like Natalie Wood in *The Wild Ones*." Candy was a strikingly pretty child, and while Clayton pretended not to know her now, Dede wondered how he would react if they were all living in the same house.

It was early, and Joyce secured the prime position in the front of the drive-in. The carhop girl took their order – burgers and fries and chocolate shakes for everyone – and five minutes later they had their food.

While the kids devoured their burgers, Joyce sipped on her shake and squinted up at the sun that was partially eclipsed by the neon sign flashing *Mel's Drive-In*. "If the weather was this nice all year round, maybe I would consider staying here." She sighed. "But I would still have to figure out what to do with all the hillbillies."

"How is the settlement coming?" Dede hated to ask – it just encouraged Joyce to start blathering about Arizona – but she really wanted to know if Ted was as accommodating as Joyce had predicted.

"Ted's being a total," Joyce peered over her shoulder and whispered, "asshole."

"Where's he living?"

Joyce laughed, but without feeling. "The man owns a hundred different apartments and houses. He could live somewhere real nice if he wanted. But not Ted. He sleeps in the construction trailer out on 60 where he's building that sporting goods store for Crutchfield."

"It's a popular form of housing these days," Dede said, and they both laughed.

"How is your money holding up?" Joyce asked.

Rollie's promise that Dancer was back on track had so far proven correct. He had sent her sixty dollars for three weeks in a row, and last week, eighty. On the envelope he had scrawled, "Take care, Dede." The bills were crisp, clean, and the handwriting on the envelope was maybe a little less herky-jerky. Dancer probably wasn't on the road to recovery, but maybe he had at least stopped falling.

"Dancer's sending money regular, and Matt's been great to work with," Dede said.

Joyce frowned. "Be careful."

Joyce saw rivals everywhere. Dede didn't want to get into it with her, especially with the kids in the car. "Jimmy, what are you doing?" she asked, looking over her shoulder. Jimmy had abandoned his straw and tilted the milkshake so he could get every last drop. His nose and eyebrows were decorated with a chocolate froth.

"Hey, Candy!" Clayton said reaching around Jimmy to tap Candy on the knee. "Jimmy looks like a clown."

Candy giggled. "Come here, Jimmy." She took her napkin and cleaned the froth off his eyebrows.

"I can help," Clayton said. He swiped Jimmy's mouth as Jimmy tried to wriggle away. "He's a squirmer," Clayton said.

Candy held Jimmy while Clayton wiped his mouth. "Me and my mom are going to see the Grand Canyon this summer," Candy said.

"Really? Neat."

"Maybe you and your brother can see the Canyon too," Joyce said. Clayton, busy attending to Jimmy and warming to Candy's company, didn't seem to hear her.

"Joyce," Dede said, her teeth clenched.

Joyce smiled serenely, as though she knew something.

"What?"

"You're not going to survive on Dancer's milk money, and Carol Gillespie and that old battleaxe Margaret Pritchard aren't going to let you hang around their Matty too much longer. My deal is much better. Sooner or later, you'll see that."

After their burgers, the five of them played miniature golf at the course Mel had built behind his drive-in. When Candy made a hole-in-one on the difficult windmill hole, Dede hugged her like she was her own daughter. And when Joyce knocked her ball off the roof of the Japanese pagoda into the parking lot, Dede and the kids laughed so hard Dede had to sit down to catch her breath. Joyce joined her on the bench as Clayton and Candy helped Jimmy to line up his shot.

Joyce squeezed Dede's hand. "This is nice," she said.

Dede sighed. They were like a family. Almost. And the thought made her feel good and bad at the same time. Good because she could sense the inviting warmth of Joyce's body. And bad because it should have been Dancer sitting next to her. She willed that thought out of her head. Thinking about Dancer would only break her heart.

43

When Matt Gillespie left for the Memorial Day weekend, he was certain their baby, already a week overdue, would conveniently arrive on Saturday or Sunday. But when Dede returned to work on Monday, Mrs. Pritchard, who had been reading *Redbook* at her desk, glanced up from her magazine and said, "Mrs. Gillespie went into labor early this morning. Mr. Gillespie said he will call when he has news."

Having fulfilled her conversational obligation, she was about to return to her magazine when the phone rang. She sighed and picked it up. After a few seconds she cut off the caller with a terse, "Mr. Gillespie is unavailable. Please call back tomorrow."

Dede stared at her, not believing what she had heard. "Why didn't you tell the caller that his wife is having a baby?"

Mrs. Pritchard's eyebrows almost collided as she considered Dede's statement. "That is none of their business. I wouldn't consider sharing personal details with a stranger."

"It's a goddamn baby, Margaret. Not syphilis," Dede said. She set her bag down on the receptionist desk, which had become her desk since the receptionist quit the day after Mrs. Pritchard took over for Carol Gillespie. "Those are customers. We need to help them, not tell them to call back again."

"How dare you speak to me with that gutter language." She sniffed. "And we don't call them customers. They're clients."

The phone rang again, and Dede grabbed it before Mrs. Pritchard could put down her magazine. "Could you hold please?" she said. She smiled at Mrs. Pritchard and said, "I'll take care of the calls, Margaret. You keep working on your magazines."

She gave Dede her famous huff and picked up her stack of magazines and walked back to Gillespie senior's office. "I plan to give Mr. Gillespie a full report on your impertinence."

At noon, Gillespie called the office sounding as if he had been in labor for twelve hours. "They tell me she's still a long way from ready," he said. "God, Dede, this waiting is awful."

She was grateful Matt couln't see her expression. "First babies take longer. She'll be here before you know it."

"She?"

"Just guessing. Go get some tasty hospital pudding. Everything's under control here."

"You better let me talk to Mrs. Pritchard. Don't want to ruffle her feathers."

"Probably too late for that." She walked over to the office and banged on the door. "Pick up the line, Margaret. Matt wants to talk to you."

Back at her desk she could hear Mrs. Pritchard's voice get louder and louder as she unloaded on Matt. Finally, she stopped talking, and the office went eerily silent. Dede didn't imagine Matt was sharing his labor pains with her. After a minute of the silence, Dede heard Mrs. Pritchard slam the phone into the receiver. A moment later, face flushed, handbag on her arm, she stormed out of the office. She marched past Dede without saying a word, but stopped at the entrance and spun around.

"I know all about your homosexual relationship. You and that woman are disgusting. You shouldn't be allowed anywhere near children."

Dede's neck prickled. She wished she had Joyce's gift for the clever putdown. Dede's impulse was to yank a good handful of Margaret's ugly black hair out of that stupid bun. The idea of working next to Margaret Prichard for the next ten years was too depressing to imagine. Would there be people like her in Arizona? Dede couldn't imagine that there could be anyone worse. She smiled as she gave Margaret the finger. "You're lucky I'm a peace-loving woman."

Two hours later, Matt called to let her know that he was the proud father of the most beautiful girl in the world: Abigail May Gillespie, eight pounds, five ounces. For five minutes he babbled happily about all the virtues of his new daughter. Then abruptly, he reverted to his office voice. "Dede, I let Mrs. Pritchard go. I'm going to need your help full time. How does ninety dollars a week sound?"

Ninety dollars. If Dancer could at least keep coming up with forty or fifty, they'd have enough to survive. She wouldn't have to break up her family or yank the boys away from their father. Joyce didn't have to rush off to Arizona. There were going to be Margaret Pritchards everywhere, so maybe it would be better to learn how to deal with them now in a familiar place instead of some strange new land called Paradise.

LEN JOY

44

When Rollie Savoy appeared in the entryway of Gillespie and Gillespie, Dede could tell by his grim look that her good luck had run its course. She chided herself for her foolishness. She had become hopeful, even though she knew better than anyone that hope had never served her well.

Reflexively, she stood up and grabbed her purse as Rollie's eyes darted furtively between her and the new girl who sat at the receptionist table. It had been a great month. Dancer had given her seventy dollars for four weeks in a row, and in the office Dede had become indispensable. That first week, freed of Mrs. Pritchard, she had hired a girl as a secretary-receptionist. The new girl typed eighty words a minute, answered the phone, fixed coffee for the clients who showed up for appointments, and kept everything filed, while Dede worked on the finances.

Matt was lousy at collecting his accounts. Dede knew all about collections. She had been on the receiving end of all sorts of collection calls. She called every past due account, and with charm and a determined steeliness, she got commitments which converted into cash more quickly than she could have hoped.

"Can I help you, sir?" the girl asked Rollie.

"I got this," Dede said, stepping around the receptionist desk. She walked toward the corner of the waiting area, tilting

her head for Rollie to follow her. "What's wrong?" she asked
him.

"Dancer got arrested. He's locked up in Mountain View,"
he said, his voice low as though that would keep the girl from
hearing their conversation.

"Mountain View?" It had to be for drinking. Dede didn't
even need to ask that. But why there of all places?

Rollie sighed. "They wouldn't let him drink in Holtville
anymore." He bit down on his lower lip. "They want two
hundred dollars for bail."

"Can I help you, sir?" Matt had just arrived. He stood in the
center of the reception area, his brow knitted with a look which
was more confusion than concern.

Dede feared that this was how her life would play out from
now on. Things were never going to be normal in Maple Springs.
Dancer was broken. She could succeed in her job, try to build a
normal life for herself in Maple Springs, but every time she got a
little bit ahead, Dancer would end up knocking that rock back
down the hill.

"Matt, this is Rollie Savoy," Dede said. She could feel the
color rising in her cheeks. "Dancer's in jail over in Mountain
View. I'll get back as soon as I can."

Matt walked over and shook hands with Rollie. "How do
you do, Mr. Savoy? Matt Gillespie." He nodded toward Dede.
"Take whatever time you need. Let me know if I can help."

Dede walked out with Rollie to the corner of Main and Harris where Rollie's truck was parked. "I appreciate you letting me know," she said.

"How are you going to--?" Rollie stammered. He knew better than anyone that two hundred dollars might as well have been two thousand dollars.

"I have a friend who can loan me the money," she said.

Dede drove over to Joyce's house, an old mansion on the north side of town. Joyce was understanding and more than willing to give her the money. As Dede sat at the kitchen table, Joyce grabbed a cookie jar from her cabinet and pulled out a wad of bills. She counted out a pile that looked to be a lot more than two hundred dollars.

"Here's three hundred." She handed the bills to Dede. "You never know with those pricks in Mountain View."

Dede didn't protest. She was relieved but couldn't shake the sick feeling in the pit of her stomach. "Thanks, Joyce. I…" She stopped herself from promising to repay her. She couldn't make the promise and Joyce would just get upset if she brought it up.

Joyce squeezed her hand. "Get him out of there, Dede. He's just a man. You can't expect too much."

The jail in Mountain View was a one-story limestone building a block west of US 60 on Pine Street. It took Dede less than an hour to get there. There was a jingle above her head when she opened the front door to the jail. The front office resembled Marshall Dillon's jailhouse. Wanted posters on the walls, gun-rack in the back, and a plank floor. The only thing missing was the jail cell.

Seated at the only desk was a stout, middle-aged woman with coarse red-hair who had managed to stuff herself into a khaki uniform that probably fit her a lot better five years ago. Pinned above her left front pocket was a nametag that identified her as Deputy Leiter. "Can I help you?"

"I'm here for my husband. Dancer—"

"Bail or visit?" Deputy Leiter flipped open the only file on her desk. The folder held a single page report which the woman scanned as she waited for Dede to answer.

"Bail."

"It's two hundred dollars cash. No checks. That's bail, fine, and lodging. Pay that, and he's all yours."

"Lodging?"

"We got expenses"

After Dede paid, the Deputy smiled at her as she put the cash in her desk drawer. "Don't be too hard on your man. That Charlotte's something else. A real firecracker. Percy's niece. Y'all know Percy Thacker, don't you?"

Deputy Leiter brought Dancer out from the cells that were in the back of the building. His lower lip was swollen, and the knuckles on his right hand looked like someone had dragged a cheese grater across them. He had a coiled, menacing look, as though he had a notion to throttle Deputy Leiter. When he spotted Dede, his expression changed, not to chagrin, so much as resignation. He started to speak, but Dede shook her head.

"Can we go now?" she asked the deputy.

The woman held up a set of keys. "Truck's in the back of the parking lot."

Dede grabbed the keys from the deputy and handed them to Dancer. She linked her arm through Dancer's and walked him out of the building like she was an usher at a wedding.

When they were safely outside away from Deputy Leiter's prying eyes, she let go of his arm. "Jesus, Dancer. What the hell were you doing in Mountain View? And Percy Thacker's niece? If you want to kill yourself, there are easier ways."

He bit down on his lower lip as he scanned the parking lot. "I just wanted a change in scenery. And all that crap about Thacker's niece is bullshit. Just a big story those Klan assholes cooked up."

A change of scenery. He was so pathetic she couldn't even be angry. "I can't do this anymore. You need help, and I hope you get it. I really do. But I'm done bailing you out. You're going to have to figure this out on your own."

Dancer's face reddened. "I didn't ask for your help. I didn't ask for anyone's help." He wheeled around and headed across the parking lot. He got in Rollie's old Ford pickup and jerked the door closed with a vengeance. The pickup turned over like it had its own hangover, and it took a half minute of grinding before the engine caught. He revved it till it screamed, then pealed out of the parking lot, the exhaust spewing a trail of oily smoke.

Dede waited until he disappeared from sight, and then she headed for home. Five miles from Maple Springs, her own trail of smoke started to pour from the hood. In what she had to consider her only lucky break of the day, she was just a hundred yards from Wally's Texaco station. She made it to the garage where Wally explained that the "smoke" was steam from the radiator that she now needed to replace. It would cost fifty dollars for parts and labor, but it wouldn't be ready until tomorrow.

She called Joyce, who answered on the first ring as though she had been expecting the call. Fifteen minutes later, with the top down, and Joyce smiling beside her like a kid on Christmas morning, they were on their way home. Dede closed her eyes and let the wind toss her hair as the sun warmed her face. It felt good to have someone who cared for her. She didn't love Joyce, at least not like she had loved Dancer. Probably still loved him. But Joyce would always be there for her. For her family. Maybe they could make it work. Maybe it would be better for Dancer if he knew she wasn't going to be there to bail him out next time. Maybe moving on was the right choice for everyone. As Joyce drove up Hill Street, Dede scooted across the seat and laid her head on Joyce's shoulder.

45

The satin sheets on Joyce's bed felt deliciously cool. A heat wave had gripped southern Missouri for the last week. The Gillespie law office had only two small windows in the lawyers' offices, and the fans Matt brought in just pushed the hot air around. At night, Dede and the boys slept in the living room because it was ten degrees cooler than upstairs, but the air was so heavy Dede felt like she was suffocating. Sleep was nearly impossible. So when Tammy Doyle invited Clayton and Jimmy to join Alex at Tammy's mother's place on the Lake of the Ozarks for the long Fourth of July weekend, Dede was happy to let them go. As soon as they rolled out of the driveway early on the Fourth, she called Joyce who was thrilled to have her stay for the weekend.

Joyce and Ted's mansion had air conditioning. Dede had never spent a night with Joyce. She expected to feel uncomfortable. Not with the lovemaking – Dede always could lose herself in the moment, make herself and her partner feel special – but sleeping together, that was in some ways more intimate. What if Joyce snored? Or worse? But there had been no awkward moments. It was as if they'd lived together for years. And with nothing to worry about – no boys to take care of, no boss to answer to, no husband to bail out – she slept the best she had in months.

Joyce was in the shower. The muffled sound of the water running was hypnotic and soothing. Dede closed her eyes and drifted semi-conscious on a satin sea. The water stopped, and a moment later, Joyce walked out of the bathroom naked except for the towel she had wrapped around her hair. When she saw that Dede was awake she grinned and scooted onto the bed. She spooned Dede, cupped her breasts in her hands, and nuzzled her neck. "Did you sleep okay, D?"

Dede moaned softly as Joyce ran her hands up and down her body. "Do you think I could stay in bed until Sunday?"

"No. You're getting up, missy," Joyce said as she slipped on her fluffy white bathrobe. "I'm going to make you my famous eggs benedict with hash browns and fresh squeezed orange juice."

Dede rolled over on to her stomach and buried her face in the plush pillow. "Eggs what?"

Joyce gently smacked Dede's butt. "See, that's why I'm taking you away from this place. No more chicken-fried steak and biscuits with gravy. And no more god-awful grits. When we get to Arizona, you'll see. A whole new dining experience awaits you."

"I like grits."

Joyce wrinkled her nose. "And tonight we can really celebrate because this afternoon I'm meeting with Ted and the lawyers, and I'm going to sign the settlement." Her face radiated with excitement as she slipped back on to the edge of the bed.

"So it's done?" Dede knew she wouldn't have to ask Joyce for the details.

"It's a great deal. Ted doesn't want me to tangle up all his properties, so I'm getting a hundred thousand dollars and maintenance." She almost bounced off the bed.

"All at once? Now?" Dede had no idea Ted Landis had that kind of money.

Joyce had crawled up next to Dede and grabbed both of her hands. "I will be walking out of that lawyer's office with a cashier's check for one hundred thousand dollars!" She hugged Dede. "And there's more," she said. "Don't I sound like that guy on *Queen for a Day?*" She laughed. "The maintenance is seventy-five hundred dollars a year."

"I thought maintenance meant he would take care of your car," Dede said. "You won't have any trouble supporting Candy with that kind of money."

A flicker of uncertainty shadowed Joyce's happy look. "He gets Candy. He insisted, and that's why we were able to get such a generous deal."

Dede grabbed the bed sheet and pulled it around her, clutching her knees. She tried to make sense of what Joyce had just told her. "You can't give away Candy," she said. "She's your daughter. Your family."

"Don't be silly. Candy will come to Phoenix for a couple weeks every summer. Once she sees what it's like out there, she'll want to be with us. And trust me, when she starts giving Ted a hard time, he'll change his mind."

Dede got up from the bed and slipped on her panties. She picked up her halter top and shorts and dressed quickly. "But you

206

haven't signed anything yet, right? What if you let him keep the hundred thousand? Would he let you have her then?"

Joyce stood with her hands on her hips and stared at Dede as though she were some stranger who had walked into her bedroom. "Give up the money? Are you crazy? With that money we are set. We can buy the house and have a nest egg. You can live like a real person. Get some decent clothes. We can go places together. Nice places. I did this for us."

"But she's your daughter. You can't sell her like a used car."

Joyce ripped the towel off her head. "I didn't goddamn sell her. For Christ's sake. This is our ticket out of here. You want a ticket you have to pay. And I'm the one who's paying, so I don't see why you're being so pissy about it."

Dede felt heartsick. Desperate. She couldn't have a life with someone who would give up her family. She walked up to Joyce and wrapped her arms around her. She pressed her body against Joyce, savored for one last time the smooth softness of her skin, and then stepped back and stared into Joyce's sad, dark eyes. "I can't go with you."

Joyce closed her eyes as though she were praying. "Oh, Dede. When are you going to learn?" She slipped back down on to the edge of the bed and covered her face with her hands as she sobbed quietly.

Dede knew there would be times when she would regret her decision. No more laughing together at the Honeymooners or playing Hearts until two in the morning. No one to caress her body or hold her on long, lonely nights. She was losing her lover and her best friend, but she had no choice. She leaned over and kissed Joyce on the forehead. "I don't know," she whispered.

46

Snowflakes swirled in the headlights of Dede's car as she drove up Hill Street toward home. Most of the houses had their Christmas lights on and their trees decorated. She had never anticipated Christmas as a child. They never had any traditions like regular families. Christmas was just another excuse for her mother to go out and get drunk. Not that she needed any excuses.

Last year with Dancer's accident and everything else, Christmas had been a nightmare. But this year, maybe things would be better. Joyce had sent her a Christmas card with a picture of her new home in Arizona. She wrote that she was studying to become a real estate agent. She looked happy. Dede missed Joyce, but it made her feel good to know her friend was able to start a new life. Maybe with Matt's help, Dede could too.

Matt was a godsend. A boss and a friend. Tomorrow, he was going to drive her and the boys out to his cabin in the hill country where he would help them cut down one of the blue spruces on his property. They would have a real Christmas tree this year. Decorated. The boys were looking forward to it and so was Dede.

As she rolled into her driveway the headlights revealed Dancer huddled under the elm tree across the street from their house. Farther up the street she spotted Rollie's pickup. She stopped the car at the edge of the driveway and rolled down the window. "What are you doing out here?" she asked. It came out harsh sounding and that wasn't what she intended. "The boys and Tammy are inside. You should have gone on in."

There was a grocery sack next to him. He picked it up and walked across the street. He still had that way of moving, so that even something as simple as walking could look graceful, effortless. "I didn't want to intrude." He half-smiled and lifted up the sack. "Christmas gifts."

Dede had not seen or talked to Dancer since the day he had driven off in a rage from the Mountain View jail. He looked better now. Sober anyway. And calm. Like he had his anger under control. His envelopes had resumed the week after she bailed him out, and they had been a reliable sixty to seventy dollars every week.

"Hold on," she said. "Let me pull the car in." She drove halfway up the drive and got out. Dancer had remained at the end of the driveway, like he was afraid to set foot on the property. She walked back to him and took the sack when he held it out. "Thank you." The packages were neatly wrapped with Christmas paper and bows. "Do you want to come in?"

Dancer shook his head. "I've got to get Rollie's truck back to him."

Dede nodded, not sure what to say.

"I was hoping I could have the boys for a weekend. Maybe on a regular basis?"

"Regular?"

He hitched his shoulders. "Couple times a month. I got plenty of room in my trailer and Matilda would take care of meals, so they wouldn't have to put up with my cooking,"

Dede took a breath. She didn't want the boys to grow up without knowing their father. But if Dancer was still drinking it might just make things worse.

Dancer seemed to know what she was thinking. "I've been going to AA with Rollie," he said. "Haven't had a drink in two months."

It felt so strange standing there at the foot of their driveway. Like they were neighbors of passing acquaintance, not husband and wife. So much had changed in a year. Their lives had gone hurtling off the tracks and there was no going back.

"Maybe we could start with Jimmy?" Dede said. "I'm just not sure about Clayton."

Dancer stared down at his shoes and took a couple of deep breaths. "Okay," he said. He began rubbing his hands together then seemed to think better of it and shoved them in the pockets of his jacket. "Thank you."

Dede shifted the bag to her right arm, and with her left arm, she made an awkward attempt at a one-arm hug. "How about the weekend before Christmas? Jimmy will be excited."

As if on cue, Jimmy shrieked, "Give it back, Clayton." From the street they could see Clayton run through the living room clutching one of Jimmy's books. Jimmy followed, fists pumping, screaming. Somewhere in the background Dede could hear Tammy, with her easy Texas drawl, telling the boys to settle down.

Dede looked at Dancer staring up at the house she had made him buy, his boys so close and yet not close at all anymore. It didn't seem fair, but he had made his choices and now all they could do was keep moving forward. She could do that. She hoped Dancer could too.

47

November 1960 – three years later

Dede parked in front of Scribner Stationary and waited for Matt to come down from the law office with the box of Kennedy campaign flyers.

Clayton twisted around and grabbed his basketball from the backseat of the Impala. "Honk the horn, Mom. We're going to be late." Clayton was playing in the Elks Club basketball program every Saturday. The program, like everything else in Maple Springs, it seemed, had grown explosively in the last couple years.

There had been less than five thousand folks living in Maple Springs when Dancer and Dede moved into the brick house on the hill east of town. Now there were twice as many. The school age population had grown even faster. A new school had been built on Pine Street, right next to the old grade school, to handle the surging enrollment in kindergarten and the first three grades.

Elks Club basketball used to be played in the Elks Lodge on Saturday afternoon with just enough boys for a game of five-on-five pickup with a couple of subs. Now they played in the new grade school gymnasium, and they had an actual league with eight teams. They even had uniforms. Caterpillar and Crutchfield General Stores and Landis Construction each sponsored two teams and McMurray Hardware and the Maple Springs Diner sponsored the other two. Dede was relieved that Clayton's team was the Maple Springs Diner. She didn't want to see the names of Caterpillar, Crutchfield, or Landis splattered across the back of his T-shirt.

Dede peered up at the law office, even though there was no way to see anything from the car. "We have plenty of time. Matt will be down in a moment."

Today was the last weekend of the presidential campaign, and Matt, who had helped manage the Kennedy campaign in Howell County, needed volunteers to hand out flyers. Dede didn't really care about the election, but she wanted to help Matt so she asked Dancer, who had Jimmy for the weekend, if he would go to the game and bring Clayton home. He jumped at the opportunity, and Dede was happy to have found a useful way for Dancer to spend time with Clayton.

"I don't need a ride home from the game. I can walk," Clayton said.

"Your dad will bring you home. No more discussion, mister."

For the last three years, Jimmy had stayed with Dancer in his trailer, almost every other weekend. After three months with just Jimmy visiting, Dancer had asked if Clayton could stay over on the alternate weekend. Clayton hadn't wanted to go, but Dede insisted. After a dinner with Rollie and Matilda that Clayton barely touched, Dancer and Clayton had retreated to the trailer. They played Crazy Eights – Clayton's favorite game – for less than an hour before Clayton said he was ready for bed. After a few minutes fidgeting in bed, he complained that he couldn't breathe in the trailer and begged Dancer to take him home.

Matilda persuaded him to sleep in her son's old bedroom. In the middle of the night, planning, he claimed later, to walk home, Clayton had crawled out of the upstairs window onto the roof of the garage and jumped off, breaking his wrist. Dancer hadn't asked again, but only because he knew Clayton would never return unless his mother made him.

Dede hoped that eventually Clayton would let go of his anger and give Dancer a chance to be a father again. Especially after Dancer started to rebuild his life. He had stuck with AA, and he'd moved up to full time work at the dairy. He now managed the ragtag group of men who loaded the trucks. But Clayton was as stubborn as his father. Dancer's contact with his firstborn son was limited to holiday visits and helping out on rides when Dede couldn't get off work.

The stairway door opened, and Matt emerged carrying a large cardboard carton. Dede jumped out of the car and opened the trunk. Matt dropped the carton in the trunk and handed Dede a map.

"Here's your territory. Start at the highway and work your way up Hill Street." Ten years ago, that would have been about twenty houses. But Ted Landis had built the Indian Hills development at the foot of Hill Street – row upon row of cookie cutter starter homes mostly owned by the men and women who worked at the Caterpillar plant – and Camelot Square at the top of the hill, for the bosses and other professionals who had moved to Maple Springs.

"That's a lot of homes," Dede said.

"I know. Just knock on the door, smile, and hand them the flyer. If nobody's home, just put it in the mailbox. We want to make sure every voter in the county hears from us."

Dede and Clayton walked into the far end of the gymnasium. Pandemonium reigned, as boys ran helter-skelter chasing basketballs, launching shots, and dribbling randomly around the court.

"My team's over there," Clayton said.

He tried to run off with his basketball, but Dede grabbed his arm. "Look for your father after the game."

"I will. Let me go."

As Clayton dribbled to the far basketball court, Dede scanned the crowd.

"Looking for someone?" Dancer asked as he and Jimmy, licking a double scoop chocolate ice cream cone, walked up next to her.

"We went to Tastee-Freeze," Jimmy said.

Dede smiled. "I can see that." She took a tissue and wiped Jimmy's face. "Try to get a little bit more of the ice cream in your mouth."

Dancer took hold of Jimmy's hand. "Let's see if that brother of yours can play any defense." He whispered to Dede. "After the game, I could take them out for pizza?"

It was a question. Dancer knew if he pushed too hard he would just drive Clayton further away. Dede sighed. "I don't think this is a good time."

Dancer nodded. "Is your man going to win the election?"

She shrugged. "I hope so," she said. She handed him a flyer from her purse. "He's much better looking than Nixon."

Dancer glanced at the handbill and handed it back to her. "His wife's not bad either."

Dede watched as Dancer and Jimmy walked hand in hand down the court to where Clayton's game had begun. Clayton stole the ball and dribbled the length of the court. He launched a shot from just inside the free throw line that swished through the net without touching the rim. Dancer's hands shot up over his head, and he clapped exuberantly.

For a moment Dede was back in Crutchfield Stadium as the little boy next to her leaped to his feet and cheered for the father who on that day had been perfect. There should be some lesson in that kind of memory – something she could hold on to. But what was it? That nothing lasts? At least nothing worthwhile. She sighed and stuffed the Kennedy flyer back in her purse.

48

Mel's Drive-In closed in the fall of 1959 and the restaurant remained vacant until the next spring when Rocco Bovenzi moved to town and introduced pizza pie to Maple Springs. Roc's Pizza Parlor was an immediate success, and when Matt Gillespie asked his daughter, Abby, where she wanted to go for her fourth birthday, she picked Roc's.

Matt asked Dede and her boys to join them. Not a party, but sort of a party-like feel he told Dede. Something to take Abby's mind off the fact that her mother was missing her birthday. A week earlier, Carol Gillespie had told Matt she had to go to Memphis to help the civil rights group she supported prepare for the "Freedom Ride." When Matt asked her what the hell that was, she explained a group of protesters, white and black, were going to ride a bus from Washington D.C. to New Orleans.

"That sounds like a suicide mission," Dede said. They were seated in a booth in the back of Roc's dining room. On the opposite side of the room, Roc had installed a bank of arcade games that filled the restaurant with the whir, pop, and whistle of electronic competition. It was the games, not the pizza, that made Roc's such a popular attraction. Right now Clayton was expertly demonstrating for Jimmy and Abigail how to play the Roy Rogers pinball machine.

"She's not riding in the bus, thank God," Matt said. "She calls herself the protest coordinator, but she's just doing glorified secretary work." He flipped through the selections on the wall-mounted jukebox console. "Want to hear Chubby Checker doing the Twist?" He fluttered his lips and flipped over another page of selections. "Damn, here's one I gotta play: 'Everybody's Somebody's Fool.'" He jammed a nickel in the slot and punched the buttons. He looked around angrily as Elvis Presley sang, "It's Now or Never."

"I guess someone else's nickel got there first," Dede said. Just as well, she thought. Connie Francis' sad tune wasn't going to improve Matt's disposition. It was selfish of Carol Gillespie to abandon her husband and daughter. Dede didn't understand why she would do that for people who weren't her family.

Matt reached across the table and gave her hand a friendly squeeze "Thanks for bringing the boys. It means a lot to Abby."

Dede had nearly forgotten how much she loved the feel of a man. She felt her face flush, even though she knew it was just an innocent gesture of friendship.

49

The Ferris wheel stopped, and Dede and Jimmy rocked slowly in the seat at the very top. From that vantage point they could see almost everything that was happening at the Howell County Fair.

"Why aren't we moving, Mom?" Jimmy asked, his chubby hands gripping tight to the safety bar.

Dede leaned forward to see why they had stopped loading passengers, and their seat tipped sharply. "Whoops," she screamed, laughing.

"Mom! Don't do that."

Dede patted his knee. "See if you can spot your brother. Or Matt and Abby."

It was the last day of the fair, and tonight the popular country singer, Johnny Horton, was performing on the main stage. Matt had invited Dede and the boys to join him and Abby. Two weeks ago, Carol Gillespie had returned to Memphis to help her group prepare for the next "civil rights stunt," as Matt described it.

Once they were inside the main gate, Matt and Abby headed over to the kiddie rides, Dede and Jimmy got in line for corn dogs, and Clayton went off with a bunch of other sixth grade boys to check out the bumper cars. They were all supposed to meet at the end of the main concourse – in front of the Ferris wheel – at four p.m. But neither Clayton nor Matt and Abby had shown up, so Dede and Jimmy decided to take a ride on the Ferris wheel.

Dede scanned the fairgrounds. Off to her left, the screams from the riders of the Sonic Coaster almost drowned out the clatter the cars made as they hurtled down the tracks. Clayton was not among the screamers.

Beyond the roller coaster was the stomach-churning Memphis Whirlygig, the Jesse James Gang Carousel, and the spinning teacups – the ride that had made Dede throw up when she was a teenager. Clayton considered those to be girly rides, and Abby wasn't old enough to ride any of them.

Stretching the entire length of the fairgrounds ran the main concourse. It was lined on both sides with fortune tellers, freaks of nature, like the bearded lady and the incredible Biloxi Siamese Twins, dozens of food booths offering fried chicken, corndogs, cotton candy, and ice cream in every shape and form imaginable, games of chance, like the Hillbilly Hustle and Benny's Magic Card World, and skill contests, like Fascination and Roller Ball and Hoop-a-Rama.

To the right of the Ferris wheel, men and boys were lined up, ready to do battle in the Thunder Road Bumper Car arcade. Beyond the arcade were the kiddie rides and the rodeo arena where in a couple of hours Johnny Horton would be singing his hit song, "The Battle of New Orleans."

"There's Matt," Jimmy said, pointing at the pony ride circuit that was just north of the main gate.

"Good eyes," Dede said. "I think that's Abby on the black pony. Isn't this a great view? You can almost see our house from here."

"Where?"

Dede pointed straight ahead. "Over those hills, at the end of the highway."

"What's beyond the end of the highway?"

"St. Louis," she said. She shaded her eyes as she twisted in her seat toward the sun. "Out there beyond that ridge is Springfield, where my mama was born." She leaned across Jimmy and pointed at the eastern horizon. "And back there is Nashville. That's where the man who is going to sing tonight comes from."

"Are those places far away?" Jimmy asked.

"No. Not really." She sighed. Her whole life had been lived in that tiny arc. She'd never been to Chicago or farther west than Wichita. Never traveled through the Deep South. Not that she had wanted to. Memphis, Little Rock, Birmingham, Jackson – those places had nothing but problems.

"There's Daddy!" Jimmy pointed to a man in a white uniform pushing a lift cart stacked with ice cream.

Dede shaded her eyes, but even in the late afternoon glare a hundred feet above the ground, with his back to her, she knew that delivery man was Dancer. He stopped at a white and red counter flanked by a streamer of blue balloons. "Your daddy's delivering ice cream."

Dancer unloaded the trays and wheeled the cart back down the concourse. He stopped at the booth where three boys were trying to get a beach ball to stay in a peach basket suspended from a pole.

"That's Clayton!" Jimmy yelled. "Hey, Clayton! Up here!"

"He can't hear you," Dede said. The Ferris wheel axle groaned, and they started down with a jolt. Dede felt like she had left her stomach at the top of the wheel. She saw the boy next to Clayton raise his hands in victory, and then her view was blocked by the crowds milling along the concourse. When they reached the summit again, she could see that the other boys had joined Dancer at the adjacent booth where customers were trying to knock over a pyramid of milk bottles with a baseball. In high school Dancer had been banned from a game like that after he won five teddy bears in ten minutes.

"Is Daddy going to play that game with Clayton?" Jimmy asked.

"I don't know," Dede said. They dipped out of sight again, and Dede had a nagging feeling that she wasn't going to like what she saw when they got back on top. As they rotated back to the top, Clayton's friends were all hurling baseballs at the pyramids in front of them. Clayton held back, thumbs hooked in his pockets. Dancer held up a baseball and beckoned him, but Clayton just shrugged. Even from atop the Ferris wheel, his contempt was obvious.

Jimmy watched with Dede but didn't say anything as they descended. He knew. When they came up and over again, Clayton still hadn't moved. The father and son stared at each other like gunfighters in a TV western, and then Dancer wheeled and fired the baseball at one of the pyramids. The pins scattered like he had blown them up with a grenade. Jimmy reached over and squeezed his mother's hand.

Dede, Matt, and the children waited in line for the gates to the rodeo arena to open. Vendors with large metal boxes strapped around their necks walked up and down the line selling soda pop, popcorn, peanuts, hot dogs, and ice cream. Dancer was one of the men selling ice cream.

Dede watched him work as he moved down the line toward them. Even missing three fingers, he was smooth and efficient. Graceful in his movements, like a dancer, she thought. That notion made her smile, despite her anxiety. She didn't want him to see her. Not with Matt. Especially not after that scene with Clayton. But there was no place to hide.

Jimmy saw him first. "Hi, Dad!" Jimmy said. He let go of Dede's hand and ran over to his father. "I saw you from the Ferris wheel."

Dancer looked startled and then smiled as Jimmy tugged on his sleeve. He scanned the line and spotted them. He continued to smile, but there was a tension in his face as he reached in his box and handed Jimmy an ice cream bar. "Here you go, sport." He walked down the line and stood in front of Matt and Dede.

Matt held out a dollar to pay for Jimmy's ice cream bar. "Hello, Dancer," he said.

Dancer stared hard at Matt. "It's on the house," Dancer said, the muscles in his jaw clenching and unclenching. He moved down the line, passing by Dede as though she were invisible. "How about you, Clayton?" He grabbed a frozen cone from the box and almost shoved it in Clayton's face.

Clayton leaned back, his eyes wide. "No, thank you," he said, his voice breaking.

Dancer slammed the lid shut on his crate and walked away from the line.

Matt started to walk after him. "Dancer, wait."

"Let him go, Matt," Dede said.

Matt steered his station wagon into the driveway. Abby and Jimmy were asleep in the backseat. Clayton jumped out of the car as soon as it stopped.

"Clayton!" Dede said.

Clayton stopped halfway up the porch. "Thank you, Mr. Gillespie," he said, looking back over his shoulder. "I have to pee."

Matt carried Jimmy up to his room, while Dede waited with Abby. "That boy's heavy," he said as he stepped back off the porch. He put his face up to the car window where Abby was stretched out.

"She's a little angel," Dede said. She leaned in next to Matt and put her hand on his shoulder. "We had a good time tonight."

Matt placed his hands on her hips. "Sorry about Dancer. I should have handled that better. Guess I messed things up," he said softly. He took a deep breath as if he were gathering his courage. "I really like you, Dede."

Dede cupped his face in her hands and kissed him softly on the lips. "Don't be sorry," she said.

Dede worried all weekend that she had crossed a line that she would be unable to uncross. The intimacy of that brief kiss was something she had been missing since Joyce had left, but she knew it was a reckless act. However, when she returned to the office on Monday and Matt acted as if nothing had happened, she felt rejected instead of relieved.

Her heart always seemed to win the battles with her head.

She remembered how Joyce had left her with that question, *When will you ever learn?* and now, more than four years later, she still had to answer, *I don't know.* And she feared that the more honest answer would probably be *Never.*

50

Some days Dede wondered what her life would have been like if she had fallen in love with Matt instead of Dancer. Without Matt, Carol Gillespie would have left Maple Springs for the bright lights long ago. Without Dede and those unexpected family obligations, Dancer might have made it to the majors. Matt and Dede would have worked out just fine in small town Maple Springs. Everyone's life would have been better.

But she had married Dancer for better or worse, so that was the hand she had to play. And lately things had been getting a little better. They had developed a routine of meeting on Saturday morning at the Foodliner parking lot. It was halfway between their houses and he would give her his envelope and, every other weekend, she would drop Jimmy off. Dancer made it to all of Clayton's basketball games, and while Clayton acted like he didn't care, Dede noticed that he would sneak a look up into the corner of the bleachers where Dancer always sat.

In January Rollie had asked Clayton if he was interested in working once or twice a month on stuff that he needed help with around his place. Since January, Clayton had cleaned up the toolshed, hauled junk out of the attic, and rebuilt Matilda's scarecrow. Dancer had helped, and then drove him home when the work was done. The projects were a chance for them to be together in a natural way, and Dede thought it had been good for both of them.

This month's project was to paint Rollie's garage, but thanks to Matt, Clayton was on his way to Springfield to take part in a basketball clinic run by one of the St. Louis Hawks. Clayton had been so excited when Matt told him about the opportunity, Dede didn't have the heart to tell him he couldn't go. Dancer would be disappointed, but he would understand.

Dancer was standing in his usual spot at the far corner of the Foodliner, away from the crowd of Maple Springers who were streaming into the store to do their Saturday morning shopping. Dede parked at the front of the lot and she could tell from Dancer's appearance that something was up. He was wearing his city clothes – pressed khakis with a short-sleeved button-down blue shirt – and there were tickets sticking out of his shirt pocket.

"Clayton's not coming?" he asked as she walked up to him.

Dede kissed him on the cheek and the aroma of his shave talcum twinged her memory. "It was a last minute thing. He got a chance to participate in a basketball clinic in Springfield. It's run by some famous basketball player."

"Bob Petit's clinic?"

"Yes. That's the name. So he is famous?"

"He's an NBA All-Star. That will be a great experience for Clayton." He took the tickets from his shirt and stuffed them in his pants pocket.

"What are those?" Dede asked.

There was just the slightest of a twitch at the corner of his mouth. "I like your dress." Dede self-consciously smoothed the front of her new dress. She'd bought it last weekend at Dalton's – a blue seersucker shirtwaist. When she was with Dancer, she hardly ever wore dresses. Wearing it now made her feel sort of like she was playing a part – acting like someone she wasn't, instead of someone she'd become. "What are those tickets for?"

He shrugged. "The Globetrotters are playing up in St. Louis. I thought he might get a kick out of seeing them."

Of all the weeks for Dancer to plan a surprise it had to be this week. Dede could feel his disappointment. "I'm sorry, Dancer. You should have told me."

He pulled his cash envelope from his other pocket. "It's no big deal. I'll just give them to Rollie. He loves basketball." He handed her the envelope.

If she had known, would she have told Clayton he couldn't go to the clinic? Would that have been better? Probably not. Some days you just can't win.

Dancer gazed out at the parking lot as though there were something interesting happening. "Looks like I might get that milk route soon," he said. He had told Jimmy he was hoping to become a milkman like Rollie.

"Being outside. That would suit you better, wouldn't it?"

Dancer nodded and his eyes seemed to light up. "Better pay. Drivers get commissions on the extra stuff like ice cream and eggnog. I'd be able to get my own place. Give Rollie back his trailer. And I'd be done by noon so I can go to Clayton's basketball games."

"If he makes the team," Dede said. "He has to beat out those eighth graders."

"He'll make the team," Dancer said. "How did you wrangle an invitation to Petit's clinic?"

Dede felt her stomach tighten. "Matt got it for him. From some client." That was a lie. Last week Matt had taken Dede to lunch. His wife had left again, and he needed someone to talk to. This time it was a desegregation campaign in Albany, Georgia. It was supposed to be for just a week, but she'd been gone for three weeks with no indication when she might return.

Matt's voice had been tight with anger as he vented his frustrations. "Carol says *we* have to make sacrifices for the cause. Like the whole movement will collapse if she isn't there to bring them coffee."

Dede had just been trying to change the subject when she told him how Clayton wanted to go to this basketball camp, which cost a hundred dollars. She wasn't asking for anything – but the next day Matt told her he had paid for the whole thing. When she protested he said, "Consider it combat pay for having me ruin a perfectly good lunch with someone who is too nice to tell me to shut up."

Dancer's face had darkened when she mentioned Matt's name. Joyce would have said that was a typical man's reaction. He doesn't want you, but he doesn't want anyone else to have you either.

"Is his wife coming back?" he asked.

"I don't know what she's going to do," she said. She knew he wanted to ask her about Matt. Were they dating? Did she love him? Did she want a divorce? She almost wished he would ask. She wanted to talk about Matt. Her boss was a man on a ledge. Every time his wife ran off he moved a little closer to the edge. She knew that with just a little effort she could pull him off the ledge and into her waiting arms. But is that what she wanted? If Dancer would just ask about her life, maybe she could come up with some answers. Or at least a plan. But she knew Dancer wouldn't ask.

He began rubbing his hands again. "Same time next week? Jimmy's going to be able to make it, right?"

"You know he wouldn't miss it."

"Yeah he likes Matilda's pies." He kissed her on the cheek and whispered, "Did I tell you how good you look in that dress?"

51

April 1963 – one year later

At the beginning of April, Carol Gillespie moved to Memphis. It was just temporary, she told Matt. Her group was preparing for a huge march on Washington that would require months of planning. They needed her down there full time until it was over.

Two weeks after she left, Matt invited Dede to his place for dinner. His timing was convenient as that weekend Jimmy was staying with Dancer, Clayton had an overnight camping trip with his friend CJ, and Abby was spending the week with her mother at her new apartment.

"Is this is a special occasion?" Dede asked.

"Yes. It's your six year anniversary," Matt said. When Dede frowned he added, "Of work. I hired you six years ago. Remember how you rescued the firm from the evil clutches of Margaret Pritchard?"

Three hours before the dinner, Dede stared into her closet even though she knew there was no dress in there she hadn't worn to the office a dozen times already. If this was a real date, and she was pretty sure it was, she wanted to wear something special. She didn't have the time or the money to buy a new dress, so in desperation she called Tammy Doyle. Ten minutes later, Tammy was in Dede's bedroom with five party dresses from her wardrobe. Most of them were low-cut – Tammy was proud of her breasts – and the dresses didn't hang right on Dede's smaller chest. She finally selected a violet floral with a V neckline and velvet trim. The waist was snug and Tammy insisted it should be worn with a petticoat, but Dede just gave her a look and she dropped the subject.

Petticoats, garter belts, stockings, girdles. Those things were not only uncomfortable, they were a challenge to take off. If Matt was interested in having sex, she didn't want to discourage him. She hadn't had any loving since Joyce left. It was time to pull Matt off that ledge. At least temporarily.

Matt had insisted on picking her up. He probably wanted to avoid having to deal with any problems from Dede's temperamental Impala, but even so, it was a nice touch. And when she opened the door, she could tell he liked how she looked. He had worn a checked sports jacket with a blue oxford shirt opened at the collar instead of his usual tie. He was still boyishly handsome, and Dede thought they made a nice looking couple. She wished they were going out where people could see them.

The lights in the dining room were dimmed. There was a candle lit in the center of the dining room table, and next to it, an ice bucket with a bottle of champagne. Matt filled her glass. "To six great years!" he said as he raised his glass.

They touched glasses, and Dede took a small sip of the champagne. It was sweet and bubbly and tickled her nose.

"And many more, I hope," Matt said.

Matt had boiled a lobster and grilled a steak. He dropped a steaming red lobster on Dede's plate.

"How do you eat this thing?" she asked as Matt tied a bib around her neck.

He sat diagonal to her so he could demonstrate. "Here. Pull off the claws and use the nutcracker to split open the tail." He crunched the body and speared the white meat with a tiny fork and pulled it out of the tail. "Go ahead."

As Dede wrestled with the lobster, she remembered that dinner when Dancer had struggled to cut his own steak. It made her momentarily sad and wistful. "Help me, Matt, before I hurt someone with this damn nutcracker."

He smiled and pulled his chair up next to her chair. He took the tail and twisted it and pulled the lobster meat out. He cut off a piece and dipped it in butter. "Open wide," he said.

Dede opened her mouth like a baby bird, and Matt placed the lobster morsel on her tongue. Butter dribbled down her chin. "Oooh, that's good." She wiped off her chin with her napkin. "But messy."

"That's what the bib is for." He held out another forkful of lobster, but Dede held him off with her hand. "You don't like it?"

She shook her head. "I better feed myself. I borrowed this dress, and I need to be careful."

"You borrowed it? It looks great on you. Hang on. I got the solution." He ran into his bedroom and returned with a grey sweatshirt with Harvard stenciled on the front. "Now you can dribble to your heart's content."

The food was great and so was the conversation. Dede couldn't remember the last time she had talked so easily. Kids, sports, politics – there didn't seem to be much they couldn't talk about. Dede told Matt how she met Dancer, how she fell in love. And the accident and what it did to their marriage. It felt good to talk to someone about her life even though she left out her affair with Joyce. She tried to tell herself that was because it was too hard to explain.

Matt told her how it had felt to lose his wife to something he couldn't compete with. The folks Carol worked with were changing the world. She never said so, but Matt could tell that she had dismissed him as just a small town lawyer. He got involved in local politics to show her she was wrong, and now he was someone the party had their eye on. He had been asked to run the Kennedy re-election campaign in Howell County next year. "Maybe one of these days I'll run for the House," he said. He smiled liked that was a joke, but Dede could tell it wasn't.

"You have my vote," she said, snuggling up beside him on the couch where they had moved after dinner.

They were having such a good time, Dede thought it might be better not to spoil it with sex. Sex would complicate everything. Maybe they could just be really good friends. If Joyce had just been a friend, things would have worked out better for everyone. But in the end when Matt stood up and offered his hand, she took it and let him walk her into his bedroom.

Matt was a different kind of lover than Dancer. More careful, more considerate, but not as passionate, which was funny because she had never thought of Dancer that way. For just a moment during their lovemaking, she wondered what Dancer was doing. Had he been with other women? She kissed Matt and did her best to drive those thoughts from her head.

She didn't think about Dancer again until Matt brought him up when he was pulling into her driveway. "If you want, I could put together the papers so you could divorce Dancer. It would be easy. The only asset you have together is this house. I can show you how to buy him out of his share."

In the moonlight, the little red brick house on Hill Street looked majestic. Like a fairytale castle. Dancer hadn't wanted to buy it, but Dede had convinced him, and he was grateful she had. He had grown up in dirt floor shacks. He was proud to own that house. It didn't seem right to take it away from him. But she knew that sooner or later she would have to let Dancer go.

"I'll talk to him," she said.

52

In the spring, the Foodliner added a greenhouse and a patio furniture outlet. It took up the far end of the parking lot where Dancer had always waited. As Dede drove into the lot, he was in the same location, but sitting at one of the picnic tables, studying a lined sheet of notebook paper, as though he were cramming for an exam. When she called his name and he looked up from his reading, he smiled at her like he used to in the old days. She suddenly wished she hadn't told Matt she would talk to Dancer about the house today.

He folded over the note paper and motioned for her to sit down on the picnic bench opposite him. "What do you have for me?" he asked, nodding at the papers she had clutched in her hand.

She avoided looking him in the eyes. She watched a father in the background boosting his son into one of the demo swing sets the outlet had for sale. "I wonder what Crutchfield thinks of this competition?" she said.

"He probably owns this place," Dancer said.

She rolled her tongue over the tops of her teeth. "I'll just say this straight out. We've been separated for over six years, and it's probably time to make things official. The first step would be to work out something on the house. We could sell it and split the money up, but the boys love the house so I was hoping to buy you out."

Dancer's face tightened, but his jaw wasn't clenched like it used to be when he got angry. "How would you do that?" he asked. His voice was calm.

"I can refinance with the bank. With the new mortgage I'd pay you off. You'd get about six thousand."

Dancer pointed at the papers. "You got it all written up? Guess it helps to work for a lawyer." He extended his hand for the papers.

Dede pushed them across the table. "There's no rush. Get back to me when you're ready, and if you don't think it's fair, let me know what you think is."

He glanced at the cover letter, typed on *Gillespie & Gillespie* letterhead. There was just the hint of a pinch around his mouth, as he stood up and stuffed the note paper he had been holding into his pants pocket. "I guess it all makes sense. I'll have someone look at it and get back to you real quick."

Dede stood up. Whatever he had written on the note paper, whatever he had been planning to say to her, she wasn't going to hear it today.

53

The sheets on the bed in the West Plains Holiday Inn were scratchy and smelled like bleach. There was a knock on the adjoining door to Dede's room. The door swung open and Matt stuck his head in. "Any more Kennedy supporters in here?" He waltzed through the doorway, beaming.

Once the sex line had been crossed, there was no going back. Matt set up the infrastructure for Kennedy's re-election campaign, and he was ingenious at using the campaign to find weekly opportunities for him and Dede to be alone together. The sex was good, but Dede was certain that he was mostly attracted to her because she accompanied him as he pursued the thing he had truly come to love: the mythic idea of John F. Kennedy. Now he had a cause every bit as important as his wife's.

He sat down on the edge of her bed. "We raised over five grand tonight."

Dede had bought a new negligee which draped her body and made her feel sexy. But she could tell by the flushed look of Matt's face that tonight would be a talking night. It was like he had already climaxed, and now it was time for conversation.

"Harper – he runs the state campaign – was very pleased. He may be looking to me to help them next year. This could be great for us."

"Us?" Dede asked.

Matt bounced himself all the way on to the bed. His eyes were red-rimmed and he smelled like a cheap cigar. "Did you stay for Collins' speech?"

"The fat bald guy with the suspenders? I left during his joke about Harry Truman and the Missouri mule."

"Rumor has it that gas bag is going to retire at the end of this term. If he does, I'm going to run for his seat in '66."

"And I'm going to be your office manager?"

Matt's forehead creased with annoyance. "No. Kennedy has changed the rules. Religion, marital status, not even race matters any more. After I get this campaign up and running, I'm going to divorce Carol."

Dede tried to smile beatifically, which further annoyed Matt.

"We can get married, Dede."

A statement of fact, not a proposal. There was a world of difference between the two, but she didn't need to make that point. Not tonight.

54

Dancer sat at the same picnic table in the far corner as he had all summer, but now he was surrounded by mountains of pumpkins the Foodliner was selling for Halloween. As Dede wound her way through the pumpkin stacks, she tried to figure out what was different about him. He looked fit – his clothes didn't hang on him any longer – and his hair was neatly trimmed, but there was something more. He had a different look about him, a stillness that might even be described as serene.

She slipped into the bench across from him. "Jimmy's looking forward to his next visit. He says Matilda's going to bake him a pumpkin pie."

Dancer laughed. "I'll do my best to keep him from eating the whole thing." He handed her his envelope. He smiled, almost coyly. "I have a speech today. Are you ready?"

"Oh my," Dede said. She grinned, but her stomach was churning.

"I was going to give this a few months earlier, but then you gave me that stuff about the house, and it didn't seem like the right time." He paused and took a breath like he was about to plunge underwater. "One of the things we learn in AA is that to move on, we have to make amends to the people we've hurt.

"That doesn't mean just saying, I'm sorry. I need to make recompense for the damage I've done to you and Clayton and

Jimmy." He had been looking at her intently, and now he looked down at the table as though his notes were there. "I don't know if I'll ever be able to fix things with Clayton, but I got a chance with Jimmy."

"Jimmy loves you, Dancer."

"I guess that's what Matilda means when she talks about God's grace, because God knows I haven't done anything to deserve his love. But it means everything to me."

"Clayton is young. He'll come around, too."

"Maybe. I know it isn't easy to forgive or forget. Especially when you're young. But that's for another day. This is your day," he said and gave her his half-smile.

Dede shook her head. "My day? You don't need to—"

"I was angry with you for a long time about Joyce. I felt you betrayed me. But I was only thinking about me. And I was wrong. I never wanted to face the fact that it was me that let you down. I was caught up in my baseball career, and when that dream died, instead of sharing my pain with you, I avoided you. Tried to get through it on my own." His voice had gone hoarse. He swallowed hard. "I'm sorry Joyce moved away. I hope you still have her as a friend. She's a good person."

Dede felt a lump rising in her throat. "Thank you." Her voice was catchy, and she didn't trust herself to say anything more. But that had always been one of the good things about Dancer. He didn't require a lot of words.

He reached into his jacket and pulled out a document. "Here's that agreement on the house. I signed it, but I don't want you refinancing. I don't need the money. Let's keep that equity for the boys. And you. You take the house. I can't think of a better way to start making my amends." He pushed the document across the table toward her and stood up to leave.

Dede thought about giving him back the document. Tell him to think more clearly about what he's going to need down the road. But she knew when he set his jaw that way she wasn't going to change his mind. She picked up the contract and walked with him back through the parking lot. "Whatever amends you think you owed me, Dancer, we're even now. Okay?"

55

Dede pulled the pumpkin pie out of the oven and replaced it with the stuffed turkey she had prepared. The tangy sweet aroma of the pie soothed her jangled nerves. Even if she screwed up the turkey, they would at least have dessert. She had four hours to get the potatoes, squash, and cranberries prepared. She wanted everything ready to go when Matt and Abby arrived at noon.

She had a plan. After the dinner was over, when the kids were off playing, she could give Matt the contract Dancer had signed. She would tell him she was ready to go forward with her divorce. A week ago, her plan made perfect sense. Now she wasn't so sure. Matt left the office in tears last Thursday when they learned that President Kennedy had been shot. On Monday when he returned to the office, he looked devastated. Dede asked if he still wanted to come over for Thanksgiving, and he told her that Abby was looking forward to it and so was he.

"Smells great, Mom," Jimmy said as he walked in from the TV room where he and Clayton were watching cartoons. "Do you want me to peel the potatoes?"

"You can peel potatoes?"

"Matilda taught me. It's my Sunday dinner job. I'm good at it."

"Okay. Let me empty this wastebasket, and I'll get you set up." She took the kitchen basket that was full of pumpkin guts and walked out the back to the garbage can beside the garage. There was a bracing chill in the air, but it felt good to escape the heat of the kitchen. As she emptied the basket into the garbage can, she heard the sound of tires crunching on the gravel driveway.

It was Matt and Abby, three hours early. So much for her plan. Matt had parked halfway up the drive, and as she walked toward him, he got out of the car with a bakery package.

He smiled, nervously. "I brought you blueberry muffins from Tag's."

She ran a hand through her hair. She hadn't had a chance to dress or put on her makeup. "You're a little early," she said.

"I know. I'm really sorry, Dede." He nodded back at Abby still seated in the car and lowered his voice. "We're going to drive to Memphis and spend some time with Carol. I had a long talk with her last night. I'm bringing her home. We want to try and work things out." He stared down at the muffin box as though he couldn't remember why he was holding on to it.

Dede should have been angry but she wasn't. Joyce had asked her when she would ever learn, and now she could answer that question. She finally understood. She didn't need anyone else. She had her family and that was enough. It had to be.

She took the muffin box out of Matt's hands. "You better get going. It's a long drive to Memphis."

"Dede I'm--"

She didn't turn around, but raised her arm above her head to wave off any pointless apology. "It's okay. Drive carefully." Whatever loss she felt for what might have been, it wasn't as bad as what Matt felt losing Kennedy.

Jimmy had been watching from the kitchen window. "Isn't Matt coming for turkey, Mom?" he asked as she walked back into the kitchen.

"No, he had to change his plans. But look. He brought us blueberry muffins."

"I love muffins. Can Dad come for dinner?"

"No. He has to work," she said.

"So it will just be me and Clayton?"

"And me. That's enough isn't it?"

Jimmy jumped down from the sink where he had perched to look out the window. "Hey Clayton, we got muffins!"

"Don't eat them all, Porky!" Clayton ran into the kitchen, almost colliding with Dede.

"Sit down, boys."

Dede put the muffins on a plate and placed them on the table. She sat down with Jimmy and Clayton, and they each took one. Jimmy had them hold hands as he recited a grace he had learned from Matilda.

Dede peeled off the paper liner and took a bite. The muffin was still warm and the blueberries were sweet and juicy. They kept the muffin from crumbling.

Clayton & Jimmy

56

July 1964

With Jimmy balanced on his handlebars, Clayton stood up to pedal as they neared the summit of Deer Lick Hill. Alex, who didn't have to haul a hefty ten year old, waited for them at the top. The brothers rolled past Lancelot Avenue, which was guarded by a wrought iron archway identifying that street as the entrance to the Camelot Square development. The houses in Camelot Square were brick or stone and most had turrets to make them look like castles.

"You're wobbling," Jimmy said. He was sitting on his hands, clinging desperately to the handlebars. There were fat dimples above his knees as he struggled to keep his legs straight in front of him.

Clayton was too winded to tell his brother to shut up. His leg muscles burned. As he reached the summit, he shouted to Alex, "Meet you at tetherball." He knew better than to stop. With Jimmy's extra weight, they could coast down Walnut, cross Main, and make it all the way to the playground without stopping.

"Here we go!" Tears leaked from Clayton's eyes as they rocketed down the north side of Deer Lick Hill. As they approached the intersection of Walnut and Main, Clayton scanned the road in both directions. There was one car headed toward downtown, but it was almost a block away.

"Clayton, don't!" Jimmy screamed.

"Hold on!" Clayton pedaled harder and they zipped across Main. The driver blasted them with his horn. Two minutes later, they rolled into the playground that had been built between the old and new schools.

They had to tear down the old playground when the new school was built. But that was okay because this new playground was way better. It had a baseball diamond, jungle-gym, merry-go-round, several swings, and best of all, a tetherball pole. Clayton and Alex were kings of the tetherball court. Clayton skidded to a stop and Jimmy tried to jump off, but his foot caught on the handlebar and he tumbled facedown into the dirt. He lay on the ground like he was dead.

"Get up you doof," Clayton said, nudging him with the toe of his sneaker.

Jimmy giggled and then jumped up and dusted off his T-shirt and shorts. "Beat you to tetherball," he said. He took off like he was running in quicksand – arms pumping furiously, legs going nowhere.

Clayton trotted past him, shaking his head. "Save your energy, Jimbo. You'll need it."

The tetherball court was next to the jungle-gym. Perched on the metal-pipe fence that circled the jungle-gym area, were four boys and little Trudy Bennett, who was in Jimmy's grade. She grinned at Clayton as he got in line behind her. "If I win, I get to play you," she said.

Something about Trudy reminded Clayton of the girl who played Pollyanna in that Disney movie his mom made him take Jimmy to last month. Maybe it was the freckles. Although Clayton reckoned Trudy's freckles might just be dirt. It wasn't her hair. Trudy's hair was mud-brown and had been chopped short like one of her wild sisters had hacked at it with a knife. It was her attitude, he decided. Trudy was fearless and she had a smart aleck answer for everyone – big kids, little kids, adults – it didn't matter to Trudy.

Clayton leaned forward, with his hands on his knees and spit into the dirt. "Yeah," he said.

The boy in front of Trudy turned around and said, "You ain't going to win, Trudy, so don't get your hopes up."

Trudy stuck her tongue out at him and then spit on the ground just as Clayton had. "Hey, Jim, why you all red-faced?"

Jimmy had finally made it up the hill. He was bent over, gasping for air with his hands on his knees. He quickly straightened himself up and wiped his face with his tee-shirt, as though he could wipe the redness off. "Hi Trudy," he said.

Clayton jumped down from the fence. Candy Landis and her gang of girls were coming over from the merry-go-round. Candy, with her long shiny brown hair, was the prettiest girl in their class, and Alex's girlfriend. At least that's what Alex said. "Hi Clayton," Candy said. She said to the girl beside her. "Clayton, Alex, and I are in the divorced parents club."

He could feel his face getting hot. "My parents aren't divorced. Neither are Alex's." If Candy hadn't been so cute, Clayton probably would not have liked her at all. She always had to bring up the parent situation.

Candy gave him her know-it-all look. "Well they're not here, are they? Alex hasn't seen his dad in over a year. And he said you've never been to your father's place, even though he just lives in Holtville."

All of Candy's friends stared at him. Girls could be so nosy. He had seen his father plenty of times since he'd walked out of their lives. He and Jimmy had even spent a few weekends in that stuffy old trailer behind those colored people's house where Dancer lived. Jimmy still went over there almost every other weekend, but Clayton told his mom he didn't want to, and she didn't make him.

Alex stopped at the ball diamond and was talking to Mr. Bilko. The year after Dancer left, Candy's dad bought Mr. Bilko's farm so he could build more houses. Clayton's mom said Mr. Bilko didn't need to work anymore, but this summer he had taken the job as Park Director. Alex waved to Clayton to come over to the field. Clayton wanted to play tetherball. He didn't like baseball. Hadn't really played it since he was a little kid, but Alex kept waving and if he stayed put, he would have to deal with Candy.

He waved back and jumped down from the fence. "I'm coming," he said. As he jogged back across the park toward the baseball field he yelled to Jimmy, "Don't let that girl beat you."

"Afraid to play me, Clayton?" Trudy said.

Clayton ignored her. He heard Candy say to her friends, "I told you Alex would show up. He promised me." Then she shouted, "Hey Alex, come here."

As Clayton approached Alex and Mr. Bilko, Alex clapped his hands together. "I've gotta go, Mr. Bilko, but Clayton can help you out. He's a better player anyway." As he ran by Clayton, he punched him in the shoulder. "I promised to buy Candy a freeze-pop over at Woody's. See you after the game."

Clayton was pretty certain the freeze-pop was just an excuse. Alex had told him that last week he and Candy had made out in the woods behind Woody's Grocery.

Mr. Bilko put his hand on Clayton's shoulder. "Can you help us out? We're short one player."

Clayton hadn't played baseball since his Grasshopper League days. And that had been a softball tossed underhand by one of the fathers. This was hardball. Real baseball. With real pitching. Clayton didn't want anything to do with baseball – basketball was his sport. But before he could come up with an excuse one of the others players spotted him.

"Hey Stonemason's going to play. We got a game."

He was trapped. They stuck him out in right field, figuring that was the safest place for him. There weren't any left-handed

253

batters so most of the hard hit balls would go to center or left field. In the first two innings, nobody hit a ball near him. He batted ninth and when he came up to bat in the third inning, there were runners on first and second.

Mr. Bilko shouted encouragement as Clayton stepped into the box. "Just stay loose, Clayton. Watch the ball all the way."

The pitcher threw the ball right down the middle, but it was faster than Clayton had expected and was past him before he could swing. He swung wildly at the next two pitches for a quick strikeout. Nobody said anything, but he knew they were all thinking he was a loser.

In the fourth inning, one of the batters on the other team hit a weak pop fly over the first basemen's head. Clayton sprinted in, caught the ball on the run, and doubled off the runner on second base who had not expected him to make the play. His teammates cheered him. When he came up to bat again in the fifth inning, Mr. Bilko called him over and said, "Keep your weight on your back foot. Follow the pitch all the way from the pitcher's hand and just try to lay the bat on the ball. See how easy you can swing. Just make contact."

Clayton settled into the batter's box. He concentrated on the ball as it left the pitcher's hand and took a smooth, easy swing. To his surprise, he lined the ball over the third basemen's head for a single. He was so excited he stumbled and almost fell coming out of the box. He sprinted to first and took a wide turn to second like his dad had taught him. When the left fielder lollipopped his throw back to the pitcher, Clayton kept on running and made it to second easily.

"Way to go, Clayton!" Trudy yelled with a high-pitched screech. She and Jimmy had come down from tetherball and were swinging on the swingset behind the backstop. The players on both teams laughed. Clayton wished he could disappear.

After the game, Mr. Bilko came over and shook his hand. "You got great baseball instincts. Just like your dad. Why don't you come out and play with us every week?"

Clayton shook his head. He wasn't like Dancer. Why did people always have to ruin things by saying that? "No thanks. I don't want to play."

Mr. Bilko held the bat bag while Jimmy and Trudy handed him the bats. "It looked like you were having a good time out there." He took the last bat from Jimmy and buckled the bag.

Clayton spotted Alex up by the tetherball court. "We gotta go home, Jimmy."

Mr. Bilko was disappointed. He was just like Dancer in that way. They thought there was something special about baseball. But there wasn't.

"How's your father doing?" Mr. Bilko asked as he hoisted the bat bag on to his shoulder.

Clayton shrugged. "I don't know. Okay, I guess. Come on Jimmy." He sprinted toward the tetherball court before Mr. Bilko could ask any more questions.

57

Jimmy leaned into Matilda's potato barrel looking for the largest potatoes he could find. When he found one that met his standards he dropped it into his gunny sack. When he had six he ran back upstairs. Matilda's kitchen was warm and full of good smells from the meat she was cooking.

"I got the potatoes," he said.

Matilda rolled out a pie crust and layered it into one of her pie pans. She nudged the edge of the crust with her fingers forming a zig-zaggy edge. "You want to help me fill this pie?"

"Okay," Jimmy said. "Where's Dad and Rollie?"

"They're no help with pie-making. I told them to take the garbage to the dump. Don't need them under foot when I'm trying to get dinner ready." She took her big wooden spoon and stirred up the brown glob in her mixing bowl. "Here. Spoon this into the crust. Don't make a mess."

Jimmy peered into the mixing bowl. "What is that stuff?"

Matilda opened the big black oven and pulled out the ham she had been baking. "That's the batter for my shoofly pie." She took a dishtowel, wiped off her hands, and then pushed a few loose hairs back behind her ears. "What you staring at, boy?"

Jimmy liked to look at Matilda. She was almost as tall as his dad. Her green eyes were catlike and her skin was dark and smooth. When she smiled at him, her teeth sparkled. He thought she was very pretty. "Nothing," he said as he finished spreading the batter.

"That looks good." She took the pie and pushed it into the oven. "Now get those taters scrubbed so I can make the cheesy potatoes you like so much."

Sunday dinner with his dad at Rollie and Matilda's house was Jimmy's favorite meal. If his mom had allowed it, he would have spent every weekend at his dad's trailer. Jimmy didn't mind that Clayton had stopped visiting. It was better without him.

An hour later, dinner was ready. Matilda covered the table with a tablecloth and Rollie put his Sunday suit back on. Dancer, who sat next to Jimmy, smelled like Ivory soap. He had shaved off his whiskers, slicked down his hair, and he was wearing the white shirt he would have worn to church if he had gone to church.

"Jimmy," Matilda said, "Would you please say the blessing you learned in Sunday school?"

Jimmy clasped his hands together and squeezed his eyes shut. He couldn't remember how it began. "Uhm."

Matilda reached over and put her hand around his hands. "Come, Lord Jesus…"

"Oh yeah. I got it. Come Lord Jesus be our guest and let this daily food be blessed."

"Amen," said Rollie as he reached for the ham. "That's my kind of prayer, son. Short and sweet. Here you go." He passed the platter to Dancer.

"Rollie, Dancer, do you gentlemen have anything you'd like to share with the Lord?" Matilda asked. It didn't really sound like a question.

Rollie eyed the forkful of ham he was about to shovel in his mouth. "Thank god for Bob Gibson."

"Amen," Dancer said.

Last Thursday, the St. Louis Cardinals Negro pitcher Bob Gibson had defeated the New York Yankees in the 7th game of the World Series.

Jimmy took a scoop of cheesy potatoes. "They set up a TV in the auditorium and the whole school watched that game." He handed the potatoes to Matilda. "It was neat."

Matilda's mouth twisted like she didn't think a World Series Championship was something to be praying about even if the winning team was the Cardinals. "And how about you, Dancer? Any special prayer requests?"

His dad set the ham platter on the table and leaned back in his chair. He rubbed his chin and then took a sip of Matilda's special lemonade. "I hope the Foodliner and A&P and IGA don't build anymore supermarkets around here."

Matilda nodded and patted his dad's hand.

"Why, Dad?"

Rollie answered Jimmy. "More and more folks are buying their milk at those damn supermarkets. Pretty soon there won't be any need for milkmen like me and your dad."

"I'm only delivering four days a week now, Jimmy," his dad said. "Not enough customers."

"We have to trust in the Lord," Matilda said. "He has a plan."

"Maybe so," Rollie said. "But I'm not sure we can wait for the Lord's plan. The writing on the wall is pretty damn clear."

His dad was massaging his bad hand again, but he stopped when he saw Jimmy staring at him. "Don't worry, Jimmy. It's all gonna work out." He dropped two thick ham slices on Jimmy's plate.

Matilda handed the potatoes to Dancer. "You know you're always welcome to come to church with us."

Rollie snorted. "Dancer could integrate the Holtville Baptists. Be just like your damn fool Freedom Riders."

"What do you mean, MY freedom riders," Matilda said. She was a teacher for the high school and Jimmy recognized that was her teacher look and voice. His dad didn't say anything about going to church. He was concentrating on his meat cutting.

Rollie stabbed a chunk of ham with his fork. "I feel just as bad as you do about those boys getting murdered, but you poke a hornet's nest and nothing good's going to happen."

Jimmy had read the story in the Dispatch. In August the bodies of three civil rights workers, missing all summer, had been found buried in a field in Mississippi.

Rollie attacked his ham slice with his knife and fork turning a good sized slab of ham into a plateful of ham chunks. While he cut the ham he sputtered about how the civil rights workers were just going to make things worse for everyone. Matilda told Rollie that things were never going to change if people didn't make an effort. His dad listened and it looked like he was going to say something, but then he grabbed another slice of ham instead.

"...and you can't say things aren't ever going to change. Dr. King awarded the Nobel Peace prize. That means something," Matilda said.

Rollie stared down at his plate of meat. He stabbed a chunk. "King's a good man. A damn fool, but he's got guts, I'll give him that."

Matilda picked up the platter of ham and the dish of potatoes and put them on the counter. "Any of you men interested in some pie?"

She brought the pie over to the table and cut it into slices. As she handed Jimmy his slice, she said, "I'm going to give you the rest of this pie to take home to Clayton and your mom. You let your brother know we miss him. Tell him he needs to come back out here and pay us a visit."

Jimmy took a big bite of the pie. He nodded because his mouth was full and because he didn't know what to say. Clayton wasn't going to visit, but he didn't want to tell Matilda. She would feel bad. So would his dad.

58

Clayton's last class on Monday was American History, taught by Mr. Hall. His favorite teacher had once played offensive tackle for Missouri State. Mr. Hall didn't just stand in the front of the classroom and lecture at them; he wanted everyone to participate. To get things stirred up, he'd read some newspaper story or an article from *Life*, *Look*, or *Time*. Today he read the headline story from the *St. Louis Post Dispatch* about the bloody battle between civil rights marchers and state police that had taken place over the weekend in Alabama.

"Suppose I own a bus company," he said, after he'd finished reading. "Should the federal government be able to force me to rent my property to those marchers when I know there's a good chance hooligans will attack my bus and destroy it?" Most of the class, even the ones who favored the integrationists, didn't think that was right. But then Mr. Hall shifted direction. "As a law-abiding citizen, shouldn't I have a reasonable expectation that the local government – in this case the Alabama State Troopers – will protect me on my journey from Selma to Montgomery?" That launched a heated argument between the kids who supported the civil rights marchers and those who thought they were all "meddling Yankee assholes." The debate might have veered out of control if Mr. Hall hadn't been six foot six and three hundred pounds.

Toward the end of the period, he called on Clayton. "Mr. Stonemason. First of all, my congratulations on your victory last Friday." Clayton had led the varsity basketball team to a win over Cabool, which secured Maple Springs a slot in the state tournament. "Please tell us where you stand on this contentious issue."

Clayton enjoyed following the debate, but hadn't said anything. Maybe because he could see that both sides had a point. Or maybe because he didn't want to be on the same side as the do-gooders. Or maybe because he still felt like he was in a spotlight. Even with his basketball heroics, he feared he would always be the kid whose father cut off his own fingers.

Clayton shrugged.

Mr. Hall frowned, his brow knitted. "Certainly you have an opinion, Mr. Stonemason."

Clayton returned Mr. Hall's look. "I think it stinks that the State Troopers didn't protect those people. That's their job."

Mr. Hall smiled. "Thank you, Clayton, for that succinct distillation of your position." He picked up a nub of chalk and scratched an assignment on the blackboard. "Good discussion, class. Now for Wednesday, I want everyone to write a short paper on 'Property Rights and the Civil Rights Movement: Pro or Con.' Just three pages."

The whole class groaned.

"Ah, stop your whining," he said as he tossed the chalk from one hand to the other. "And don't just give me regurgitation from *The World Book*. Take a position. There are important things happening right now. This is going to affect the world you inherit, so you better start thinking about it."

After the big victory on Friday, the coach canceled Monday's practice. Clayton had been looking forward to his first day off from basketball practice in three months, but now he would have to spend his one free day working on that lousy paper.

As hegathered up his books, Candy Landis sidled up to him, clutching her books to her chest, her face framed by her long brown hair. "You played great," she said. "I can't wait till the tournament starts." She set her books down on his desk and pushed her hair behind her ears. Candy was a cheerleader on the Junior Varsity squad, but that was only because they didn't let sophomore girls cheer for the varsity. Clayton thought she was a fox.

"Thanks." He tried to think of something clever to say to keep her standing there by his desk. She was wearing a leather mini-skirt that made her legs look extra-long, and a white cashmere sweater that snugged her breasts. The sweater distracted him. It had been easier to talk to Candy before she had breasts.

She flicked her hair back. "I was wondering," she said, her smile almost dazzling enough to distract him from her body, "if you could come over to my house after school and help me with that paper?"

Clayton stared at her, his mouth open.

"I thought since I don't have cheer practice, and you don't have basketball, this might be the best time to get it done."

"Okay," Clayton said, his brain still struggling for words. "But how do I get there?" Candy lived west of town in a huge plantation-style house Ted Landis had built the year after his divorce.

"Vicki Bennett can give us a ride." Candy giggled. "It'll be a little crowded in her GTO – she has to pick up her sister from junior high – but we'll make room." The Bennett girls all had reputations. Darlene Bennett, who was in their class, had been kicked off the cheerleading squad for smoking. Her older sister, Vicki, mysteriously left town in the middle of her junior year and didn't return for twelve months. And little Trudy, according to Jimmy, had a permanent seat in the junior high detention hall.

There were three girls, and Clayton squeezed in the backseat when they stopped for Trudy. She scowled at her sister as she stared into the full backseat. "Where am I supposed to-- Hey Clayton, what are you doing back there? I guess I'll have to sit on your lap."

"That's okay," Candy said, "he's my guest." She scooted up into Clayton's lap and draped her arm around his neck.

Trudy wrinkled her nose and slipped into the backseat. "Way to rub your boobs in his face, Candy."

"Shut up, Trudy, or you'll be walking your sorry little ass home," Vicki Bennett said from the front seat. Her boyfriend popped the clutch, and the tires squealed as they pulled away from the school. Candy's body pressed back hard into Clayton's chest. Her silky hair tickled his face. It smelled of nutmeg.

Candy's house was set back from the highway in the middle of a small grove of willow trees that had grown up around a stream that meandered through the old farmland. The house had four pillars that supported an impressive front portico. The recreation room on the lower level resembled something out of a Hollywood movie. It had a walnut parquet floor, sleek metal-framed sofas, and chairs with light-green foam cushions. In the center of the room there was a circular fireplace, and in the back, a bar. Next to the bar was a felt-covered poker table. A ceiling-to-floor expanse of glass along the far wall had sliding doors and opened on to the backyard patio where there was a hot tub and a large brick grill.

"Just you and your dad live here?" Clayton said, and then he kicked himself.

Candy was unfazed by the question. "And Daddy's not here half the time," she said. "He's building all those new sports stores for Mr. Crutchfield."

"Old man Crutchfield always scared me when I was a little kid," Clayton said. "When we would go to his store, he would appear out of nowhere – really spooky-like. He'd shake my dad's hand and try to smile. He wasn't any good at it, though."

"And those black suits. He looked like a preacher in an old western."

"I'll bet Seymour would be on the property rights side of this debate," Clayton said.

"And how about you?" Candy said. She sat down at the poker table and ripped a sheet of paper from her spiral notebook. "What side of the issue are you taking?"

Clayton felt a twinge of disappointment. Alex told him about making out with Candy, and Clayton hoped this might be his big chance. The only girl Clayton had ever kissed was Karen Savadelle and that didn't really count because it was a kissing game for her fourteenth birthday party last summer. But it appeared that Candy really did want to work on the paper.

"Those folks should be able to ride a bus without getting attacked," he said.

Candy smiled at him and drew a line down the middle of the paper. Her lower lip rolled out as she concentrated on writing down what Clayton had said. When she was finished writing she asked him, "But what about the poor man who owns the bus? Doesn't he have a right to protect his property?"

"That's what those state troopers are supposed to do. Instead they let the mob attack," he said.

They talked for almost an hour. Candy suggested that maybe if the civil rights folks had property of their own, they'd feel more strongly about property rights. Clayton countered that if they had been treated fairly all along they'd have acquired their own property, so maybe the civil rights laws were needed to fix things.

"Fix things?" Candy said. She had filled three pages with her notes. She tilted her head to the side as she thought about that. "Maybe." She smiled at Clayton as she stood up. "I'm going to make a copy of these notes for you. I'll be right back."

"How are you going to do that?"

"My dad has his own Xerox machine." She rolled her eyes. "There are cokes in the refrigerator behind the bar. Help yourself and get me one, too. But don't touch his beer," she said as she disappeared up the stairs.

Clayton grabbed two bottles of coke and pried off the caps. He sat down on the sofa in front of the circular fireplace and set the bottles on the brick hearth. He imagined sitting on the sofa with Candy, a fire crackling, the room dark. Mood music playing on her stereo.

"Comfortable?" Candy came up from behind him and whispered in his ear. She handed him the photocopies. The paper was dry, not wet and smelly like the school copier.

"Neat," Clayton said. "Now we just have to write the paper."

She came around the sofa and sat down next to him, her hip tight to his. "You made some good arguments. You almost convinced me."

"Almost?" Clayton twisted slightly and put his arm over the back of the couch. Candy snuggled in next to him. Her skirt rode higher and Clayton thought he might have seen a flash of panties as she shifted her position. He could feel the softness of her cashmere breast on his ribcage as she leaned into him.

He moved his hand to her shoulder and squeezed lightly.
Candy turned her face toward him. Her eyes were closed and her
lips, slightly parted, were inches from his face. His heart
pounded. Their mouths came together and everything slowed
down. Candy's lips were smooth and soft and sweet. He broke
the kiss after what he thought was the appropriate length of time
for a first kiss, but Candy pulled his head back to her and they
kissed again. And then her lips parted and she probed his mouth,
playing tag with his tongue. She tasted like Dentyne and Coke.

The kisses got longer. Soon they were only pausing to
breathe. When Candy draped her arm across Clayton's chest, his
hand drifted down from her shoulder. His thumb rubbed the side
of her breast.

"Clayton." Candy broke off the kiss. She tucked her knees
up under her so she was facing him straight on. "Does your
father ever talk about my mother?"

Clayton's hand moved back to the top of the couch when
Candy changed positions. "No. Why would he?"

"You know. Because of the affair. Do you think he loved
her?"

"My dad and your mom?" Clayton cringed. Could that be
possible? That day on the old school playground when Sammy
Kellerman had told him his dad had cut off his fingers on
purpose, Clayton felt like he had been stripped naked. It seemed
like everyone on the playground was staring at him. He hadn't
done anything wrong, but he felt guilty. And humiliated. That
same sense of helplessness swept over him now. He didn't want

to believe Candy, but of course it was true. He knew his father was guilty of far worse.

Candy put her hand on his chest. "Oh my god! You didn't know?"

Clayton closed his eyes, willing Candy not to tell him. But he knew she would.

Candy leaned into him and with the I've-got-a-secret-voice he had heard her use with her girlfriends, she said, "A few weeks before my dad moved out, I heard my parents fighting. They were trying to keep their voices down, but I could hear my dad say, 'Stonemason' over and over again and he sounded awful. Like he was going to cry."

Clayton stood up and walked over to the sliding doors. Beyond the patio and the imposing brick oven was a large expanse of well-groomed lawn. Something about the lawn, maybe it was the eerie effect of the twilight, reminded him of the manicured grass of Crutchfield Stadium and that day so long ago when his dad had been perfect. Why did his father have to screw everything up?

Candy got off the couch and joined him. "It doesn't have anything to do with us," she said.

Us? Clayton liked the sound of that. He took hold of her hand, and together they watched as shadows slowly cast the backyard into darkness.

59

Jimmy was at the kitchen table copying numbers from a leather-bound ledger onto the monthly invoices for Rollie and Dancer's newspaper delivery business when his mom walked in the house carrying a bucket of Kentucky Fried Chicken. The restaurant had opened last year, a block from the law office, and Dede had been bringing home a bucket almost every Monday since they opened.

"I'm almost done, Mom." Jimmy scooped up the completed invoices.

"Just leave them. We can eat in the TV room. How's their new business looking?"

"Twice as many customers as last month." Dancer had lost his milkman job just before Christmas. With all the supermarkets popping up, fewer folks were having their milk delivered. Rollie figured it wouldn't be long before he would be let go too. He started a business delivering newspapers to the people who didn't live in town, and he made Dancer his partner. Jimmy had been helping them on the weekends, folding the Sunday supplement and rubber-banding the papers. Today he was helping them prepare their monthly statements.

Dede set the bucket down on the coffee table in front of the TV, and Jimmy loaded his plate with a large scoop of mashed potatoes, a handful of biscuits, and three chicken breasts.

"Save some for Clayton." Dede turned on the television. Walter Cronkite was reporting on the bloody clash in Selma between the Alabama State Troopers and the civil rights marchers. The film footage of the confrontation showed the troopers, outnumbered, but with shields, clubs, and attack dogs driving back the demonstrators who blocked the highway to Montgomery. Suddenly the cameraman was running and the scene became a jerky swirl of men and women fleeing from the dogs. Some of the marchers scaled the chain link fence that bordered the highway. The camera zoomed in as one of the dogs tore at the pant leg of a young black man trying to climb the fence.

Jimmy stopped devouring his chicken to stare at the TV. "I'll bet Matt's glad his wife isn't out there with those marchers." They had had a baby boy just before Christmas.

Dede picked through the bucket and grabbed a wing. "She was never out there marching. She worked in an office."

The door in the kitchen slammed, and Clayton walked into the room. He was wearing his school jacket with the coveted M sewn on the chest. He earned his athletic letter as a starter on the basketball team. He bragged to Jimmy that he was the only sophomore in the school who had earned a letter. "Hey, Porky, you don't get all the breasts." He snatched the last one off Jimmy's plate.

Jimmy tried to grab Clayton's hand, but his brother sidestepped him and put him in a headlock while he took a large bite. "You're not quick enough, Jimbo. Or strong enough." He released Jimmy's head and shoved him toward the sofa.

"Jerk." Jimmy's ear burned from the grappling, but he wouldn't give Clayton the satisfaction of knowing he had hurt him. He resisted the urge to rub it and plucked two thighs from the bucket to replace the breast.

Dede handed Clayton a napkin and silverware. "How was practice?"

"Coach gave us the day off. I was over at Candy's doing homework." He flopped down on the couch and poured himself a glass of milk.

His mom scrunched her face when Clayton mentioned Candy. She should have been pleased he was actually doing his homework, but she didn't seem to like Candy very much anymore.

It was easy for him to talk to girls. He never got nervous or tongue-tied. The only time a pretty girl would talk to Jimmy was to ask him a question about Clayton. Lots of girls in his school had crushes on Clayton just because he was an athlete. That's what girls liked. They didn't care if you got good grades or worked hard.

Jimmy stuffed the last biscuit into his mouth. "Hey Clayton, I'm working for Dad and Rollie on their newspaper business."

"What are you talking about?"

Dede said, "Your dad and Mr. Savoy have a business delivering the morning newspapers to rural customers. You'd know that if you spent some time with your father."

Clayton shook his head. "You got to be kidding me. Now he's a newspaper boy?"

When he made bad comments about their father, his mother's mouth would get all pinched like she was trying to keep from saying anything.

"I fold their Sunday flyers and help them with their accounts," Jimmy said. "And this summer, Dad told me I can ride with him when he delivers the papers."

Clayton looked angry. He always got angry when they talked about Dancer. What was wrong with delivering newspapers? "Dad and Rollie are going to take me to your playoff game," Jimmy said. Clayton couldn't get angry about that.

His brother laughed, but it didn't sound like he thought it was funny. "Great," he said, rolling his eyes up toward the ceiling. "What are you going to do when he sneaks out with two minutes to play?"

His mother put her chicken wing back on her plate. "Clayton," she said sharply. His brother gnawed on the chicken breast like he hadn't heard her. "Clayton," she said again, and finally he had to look at her. "He leaves before the end of the game because he knows you don't want him there."

"That doesn't make any sense," Clayton said.

"Neither does getting mad at everything your father does."

Back and forth they went, covering the same ground they'd covered a dozen times before. Jimmy wanted to tell Clayton to just shut up for once. He always had to have it his way. He'd never give in, even to his mother. Couldn't he see she was worn out after working all day?

Even when she was arguing, his mother's face remained pale, like she hadn't been outside in months. And her clothes hung loose on her. She was too skinny. Jimmy worried as much about her not eating enough as she worried about him eating too much. When Clayton finally paused to catch his breath, Jimmy jumped in to change the subject.

"Look at that neat helicopter," he said pointing to the TV. A reporter in army fatigues was holding a microphone and trying to talk over the *whop-whop-whop* of the helicopter that had just landed behind him.

"8,500 troops from 1st Marine Division arrived here at the Tan Son Nhut Air Force base, just outside of Saigon. These are combat troops, ready to take the war to the insurgent forces of North Viet Nam."

The reporter stopped a Marine lieutenant and asked him how he felt about fighting in a war halfway around the world in a country most folks back home had never heard of. The soldier – he didn't look much older than Clayton – talked about duty and honor and how they had a job to do and how they were going to take care of business. When the soldier finished his assessment, the reporter asked him how long it would take to get the situation under control. The boy grinned. "We'll be home for Christmas."

60

For the first round of the Class C State Championship, Maple Springs was playing Poplar Bluff at the old amphitheater in West Plains. The tipoff wasn't until 8 p.m., but Rollie had driven over with Dancer to pick up Jimmy just after six so they could get a good seat.

They had to wait in line to pick up their tickets, and then Jimmy asked his dad to buy him a Coke and a box of popcorn. By the time they made it through the refreshment queue and walked into the arena, it looked like everyone from both towns had already arrived.

They found an opening around twenty rows up on the Maple Springs side of the court. Jimmy was squeezed between his father and Rollie, his arms pinned to his sides. He tried to set his Coke on the floor so he could get at the popcorn, but he couldn't move. From behind him he heard a girl yell, "Hey, Jim! You want to sit here?"

Trudy Bennett. Jimmy knew who it was even before he twisted his head around to see. She was three rows back, sitting with her two sisters and two boys Jimmy didn't know. Jimmy liked Trudy. Mostly when she talked to him it was to ask about Clayton, but once, after Jimmy had done a report for their fifth grade class on the Missouri Compromise, she had told him he was the smartest kid in the class.

When Trudy called for Jimmy, his father smiled like he had remembered some funny story.

Trudy patted the open space beside her. "Come on, Jim. Bring your popcorn."

Jimmy felt his face getting warm.

"Go ahead, Jimmy," Dancer said. "Rollie could use a little more breathing room."

"Is Clayton ready for the game?" Trudy asked as soon as he sat down.

Jimmy put his Coke on the floor and grabbed a handful of popcorn. He offered the bag to Trudy. "I don't know. I guess," he said.

The teams ran out of their locker rooms and started doing layups. Clayton made it look so easy. He seemed to glide like a skater. Jimmy wished he could move like that.

Poplar Bluff was bigger and taller, but Maple Springs had more speed and got off to a good start. Clayton hit his first two jump shots and harassed the player he was guarding up and down the court. In the first quarter he stole the ball three times. By the end of the quarter, Maple Springs led 16 to 11.

Early in the second quarter, Clayton had a clean block on a shot but was whistled for a foul. "Goddammit ref, that's not a foul!" Trudy screamed, causing a number of heads to turn. It was his second foul. "Now he's going to have to come out of the game."

"Doesn't he get five fouls?" Jimmy asked. Every time he thought he had figured out the rules, something happened he didn't understand. It made him feel stupid.

Trudy squinted at him. "Are you really Clayton's brother?" she said. And then when Jimmy frowned at her she added, "I'm just kidding. Don't get all mopey. They don't want him to get three fouls in the first half. They need him playing hard in the second half."

Without Clayton's defense, Poplar Bluff pounded the ball inside. By halftime they led 29 to 26.

As the teams headed off to the locker room, Dancer and Rollie stood up. "You want anything, Jimmy?" Dancer asked

Trudy had sent the box of popcorn down the aisle to her sisters and their boyfriends. By the time it came back, the popcorn was nearly gone. Jimmy was still hungry, but he didn't want Trudy to think of him as Clayton's fat little brother. "No, thanks."

"Can I have a sip of your Coke?" Trudy asked. She picked up the cup from the floor and sucked on the straw, slurping up the last drops of melted ice and soda. "We'll catch them in the second half when Clayton gets back in the lineup," she said.

"I hope so." Jimmy rattled the ice in his cup.

"You know what I love about Clayton?" Trudy said.

Jimmy really didn't want to know. He wanted to say something funny that would make Trudy laugh and forget about Clayton for a while. But he couldn't think of anything. All he

could think to talk about was how he was helping his dad and
Rollie with their delivery business. That wasn't funny or
exciting.

"He never quits," Trudy said. "When he's guarding
someone, he's on them like white on rice. All over the court.
Never lets up."

Jimmy nodded. Trudy was right about Clayton never giving
in. Even when he was wrong, like he was about their dad. It
didn't do any good to tell him, though. That just made him
angry. And Trudy had been right when she predicted that with
Clayton back in the lineup, Maple Springs would regain the lead.
But with four minutes left in the third quarter, he picked up a
charging foul and then committed a foolish reach-in foul on the
in-bounds pass. With four fouls he had to come out of the game.
Trudy held her head in her hands and stared at the floor. "Shit,"
she said.

In the next row Rollie was muttering and his father was
gripping his bad hand so fiercely that it had turned an angry
shade of red. With Clayton on the bench, Poplar Bluff began to
pull away. When Clayton finally returned to the game with four
minutes to play, Maple Springs was down by ten.

Clayton played like a madman. Jump shots, steals, layups,
rebounds – he was everywhere. With twenty seconds to go, and
Maple Springs down by one point, he forced another turnover.
Maple Springs called time. The crowd had been standing for the
last ten minutes. Somewhere in those final minutes, Trudy had
grabbed hold of Jimmy's hand like he was her protector. And
even though she squeezed so hard it hurt, it was exciting. Trudy
needed him. As he watched his brother running from one corner

of the court to another, the envy for his brother's athletic prowess was swept away by a surge of pride. From the intense look on his father's face, Jimmy could tell he felt the same way. His dad loved Clayton. Jimmy wished his brother could see that.

Poplar Bluff tried to keep the ball out of Clayton's hands, but he was too fast for them. He caught the inbounds pass at the center court line. He dribbled hard toward the basket. As he reached the foul line, their center left his man to double team him. Clayton crossed over his dribble to his left hand and shifted directions so quickly, both defenders fell down. He drove toward the rim as another player slid over to get in his way. Clayton banked his shot against the backboard as he collided with the player. The shot rimmed around but fell out as Clayton and the boy crashed to the court. The referee whistled a foul. Trudy had grabbed hold of Jimmy's arm, and he could feel her fingernails digging into the fleshy underside. The crowd waited for the ref's call. Was it a charge on Clayton? Or a shooting foul against Poplar Bluff?

Finally the ref held up a fist and two fingers and the Maple Springs crowd went crazy. Trudy hugged Jimmy. He wasn't sure what had happened. There was no time left on the clock.

He looked at Trudy. "What—"

"Clayton gets two free throws," she said. "He makes both, we win. If he makes one we go to overtime."

The players from both teams stayed back at half court, and Clayton stood at the foul line all alone. The referee bounced him the ball and held up two fingers again. Trudy was back to squeezing Jimmy's hand. His father stared down at Clayton, his eyes steely. Jimmy's heart was pounding so hard he didn't think he would have been able to even hold on to a basketball. But his brother appeared calm, determined.

Clayton bounced the ball twice and lofted his free throw. It clanked against the front of the rim. A nervous, collective groan arose from the Maple Springs side. On the other side of the court, the crowd cheered wildly and someone yelled, "Choke."

Clayton stepped off the line. He ran his hand through his hair and flexed his shoulders. Trudy had her hands clasped together, and she was practically vibrating. Jimmy reached over and took her hand. She clasped it with both hands and pressed it against her chest. Clayton stepped back to the foul line, and the referee handed him the ball. He bounced it twice, bent his knees, uncoiled and lifted the shot. As the ball left his hand he kept his arm poised as though he were guiding it to the basket. Trudy, still clutching Jimmy's hand, extended her arms as though she were taking the shot. The basketball hit on the right side of the rim, swirled around slowly and then faster, faster, and then...

It rolled out.

Trudy dropped Jimmy's hand and collapsed into her seat with an anguished sob. She covered her face with her hands. Clayton's teammates sprawled on the ground, a couple of them buried their heads in their towels as the Poplar Bluff players and crowd celebrated their victory. Clayton had failed, and Jimmy felt as bad as if he had missed the shots himself. Clayton hung his head. Jimmy had never seen his brother defeated. It seemed wrong.

Jimmy patted Trudy on the back. "Don't cry, Trudy," he said. It was a stupid thing to say, but his brain had frozen again and he couldn't come up with the right words. He wanted to hold her hand and be her protector again, but he couldn't make his hand move. There was a murmur of surprise from the crowd around him. His dad was standing on his seat staring down at the court with his hands clenched together over his head. A triumphant pose that said, "You're a winner, son." There were tears of pride in his eyes. Jimmy willed Clayton to turn around, but Clayton walked dejectedly off the court with his head down.

61

Clayton primed the Roth's Briggs & Stratton power mower, stepped on the housing to brace himself, and pulled hard on the starter cord. The lawnmower rattled and coughed, the exhaust belched blue smoke, and then the engine caught. He adjusted the throttle until the mower purred.

He liked cutting the Roths' lawn. It was flat, and except for a few bushes around the front door, they just had grass – no flower beds, fountains, or statues to maneuver around. And their mower was new. He could usually get it started with one pull, and the wheels were powered, not just the blade, so mowing the grass was like a walk in the park. He could daydream. Sometimes he would try to calculate how many more lawns he'd have to mow before he had enough money saved to buy Andy North's '55 Buick. Andy wanted two hundred, but Clayton figured he'd take one fifty. When he got tired of arithmetic, he'd imagine being on a date with Candy, in his Buick, parking down by the tracks. Getting to second base. Or maybe third. But it was hard to think about that stuff too long, and usually by the time he mowed the side yard, he was back on that foul line with no time left on the clock, shooting free throws to win the game. He never missed.

It was Jimmy who came up with the idea of mowing lawns. Clayton had needed a summer job, but he didn't turn sixteen until the end of August, and none of the stores or restaurants would hire a fifteen-year-old. Jimmy was helping Rollie and

Dancer with their delivery business, and he said they could use more help, but Clayton didn't want to work for his father, so Jimmy had suggested the lawn mowing business.

"You don't even mow our lawn," Clayton said. "And you're not strong enough to start the mower."

Jimmy laughed. "You and Alex are going to mow the lawns. I'm going to keep working for Dad and Rollie, but I'll find you the customers."

"Nobody's going to pay us to mow their lawn," Clayton said.

"Not here. But up the hill in Camelot they will."

"What are you going to do, knock on their door and ask them if you can mow their lawn?"

"That's how you get business, Clay. You ask for it. But I'll have a flyer printed up, too. We'll charge five dollars."

Most of the summer jobs in town paid minimum wage – a dollar and a quarter. The Camelot development had big lawns, but they wouldn't take more than two hours to mow. "If you can find suckers to pay us five dollars," Clayton said, "I'll do all the lawns. The hell with Alex." Clayton would be getting his learner's permit at the end of the month, and he wanted to buy Andy's car as soon as he got his license.

"No. We need Alex. That'll give us scheduling flexibility," Jimmy said. "You'll get four dollars for each lawn, I'll get a dollar."

"A buck? For doing nothing?"

"Sales commission. And I have to pay for all those flyers."

Clayton had to hand it to Jimmy. He was a pretty shrewd eleven-year old. By the beginning of July, he had signed up twenty houses and he kept finding new customers. So far in August, Clayton had mowed two lawns almost every day.

Clayton had waited until 3:30 to start the job. Mr. Roth tipped better than his wife, so Clayton didn't want to finish before he came home from work. With perfect timing, Mr. Roth pulled into the driveway just as Clayton finished cleaning the lawn mower.

"The grass looks great, Clayton." Mr. Roth pulled out a wad of bills from his pants pocket and peeled off a five and three ones. He pointed to the basketball next to Clayton's bike. "You play ball in this heat?"

"Free throws. I shoot a few every day."

It was more than a few. Every day since the playoffs last April when he had let his team down, Clayton had been riding his bike over to the playground to practice. He shot at least three hundred every day. His record was fifty-five in a row. Next time the game was on the line, he would not fail.

From the Roths' house on top of the hill it only took him five minutes to get to the park. All the little kids had left for the day, and he had the basketball court to himself. He purposefully chose the west end because the setting sun would be in his eyes and that forced him to concentrate more on the shot. The rims were bare, but Clayton had brought his own net.

He stood under the strut that fastened the fan-shaped backboard to the basketball stanchion. After flexing his knees he jumped straight up, grabbed the strut, reached around the backboard and hung from the basket bracket while he hooked his net onto the rim.

He dropped to the ground, picked up his basketball, and dribbled out to the foul line. He took a deep breath, exhaled and bounced the ball twice on his right side, keeping his eye on the rim. With the ball cradled in his left palm, he gripped it with his right hand, reading the nubby surface with his fingertips. He coiled slightly, and then, as he uncoiled, his hands rose and the weight of the ball shifted from his left hand to his right. He released the shot with a snap of his wrist, imparting a slight backspin so it flew straight and true, and with enough forward thrust so it arced upwards for two thirds of the flight and descended gently toward the target.

Tchaa.

Clayton loved that sound. The shot kissed the inside of the rim, rippled through the net cords and bounced off the end of the court.

"I got it, Clayton."

Clayton smiled. Trudy Bennett was on her sting-ray bike pedaling toward him. Almost every time he shot free throws, Trudy showed up. She had become his official ball returner. As she rolled past, she grinned at him, revealing new, shiny metal bands on her top teeth. She parked her bike under the basket and bounced the ball back to Clayton.

"What happened to your mouth?" he asked.

"Shut up."

He clanged the free throw off the front of the rim.

"Concentrate," Trudy yelled.

"Could you keep your mouth closed? The reflection from those braces is blinding me."

"Ha ha." She clamped her mouth shut.

Tchaa.

The ball ripped through the net and bounced at Trudy's feet. She fired it back to him. Her lips pressed tight.

"Aren't you going to count?"

She shook her head.

Tchaa.

She bounced the ball back to him.

"If you don't open your mouth soon, you're going to run out of breath and die."

Tchaa.

"I guess I'm going to have count for myself. That's five in a row. Fifty more for the record."

"That's only four," she said, then clamped her hand over her mouth.

Clayton laughed. "See, I need your help. I can't shoot and count, too."

She grinned broadly, "Okay, I'll count."

Clayton covered his eyes. "Oh my god, I've been blinded again."

Trudy took two steps toward him and hurled the ball at his head. "You asshole."

He got his hands up in time to knock the ball away. "Sorry. Let's get serious now."

He made twenty-three in a row, and then the ball caught the back of the rim and bounced out.

Trudy tracked the ball down and fired it back to him. "Not bad, but you can do better."

Clayton caught the ball and re-set himself on the foul line. Trudy waited under the basket, and as the sun set behind her, it gave her a bright, hazy look, like an angel in one of those TV movies.

She was right. He could do better.

Tchaa.

62

June 1966 – one year later

Jimmy was grateful that Rollie's new truck had a backseat so he didn't have to be squeezed between Rollie and Dancer. Rollie accelerated as the truck pulled on to Highway 60. They were on their way to Mr. Crutchfield's office to pitch him on the idea Jimmy had come up with.

In the spring, Crutchfield had hired boys in the town to hand out flyers for his chain of sporting goods stores. Jimmy had figured it wouldn't cost them any more to deliver the Crutchfield flyers to the out of town customers to whom they were already delivering a newspaper. His dad had called Seymour, and he was willing to listen to their proposition.

The toothpick in Rollie's mouth was bobbing up and down. He cracked his neck and looked over at Dancer. "About the sales call…"

"What?" Dancer asked.

"You and Jimmy need to make this call without me. Better if I stay in the truck."

"Are you crazy? We're partners."

"You saw the paper today. Crutchfield don't need any uppity Negroes in his face right now."

Jimmy had seen the photo. A Negro named James Meredith had been shot by a sniper soon after he had begun his one-man protest march to Montgomery. The photographer had snapped the photo of Meredith, his face contorted with pain, as he attempted to crawl off the highway.

His dad frowned at Rollie and began to rub his hands together. "No. We go in together. You're not that uppity."

"This ain't a joke, Dancer. This is a big deal for all of us."

He shook his head. "It's not right. For Christ's sake, you're the one who put this business together."

"Right ain't got nothing to do with it. This is the way the world works. Sitting in the truck hoping you don't step on your dick, ain't the worst indignity I've had to suffer. Not by a longshot. But--"

"What?"

Rollie caught Jimmy's eye in the rearview and winked. "Maybe you ought to let Jimmy do the talking."

Mr. Seymour Crutchfield's office was in the original Crutchfield store on Main Street. One of the sales clerks led them up to the mezzanine walkway that circled the sales floor. As they approached he opened the door to his office and stepped out on to the walkway.

"Dancer! Great to see you. What's it been? Five years?"

"More like ten," his dad said. He half-turned toward Jimmy. "Mr. Crutchfield, this is my son, Jimmy."

His mom had told Jimmy that Mr. Crutchfield reminded her off an old-fashioned preacher. She said he was very serious. But the man welcoming him to his office was as friendly as any adult Jimmy had encountered who wasn't trying to sell you something. "Jimmy, this is a pleasure. I understand you're quite the basketball player."

"That's my brother," Jimmy said. Clayton had led the basketball team to the quarterfinals in the state tournament. For the last two months, it was all folks in town could talk about. Everyone was predicting that next year they would be state champions and Clayton would get a scholarship to Missouri State, maybe even Kansas.

"Jimmy's the businessman," Dancer said.

"Well, we can't all be athletes, can we?" Mr. Crutchfield said. "Please come inside."

Jimmy was always being compared to his brother. It was nice for once to have his own identity.

Crutchfield led them into his office and indicated they should sit down at the chairs that were placed in front of his desk. It was probably a good thing Rollie had not come along as it didn't look like there were any more chairs and the office was crowded with just the three of them.

His father had walked over to study the photograph that hung on the back wall of the office. "Last time I was here, there was only one girl in the picture," he said.

Crutchfield beamed. "Three girls. Wilbur and Melissa have their hands full." He fake whispered to Jimmy, "Wilbur's my son-in-law. He used to be your father's baseball manager."

His dad smiled. "That was long ago. Before you were born Jimmy."

"They grow up fast, don't they?" Crutchfield said. He addressed Jimmy again. "My granddaughter, Cynthia, wants to go see those Beatles when they come to Chicago next month. Are you a Beatles fan, Jimmy?"

"Not really," he said. The only Beatle he could name was Ringo. And that was just because it was such a cool name.

"Me neither," said Crutchfield. "But they are good for business. I sell a lot of their records. Speaking of business," he turned back to Dancer, "tell me about your delivery company."

Dancer gave him the background of the business. Following Rollie's directions, he didn't mention Rollie's name.

"So how many delivery vehicles do you have?" Crutchfield asked.

"Two. I drive the north counties and Rollie Savoy drives the south. So if you have a flyer or ad special you want to get to the people who don't live in town, we can deliver it."

"This Rollie – he's your employee?"

His dad cleared his throat. "We work together," he said.

"Hmm." Crutchfield pulled a pencil from the cup on his desk that held at least a dozen lethally-sharpened No. 2 pencils. He made a quick mark in his notebook. "He's a Negro, is he not?"

"Yes, sir."

Crutchfield nodded and put the pencil back in the pencil cup. He picked up the morning paper and frowned at the front page photo of James Meredith. "That's a good business move."

His father's eyes narrowed and he leaned forward like he wasn't quite sure he heard Mr. Crutchfield correctly.

"Having a Negro in your business is smart. Times are changing." He slapped the paper down on the desk and shook his head. "Idiots."

Now he looked serious.

Crutchfield sat back in his chair. "You'll appreciate this, Dancer. Lowell Thacker has made a similar proposal to us. He has four trucks. Been in business a couple years now. So he's got a track record."

Mr. Crutchfield had smiled when he said that, like it was good news. But it didn't sound good. Jimmy knew that Percy Thacker was the head of the Klan in the county. From the way his mom had talked about him, he sounded like a creep.

His father's lips were pressed tight. "Thacker?" he said.

Crutchfield stifled a burp. "Some relation of Percy's. Cousin or some such thing. Who knows? Those folks are all related one way or another."

His dad began to knead his hands but stopped when Crutchfield jabbed his finger at the newspaper. "Look at Meredith. Now he's a martyr. And that preacher fella, King." Crutchfield shook his head with an air of resignation. "They're just going to keep coming. We need to accept that, like you have. We don't have to like them. We just have to deal with things we can't change and make the best of it. Percy Thacker and his ilk are dinosaurs. They do stupid things like shoot down this rabble-rouser, and what does it get them? More government interference in our lives. The Thackers are bad for business."

Crutchfield stood up and walked around his desk. He extended his hand. "It's going to be a pleasure working with you, Dancer. And with you, Jimmy."

Rollie was so pleased with the news that he insisted Dancer and Jimmy join him at Hecky's Barbeque Joint on the outskirts of Holtville for a celebratory meal of pulled pork sandwiches, cornbread, and sweet ice tea. A wiry black man in a greasy apron brought the sandwiches to their table.

Rollie wrapped his arm around Jimmy's shoulders. "Hecky, this here is James Stonemason. You need to remember his name. He's one smart businessman."

Jimmy smiled so hard his face hurt. He had seen his future. He was a businessman. Right now the athletes ruled, but someday school would be over, and it would be Jimmy's time.

63

Clayton and Dede sat on the back porch sipping lemonade. It had been uncomfortably warm all week, but it was still spring and the temperatures dropped back to comfortable by the time Dede got home from work. While his mom read the rejection letter he just received from the East Texas State Athletic Department, Clayton gazed out at the backyard.

The lawn needed cutting again. Clayton had mowed it only a week ago, but with the heat and spring rain, it was already so thick and long he could barely locate the spot where Dancer had scuffed the grass down to the bare dirt for pitching practice. Clayton remembered how all through the offseason, even in the winter, his father would hurl fastballs against the red brick wall of the garage. Over and over and over again. Pursuing his dream.

The East Texas letter was just like all the others: *Congratulations on a great season. We regret that we cannot offer you a scholarship. Wish you all the best.* Etcetera, etcetera, etcetera. It hadn't been a surprise. The Maple Springs Eagles had made it to the state championship, thanks to Clayton. But in the finals they were beaten soundly by the South Joplin Raiders, who were led by high school All-American, Leroy Washington. Leroy was awesome. Far better than any player Clayton had ever faced. Leroy was on his way to UCLA, and Clayton knew he was not in the same league as Leroy. But that was okay.

His dad had been driven by his dream to make it to the majors. When he failed, it broke him. Clayton wasn't going to have that problem. He didn't have a dream.

Dede folded the letter and handed it back to him. "I'm sorry, Clayton. I think you would have liked Texas."

Clayton laughed. "You're just trying to get me out of the state. Away from Candy."

"There are other girls," she said. She held the lemonade glass up to her cheek. "Ah, that feels good." She moved the cool glass to the other cheek. "You need to send in your acceptance to Southwest."

"I don't know," he said. Dede insisted he apply to Southwest Missouri State in Springfield, just in case he didn't get a basketball scholarship. They accepted him immediately, but SWMS took anyone with a pulse. They even wanted him to play basketball, but couldn't offer a scholarship. Clayton didn't want to go there. He was tired of school.

"Clayton!" Dede leaned forward and set her lemonade on the porch table. "You have to go to college."

Her face was drawn. He didn't want to fight with her about his draft status again. He wasn't even eighteen yet. There was plenty of time. "Want me to go to Hardee's? Pick up some burgers and shakes?"

His mother smiled weakly. "I swear you are just like your father. And I'm not talking about your love of cheeseburgers."

Before he could respond, there was the crunch of gravel and Rollie's truck rolled into the driveway. Something was wrong. Rollie wasn't smiling and Jimmy was slumped forward in the passenger seat. Every afternoon after school, Jimmy had been helping Dancer and Rollie with their deliveries. He'd ride with whoever had the longer delivery, keeping everything organized.

As Rollie jumped out of the truck, Clayton could see his face was puffy and his clothes covered with mud. A bloody rag was wrapped around his right hand.

Rollie caught Clayton's eye. "Help me with Jimmy."

"Jimmy!" Dede yelled. She knocked over her lemonade as she ran off the porch. She pushed herself in front of Rollie who was trying to help Jimmy out of the truck. "What happened?"

"Bunch of Klan thugs jumped us over in Mountain View," Rollie said.

Jimmy's bottom lip was split, and his left eye was swollen shut. His T-shirt was bloody and his neck was caked with blood that had gushed from his nose.

Clayton tugged on Dede's sleeve. "Mom. Get out of the way. Let me help Rollie." As they eased him out of the truck, Jimmy grimaced and hugged his gut.

"He might have a couple broke ribs," Rollie said.

Dede walked alongside them, her face showing almost as much pain as Jimmy's. "Clayton," she said. "Get your car. We need to take him to the hospital."

Jimmy winced. "I'm okay, Mom. I just want to take a shower and lie down."

Rollie and Clayton supported Jimmy as he climbed the porch steps and shuffled into the kitchen.

"I can make it from here," Jimmy said. "Thanks, Rollie," He leaned on the bannister and headed up the stairs to his bedroom.

"I'll get some witch hazel. Clean out those cuts," Dede said.

Jimmy groaned and as he reached the upstairs landing he looked down at his mother and shook his head. "I don't need anything," he said, his voice breaking.

"Let him be, Mom." Clayton stared at Rollie. "What happened?"

Rollie frowned. A droplet from the blood-soaked hand-bandage had splattered on the dining room floor. He knelt to wipe it up.

"Let it go," Dede said. She walked him back into the kitchen and pulled out a chair from the table. "Sit down. I'll get you some lemonade. Tell us what happened."

Rollie eased himself into the chair. He wrapped his two hands around the glass of lemonade and shook his head slowly. "This was my fault." He lifted the glass with both hands and took a sip. "We were out on 386, a couple miles south of Mountain View in that patch they call Colson Hollow. Those hillbilly shacks down there in the holler are all on private roads so those folks have to come up to the highway to get their mail. I started filling the boxes on the east side, and Jimmy worked the west side."

Rollie took a long swallow of lemonade.

"The road ain't nothing to brag about out there. And what with the rain last night, those potholes were sloppy. I'm about half finished stuffing them boxes when this pickup comes bouncing over the hill. I hear them whooping it up, and I knew it was trouble. They was heading south, coming down the west side of the highway, but when they seen me filling them boxes, the driver swerved over to my side and splashed me with that red slop."

Clayton stared at his mom. She'd always been so strong. A fighter. But lately everything seemed to weigh her down.

Rollie sighed. "If they hadn't called me a nigger, I probably would have let it go. Should have. It was just a little mud."

He held his head in his hands and stared down at the table. Clayton wanted to reach over and smack him. The man took forever to get to the point.

"I should have let it pass. Instead I told them dumb ass crackers they could go fuck themselves." He rubbed the back of his neck. "Excuse my language. Them boys did a quick U-turn and I thought they were going to run me down. There were three of them. They came running out of that truck like it was on fire. I surprised the hell out of the first one. Guess he thought I was just going to lie down and beg for mercy. Busted him solid, might have broke his nose. Them other two got me down on the ground, and the one I hit kicked me in the gut. Knocked the wind out of me. I was goddamn helpless. Jimmy saved my ass."

Rollie reached across the table and grabbed Dede's hand with his good hand. "Jimmy came across that highway like a freight train. Knocked that kid smack into the ditch. Them other two boys let me go and went after him. I tried to get up, but I couldn't get my wind. If that sheriff hadn't shown up, them boys might've killed Jimmy." Rollie let go of Dede's hand and hung his head. "I'm sorry, Dede."

"What'd that sheriff do?" Dede asked.

"Nothing. Told them Klan assholes to go home. Told us if we didn't get out of town he'd arrest us for disturbing the peace."

"Who were they?" Clayton asked. He flexed his hands. They were stiff. He hadn't realized that they'd been clenched ever since Rollie started telling his story.

Rollie sighed again and pushed back from the table. "It don't matter now, Clay. They ain't going to do nothing about it. That's Thacker's town."

Clayton pounded his fist on the table. "I don't care if it's Thacker's town. Who did this?"

"Was it Brandon Thacker?" Dede asked.

Rollie shook his head. "It wasn't Brandon." He stared hard at Clayton. "I didn't know the other two, but the kid doing the kicking was Lowell Thacker's boy. Bobby Joe or something like that."

300

"Billy Joe Thacker? Bullet head, pineapple face?" Clayton asked. He knew Billy Joe.

"That's the guy. Dog ugly little shit. The Thackers are all bent of out shape because we took that Crutchfield business from them."

Dede pulled open the door for him. "You need to see a doctor."

Rollie nodded. "There's a doc over in Holtville who can check me out. And I'll tell Dancer about Jimmy as soon as he gets back from his route."

Clayton stayed on the porch as Dede walked Rollie to his truck. After Rollie pulled out of the driveway, she headed back, her face pale. "We need to take Jimmy to the hospital," she said.

Clayton had his car keys in his hand. "I'll be back in a couple hours. Jimmy will be okay."

"Where are you going?" Dede asked even though she had to know that he was going to Mountain View. "Don't do it, Clayton."

"I have to," he said.

64

Despite the pain in his gut, Jimmy felt oddly satisfied with himself. He had fought bravely and saved Rollie. But Clayton couldn't leave it at that. He had to jump in and be the big hero – take on the whole Thacker gang all by himself. And Dede did nothing to stop him. She was more worried about Jimmy than she was about Clayton. She wanted to take Jimmy to the hospital and when he refused, she drove off to the drugstore for bandages and aspirin.

Five minutes after she left, Jimmy heard a vehicle pull into the driveway. The kitchen door slammed open.

"Dede! Jimmy! Anybody home?" Dancer yelled from the living room.

Jimmy rolled off the bed and clutching his ribs as tight as he dared, stumbled out to the upstairs landing. "I'm coming down, Dad."

His dad intercepted him on the stairway. He gripped hard on Jimmy's arm as he studied his face. "Matilda told me what happened. Are you okay? Where's your mom?"

Jimmy eased down the steps. "I'm okay. Mom went to get some aspirin." His ribs hurt, but not as bad as before. "Clayton went after them."

"After the Thackers? Over to Mountain View?"

Jimmy nodded.

His father knew what a stupid move that was. He ran his hand over his face. "Tell your mom I've gone to get him back."

"I'm coming with you," Jimmy said. He walked toward the kitchen door.

"No. You stay here."

He glared at his father. This had been his fight, not Clayton's. He wasn't going to sit home like a bookkeeper while the warriors went off to battle. Not this time. Not anymore. "No. You're not leaving me out of this. We're a family."

His father looked around the room as though Dede might magically appear and talk Jimmy out of going. Finally he shrugged in resignation. "Okay. Leave a message for your mom that doesn't scare her too much."

It wasn't difficult to find Clayton. His father figured he would be looking for Billy Joe Thacker at one of the Thacker hangouts, and the first place they checked out was the Tip Top Lounge, which was on the main drag of Mountain View. As they approached the bar they could see the flashing lights of two police cars blocking the entrance to the parking lot. Clayton was being held face down in the middle of the parking lot, and one of the cops was about to handcuff him.

Dancer parked in the street. "We're just here to talk, Jimmy," he said, as they jumped out of the truck. Clayton was surrounded by a semi-circle of men, some holding beers like they'd taken a break from the bar to check out the action. Outside the circle, a pimple-faced kid with a bloody nose sat on the ground, looking dazed.

As they made their way across the parking lot, Percy Thacker emerged from the bar. He bent over to say something to the kid with the bloody nose. Then he shouted something and the deputies stepped away from Clayton. Percy ran over and kicked Clayton in the gut.

Before Jimmy could even make sense of what happened, his father surged toward Percy Thacker, roaring like a wounded animal. Jimmy saw the surprised looks on the faces of the men in the circle as they scrambled to get out of his way. As Thacker brought his leg back for another kick, Dancer caught him flush on the jaw with a roundhouse right-hand. The punch made a sickening *splat* and Thacker's head snapped back as though someone had yanked it. He dropped to the ground like a dead man.

Dancer stood over Percy Thacker. Before he could decide what to do next, he was knocked to the ground by the deputy who wasn't holding Clayton. The cop raised his club to hit Dancer, but a reedy-voice from outside the circle yelled, "Leave him alone. Stop it." The cop froze. The man who yelled resembled a younger version of Percy Thacker. He walked over to Percy, who lay on his back staring up at the sky and said, "Dad, are you okay?"

The pimple-faced kid cursed. "What the fuck you doing here, Brandon? You quit on us. You're a traitor to the cause." He pulled a hunting knife from his boot.

"Put the knife away, Billy Joe. Don't be stupid," Brandon said.

"I'm going to gut that asshole," he said pointing the knife at Clayton. "Motherfucker sucker-punched me."

Clayton had been dragged to his feet by the deputy. His hands were cuffed behind his back, and his face was twisted with pain from Percy's kick.

Brandon held up his hands. "Enough, Billy Joe. Let it go."

"Screw you." He spit blood out of his mouth and ran toward Clayton.

Everything seemed to slow down. The deputy released Clayton and tried to pull his gun from his holster. Dancer twisted out of the grasp of the other deputy and was about to grab Billy Joe when Brandon crashed into both of them. The bodies converged like some kind of bad square dance. There were shouts and curses and Jimmy saw Billy Joe raise the knife above his head. Jimmy lunged for it, but he was too late. Billy Joe plunged the knife into the scrum and when he pulled it back, it was bright red. He dropped the knife and ran. As the knife floated to the ground, Jimmy could see blood pooling on the asphalt.

A piercing scream silenced the mob.

Percy Thacker was cradling Brandon's head as blood poured from a wound in his chest. Dancer and Clayton stood behind them. Brandon was breathing rapidly. Bloody air bubbles oozed from his mouth. He looked around the circle of men who surrounded him, as though he were trying to understand what had happened. He spotted Clayton and Dancer and his body seemed to relax. He closed his eyes. The heaving in his chest slowed and then stopped altogether.

Percy Thacker sobbed.

65

Brandon Thacker was dead. Billy Joe had vanished, but no one was looking for him. Jimmy's mom said Percy Thacker wasn't interested in his useless nephew. He wanted Dancer to pay for his son's death and for shattering Percy's jaw so badly he had to have it wired shut by some specialist in St. Louis. The Mountain View police hauled Dancer away to the Howell County jail in West Plains. They charged him with first degree assault, and the county prosecutor, under pressure from Percy Thacker, convened a grand jury.

Dede hired Matt Gillespie to be Dancer's lawyer. The Monday evening after the grand jury convened, he came over to the house to update Dede, Clayton, and Jimmy on what was happening. They sat down at the kitchen table, and Jimmy knew instantly that Mister Always Smiling didn't have good news.

"The prosecutor has offered Dancer a deal," Gillespie said. "One year in county jail." Dede gasped. "I know. It stinks. I've told Dancer not to take it, but he says he wants the deal. I'm hoping you can talk some sense in to him."

Dede leaned across the table, her eyes squinty. "Why would he agree to that? You said we had a good case."

"We do. But it's not a guarantee." Gillespie sighed. "And they're using leverage."

"What leverage?" Clayton asked. Since the incident Clayton had barely said a word to anyone. He had stayed home from school and just sat in his bedroom and played his rock albums so loud it made Jimmy's teeth vibrate.

"They're threatening to charge you with felony assault against Billy Joe Thacker and resisting arrest. Any place but Mountain View I'd tell you those charges would get laughed out of court. But Mountain View, that's a different story."

Clayton scowled. "That's bullshit. Let them charge me."

Dede put her hand on Clayton's sleeve. "Wait, Clayton. We need to find another way. What other options do we have, Matt?"

Matt shrugged. "We fight them in court and take our chances, or take the deal. Dancer says he doesn't want to take the risk. He was pretty adamant."

Clayton pounded the table. "No. He doesn't get to decide. I don't want him doing that. We can fight these guys."

Dede put her arm around Clayton. "We'll talk to Dancer. Matt and I. Tomorrow."

When Dede got back from the jail, she went up to Clayton's room. The music went silent. Jimmy could hear Dede's voice, her tone soothing, as she reported on the meeting with Dancer. Clayton shouted, "That's not fair." The bedroom door slammed opened, and a moment later, there was a squeal of tires as Clayton's car disappeared down Hill Street.

Dede slipped into Jimmy's room and sat on the edge of his bed. She looked too tired to cry. "Your father took the deal. He said he didn't want to take the chance with Clayton's life. He said it wasn't Clayton's fight."

Jimmy swallowed hard. He had been scared to think his brother might go to jail. His father was right – it wasn't Clayton's fight. But Clayton was right, too. It wasn't fair. His dad had done nothing wrong.

"There's nothing we can do, Jimmy. Your father can be very stubborn. I told him Clayton wants to fight them. I said if you do this, you're going to lose him. But he told me it was too late. He said he lost Clayton a long time ago." A tear trickled down his mother's cheek, and she brushed it off with the back of her hand.

She tried to smile as she pushed a wisp of hair out of her eyes. "He acted like his life was over. He said, 'I had my chance. Someday Clayton will understand.'"

Jimmy wrapped his arms around his mother and hugged her close. He whispered in her ear, "I think he will, Mom. Someday."

66

July 20, 1969 – fourteen months later

Jimmy lifted the cover of the pizza box, hoping there was one more piece, but the box was empty. It had been almost a whole pizza when his dad brought it over at six in the morning, left over from Jake's poker game. Dancer knew Jimmy would be up watching the Apollo 11 coverage.

When Dancer got out of jail he went to work for Jake, and now lived in the backroom at the bar. Dede thought that was a really bad plan, but Rollie had closed down their delivery business and gone to work for Mr. Crutchfield managing a bunch of his stores. Dancer needed work. He did a lot of different stuff for Jake. On Saturday nights he kept order at the poker game Jake ran in the backroom where Dancer slept.

His dad had been impressed with how successful Jimmy's lawn mowing business had become. Jimmy had four boys working full time, and they were having trouble keeping up. Dancer told him that if he got in a bind, he should call him. Said he'd be glad to help out.

Jimmy pushed the empty pizza box off the coffee table to make room for his scheduling calendar. Every Sunday he plotted the coming week. Each boy would have to do at least three lawns a day to keep up. As he marked the jobs on the calendar, he kept one eye on the television.

Five hours ago, the lunar module had touched down and now the astronauts were preparing to walk on the moon. Jimmy had been waiting for this day since he watched Alan Shepard blast into space.

"Hey Mom, he's going to come out of the module soon."

"I'll be down in a couple minutes. Tell him to wait," Dede said. She had slept all afternoon. She was tired all the time lately.

The sound of a car with a deep-throated muffler raced up Hill Street.

"Is that Clayton?" Dede's slippers made scuff sounds as she shuffled down the stairs.

"He's out with Candy," Jimmy said. "He's not coming home at nine."

Dede settled onto the couch. "I guess if he gets her pregnant at least he won't get drafted."

His mom was obsessed about Clayton and the draft. She had convinced him to go to Southwest Missouri State – a two year school. But when he graduated last month, he refused to go on to a four year school. Instead, he had gone to work for Lexington Industries. It was a cool job – he got a company truck and drove all over the state servicing filling stations and auto parts stores. But he lost his student deferment, so now he was 1-A draft status and Dede was more worried than ever.

"When did you get the pizza?" Dede flipped open the box. "Did you eat the whole thing?"

"Dad dropped it off this morning. It was left over from Jake's poker game – just a couple slices."

"How did he look?" She tried to sound casual, but Jimmy could tell she was worried about Dancer too. "Tired. He said they played until four."

"But he was okay?"

She wanted to know if he had been drinking. Or worse.

"He was fine, Mom. Really."

Jimmy marked another job on the calendar and took a sip of Tab. On the TV screen, a man with a headset asked a question about some piece of equipment. A few seconds later another voice, crackly, said, "That's a roger."

"What's going on? Is he on the moon yet?"

Jimmy put down his pencil and squinted at the screen. "They're going through a final checklist, and then Neil Armstrong is going to leave the Lunar Module."

On the television there was a bunch of men in short-sleeve shirts and ties squawking questions to the unseen astronauts. They were methodical, and there was a delay after every inquiry because it took nearly three seconds for the voices to be transmitted back and forth from the moon.

"How's business?" Dede asked.

"Great. Going to be a record. Mr. Baker offered me a real job next year, working at his dealership."

312

"Wendell Baker?" Dede said. It didn't sound like she liked Wendell Baker.

"Yeah, he owns Baker Ford out on Highway 60."

"I know who he is. He's a pompous old fart. Sick of seeing him on the television dressed like some ignorant hillbilly. The man has the biggest house in Camelot Square."

Jimmy had to admit that the commercials were awful. But people remembered them. "Maybe I can help him with his commercials." Jimmy was hoping to get a smile out of her, but his mother just sighed and sat back on the couch.

Suddenly the scene on the TV screen switched from the control room to a grainy black and white image of a man in a spacesuit descending slowly from a ladder.

"How did they get the camera up there?" Dede asked.

Jimmy slipped off the couch and scooted up close to the television. "The camera was attached to an equipment pallet on the side of the Lunar Module. It unfolded when Neil Armstrong stepped down the ladder. This is so cool!"

The astronaut, a white blob with a backpack, stood on the bottom rung of the ladder and put his foot down several times, like a man testing the water temperature in the pool. Finally, he slow-motion jumped off the ladder. "That's one small step for man...one giant leap for mankind."

Jimmy stood up and clapped his hands. "They did it!"

313

Dede jumped up from the couch and clapped too. She took hold of Jimmy's hand and squeezed it hard. Tears were running down her cheeks.

"Why are you crying, Mom?"

"I don't know. I think I'm actually happy. Scared, but happy. My boys are going to make something of their lives. I never doubted that you would, Jimmy, but now even your brother seems to have his act together." She sighed. "Maybe this moon landing will change everything. Maybe they'll decide to end that stupid war."

"Do you think you'll fly to the moon someday, Mom?"

Dede smiled. "I think you'll have to go for me."

67

As Clayton pulled out of the parking lot of West Plains Transmissions after his last service call of the day, the deejay at KWPM was reminding his listeners that at eight p.m. the station would be broadcasting the first Selective Service Draft Lottery since World War II. There were a half million troops in Viet Nam, but even with Nixon promising to wind the war down, the draft board needed a better way to keep their pipeline filled. Clayton suspected he was the only draft-eligible guy in Maple Springs who was actually looking forward to it.

If he drew a high number, he'd be out of the draft forever, and his mother could stop hassling him about returning to school. And if he got a low number he'd probably get drafted. But that might not be such a bad thing. It wasn't like his job with Lexington was all that special. Customer Service Tech. Fancy title for a delivery driver. He serviced the garages and machine shops in every map-dot between Springfield and Little Rock.

When Clayton walked in the door at five past six, Dede and Jimmy were already eating. Dede had picked up burgers from Hardee's. Clayton reached over and grabbed a container of onion rings off Jimmy's plate.

"Hey, I already gave you your fries." Jimmy gripped hard on Clayton's arm until Clayton dropped the onion rings back on his plate.

"Just trying to help you with your diet," Clayton said.

At his high school physical in the fall, Jimmy weighed in at 205. Dede freaked out. Except on burger day, she had been cutting back on his portions and discouraging him from seconds. He had dropped about ten pounds, but he could afford to lose more.

"I can't eat this." Dede held up the remaining half of her grilled chicken sandwich. "Clayton, do you want it?"

"Let Jimmy have it. You're starving the poor kid," Clayton said. His mom gave him a look as he unwrapped his cheeseburger and consumed it in three bites. He pushed back from the table.

"What's your hurry?" Dede asked.

"I gotta shower. Going out tonight."

"On a Monday?"

"Yeah. Victor's driving."

Jimmy grabbed Dede's sandwich. "Victor's a cool guy."

Dede frowned as he stuffed the sandwich in his mouth. She stood up and began to clear the table. "I like Victor. He's very polite."

Victor Sanchez and his mother had moved up from Juarez last June to work in her brother's restaurant. Victor looked like a body builder. He drove a muscle-bound midnight-blue '63 Chrysler 300 with tinted windshield, and when he wasn't working, he wore black jeans and T-shirt and shades, even when it was dark out. Clayton thought that his mom liked Victor because most of the god-fearing Maple Springers were afraid of him.

"Alex is coming, too," Clayton said.

His mom frowned. "Does he ever hear from his father?"

Clayton shrugged. "Beats me."

"Where are you going?" she asked again.

"There's a draft lottery party out at Landis Field." When Ted Landis donated the land that became Landis Park, the southern stub that was cut off by the Burlington tracks never got developed. It had become a convenient place for keg parties and making out.

Dede frowned. "That's no reason to have a party. I wish you would think about college. It's not too late."

"That's the beauty of the lottery. If you get a high number, you don't get drafted, even if you aren't in college."

Ever since the Mountain View disaster, Clayton felt as if his life had jumped the tracks. The more he brooded on it, the better the draft looked. It would free him from a dead-end job, derail Candy's marriage plans, and allow him to escape from Maple Springs and all the drama that had come with being Dancer Stonemason's son. It was his ticket out of town.

Clayton stretched out in the backseat of Victor's car as Victor raced south on Hill Street. Alex, riding shotgun, looked over his shoulder. "Better be careful where you sit, dude. Candy's not going to like it if you get cum stains on your jeans."

Victor gave Alex a backhanded punch in the shoulder. "I'm not like you, Doyle. This car is my temple."

Alex threw his arm around Victor. "Sorry, dude. No action, huh?"

"Serious fucking dry spell."

"How you doing with Candy?" Alex asked Clayton.

"Fine."

"Why you sound so down? That girl is perfect. Nice rack, perfect ass."

"Yeah, she's great," Clayton said, his voice flat.

"Candy told Darlene that you guys were planning to get married," Alex winked at Victor.

Clayton sighed. "We talked about it. Well, mostly she's talked about it." It usually came up just before sex.

Alex leaned over the front seat and grinned. "Dude, let Kellerman have her. He's had a crush on her since grade school. He'd be eternally grateful. Might even forgive you for that beat down you gave him back in grade school."

"I couldn't do that to Candy. That fat asshole would crush her." Sammy Kellerman was pushing two fifty.

Clayton braced himself as Victor steered the car into the rock-strewn vacant lot. "Jesus Christ. It looks like she invited the whole town."

There were two dozen cars parked in a semi-circle in the northeast corner of the field, just south of the Burlington Northern tracks. Kids from his class and a bunch from classes that graduated ahead of Clayton. This first lottery was going to sweep up everyone from eighteen to twenty-five.

Victor pulled alongside a day-glow orange GTO convertible driven by Darlene Bennett, Alex's latest girlfriend. She had brought along her kid sister, Trudy. In the middle of the circle, a bonfire of discarded railroad ties burned. As Clayton jumped out of the car, he could smell the burning creosote. Sparks from the fire danced in the December night sky like fireflies in winter.

Alex strolled up to the GTO and gave Darlene a kiss. He glanced over at her sister. "Hey jailbait, what are you doing out on a school night?"

Darlene answered for her. "The folks went into Springfield, so I'm babysitting. They don't want sweet little Trudy to have another one of her parties."

"Oh, yeah. I heard you're grounded until 1990," Alex said.

Trudy gave him the finger and jumped out of the car. Clayton laughed. He remembered those summer nights at the playground. Trudy was fifteen now, but with her baby-face and flat-chest, she could have passed for a twelve year old. She

319

skipped over and jumped up on the hood of Victor's car. She smiled at him and gave him a wink. "Hi, Victor."

"Yoo-hoo, Clayton." Candy waved to him as she stood next to a flatbed truck that was parked near the bonfire. She had an old school blackboard propped up on the truck bed. "Come over here. You and your friends need to register for the draft."

Candy looked perfect, as usual. She wore a powder-blue cashmere sweater that showed off her perfect breasts and tight-fitting stretch jeans that did the same for her ass. Her long, straight brown hair shimmered in the firelight. She always had a smile, even when she was angry. She was scary that way, because sometimes Clayton didn't realize she was angry until it was too late.

She wasn't angry tonight. Just a little drunk. She kissed him hard. She wasn't wearing a bra and he could feel her soft breasts through her sweater.

She turned toward Victor. "This handsome man must be your new friend I keep hearing about."

"I don't have any handsome friends. This is Victor."

Victor removed his shades and held out his hand. "Victor Sanchez. Pleased to meet you."

"I love that accent." She ignored his hand and gave him a hug. She waved at a group of guys standing around the bonfire. "Sammy, honey, would you write these boys names and dates on the board?"

Sam Kellerman lumbered over, a big smile on his face, until he saw Clayton.

"You know Clayton and Alex, right?" Candy said. "This is Victor Sanchez."

"How ya doing, Clayton," Kellerman said. It didn't sound like he wanted an answer.

"Hey, Sammy. August thirty-first," Clayton said. He elbowed Alex who was staring at Candy's chest.

"June third, dude."

"February fourteenth," Victor said.

"Oooh, you're a Valentine," Candy said. "That's good luck." She planted a kiss on his lips, which surprised Victor and made Kellerman blush.

"You ain't in the draft. You're not a citizen," Kellerman said, his voice whiny.

"I'm getting my citizenship," Victor said, his tone surprisingly mild. "But you don't have to be a citizen to be drafted."

Clayton figured Victor was playing the role of a gentleman to impress Candy. Most days Victor would have stomped Kellerman just for looking at him cross-eyed.

When the lottery was about to start, Candy ran out in front of the bonfire, put two fingers in her mouth and whistled like a construction worker. "Welcome, everyone. Thanks for coming.

321

Now turn your radios to 560 AM – KWTO in Springfield. Good luck guys."

Candy skipped back over and sat next to Trudy on the hood of Victor's car. With all the radios tuned to the broadcast, it was like a drive-in movie without the picture. The lottery commenced with a prayer and the announcer began to call the numbers.

The boys of Maple Springs seemed to be leading charmed lives – the only guys with low numbers were college boys who could hide behind their 2-S deferments. Then the radio voice announced:

"February fourteen is…"

Candy squealed, "Victor, that's your day."

"… number four."

Victor hung his head. "Damn."

Without thinking, Clayton said, "Let's sign up together." The tequila had somehow made enlisting seem like a reasonable proposition.

Victor grinned. "That'd be cool, man. What are you thinking? Marines? A few good men? We'd be kickass Marines."

"Are you crazy?" Clayton said. "Marines get all the shit jobs. Why not the Air Force or the Navy?"

"I ain't flying no goddamn airplane. And I get seasick."

They had a couple more shots as they debated the pros and cons of the various branches. Victor was filling Clayton's glass when the announcer called his birthday.

"August 31 is... number eleven."

The number brought him back to reality. Enlist or get drafted, he was going away.

Candy tugged hard on his sleeve. "Clayton, now you have to go to school," she said. There was a tremor to her voice. She was close to crying.

"Why should I get to hide away in college while Victor goes off to fight? How is that fair?"

"But what about us?" she said, her eyes welling.

Clayton couldn't stand to see her cry. He didn't love Candy, but he didn't want to hurt her. He wrapped her in his arms. "Don't cry."

She buried her face in his chest. "Please, Clayton."

Clayton sighed. He whispered in her ear. "I'll think about school."

She stared into his eyes as if she could read his mind and know whether he was telling her the truth. She smiled and kissed him. "I love you, Clayton."

She wanted so badly to be in love. Convinced of Clayton's good intentions, her good humor was restored. She grabbed

Victor by the arm and dragged him across the circle to introduce him to one of her unattached friends.

Clayton jumped on to the hood of Victor's car next to Trudy and took a long pull from the tequila bottle. His head was spinning, but it was a controllable spin.

"You don't look very happy for a man who's about to marry Miss Perfect Tits and Ass," Trudy said.

"Who says I'm getting married?"

"She does. You played great in the finals."

Clayton smiled at her. "That was two years ago. We lost, remember?"

She shrugged. "You were never going to beat Leroy Washington." She grabbed the bottle and took a gulp. "You weren't that good."

"You're too young to be drinking."

"Don't marry her."

"Why not?"

"Because you don't love her. She doesn't make you happy."

Clayton twisted slowly toward Trudy so as not to lose his grip and go spinning off into space. He had never noticed her eyes before. They were deep brown, hungry eyes. He had to look away. She was only fifteen. "How do you know what makes me happy?"

"Remember when you used to spend all those hours practicing your free throws? Shooting free throws made you happy. Making fun of my braces made you happy. You liked me even back then."

"You're crazy."

Darlene honked her horn. "Hey Trudy, come on. We're going to take Alex home. He's no fun anymore."

Alex had celebrated his good luck at getting number 301, and was now passed out in the passenger seat. "Damn. I have to go. Kiss me," she said.

"What?"

"A real kiss. Not some little-sister peck on the cheek. Come on. Your girlfriend kisses everyone. Why can't you?"

She put her hand on his thigh and peered at him expectantly. Her eyes glistened and her lips trembled. Clayton cupped her head in his hand and guided her face toward his. She held on to the front of his shirt with her small fists. Her tongue darted between his teeth.

"Clayton, what are you doing?" Candy had returned from her matchmaking. She stood with her hands on her hips, her mouth open. Sam Kellerman stood behind her, arms folded across his chest like an angry parent.

"What kind of pervert are you, Stonemason? You're as sick as your old man."

Clayton slid off the hood of the car. The world was starting to spin out of control.

"Jesus Christ. When you're drunk you look just like your dad," Kellerman said.

He should have ignored him. He should have walked away or jumped into the back seat of Victor's car and gone to sleep. But he really wanted to hurt Kellerman. Wanted to beat his fat face bloody. Pay him back. Maybe he wasn't as different from his father as he wanted to believe.

Clayton stepped toward him, but stumbled and went down on one knee.

"See. Falling down drunk. Just like Dancer."

Clayton paused to let the world stop spinning and then climbed back to his feet. Kellerman appeared to be leaning about thirty degrees to the right. Clayton lunged and fired a right hook at his smirking face. He missed and tumbled to the ground. He landed hard on his right shoulder. The pain invigorated and revived him.

Sam Kellerman laughed. Clayton wobbled to his feet. His right arm hung limp at his side. He squinted at Kellerman, trying to bring him into focus.

"Your old man fights better when he's drunk. Of course, he's had more practice." Kellerman pulled his fist back, preparing to deliver a knockout punch, but Clayton struck first. This time he caught Kellerman flush on the right cheek with a straight left hand. The punch sent shock waves up Clayton's arm. It must have hurt, but Kellerman didn't go down.

"You son of a bitch," Kellerman said. He flung Clayton to the ground, driving his busted-up right shoulder into the rock-strewn turf.

Clayton got to his knees and waited for the ground to stop spinning. Sam Kellerman stood over him, fists clenched and blood dripping from his cheek. When Clayton remained kneeling, Kellerman began to walk away. Clayton charged him, and as Kellerman looked back, he rammed him with his good shoulder at mid-thigh and wrapped his left arm around his legs. A perfect form-tackle, but he could only use one arm, and Kellerman refused to go down. Clayton bounced off him and slid to the ground. Kellerman kept on walking.

"You're fucking crazy, Stonemason."

Now both shoulders burned. It didn't feel invigorating anymore. Clayton staggered to his feet, but this time Victor held him back. "He's had enough, Clayton. Let it go."

He looked over Victor's shoulder at the crowd of onlookers. Candy stared at him as though she were seeing him clearly for the first time. She sighed, then headed back across the field toward her car. The GTO convertible, with Trudy in the backseat, pulled out of the ring of cars and rumbled across the lot toward the road. It stopped. Trudy jumped out and ran toward Clayton.

Victor held tight to Clayton's arm. "Not a good idea," he said.

"Maybe not. But it's my idea."

Victor let him go, and Trudy threw herself into Clayton's arms. She smothered him with kisses. "I love you, Clayton."

He smiled at her. "Yeah. I think you do."

68

Jimmy stripped down to his underwear and stepped on the new scales his mother had bought him. The needle shimmied just beyond the 200 mark. He exhaled and tried to make himself lighter, but the needle refused to budge. Downstairs, Clayton, Alex, and Victor were watching the Super Bowl, but all Jimmy could hear was Alex blathering on and on about Trudy Bennett.

Alex had landed a job working for Ted Landis. Condominium conversion was Landis' big new business venture. He had hired his daughter, Candy, Alex, and a half-dozen other recent Maple Springs graduates to blanket the Springfield market hunting for apartment buildings that would make good conversion prospects. Alex and Candy drove together to Springfield each day, so now Alex was full of gossip about what Candy Landis thought of the whole Trudy thing.

All the kids at school had heard about Clayton's fight with Sammy Kellerman, how he had kissed Trudy and broke up with Candy. For two weeks it was all anybody seemed to want to talk about. Jimmy hadn't wanted to believe it. His brother had a beautiful girlfriend, but that wasn't good enough for him. He had to go after the one girl that Jimmy had hoped to ask out for a date.

Jimmy studied himself in the mirror. His belly oozed over his jockey shorts even when he tried to suck in his gut. A date with Trudy? That was never going to happen.

It was a relief that after the Christmas break kids returned to school with new stuff to gossip about. But now stupid Alex had come around and dredged the whole thing up again. It made Jimmy angry and for a moment he considered not telling Clayton what he discovered about the draft lottery. But he couldn't do that to his mother. He would save his brother from the draft.

He wished he could save Victor, too. Victor was a good guy – he didn't treat Jimmy like a kid. But instead of waiting to be drafted, Victor had enlisted in the Marines. He was heading off to Parris Island for basic training in two weeks.

"Touchdown!" Victor and Clayton yelled, their cheers drowning out Alex's babbling. "Hey, Jimmy!" Clayton had walked to the foot of the stairs. "You're missing a hell of a game. KC's up sixteen to nothing."

"I'll be down in a minute." Jimmy put on his sweatpants and the Kansas City Chief's football jersey Dancer had given him for Christmas. It was loose-fitting, comfortable, and he wore it everywhere. He grabbed the *Time* magazine with the article on the draft and the Sunday newspaper from the week after the lottery that showed all the lottery numbers and dates.

"Hey Jim, want a beer?" Victor asked, as Jimmy walked into the TV room.

"No thanks." Jimmy put the magazine down on the end table away from the chips, dips, and empty beer bottles.

Alex laughed. "Jimbo don't drink. He's a scholar. What you studying there?"

"Where's Mom?" Jimmy asked Clayton. The only good thing about Alex was that he didn't really notice if you answered his questions or not.

"Foodliner," Clayton said. "We're grilling steaks after the game. She wanted to give Victor a last supper before he ships out."

Victor grinned. "Not too late for you. Go down Monday, and see the Marine recruiter. We could go off to war together."

Clayton half-smiled. "Marines only want crazy fuckers like you."

Victor chugged the rest of his beer and forced a loud burp. "Just kidding. You're too tall to be a Marine."

Jimmy grabbed a Tab and sat down on the floor in front of the TV. For the first time all half, the Vikings had crossed the fifty yard line.

"You look like you lost some weight, Jimbo. Got yourself a girlfriend yet?" Alex asked.

Victor pounded the floor as the Vikings' desperate last second field goal fell short. "Hey, Jim. Where did you get the jersey? It looks like the real thing."

Alex grabbed the neck of Jimmy's jersey and twisted it so he could read the label. "This looks like it came from one of Jake's 'fell-off-the-truck' specials. He was selling these like gangbusters just before Christmas."

Jimmy knocked away Alex's hand. "My dad gave it to me." He could feel his face getting hot. Kids at school said Dancer did illegal stuff for Jake, but Jimmy didn't believe it.

"Cool," Victor said. "I like it. Sure you don't want a beer? That diet stuff could kill you."

Jimmy shook his head and walked over to the end table where he had stashed his articles on the draft. He picked up his papers and headed for the kitchen. "Clayton. I got something to show you."

Clayton frowned, but was curious enough to follow Jimmy to the kitchen. Victor and Alex remained in the TV room debating the merits of the halftime show.

Jimmy sat down at the kitchen table and opened up *Time* to the feature story on the draft and the lengths some would-be draftees were taking to avoid it. "Read this," he said.

Most of the stories were about conscientious objectors, boys coming up with heretofore undetected heart ailments, or announcing they were homosexuals. But in a sidebar, which Jimmy had circled in red pencil, *Time* reported on the story of Billy Nanapush, who was born at home on a Sioux reservation in North Dakota. When his mother brought him into the hospital the next week, the res doctor had recorded the birth on that day, October 5, 1950, instead of his actual birthday of October 1. The lottery number for October 5 was 24 – a guaranteed ticket to Viet Nam. The number for October 1 was 359. Billy Nanapush appealed his number to the draft board, and with testimony from the midwife who helped deliver him, the board ruled that his true birthday was October 1, so he was home free.

Clayton shrugged. "We don't live on a reservation."

Jimmy laughed. "That doesn't matter. You were born on the 30th, not the 31st. Do you know what the draft number is for August 30?"

"333. Cool number," Clayton said. He didn't act surprised.

"You knew?" Jimmy asked.

The kitchen door opened, and Dede walked in with a bag of groceries. "There's more out in the car."

Clayton closed the magazine and threw it on the counter. "Come on, Jimbo. We'll talk later." He gave Jimmy a look, which meant keep your mouth shut. He held the door open for Jimmy and followed him out to the car.

"Don't show that story to Mom," he said. He grabbed two sacks of groceries from the trunk and shoved them into Jimmy's arms.

"Why not?" Jimmy asked. Clayton always had to control the agenda.

"Because you'll just get her hopes up for nothing. She was finally getting used to the idea I was going." He grabbed the remaining bag and slammed the trunk shut.

"But—"

"Drop it."

When they walked in the door, Dede was seated at the kitchen table reading the story.

"Clayton, you've seen this?" she said. Her mouth was curved into a smile of pure joy, but her eyes were still narrowed with confusion. "This applies to your situation. What was the number for August 30th?"

"Three-thirty-three," Jimmy said. Clayton stared daggers at him, but he didn't care.

"Oh my God! That's wonderful. We have to tell your draft board now, before your number gets called."

"Mom, it's not that easy. That was on some Indian reservation. The draft board was probably looking for any excuse they could find to keep their boys out of the white man's war. It's not the same here. They're not going to take your word for it."

"I'm going to call Matt. I think he can help us with this."

"I don't want his help. I'm ready to go. Just drop it," Clayton said.

Dede slumped back in her chair and ran her hands through her hair. She glanced toward the TV room where Alex was talking to Victor about the economics of condominiums. Pitching Victor like he was a prospect. She lowered her voice. "You don't know what you're getting into. Do you see the casualty figures? Five hundred boys killed last month. This isn't a game. You have your whole life ahead of you. This war is insane. Please, Clayton." Her voice broke and her eyes welled with tears.

It made Jimmy's stomach churn to see her cry. Clayton sat down and rubbed Dede's back. He sighed and for once, Clayton gave in. "You can call Matt. See what he says. But don't get your hopes up."

He got up from the table and stared hard at Jimmy. He picked up the magazine from the table and pushed it into Jimmy's hand. "Here," he said. As he passed by he whispered, "Thanks a lot, asshole."

69

Demonstrators, young and old, incited by the killing of four students at Kent State by the Ohio National Guard two days earlier, clogged the sidewalks around City Hall. The Kent State students had been protesting Nixon's decision to allow troops to pursue the Viet Cong into neutral Cambodia. Their deaths sparked nationwide protests. With the marchers spilling out into the street, it took Clayton and Dede ten minutes to walk the two blocks from the parking lot on South Main Street.

"This ain't going to help," Clayton said as they wound through the crowd.

Dede held tight to his hand, like she was afraid they might get separated. "I hope Dancer doesn't get held up with all this traffic."

Clayton snorted. "Yeah, can't go on without our star witness." Matt Gillespie had arranged for the draft board to hear their appeal. He explained that the only relevant testimony would be from Dancer since the board did not believe that Dede, having just given birth, would be aware of the hour.

The Howell County draft board met once a month in the county clerk's office on the second floor of the Maple Springs City Hall building. Miss Lillian Karp, the county clerk, had held that position forever. Now she was also the head of the draft board that included Gordon Baldwin, a retired high school math teacher, and Dan Ivy, Jr., the owner of Ivy Drugstore, a block down the street from Crutchfield's General Store.

Matt Gillespie sat in the hallway outside a door with a window of pebbled, opaque glass. "County Clerk" was stenciled on the door. He waved his arm. "Over here, Dede," He stood up and shook Clayton's hand. "It's a madhouse out there. I think the board members are a little frazzled by the demonstrators. That might help. Ah, there's Dancer."

Dancer stood at the top of the broad stairway, looking lost. "Wow, Dad's wearing a tie," Clayton said. Dancer had on his churchgoing short-sleeve white shirt and khaki pants that still had the new crease in them. He was clean-shaven and it looked like he just got a haircut.

Dancer walked over to them.

"You look nice," Dede said.

Matt stood up and shook Dancer's hand. "Let me explain how this is going to work."

Dancer sat on one side of Matt and Dede, and Clayton sat on the other side on the varnished bench outside the clerk's office. "Lillian Karp runs a tight ship. She's fair, but she doesn't want any long-winded lawyer explanations. They read the affidavits from Kelly Doyle and Ron Bilko, but those only relate to what Dancer told them with respect to the birthdate. It's secondhand information, and they don't give it much weight. Your testimony, Dancer, is the key. I can help you if they ask a confusing question, but other than that, I'm not going to talk."

"Then what?" Dede asked. "Will they want to hear from Clayton?"

"They might, but I doubt it. You don't remember anything about the day, do you Clayton?" Matt asked with his know-it-all lawyer smile.

Clayton's neck itched. Dede insisted he wear his button-down blue shirt with the dorky navy blue pants and that he get his hair buzzed. He looked like he'd already been processed. "Guess not," Clayton said in the disinterested tone he usually saved for his father.

Miss Karp had a small desk in the corner of her office and a large mahogany conference table in the center. The three board members sat on one side of the table and a court stenographer sat at the foot. Clayton and the rest of the group took seats opposite the board members.

Lillian Karp began. "Welcome, Mr. Stonemason," she said, addressing Clayton. "We have here the affidavits," she paused to recheck the names, "of Mr. Kelly Doyle and Mr. Ronald Bilko, testifying as to the story your father allegedly told each of them regarding your birth date. Their testimony, however, is hearsay and really of limited value. We need to hear from your father." She addressed Dancer. "Sir, we have a couple perfunctory questions for you, and then we will listen to your statement regarding this matter. Okay?"

Dancer nodded. He stared at each of the board members. Clayton remembered that look. It was how he appeared when he was facing a batter for the first time. He told Clayton he would decide how to pitch someone just by the way they walked up to the plate.

"Please state your name and occupation for the record," Lillian Karp said, looking at Dancer over her half-moon, librarian glasses.

"Dancer Stonemason. I work for Jake's Bar & Grill."

"In what capacity?" she asked.

"Security," Dancer said.

Lillian Karp frowned. "Could you elaborate?"

Dan Ivy sighed and his face was screwed up like he had gas. "What difference does it make what he does?"

Gordon Baldwin leaned over and whispered in Lillian's ear, using his hand to shield his face from Dancer.

Lillian Karp ignored Dan Ivy's question. She stared at Dancer. "Like a bouncer?"

"Sometimes," Dancer said.

"Have you ever been convicted of a felony?" Karp asked, looking down at her notes.

Dan Ivy sighed and shook his head. "This is not necessary," he said. He looked over at Baldwin, but the math teacher just stared back at him, stone-faced.

Matt leaned over and whispered in Dancer's ear. Dancer nodded. "No," he said.

Lillian Karp frowned, and reread her notes. "But were you not incarcerated from May 21, 1967 to May 5, 1968."

Matt leaned forward. "That was a misdemeanor assault charge. Not a felony."

The chairwoman nodded. "I see." She sat back in her chair, her half-glasses, suspended from a cord around her neck, rested on her arms, which were folded across her chest. "Mr. Stonemason, we're ready to hear your story."

His father stared down at his hands. He had frozen. Clayton wanted to tell him it didn't matter. That this was no big deal. There was no need to torture him. The room was silent, except for the *tick* of the big round clock on the wall behind Miss Lillian's head. Matt leaned over and put his hand on Dancer's back. "Go ahead, Dancer."

Dancer focused on Lillian Karp. "A man doesn't forget the day his son was born." He paused and stared down both Baldwin and Ivy. Each man in turn nodded at him. He continued. "We had a doubleheader in Tulsa that day. Second game got over just before five p.m. We could have showered, but Doc – he was our manager – told us to get on the bus so I could get home to Dede." His father smiled as he recalled the manager's consideration. "We were hot and tired and sweaty, but not one of those boys complained. We were a team. We looked out for each other. And our bus driver? He drove like his wife was expecting. We got into Rolla before 9 pm. I drove the sixty miles to Maple Springs and made it home just after 11. And I swear to God, when I walked in that door, the first thing I saw was Dede on a mattress on the floor in the living room, holding Clayton." Dancer stopped to clear his throat. His eyes were shiny.

"I got Dede and Clayton out to the car, and we made it to the hospital in West Plains a few minutes after midnight."

Dancer paused, and Lillian Karp, assuming he was finished began, "Well, thank you—"

Dancer held up his hand. "I'm not done," he said. He stared at her like she was the last batter in the bottom of the ninth. "I've made mistakes. I've done things I'm not proud of. My wife deserved better. So did my sons. But don't punish Clayton because I've been in jail, or because I'm a bouncer in a bar, or because I'm an alcoholic. I've told you the truth. Clayton was born on the 30th. I know that and y'all know that." He looked at each of the board members. He had captured their attention. "Okay. Now I'm finished."

Lillian Karp smiled at him. "Thank you, Mr. Stonemason. Now we will confer among ourselves and render our decision." She put her half-glasses back on. "Give us about ten minutes, Matt."

The four of them sat in the hallway outside of the office and waited. The voices were muffled, and Clayton couldn't make out any words. Couldn't tell whether they were arguing or agreeing. Dede held her face in her hands and stared down at the floor. Clayton rubbed her back. "Mom, take it easy. They're not sentencing me to jail."

Dede smiled weakly and patted his knee. "I know, hon. You're right."

The door opened. Dan Ivy beckoned them. "Okay, Clayton, come on in. You can bring your lawyer and your parents."

Lillian Karp waited until they had sat down, and then she looked at Clayton over her little-half glasses and smiled like teachers did when they had to deliver bad news. "I'm sorry Clayton, but your petition is denied."

That was all. No discussion. Miss Karp banged her gavel and they were dismissed.

Dancer and Dede lagged behind as Clayton hustled out to the parking lot. He was anxious to get home and call Trudy. She'd be upset, but she'd understand. She wanted out of Maple Springs as bad as he did. He jumped into the car and started the engine. He drummed on the steering wheel waiting for Dancer and Dede to make it through the crowd of protesters. He reminded himself that he should thank his dad. Dancer had done a decent job with his statement. Much better than Clayton had expected.

After five minutes of waiting, Clayton turned off the car and headed back to City Hall. Except for a clump next to the entrance to City Hall, the protesters had mostly dispersed. There were shouts coming from the final group of protesters. As he neared the group, he realized they weren't calling for Nixon's impeachment, they were yelling for someone to call an ambulance. Clayton pushed his way through the throng. In the center of the circle of onlookers, his mother lay on her back and stared blankly up at the faces that surrounded her.

Dancer knelt beside her, holding her hand.

The Stonemasons

LEN JOY

70

June 1970

Chronic myelogenous leukemia. Dancer stared at the words
on the glossy brochure that the nurse handed him when he
brought Dede to the hospital for her treatments. He wanted to
read it. Wanted to understand what Dede was dealing with, but
he couldn't get beyond those three ugly words. He set the
brochure on the end table and tried to follow the bright yellow
fish with black dots on its tail that was in the aquarium at the
opposite end of the waiting room.

This was a different kind of waiting room. Plush mint-green
carpet, with comfortable over-stuffed leather chairs.
Windowless, but it had a huge aquarium of exotic fish and the
sidewalls were covered with awe-inspiring mountain range
photographs.

The fish disappeared into a coral contraption and Dancer
picked up the brochure again. Dede told him that "chronic" was
the key word. Acute leukemia was a death sentence, but chronic
meant she might live a long time with the disease, and now there
was a new treatment, chemotherapy, which might knock the

345

disease into remission. According to the brochure, CML was a form of cancer where the bone marrow makes too many white blood cells. "Like a thermostat stuck in the on position," it stated.

Now Dede was on the other side of that aquarium someplace, strapped to a gurney while they pumped poison into her veins. The idea was for the poison to unstick her thermostat so she wouldn't be making all those bad cells.

Dede was going to have the chemotherapy, Monday through Friday, for four weeks. Then they'd take a break for a month and do it all over again. Her doctor was hopeful that three month-long sessions would be enough. This was the first day. Dancer had volunteered to drive her and Jake told him he could borrow his Cadillac. Clayton wanted to drive her, but the process – two hours of treatment plus an hour driving each way – took up the whole morning, and he couldn't make that commitment and keep his job. Even though he was expecting to be drafted any day, Dede didn't want him to quit. She still hoped something would happen.

So far there had been no notice from the draft board and, on the drive over, Dede speculated that maybe his file got lost after the draft board hearing. Dancer knew that was not likely. The government never screwed up in good ways. But it did look like the war was starting to wind down. Kent State had been the last straw, and now more and more politicians were calling for an end to the "debacle." Even Walter Cronkite had come out against the war.

The door next to the aquarium opened, and the nurse backed through the door pulling Dede in a wheelchair. Her face was drained of color, but it wasn't white. It was a sickly gray, like a corpse. Dancer rubbed his hands together and tried to smile.

"It's okay, Dancer. I don't feel as bad as I look." Her voice was croaky. She looked like she was trying to smile.

They wheeled Dede out to the hospital entrance while Dancer retrieved the car. He pulled the Cadillac up to the curb and helped the attendant lift Dede into the car. She felt lighter than she had when they first met in high school. In five minutes they were back on US 63 headed for Maple Springs.

Dede reclined the seat and played with the power windows. "Jimmy would love to drive this beast. It was good of Jake to loan it to you." Jimmy had started working for Baker Ford and become a car nut. Dede ran her hands over the beige leather seat. "Hope I don't puke on the nice upholstery."

Dancer glanced over at her. "You let me know if you're feeling sick."

She opened the window and let the wind blow through her hair. "This feels nice."

As they neared the Pomona intersection, the Mercantile Bank sign showed the temperature was 85. Dede twisted in her seat and stared at Dancer,

"What?" he asked.

"Are you going to be okay in Jake's backroom? It's going to be a hot summer."

Dancer grinned. "I grew up in a dirt-floor shack. His backroom is like the Ritz."

Dede pointed out the window at the mileage sign for Maple Springs and Rolla.

"Do you want me to stop?" Dancer asked. He slowed the car.

Dede shook her head. "That sign for Rolla got me thinking. Does Doc still coach the Rebels?"

Dancer laughed. "No. He stopped when Seymour sold the team. Why?"

Dede's head lolled back and she closed her eyes. "Maybe we could go to a game next month, when I'm off the treatment."

He looked over at her. Some color was starting to creep back into her cheeks. It occurred to him that he had never gone to a baseball game with Dede other than when he was playing. "I'd like that," he said.

When Dancer drove over to pick up Dede the next morning, he could tell something was wrong. "Rough night?" he asked. "Maybe you need a day off between sessions."

Dede settled into the seat and buckled her seat belt. "Clayton got his notice yesterday. He has to report to Fort Leonard Wood in two weeks." She sighed. "Those sons of bitches didn't waste any time."

Fort Leonard Wood was just ninety miles north of Maple Springs and Dancer offered to drive Clayton, but there were twenty draftees from Howell County headed to the Fort, so the Army sent a bus. The bus was leaving from the City Hall parking lot at 8:30 a.m. Dede was starting her third week of chemotherapy, so it was decided that Dancer would pick up Dede, Jimmy, and Clayton and drive them all to City Hall to meet the bus. After Clayton left, Dancer would take Dede on to the hospital.

They were sitting on the porch when he drove up. Clayton was fit and tanned, and instead of his usual jeans and T-shirt, he had dressed in khaki's and a perma-press short-sleeved white shirt. With his buzz-cut he looked like a soldier on leave.

Jimmy wore a Baker Ford work shirt with his name on the pocket. It reminded Dancer of the uniform he used to wear at the foundry. Dede was still gaunt, but her color had improved. She sat on the porch between her two boys and was holding on to Clayton's hand like she was never going to let go.

Jimmy jumped off the porch and ran over to the Cadillac as Dancer stepped out of the car. "Can I drive it over, Dad?" In April, on his sixteenth birthday, he had made Dede take him to the Motor Vehicle department for his learner's permit. Clayton was leaving his car for him, so Jimmy was desperate to get his license so he could drive it to work.

"No way, Jimmy," Clayton said. "I don't want to get injured before I'm even a soldier."

Dancer could see Dede's tight smile, straighten into a frown.

Clayton grabbed his gym bag and headed to the car. "Come on, Mom. I don't want to be late."

Dancer opened the trunk and took Clayton's bag, which felt like enough clothes for a long weekend. "I guess the army's going to give you everything you need," he said.

"And free room and board. Hard to beat."

As he drove the mile and a half into town, Dancer thought about how much this was like the old days – Dede beside him in the front and the two boys horsing around in the back – and how much it was different – Dede fighting for her life, Clayton going off to fight for his country, and Jimmy practically grown up. Everything about Dancer was different, too.

He pulled the Caddy into the lot, and they all piled out. There were clumps of families surrounding the khaki-green army bus. A barrel-chested soldier stood in front of the bus with a clipboard. He looked like he meant business. As they walked toward the bus, Clayton scanned the crowd, as though he were looking for someone.

"Hey, Jimmy. Will you take my bag? I'll meet you guys at the bus."

Dede said, "Where are you--" Clayton was double-timing toward the back entrance of City Hall. A girl was standing on the waist-high brick wall that ringed the parking lot. She was staring at Clayton with the same sad squinty look as Dede. "Who's that, Jimmy?" Dede asked.

"That's Trudy Bennett," he said. He smiled, but he looked almost sad. "She's in my class."

Clayton reached up and plucked Trudy off the wall. She wrapped her arms around his neck and plastered kisses up and down his face and neck. Dancer could see that she had started to cry.

Dede stared open-mouthed. "Jeez. You get sick and nobody tells you anything."

The sergeant's voice boomed over the crowd, telling all the inductees to get their names checked off and to get their butts on the bus. Clayton broke his embrace with Trudy and trotted over to his mother. He looked flustered and excited and a little scared. "Gotta go now, Mom." His voice had become husky.

He let Dede hug him, and then he grabbed his bag from Jimmy and punched him in the shoulder. "Do not fuck up my car, I'll be back in eight weeks."

Jimmy's lips trembled slightly. "I won't."

Dancer held out his hand. "Be careful, Clayton."

Clayton hesitated, just for a half heartbeat, then grasped Dancer's hand. "I will," he said. He spun on his heels and trotted over to the Sergeant.

Five minutes later, the bus rolled out of the parking lot, but not before the crowd of friends and family heard the Sergeant welcoming the new recruits. It reminded Dancer of his first day at the county jail.

As the bus pulled out of the lot, Dancer reached in his pocket and handed the car keys to Jimmy. "Why don't you get it started and you can drive over to Baker Ford and show old Wendell what a real luxury car looks like."

"All right!" Jimmy said. He hoofed it across the parking lot to the car.

"Fastest I've seen that kid move in years," Dancer said.

As he walked with Dede over to the car, she held on to his arm. "It's silly for you to be living at Jake's. Why don't you stay with us?"

Dancer smiled. "Where would I sleep?"

Dede shrugged. "Clayton's bed for now. Maybe later you can get a promotion." And then she giggled like the girl who had fallen for that high school idol so many years ago.

72

October 12, 1970 - Eighteenth Engineering Brigade, Company B

Dear Trudy,

Just landed in Tokyo at some air force base. 10 hour flight from Seattle. Boy is my butt sore. Only here for 2 hours so I won't get to see anything. Then it's on to Nam. Thanks for all the letters. Sorry I haven't written. I'll do better once I get settled. I lucked out I think – they trained me for the Engineer Corps. More later.

Clayton

October 20, 1970

Dear Trudy,

We landed in a place called Cam Ranh Bay. It was like a tropical island. Beautiful white sand beach and the water is like turquoise. I was starting to think this isn't going to be so bad, but I only got to stay there a day.

The officers got to go to the beach, but us peons had to stick around the base, and then the next day they flew us over to my new home – a garrison at Long Binh. This place is huge. You can go 30 miles in any direction and still be inside the perimeter.

It's bigger than Howell County. And forget about the nice beaches. This place is all red clay and dust. I guess there used to be trees and bushes, but part of what we do over here is chop all that shit down. The VC don't like crawling around in the open so they leave us alone.

I'm in a squad with 8 other guys. Mostly farm kids who knew how to operate machinery. Our group builds roads. Lot of the guys don't even carry their weapon. They aren't expecting us to fight. They didn't even issue us an M-16 like the real soldiers. We got the old M-14s, which aren't worth a shit.

The lieutenant who heads up the four squads in our unit is Terry Ryan. He was a point guard at Vanderbilt, but he flunked out and that's how he ended up over here.

He's pretty cool for an officer. Most of those assholes act like you're invisible. But TR's different. I was shooting baskets at the enlisted men's court (the officers have a full court – we just get a lousy half court), and he challenged me to a game of horse. Beat me like a drum. But I was rusty.

Next week, they're going to train me to operate one of those big-ass bulldozers. When I get back, maybe I can get a job working for Candy's dad on one of his new housing projects. Haha.

I got a letter from Mom yesterday. She's done all her chemotherapy, and says she's going back to work. Says the doctor told her they think they got rid of her cancer. She said she feels better than she has in years.

Keep an eye on Jimmy. Make sure he doesn't fuck up my car.

Behave yourself.

Clayton

November 28, 1970

Dear Trudy,

Hope you had a good Thanksgiving. I had a three day pass and hitched a ride into Saigon with this corporal from Arkansas named Joe Collins. He's TR's driver, but TR was in Japan on R&R, the lucky fucker.

Saigon is a shithole. At least the part we saw. Stinks like a sewer and the houses are like those shacks out in the boonies, but here they're all squeezed together – like one big happy family. Collins got totally shitfaced and I had to drive us back to the base on Sunday night. Scared the hell out of me. Drivers here are crazy. Especially the idiots on those Jap motorbikes. And we have to share the road with cyclos, which are like rickshaw bicycles.

Thanks for the picture. You look real cute. How old are you now, 13? Haha.

My mom said Dancer's living in the house now. I guess he's been there for a while, but nobody wanted to tell me.

I don't care where he lives. When I get back I'm going to move out of that goddamn town.

287 days to go. Do you miss me?

Clayton

December 8, 1970

Dear Trudy,

Guess what? I got a new job. Joe Collins shipped home, and he recommended to TR that he make me his driver. That means no more road building. Now I drive TR around to all the job sites.

TR's a wheeler dealer. He has pretty-boy good looks, like Robert Redford, but with a southern accent. He's friends with everyone – generals and cooks and pimps and hookers and supply sergeants. He gets stuff. I'll tell you more about that some other time. But right now I'm thinking this tour is going to work out okay.

Except for these goddamn flies. Fucking flies are everywhere. People here don't even notice them. It's like they're part of the atmosphere.

Did you hear about Jimmy? Son of a bitch got his license, and now he's a bona fide used car salesman, working for Baker Ford after school. Told me he sold three cars his first week on the job. Kid will be a millionaire before he turns 20.

277 days to go. Do you still miss me?

Merry Christmas,

Clayton

December 20, 1970

Hi Trudy,

I saw Victor last night. He says hi. He's been out in the bush for 60 days and just got back last week. He's being redeployed to Quan Loi. He thinks you're the best thing that ever happened to me. But remember he's the guy that enlisted in the goddamn Marines, so he's not that bright.

His squad got a lousy assignment - support for ARVN. That's the South Vietnamese army. The Vietnamization of the war you keep reading about. Brass like to think it's a big fucking success, but it sucks.

The ARVN are the laziest assholes on the planet. They're supposed to be working with us on the repave of QL-1 – that's the highway to Saigon. Fuckers work about 3 hours a day. Victor wasn't happy about having to support their lazy asses in a fight. But he says they can go over the border - places the Marines can't go.

Victor said his mom moved back to Mexico to take care of her father. But he says when he gets shipped home he's going to buy a bar in Maple Springs and never going to leave. I told you he's not too smart.

Okay here's the big news. TR knows this supply sergeant at Long Binh. Big Polack from Chicago named Bosowski. Bos has to take care of all the damaged shipments. Turns out a lot of cigarettes get damaged on the way over here. They don't ship back the damaged stuff, just destroy it and get a credit. Well TR and the Bos, being enterprising kind of guys, decided it was a shame to see all those cigarettes go to waste, so Bos sells the damaged cartons to TR for a buck.

There's big demand on the black market for US cigarettes. My job is to pick up the cartons each day and stash them at one of our storage lockers near Saigon. TR sells them to Big Minh. He's a honcho in the SVN government. TR met at him some officer's party in Saigon.

Minh's an ugly fucker, and he ain't that big either. Maybe five ten, and he could have used your braces – I think he opens beer bottles with his teeth.

So far we've delivered about a thousand cartons. TR pays me $1 for every carton. He's been holding my money in his officer quarters cause it's not safe where I am.

Bosowski says he has an unlimited supply. He's the one who has to decide what's defective. All I can say is that he has very high quality standards.

265 days to go.

Clayton

January 8, 1971

Hi Trudy,

Happy New Year. Got your Christmas package. Thanks for the Velvet Underground tape. Great album. Love that first track, "Candy Says." Candy is such a cool name. Hah. I guess you couldn't find any songs with Trudy in the title.

For New Year's we expanded our product line. Hard to believe, but Bos ended up with a lot of defective scotch and bourbon that we were able to take off his hands. We're the place to go for booze and smokes.

Did I tell you TR has an apartment in Saigon now? He rented it with some bird colonel whose doing liaison work for the State Department and is never around. Now I see a whole different side of Saigon. Some of these French villas are amazing. TR's apartment is on this wide boulevard, lined with droopy looking trees. You wouldn't believe it's the same city I toured with Collins. Air smells almost fresh here.

Got a letter from Victor. He's back in country still shepherding the ARVN. Says something big is going down soon. Said he'd send me a note when he gets back.

I can't believe Mom and Dancer went to a high school basketball game. Thanks for telling me. That's another detail Mom left out of her letters. Mom sounds good, but she wouldn't tell me if she was hurting. How did she look to you?

256 days to go.

Clayton

February 14, 1971

Trudy – been a crazy month. Big Minh has set us up with a bunch of distributors. I've been driving two hundred miles a day making deliveries, collecting accounts receivable. Just like my dad – but I get to carry a 45.

Not that I need it. Minh's dealers are happy to get the merchandise. I've got a lot of money saved now – over twenty gs. TR keeps track. He's good with the books. He says we should start sending it home soon.

Looks like I may be the millionaire before Jimmy. Hah.

TR doesn't rotate out of here until September '72 and since we got such a good thing going, I re-upped for another year. So I won't be back until next Christmas.

No word from Victor yet.

Be good.

Clayton

P.S. Happy Valentine's Day. I'll send something next week.

April 24, 1971

Trudy,

You've probably heard by now how I'm a decorated war hero.

It's all bullshit. You deserve the truth.

Last month I was making my deliveries and we had a big load – about 400 cartons and a couple cases of booze – so TR came along to help. We were about four clicks north of Saigon when a van cut me off and forced the jeep off the road. Hijackers. Big Minh was supposed to make sure that didn't happen. We stood aside and let them have our cargo. In less than five minutes they'd packed their truck and were on their way. But as we walked back to our Jeep a kid roared up on a Jap bike and shot TR.

So what did I do? Not a goddamn thing. My best friend gets gut shot, and I just stood there too scared to even reach for my 45. But not TR. He shot the son of a bitch in the back as he was riding off.

They were both dead before I pulled out my 45. That's when everyone showed up – MPs, ARVN big shots, local police. They needed a hero so I became the brave soldier who took down the notorious VC cycle bandit. The kid wasn't even VC. He was a two-bit mobster, just like me.

They gave me the Bronze star for "exceptionally valorous action against hostile forces," and they sent TR home in a body bag.

TR's replacement asked me to continue as his driver, but I wanted to go back to my squad. Do what I'm supposed to for once. So now I clear brush for new roads. I think our goal is to pave over every square foot of South Viet Nam before we leave.

I wish I had listened to my mother and gone to school, and I wish I had forgiven my father for not being perfect.

And I really wish I were the guy you thought you fell in love with. But I'm not.

Get on with your life, Trudy. Don't waste any more time on me.

Clayton

August 11, 1971

Trudy,

I know I've never answered your letters, and I don't blame you if you hate my guts, but I need a favor for Jimmy.

Victor's dead. I just got word from his squad leader. He was part of that FUBAR in Laos where the ARVN got their ass kicked all the way back to Saigon. His helicopter was shot down. No bodies recovered, so they're saying he's MIA, but that's bullshit. He's gone. Can you tell Jimmy before he reads it someplace?

Victor was too good a man to waste on this country. I hate everything about this place.

They cancelled my re-up 'cause they don't need me anymore. They're deactivating the Engineers. I guess they decided we've won the war. Doesn't matter. The ARVN will undo everything as soon as we're gone.

I hope Ho Chi Minh, or whoever the fuck is in charge now, appreciates all the nice roads and bridges we built for them.

Clayton

P.S. Looks like I'll be home for Christmas.

73

April 1972

Matilda set the table in the dining room. In all the years Dancer lived with Rollie and Matilda, he'd never seen them eat in their dining room. A week ago, Matilda called Dede and invited her, Dancer, and "the boys" for Easter Sunday dinner. She added that the Stonemasons were welcomed to attend services with them if they didn't have other church plans.

Of course they had no plans for church. Dancer and Dede hadn't been to church in years, so Dancer was surprised when Dede told Matilda they would love to attend services with her and Rollie. Clayton was living in Springfield with Alex Doyle and told Dede they had made plans for Easter, but Jimmy was looking forward to seeing Rollie and Matilda again.

So was Dancer. He had hardly talked to Rollie or Matilda since he got out of jail. He missed his friends and he was proud of what Rollie had accomplished working for Crutchfield. When they embraced in the parking lot of Coventry Baptist Church, Dancer almost choked up.

After the service, they drove back to the house and sat on the porch sipping lemonade while Matilda finished preparing the meal and giving orders to Rollie. She had prepared most of the meal in advance, so fifteen minutes after they arrived, Rollie stuck his head out the kitchen door and said, "Come on in, Stonemasons. It's time for dinner."

Rollie draped his arm over Jimmy's back as he led them all into the dining room. "You done grown up while I wasn't looking, Jimmy. Come sit beside me on the roomy side of the table."

Dancer and Dede squeezed into the seats on the opposite side. Behind them loomed Matilda's prized breakfront – a walnut china cabinet she had inherited from her mother. Matilda brought in a steaming tray of sweet potatoes, creamed spinach, and green beans and set it on the end of the table. "Are you going to have enough room there, Dancer? Or do you want to sit at the end here?"

Dancer held up his hand. "I'm good here."

"Dad can fit in tight places," Jimmy said. "He's skinny."

Dede reached over and squeezed Dancer's shoulder. "No, your father's lean. Not skinny." Matilda came back from the kitchen with a large baked ham and gave it to Rollie to carve. "That smells delicious," Dede said." I'm getting hungry."

Dede had regained most of the weight she had lost during chemo, and while the whole ordeal had aged her in some hard to pinpoint manner, the changes made her hauntingly beautiful. Maybe it was the eyes. They had always mesmerized Dancer, but now they seemed to burn. As though everything she saw was special. And with Clayton back safe from the war, her laugh had returned. Just hearing her laugh made Dancer happy.

Four months after he moved back into their house, Dede invited him back into her bed. That was the happiest day of his life. He had fallen in love with his wife all over again.

"Seymour mellowing any in his old age?" Dancer asked Rollie.

Rollie speared another slice of ham. "How about you, big fella?" he asked Jimmy with his fork poised over the platter.

Jimmy, his mouth full of sweet potatoes, nodded and lifted up his plate.

Rollie handed the platter of ham to Dancer. "Mr. Crutchfield does have a powerful interest in sports." Rollie had been given responsibility for the chain of sporting goods stores Crutchfield had opened in southern Missouri. "I'll bet I get three calls a day from him. Of course, they're just suggestions, he says."

"Doc used to get a lot of those suggestions when he was managing the Rebels," Dancer said.

"He gave Jimmy a very nice letter of recommendation," Dede said. Jimmy was graduating from high school in June and in the fall he would be heading to the University of Missouri. Crutchfield's letter to the admissions office was classic Seymour. He suggested that if the school were foolish enough to pass on James Stonemason, he planned to hire him and give him a real education.

"What are you going to major in Jimmy?" Matilda asked. "You want more sweet potatoes to go with that ham slice?"

Jimmy glanced over at Dede and shook his head. He was fighting a losing battle with his weight. For most of high school he managed to yo-yo around the two hundred mark, but now he was pushing two twenty-five. He put his fork down to answer Matilda's question. "Business."

Rollie clapped his hands together. "Business? You got more business savvy than any of the professors in that school. You could teach them a thing or two."

While Rollie ruminated on higher education, Jimmy finished his second slice of ham. He set his fork in front of his plate as if that might prevent him from using it again. "I need accounting and business law," he said. "I'm going to buy Wendell's dealership when he retires."

Rollie laughed. "Wendell Baker? He's younger than Seymour. Those old boys like to hold on forever. You best get a backup plan."

Jimmy smiled confidently. "Japanese imports," he said.

"Those Jap cars are junk," Rollie said.

Jimmy shook his head. "Not anymore. They're cheap and the quality's getting better every year. Gas prices go up, the import market will explode. I could get a Datsun dealership right now if I wanted. Clayton said they were all over Viet Nam."

Matilda began clearing dishes. Dede rose to help, but Matilda waved her back down. "Just sit, Dede. You're our special guest today." She said to Jimmy. "You tell your brother he needs to come by and see us one of these days. Haven't seen that boy in years. Tell him I have a pecan pie waiting here for him."

"Pecan pie? Where?" Rollie mocked getting up and looking around the table.

"I'll make it when he comes over. You come with me. I need help with the dessert."

"Yes, ma'am." Rollie threw his napkin on the table and pushed his chair back. He winked at Dancer. "You don't have to tell me twice."

"I don't know if I have room for dessert," Dancer said.

"You always manage to find room," Dede said. "I wish Clayton had come. Have you talked to him lately, Jimmy?"

Clayton had gone back to work for Lexington, and they promoted him to field sales rep. He called on the same machine shops and garages, but he no longer had to deal with servicing the equipment.

"Talked to him Monday. He's coming down next week to buy a new car."

"A new car?" Dede said. "How can he afford that?"

"It's a company car. He convinced them he could get a better deal for them," Jimmy said. "Sometimes he's a pretty good salesman."

Rollie pushed opened the kitchen door and held it as Matilda walked into the dining room holding a chocolate sheet cake, ablaze with candles.

"Is that Matilda cake?" Dancer asked. Matilda was famous for her double fudge chocolate cake.

"Yeah, and you better blow out those candles, Dancer, before that bonfire melts all the frosting," Rollie said.

"My birthday's not until next week."

Jimmy tried to count the candles. "I've never seen so many candles on a cake," he said.

"There's forty-two, son. Trust me," Rollie said.

As Matilda positioned the cake in front of Dancer, she led a surprisingly well-harmonized version of "Happy Birthday."

It took Dancer three tries to blow out all the candles.

"That's what smoking does for you," Rollie said.

"I never smoked. Don't drink, don't smoke. Perfect guy to run a bar." Dancer now managed Jake's Bar, while Jake concentrated on his other business ventures.

Matilda cut the cake and distributed it around the table. "I have a proposition for you, Dancer."

Everyone at the table stopped their conversation. "Heavens, it's nothing serious. But I think this is something you might find interesting. The Holtville varsity baseball coach had a heart attack last week."

Rollie fluttered his lips. "That old boy loved his fried chicken."

Matilda gave Rollie the shut-up-I'm-talking look. "Obviously he can't coach, and that's a real shame because we have a pretty good team, I'm told. We need a coach, Dancer. Are you interested?"

Dancer sat back in his chair.

"Oh, and it pays nothing," Matilda said.

"Way to give him the hard sell, Mattie," Rollie said.

"Don't you have to be a teacher in the school?" Dancer was flattered, but he had never considered coaching.

"No," Matilda said. "I already cleared it with the principal. And your boss."

"Jake?"

Dede reached over and put her hand on Dancer's forearm. "You'd be a great coach."

Dancer smiled. "Oh. That boss."

"Looks like you're the last to know, Dancer," Rollie said. "I know the feeling."

"How do you think those boys would take to a white coach?" Dancer asked.

Matilda gave him another of her looks and her voice rose an octave. "Don't you read the papers? We've been enriched. We aren't just Holtville High anymore. We're Holtville *Central* School. We get kids from all over the county – white and black and brown and yellow. We are a melting pot."

Rollie snickered. "I wouldn't say one Chink family and some white trailer trash makes us much of a melting pot."

Matilda stared hard at her husband, her mouth twisted downward. "Dr. Park is Korean."

Dancer was surprised at how fast the idea took hold of him. Despite the melting pot comments, Rollie was sold on the idea. He told Dancer that Holtville had some great athletes, but they never got a chance to develop their skills because Holtville didn't have programs like Little League or American Legion baseball. "Lots of diamonds in the rough for you."

Dancer grinned at Rollie. "It takes a long time to develop a diamond."

Matilda said, "And there's no budget for uniforms, equipment, or field maintenance."

"There you go again, with more of that hard sell," Rollie said.

Jimmy jumped into the conversation before Matilda could take umbrage at Rollie's comment. He suggested they organize a "Fix the Field Day" and bring the community out to work on putting the ball field in playable condition. "And for uniforms, we could get donations from local companies."

Rollie said, "I could bring up the idea to Seymour. Maybe after I follow up on one of his suggestions."

"Lexington has a warehouse outside Holtville," Jimmy said. "Maybe Clayton could get them to contribute."

Thinking about Clayton brought Dancer back to earth. When Clayton had been drafted, Dancer felt like they were getting closer. But he came back from the war more distant than ever. Less connected to anything – his family, his friends, his whole life. He seemed, to Dancer, to be just going through the motions. Dancer knew that feeling.

He tried not to think about Clayton because thinking about him made Dancer feel bad for the past he couldn't go back and change, and sad for a future he wanted to be a part of but had no way into.

"I don't think that's going to happen," Dancer said to Jimmy. "Hard for those big companies to contribute. There are too many groups with their hands out."

Matilda smiled wistfully. "Thank God he made it home safe."

"And he's a hero," Rollie said. "Got the Bronze Star."

"He threw it away," Jimmy said.

"What?" Dede said. "Who told you that?"

Everyone stared at Jimmy.

"Clayton told me," Jimmy said. "He said he threw it in the river the night after they gave it to him. He thought it was an insult to the memory of guys like Victor. He said they were the real heroes."

Matilda sighed. "That boy needs to give himself a break."

74

Holtville finished their season on the road with games against Mountain View on Friday and then the finale – a Memorial Day game against Maple Springs. As they passed the "Welcome to Mountain View" sign, Dancer shuddered. The last two times he traveled to Mountain View he ended up in jail. There was the bar fight back in the 50s when Dede had to come in and bail him out, and then later the melee with Billy Joe Thacker and Clayton. It had been five years since that fateful encounter. It cost Dancer a year of his life and cost Brandon Thacker all of his life. For Dancer, the memory was still raw and he didn't reckon Percy Thacker had forgotten either.

He was right.

In Mountain View, high school football was a religion and baseball was, at best, an afterthought. When Dancer was playing high school ball, the Mountain View diamond had been carved out of a rocky pasture with a rickety snow fence to mark the outfield boundaries. But as their team bus rolled into the asphalt-paved parking lot, Dancer could see that things had changed. Now they had a real stadium with lights and enough seats for everyone in the county. A sign on the outside wall of the brick stadium identified it as, "Brandon Thacker Memorial Park."

Dancer started coaching the Holtville baseball team the Monday after Easter. There were four white players on the team. Two of them, Bob and Steve Wade, had pitched for Darien for the last two years before the redistricting resulted in them being bussed into Holtville.

Dancer's first order of business had been to develop more pitchers. After thirty minutes of drills, he recruited the Blues Brothers – Willie and Richie Blue, both freshmen even though Willie was two years older than Richie. Neither had ever pitched in an organized baseball game, but Willie had a decent arm and pinpoint control. Dancer was confident he could mold him into a competent high school pitcher. And then there was his younger brother, Richie. Richie Blue threw heat and didn't even break a sweat. No telling where the ball was heading, but it got there fast. Dancer reckoned Richie's fast ball was over 90 miles per hour.

The team had three games in the first week of the season. Dancer used the Wade brothers as his starting pitchers in the first two games, and they were both shelled in lopsided losses. In the final game of the week, against Cabool, he made Richie Blue his starting pitcher. The kid struck out 15, but walked nine – five of them in the fourth inning--which forced in two runs. That was all Cabool needed, and they won 2 to 1.

The next Monday, Dancer had Richie come in early so he could work with him. They started by playing catch. "See how easy it is to throw the ball to me? Pitching is just playing catch with one guy wearing a chest protector," he said. "You got natural speed. You don't have to muscle up and throw the ball through the wall. Just throw to the catcher's mitt. Nice and easy." Richie followed Dancer's directions. The next time he pitched, he only walked five batters and Holtville won 4 to 2. Willie won his game, too.

The following week, Dancer moved the Wade Brothers to the bullpen and Willie and Richie started the rest of the games. With the Blues brothers pitching, Holtville won every contest. Richie Blue had an earned run average of less than one, and the only earned runs were from walks.

As Dancer sat in the dugout making out his lineup card, he had to admire the new Mountain View ballpark. The infield and outfield were groomed to major league standards, there were individual seats, not just plank bleachers, and there was even a press box at the top of the stadium behind home plate. Dancer decided Percy Thacker had built an impressive memorial to his son.

The day after Don Larsen's World Series gem, Brandon had told Dancer how proud he was of his perfect game. Of course, Brandon had wanted a favor. He had practically begged Dancer to go to that one lousy Klan meeting and make Brandon look good to his old man. If Dancer had done that, everything would have played out differently. He wouldn't have dunked Brandon in the sink. Percy wouldn't have sent him to Specialty Fab. He wouldn't have cut off his fingers. He wouldn't have lost Clayton. And maybe Percy wouldn't have lost his son. Maybe Brandon would have stayed in the Klan, and then he wouldn't have ended up dying in the parking lot of the Tip Top Lounge. Dancer shook his head. He could drive himself crazy playing that game. And he could never win.

When he brought his lineup card out to the umpire before the game, he got a better surprise. Ronny Bilko was the umpire. He tapped Bilko's chest protector as he handed him the lineup. "You get tired of being playground director?"

Bilko bear-hugged Dancer. "This is just one of my side jobs. You're looking good, buddy."

"Doing okay."

"I've been reading about your team. You done more than okay. Coaching suits you."

The Holtville manager, who was barely out of high school, handed his card to Bilko. He shook hands with Dancer. "Damn. It's bad enough we have to face Richie Blue, but you got the umpire on your side, too." He winked at Dancer.

"Actually, I'm saving Richie for my hometown. Willie's pitching today," Dancer said. "This park is a lot nicer than when Bilko and I used to play here."

The young manager nodded enthusiastically. "Mr. Thacker spared no expense." He glanced up at the press box and frowned. "That's funny. I don't see him up there today. He never misses a game."

Bilko took out his broom and gave home plate a ritual brushing. "Well, we can't wait for Percy. Let's play ball."

Richie Blue knocked in four runs and his brother held Mountain View to three runs. After the game, the two teams – one mostly black, the other all white – lined up and shook hands. Together, they all filed out of Brandon Thacker Memorial Park.

Jake had given Dancer the night off. After the game he drove straight home and pulled into the driveway just as Jimmy arrived in a tomato-red Mustang with a fancy air scoop. "I like your new ride," he said. Jimmy brought home a different car every week. One of the perks of being a car salesman.

Jimmy flashed his salesman smile and pitched Dancer like he was a prospect. "It's a Cobra Mach 1. This baby really hauls ass. 428 cubic inches. Just took it in trade. It won't be around long."

"Maybe we should buy it for your mother," Dancer said.

Jimmy laughed. "You couldn't afford the speeding tickets. But I really wish I could hold on to it until graduation. It'd be a great prop for my speech."

Jimmy had been voted "Most Likely to Succeed," and had been selected to be one of the student speakers at his graduation next month.

"With your salesman bullshit you don't need any props," Dancer said. He wrapped his arm around Jimmy's shoulders as they walked into the kitchen. "Come on. Supper's waiting."

Dede had prepared meatloaf and mashed potatoes with fresh green beans. "Is it my birthday?" he asked. She was serving all his comfort foods. She didn't even like meatloaf.

"I thought Mountain View might be a bad experience for you, so I figured it best not to put a steak knife in your hands."

Dancer slathered his meatloaf with ketchup. "Just another game. Didn't even get in an argument with Bilko." He told them about the field and how Percy had been a no-show. "Just one game left," he said. "You want that last piece of meat, Jimmy?"

Jimmy hesitated for an instant, then reached over and stabbed the piece with his fork.

Dede frowned. "Jimmy."

"Mom, we can't all be skinny like Dad and Clayton. I need my energy. This speech is driving me crazy. I can't think of anything interesting to say."

Dede got up from the table and walked around behind Jimmy. She wrapped her arms around him. "We're very proud of you. I know you'll come up with something brilliant."

"Thanks, Mom." He pushed his plate aside. "I guess I don't need this. I better get to work now."

As Jimmy thudded up the stairs, Dancer yelled after him, "I'll save it for you."

Dede punched him in the arm. "You're not helping. Are you nervous about the Maple Springs game?"

Dancer wiped his mouth and pushed his chair back from the table. "Nah. Those boys haven't faced anybody like Richie Blue."

"I'm not talking about Richie Blue."

Dancer wanted to pretend it was just another game, but he knew it wasn't. The last time he set foot on that diamond, he'd been The Man. The greatest ballplayer to ever come out of Howell County. A sure thing to make the big leagues. Now the best he could hope for was that everyone had forgotten him. "I'm a little nervous. At least they didn't name the field after me."

Dede smiled. "They should have.The first time I saw you was at that ballpark. You were so…"

"Handsome?"

Dede shook her head. "Confident." Her mouth curved downward, and her eyebrows peaked. "Maybe it wasn't even you I wanted. I just wanted your confidence. God, we were so young."

"So you were using me, huh?"

"I suppose I was."

"Well, I hope you learned your lesson. Is there any ice cream?"

The game with Maple Springs was never in doubt. Holtville scored four runs in the first inning and Richie Blue allowed only two scratch hits in the first six innings while striking out fourteen. Then in the seventh and last inning after two were out, his control went haywire, and he walked three batters in a row. Dancer called time and walked slowly out to the mound. As he crossed the foul line, someone on the third base side began to chant, "Dancer, Dancer, Dancer." Others joined in, and by the time Dancer got to the mound, it sounded like the whole crowd had picked up the cheer.

Richie Blue grinned at Dancer. "Maybe you should finish the game, Coach."

Dancer took the ball from Richie and pounded it back in the boy's glove. "Quit farting around and strike this kid out so we can go home."

"Okay, Coach."

As Dancer headed back to the dugout, the crowd stood up and cheered. The ovation continued until Dancer finally stepped out of the dugout and tipped his hat.

Richie Blue struck the next batter out on three pitches. As the team boarded the bus to go back to Holtville, Dancer stayed in the dugout. It felt like something had broken loose inside of him. Whatever it was, it made him feel good.

75

There were 334 students in the Maple Springs Class of 1972. The year before there had been 280 graduates and that had proved to be too many for the poorly air-conditioned gymnasium. A couple of the elderly relatives of graduates nearly fainted from the heat. So this year they decided to move graduation to the parking lot and take their chances with the weather. Dede was grateful to be outside. It was a typical Missouri summer night, with the temperatures and humidity clinging to the eighties, but there was a whisper of a breeze, and the air was at least breathable.

They set up a stage at the far end of the student parking lot. The band was arranged on the back half of the stage. In front of the band, in the center of the stage, was a podium, draped with a purple sash and the Maple Springs logo. There were twenty rows of folding chairs arrayed in front of the stage for the students, and ten yards behind the student section were seats for families and friends. Those seats filled the remainder of the parking lot. Dede sent Clayton to save them seats as close to the front as possible. She wanted to make sure Jimmy could see his family supporting him when he gave his commencement address. Dede suspected she was more nervous than Jimmy.

Dede and Dancer stood at the back of the parking lot scanning the crowd for Clayton.

"There he is." Dancer pointed to Clayton, who was smiling and waving his hand back and forth over his head to get their attention. He had staked out three seats in the front row, on the aisle the graduates would march down to get to their seats.

Clayton had been home from the war for six months. Dede was so happy he had made it home that at first, she hadn't noticed how he had changed. Not angry, or bitter, or all full of himself like some of the vets. He seemed distant, distracted, and sad. Mostly he seemed sad, she had decided, so it was good to see him smile. She wished he hadn't moved to Springfield, especially to live with Alex Doyle. She wanted to ask him about Trudy. Dede thought that spunky girl had been just right for Clayton.

Dancer took her hand as they slipped through the crowd. "Remember how hot it was for my graduation?"

Dede remembered. She had sat alone in the last row of the bleachers, barely able to breathe in the stultifying atmosphere of the sweat-box gymnasium. There had been barely a hundred graduates in the Maple Springs Class of 1948, but the ceremony seemed interminable until they announced the class awards and Dancer won for Best Athlete. Dede had leaped to her feet and cheered unabashedly.

"I was so proud when you won that plaque for Best Athlete."

"I won an award? Are you sure?" Dancer asked.

"It probably meant more to me than to you," she said. Dancer's only goal in life had been to become a St. Louis

Cardinal. The day after graduation, he signed with the Hannibal Stags for five dollars a day. Hannibal was the very first rung on the ladder that would lead him to the Cardinals. The next year they moved him up to St. Joe and paid him a regular salary. And then Dede got pregnant. She was only sixteen, Dancer not quite nineteen.

Instead of attending Dede's Valentine's Day Junior Prom, she and Dancer went down to the Justice of the Peace and got married. Dede had to get her mother's consent, but that wasn't a problem – her mom had always liked Dancer. She even offered to stand up with them as a witness. Of course, Dede knew she wouldn't actually show up for a morning ceremony. Her mother seldom sobered up before noon.

After the ceremony, Dede moved into Dancer's apartment in St. Joe. Five months later they moved back to Maple Springs when Dancer got promoted to triple-A ball with Rolla. And then Clayton was born, and Dancer pitched his perfect game, and then Jimmy arrived, and then...

Dede hugged Clayton and took a seat between him and Dancer.

The band played "Pomp and Circumstance," and the audience all stood as the graduates marched solemnly up the aisle toward the stage. Their shiny maroon gowns rippled in the evening breeze. Trudy Bennett was the first graduate Dede recognized. She radiated energy, smiling at folks to the right and left. But then she spotted Clayton standing on the aisle, and her lights went out. As she walked past, she stared straight ahead, her face expressionless.

Dede looked at Clayton, his expression the same as Trudy's. She tugged on his elbow. "I really liked that girl."

Clayton's eyes crinkled. "Yeah. Me too." The edges of his mouth twisted up like he wanted to smile, but it hurt too much. "I wish I'd--" His voice faded to nothing.

"What?"

"There's Jimmy," Clayton said.

Dede nudged Dancer with her elbow.

"I see him," Dancer said.

Jimmy smiled and gave a thumbs up as he marched past their row.

After the invocation, the class president presented the Excellence in Teaching award to Mr. Hall.

"Good choice," Clayton said. He put his fingers in his mouth and produced an ear-splitting whistle.

"Did they teach you that in the Army?" Dede said.

Clayton smirked. "Probably the only useful thing I learned." He whistled again as the crowd rose for a standing ovation. "Mr. Hall was a good teacher."

After the last diploma had been handed out, the principal walked slowly to the podium.

"I recently paid a visit to Baker Ford, as I had a vague notion I might have need for a second car. Two hours later, I was the proud owner of a low mileage 1967 Belvedere, thanks to the persuasiveness of the young man whom the Class of 1972 has voted most likely to succeed. Ladies and gentlemen, please welcome, James Carter Stonemason!"

Jimmy marched proudly across the stage. He stood at the podium, glanced at his speech for a moment, then dropped it on the lectern. He reached for the microphone and detached it from its holder. Now he was in the center of the stage, like a revivalist preacher or a game-show host. Dede held her breath.

"Thank you," he said, nodding to his classmates. He grinned. "It occurs to me that I may be the first used car salesman to ever deliver a commencement address." The crowd laughed. "I've thought a lot about what I should say here today. I asked my family for advice, because I figured if the speech is really bad, I can blame them. First thing I did was ask my mom, because she's always had plenty of advice. She told me that whatever my message is, I need to tell it from the heart, because y'all will know if I'm not being straight." He walked over to the edge of the stage and spoke to one of the girls in the front row. "She's right, isn't she?" The girl nodded and murmurs of agreement rippled through the rows. "And then I asked my brother Clayton who has always been a pretty persuasive guy." A few catcalls from the boys and some giggles from the girls. "And he said to suck in my gut and make eye contact." Jimmy looked down at the graduation robe which made his gut invisible. He paused theatrically, and the titters rolled through the class. He made a sucking in sound and walked over to the band. He stared at the Chinese girl who was first chair clarinet. "How'm I doing?" he asked.

386

The girl smiled and blushed, and Jimmy moved back to center stage. "Finally I asked my father, who is a man of few words. Dad said, 'It's Missouri. It's June. Keep it short.'" The class whooped and clapped wildly. Jimmy held up his hand. "I thought that was pretty good advice."

He walked back to the podium and glanced at his speech again. He paused and rubbed his chin.

"There's probably been a million commencement addresses delivered in the last fifty years. Sort of hard to come up with something new. I'm supposed to talk about success. For the last two weeks I've been coming home from work and going up to my room and thinking about that topic. Trying to come up with an angle." He wandered away from the podium, rubbing his hands together as he approached the front of the stage again.

"I even went to the library and checked out *Bartlett's Familiar Quotations*. Emerson said the secret to success was self-trust. Disreali believed that success required constancy of purpose. And for Albert Schweitzer, the secret was to never get used up. I needed more so I turned to the self-help books. There are dozens of those books, and every writer seems to have come up with a pithy quote that illuminates the road to a successful life. Old chestnuts like 'Get knocked down nine times, get up ten.' Or my personal favorite, 'People don't plan to fail, they fail to plan.' I love the symmetry."

Jimmy strolled back across the stage to the podium and poured himself a glass of water. He walked back toward the front of the stage, his face creased with a look of genuine puzzlement.

"Okay. Here's what I figured out so far: We're all going to fail." He paused to let that sink in. "We're not going to fail to plan. We're going to make all sorts of ridiculous plans. And you know what? God's going to laugh at our plans. Most of us are going to fall on our face. The unlucky ones are going to grab the brass ring, and then they're going to realize they didn't even want a brass ring."

"A lot of those self-help books have ten-step programs for the reader to follow. I wanted to come up with my own program, but I figured, ten steps are too many. My dad would probably walk out before I got halfway through, so I figured a three-step program would be better."

He walked back to the lectern and glanced at the notes from his speech again. "Okay are you ready for this? The Jim Stonemason three-step program for a successful life?

"Step 1. Forgiveness.

"It's not a perfect world. Sometimes the people we count on – our parents, our teachers, our friends – they are going to break our hearts.

"Guess what? They're human. We have to forgive them. Because if we can't forgive the people who helped to get us to this point, we won't be ready when we move into the real world. Because if there is one thing I am certain of, it is this: we are all going to fail."

He stopped smiling. He swallowed hard and took a deep breath and slowly exhaled, then continued, with a slower cadence, as though he were searching for just the right words.

"When we fail, even if the failure is catastrophic, it doesn't have to be forever. We have to forgive ourselves. Let me repeat that. We have to forgive ourselves. As long as we're still breathing, we have a chance to make things right. But we can't if we're spending all of our energy blaming ourselves. So when you stumble, give yourself a break."

He took another deep breath and his shoulders sagged into a more relaxed posture. "I thought to myself, that is a damn good first step. And, after I sat in my room for a few more days and hadn't come up with any more steps, I had an epiphany. Why not a one step program?" He scanned the crowd. "I don't see y'all taking any notes so this will be easier for you to remember. Right?"

He walked back to the podium and picked up his speech. And then he raised his hand, like a minister giving a benediction. "Now as you all go out in to the world, just remember, you're going to need a good car. So come and see me out at Baker Ford."

Dede felt like the air had been sucked out of her. She was aware that the crowd was on its feet, and she was aware they were cheering and clapping, but it was as if she were watching a movie without any sound. The graduates began a much less orderly procession back down the aisles. Jimmy remained near the stage swarmed by several of his classmates – girls and guys – extending their congratulations.

Clayton stood at the end of their row as the students marched by. He had that confident Stonemason smile and it looked like someone had lifted a fifty pound pack from his back.

As Trudy approached he stepped toward her and she embraced him, her robed body pressing tight against his.

Dede leaned into Dancer, and he wrapped his arm around her. She took hold of his bad hand and pressed it against her heart.

76

It was nearly noon when Dede woke. Dancer had just opened the living room curtains. The sun, reflecting off the light snow that fell in the night, gave Dede's face a soft, warm glow. Her cheeks were sculpted, and the fever gave her a flush, almost healthy look. She was dying, and she was beautiful.

When she visited her oncologist for a six month checkup two weeks after Jimmy's graduation, he found a disturbingly high number of white blood cells. He sent her to St. Louis for more tests. They confirmed his fears – Dede's leukemia had reached the blast stage. Her bone marrow was pumping out useless white blood cells, and there was nothing, no chemotherapy, radiation, or any other treatment her doctors could offer to slow the onslaught of bad cells. Her body would soon be unable to fight off any kind of infection or cold virus.

Jimmy wanted to postpone college, but Dede insisted he go. She told him the University of Missouri was only a hundred miles from home, so he could visit any weekend he wanted. She rallied in September and she, Dancer, and Jimmy all made the trip to Columbia to get Jimmy settled into college. In October, she caught a cold and was in the hospital for two weeks. Dancer and Clayton held vigil. Dancer was inspired by the support from their friends. Every day Trudy brought them a home-cooked meal, Rollie and Matilda tended to the needs of the house, and Jake made sure all the bills were paid. And he kept paying Dancer, even though Dancer seldom showed up for work.

Dede came home in early November. For Thanksgiving, Matilda took over the kitchen, and with help from Trudy, prepared a feast. Ronny Bilko, Jake, and his wife joined Rollie and Matilda for Dede's last Thanksgiving. Two weeks later she was back in the hospital with pneumonia. This time, Dancer knew, there would be no comeback. She was getting weaker, with no reserves left to fight off the disease.

Dancer and Clayton moved Jimmy's bed into the living room, and they brought Dede home on Christmas Eve. Jimmy had come home for the semester break and would not be going back until mid-January. The three men tended to Dede, feeding her ice chips, giving her morphine, doing whatever was needed to make her comfortable. She slept more and more each day.

As Dancer adjusted the curtains, Dede furrowed her brow. He walked over to the bed. "Do you want me to close the drapes? Is it too bright?" he asked.

"Water," she said. Her voice was raspy.

Dancer pulled his chair up next to the bed. He held her water bottle with its flex straw up to her chapped lips. She took a long sip and settled back on to her pillow.

"Thanks."

He took a damp cloth and wiped her brow and moistened her lips.

Dede smiled at him, like she had thought of something funny.

"What?"

"You make a good nurse."

She took hold of his hand and held it across her chest. Her arm was skeletal.

"Hi, Mom," Jimmy yelled from the kitchen. "Hey, Clayton. Mom's awake."

Clayton, who had been making sales calls from his room, clumped down the stairs and joined Jimmy and Dancer next to Dede's bed.

The three men sat in their chairs, Jimmy and Dancer on one side of her bed, and Clayton on the other. Dede held Jimmy and Clayton's hands. "Talk to me," she said.

Jimmy took a deep breath and sat up a little straighter. "I've lost another five pounds, Mom. Almost under two hundred now."

"You should see him in his red jogging shorts," Clayton said. "Dude looks like a runaway caboose."

Jimmy grinned, "Six months and I'll be outrunning your skinny ass."

Dede smiled faintly. "Did you get your grades?"

Jimmy nodded. "Yesterday. I did okay."

Clayton punched him in the shoulder. "Kid made Dean's List. How come you gave him all the brains?"

"It's not brains. You have to go to class," Jimmy said.

Clayton gazed up at the ceiling. "Now you tell me."

"Are you treating Trudy, right?" Dede's voice had faded to barely a whisper.

"Do you want some water, Dede?" Dancer asked.

She shook her head.

"Trudy got a job working at the Post Office. She's just a sorter now, but they promised her that by spring she has a shot to move up to carrier. She'll get to drive one of them cute little trucks."

"I like Trudy," Dede said. "She reminds me of me." She winked at Clayton. "When I was young and pretty."

Clayton's eyes watered, and he bit down on his lip and tried to smile.

Dede raised herself up and pulled the boys closer. "You boys help your father. He needs you. And you need him."

"We will, Mom," Jimmy said. He kissed Dede on the forehead and sat back in his chair as she released his hand.

"I know you will. You're a good boy, Jimmy. I love you." She smiled at him and turned toward Clayton. She clasped both her hands around his, and she closed her eyes.

Clayton bowed his head. "I'm sorry I was such a jerk for so long, Mom. You were right about school, and the war, and you're right about Trudy. And Dad. I'm sorry." His voice broke, and he buried his head in her lap.

Dede stroked the back of his head. "We love you, Clayton." She sighed. "Dancer, I'm going to rest for a while. Okay?"

Dancer nodded and the boys filed out as Dede drifted back into sleep. He closed the drapes and sat back in his chair. He had had plenty of time to prepare for this day. He knew everything that had to be done. He had figured out all the details, but he hadn't accounted for how he would feel. He closed his eyes and prayed. "Just give me one more day, God. Don't take her today. Please. I'm not--" His prayer ended with an anguished sob. He felt faint with hunger. According to the clock by Dede's bed, it was five fifteen. The sun was setting and the drip of melting snow from the eaves had stopped.

"Don't cry, Dancer." Dede was sitting up in her bed. Her eyes were bright and shiny. "Hold me, dear." She extended her arms to him.

Dancer leaned over and put his arms around her. "I love you, Dede."

"I love you too, hon." She pressed her lips against his, and then she sighed and let go.

Dancer rested his head on her chest. He was still holding on to her when the boys returned at six with a pizza from Valentines.

77

After Dede's funeral, Dancer asked Clayton to move back home. Clayton could tell his father was nervous about asking him. His request had sounded formal, as though he'd rehearsed his proposal about how Clayton would be able to save money on rent, groceries, and his clincher – that he would be closer to Trudy. What he didn't say, but he didn't need to, was that he was lonely. So was Clayton. He was grateful for the offer and moved back at the end of January.

As Clayton pulled into the driveway late on Monday afternoon, Dancer had just finished painting the garage door. Every day a project. Already he'd painted the master bedroom, fixed all the leaky faucets in the house, sanded the floors in the living room and dining room, and cleaned out the attic and basement.

"It's a little cold to be painting outside, isn't it?" Clayton said as he stepped out of the car.

Dancer shrugged. "Need to get these projects done before baseball starts." Dancer had agreed to coach the Holtville team again.

"The season doesn't start for two months. You better slow down, or you're going to run out of things to paint. You working tonight?"

Dancer shook his head. "The Monday Night Football crowd is too noisy. I hired Jake's kid to bartend on Mondays and weekends. I'm getting too old for that shit."

Clayton laughed. "Maybe you should tell them football season's over."

"It doesn't matter. It's just an excuse to get out on Mondays. " Dancer stepped back to admire his handiwork. "Maybe I should become a house painter."

Clayton snorted. "Come on inside, Dad."

As they stepped into the kitchen, the phone rang. Dancer answered, and Clayton grabbed a beer and walked through to the TV room. His father had painted it a soft yellow, and Clayton imagined his mom would have liked the color. The floors had been sanded and buffed, and Dede's hook rug cleaned. Everything was much neater and better organized, but it was clear that Dancer had not disposed of any of Dede's things. Her *Life* magazines and *National Geographics* had been sorted and stacked in a small bookshelf Dancer retrieved when he cleaned out the attic.

There was a stack of restaurant menus on the coffee table in front of the TV. Clayton turned on the television and flipped through them. Kentucky Fried Chicken. He remembered how his mother brought home a bucket every Monday night. Back then, KFC had been the only takeout place in town. He walked back into the kitchen where Dancer had just hung up the phone. "Hey Dad, you want chicken tonight?" His father held the phone in his hand, poised over the wall carriage, as though he had forgotten what to do with it. "Is everything okay?"

His father grinned as he hung up the phone. "Remember Connie Ryan?"

"No. Who is she?"

"Not she. Connie Ryan was a ballplayer. I pitched against him in the perfect game. He's the general manager of the Little Rock Lions. It's the Dodger's double-A affiliate."

"What did he want?"

"He said he'd heard about my coaching Holtville. Asked me if I might be interested in a job as their pitching coach."

Clayton steeled himself. First his mother, now Dancer was going to leave. Again. "You'd move to Little Rock?"

Dancer shook his head. "Told him no. I can't consider anything until our season's over. I made a commitment to coach those kids." Dancer picked up the menu. "Let's go for a bucket tonight. I'm hungry."

Clayton took a breath. "Are you sure? Holtville has time to find another coach." Clayton was amazed at his ability to argue for something that was the opposite of what he really wanted.

Dancer picked up the phone and handed it to Clayton. "You order. And get some extra biscuits and honey. I need to get cleaned up." He paused and smiled at Clayton. "I don't want to leave right now. Haven't finished my 'honey-do' list."

They had finished half of the bucket by the time Harry Reasoner came on with the ABC Nightly News at six. His lead story was a report by Peters Jennings from Clark Air Force Base on the POWs who had been released from North Vietnam.

Clayton put down his beer and edged closer to the television. Jennings described the flight over from Hanoi and then they showed the servicemen walking down the ramp. USN Captain Jeremiah Denton was the first man off the plane. He shook hands with the commander-in-chief of the Far East command and walked up to the microphone. With incredible poise he thanked everyone who had made this day possible. And when he finished with "God Bless America," Clayton felt his eyes welling with tears.

"Dede would have loved to have seen that," Dancer said. He blew his nose with one of the KFC napkins. "I got an idea." He jumped up and ran into the kitchen. He returned with a bottle of champagne and two wine glasses.

"Where did you get that?"

"We had it for when you came home from Vietnam. But then you sort of didn't come home, and we never got to open it. I think this is a good time." Dancer tucked the bottle under his armpit and twisted the cork out of the bottle. He filled one glass with champagne and filled the other from his Coke can.

"Not going to indulge?" Clayton asked.

"Nope. I'm staying up here on the wagon. More for you." He raised his glass.

"Oh my God!" Clayton was staring at the TV screen. They had finished reporting on the POWs who had been returned from Hanoi and were now showing the plane that had arrived later in the day with the men who had been held in South Vietnam by the Viet Cong. "Oh my God," he said again. "I can't believe it." He pointed at the third man off the plane. The soldier walked stiff-legged, but with a swagger that looked familiar to Dancer. "It's Victor, Dad! He's alive. The son of a bitch made it."

78

July 4, 1973

Dancer zipped up his gear bag and carried it down to the kitchen. He set it next to his clothes suitcase. He'd be able to get both bags in the passenger seat of the new pickup Jimmy sold him the previous week. Gave him a super deal on a midnight-blue F-100. A "year-end closeout" Jimmy said. If Dancer ended up taking the job in Little Rock, he could use the truck to haul the rest of his stuff down there. He didn't have that much.

Last week, after Holtville had won the state championship, Connie Ryan called again. He said his team would be back in Little Rock for a two week homestand starting July 5th. He needed to find a pitching coach now. Ryan told Dancer he needed help with a young hotshot the Dodgers wanted to move up to the big leagues before the end of the season. If Dancer came through this year, Ryan said there was a damn good chance he could move up to the triple-A club in Albuquerque next year. There were no guarantees, but the Dodgers were a first-rate organization that were loyal to their coaches and treated them well. Connie thought Dancer had a great chance of making it to the major league club if he made the commitment.

The major leagues. Dancer had tried to kill that dream a long time ago. It amazed him how quickly it came back to life. He was smarter now, though. Talk was cheap. Connie Ryan was a straight shooter, but Dancer needed to make sure of what he was getting into.

He said to Ryan, "I can make it down there by the fifth to check out the situation. If I think I can help and if you think an old Missouri hillbilly can get along with your crew, then I'd like to give it a shot. If it's not a good fit, I'll be out of your hair by the eighth."

Ryan agreed. He was confident Dancer was the right man for the job. "Once you get a taste of real southern hospitality, you ain't never going to want to go back," he said. "I'll see you first thing Friday morning."

Dancer had figured to leave early on the fourth so he'd get to Little Rock and have most of the day to get settled in and check out the town. But the Maple Springs city fathers had made Victor Sanchez the lead attraction in their Fourth of July parade, and Clayton wanted Dancer to come with him to the parade to honor his friend. Even if Dancer delayed his departure until the parade was over, he would still have time to get to Little Rock before dark.

Dancer filled Jimmy's old school book bag with a lunch and the scouting reports on the Little Rock pitchers, which Connie Ryan had mailed him so he could prepare. He walked back through the house one more time to see if there was anything else he needed. He stopped at the hutch and picked up the framed photo of Clayton on his shoulders as they marched around the field after the perfect game. Next to that, Dede had one of those department store photographs of her and the boys. Clayton must have been fifteen at the time – he had that know-it-all smirk. Jimmy was ten and smiling as if there were nothing he wanted more than to be in this family photo wearing a stiff sports coat and a clip-on tie. Dede sat dead-center wearing her church dress and staring straight into the camera with those crazy blue eyes. Her smile was coy, as if she knew something no one else knew.

Dancer put the family photo back on the hutch and picked up the baseball photo again. When he closed his eyes he could feel Clayton's sticky hands and hot breath on his neck. He set it down and stuffed the family photo in the bag.

With all the traffic and limited parking, Dancer decided it would be quicker to leave the truck at home and walk to the parade. It was only a mile and a half and Clayton and Trudy had gone ahead to save a spot. It was perfect Fourth of July weather. Not a cloud in the sky. The winds from the night before had blown the humidity down to Arkansas, and even at mid-morning the air was still cool. Dancer strolled up Hill Street past the Indian Hills development where he'd discovered Dede with Joyce. He tried to remember which of those houses had been the model home, but all the houses looked so different now. He wasn't sure anymore.

Another ten minutes and he had reached the top of the hill and the Camelot Square development. That had been the exclusive place to live in Maple Springs, but now it was more of a stepping stone. Those that had really made it were building bigger houses on four and five acres lots outside of town. As he headed down the other side of the hill, he could see the parade forming at the west end of Main Street. He heard the squawk of a loudspeaker announcing the start of the parade, the pop of firecrackers, the cacophony of the marching bands, and the drum and bugle corps warming up.

Clayton and Trudy had staked out a prime spot right in front of Crutchfield's General Store. Clayton put his beer cooler in Dancer's folding chair, which was flanked by him and Trudy.

"You saving that seat for someone?" Dancer said as he stepped up behind Trudy.

"Dancer!" Trudy said. She jumped up from her seat and hugged him around the waist.

Clayton hauled the cooler off the chair and set it on the curb. "Want a Coke, Dad?" He handed him a can.

"Thanks," Dancer said. He took the can and settled down in the folding chair. The parade was two blocks away and heading their way. At the front of the parade a banner carried by two husky and sweating high school boys announced the Maple Springs Drum and Bugle Corps. The boys were flanked by baton twirlers and followed by a phalanx of drummers and horn players.

"Did you get packed?" Clayton asked, leaning in close to Dancer so he could be heard over the din.

"Yeah, I'm all set."

"Hey, Clayton!" Alex Doyle was standing on the opposite side of Main Street, holding a can of beer with one hand and waving at them with the other. He glanced to the right and left and quick-stepped across the street, weaving effortlessly through the rows of drummers, like he was part of the choreography.

"You idiot," Clayton said, as Alex pulled the beer cooler over and sat on it.

As Clayton and Alex talked, Trudy leaned over and whispered in Dancer's ear. "He doesn't want you to go. He's trying to be all business-like and grown-up, but he really wants you to stay."

"It's just a look see," Dancer said. "I might be back by Monday, so don't be moving all my stuff to the attic just yet."

Trudy grinned at him, like he had just said something very foolish. "They're never going to let you come back. You're too good. I just wish you were working for the Cardinals instead of those sucky Dodgers."

Dancer laughed. "Hey, at least it's not the Cubs."

"If it were the Cubs, we wouldn't let you come back."

Twenty yards behind the drum and bugle corps was the VFW contingent. In the front row were the three surviving vets from World War I, then several rows of World War II and Korean Vets, and following them was a caravan of convertibles carrying the Vietnam Vets.

"Here comes Jimmy, driving your new bartender," Clayton said to Dancer. Jimmy was driving Victor Sanchez in a burgundy 1958 Lincoln Mark III convertible that had been provided by Wendell Baker from his classic car collection. Victor, dressed in his Marine dress blues, sat on the top of the

backseat and waved to the crowd like he was running for
governor. He had a million dollar smile.

When Victor returned to Maple Springs in early May,
Dancer hired him as a bartender and bouncer. Victor had broken
his leg when his helicopter crashed and it had never been
properly set. He would always have a limp, but he told Dancer
that was a small price to pay. He was a hard worker and Dancer
told Jake if he did decide to take the Little Rock job, Victor
could replace him. "He's honest and well-liked. And he'll be a
better bouncer than me. Nobody wants to mess with him," he
said.

As Victor's car approached, the spectators who were seated
stood up. Alex pumped his fist in the air and let out a whoop. He
nudged Clayton in the shoulder. "How come you're not out
there?"

Clayton shrugged.

Trudy slid in front of Dancer and wrapped her arm around
Clayton. "Hey, Victor!" she yelled.

Her shrill voice cut through the motorcycle backfires and
the firecrackers and the band noise. Victor jerked his head
around. "Yo, Clayton! Get up here." He patted the seat top next
to him.

Clayton shook his head, his lips pressed tight. He squared
himself and crisply saluted Victor. He held the salute as the car
rolled past. Victor stopped smiling and snapped off a salute.
"Hoo rah, brother. Semper fi."

a bicycle brigade, a mounted squad from the 4-H Club, and then all of the civic organizations from the K of C, to Kiwanis, to Elks. Trudy sat in Clayton's lap as the parade wound down. "Jeez, how many clubs do they have in this town?" she said. "I'm surprised there's anybody left to watch."

It was the kind of thing Dede might have said, and it gave Dancer a quick pang. Those memory shots weren't quite as frequent as they had been in the first weeks after Dede's death, but he didn't think they would ever stop. He didn't want them to. He looked at his watch. It was nearly one p.m. Time to go.

"I'm going to head back to the house now," he said to Clayton. "Are you going on to the picnic?" Ted Landis had sponsored a picnic at Landis Park – food, drinks, games for the kids, and a softball challenge match between the youngsters and the oldsters.

Trudy stood up and hugged him. "You can't leave yet. Those old guys are going to need your help."

Dancer smiled. "They'll do fine without me." He looked at Clayton. "Are you playing?"

"Oh yeah. We're going to kick some serious old-timer ass."

It had been a long time since he'd seen Clayton play ball. He thought of all the games he missed, but he didn't want to get to Little Rock in the middle of the night. "Sorry. I'm going to miss that, but I better get on the road before I lose my nerve."

Clayton nodded. "You're going to do great, Dad." His voice broke.

Dancer put his hand on Clayton's shoulder. "We'll see how it goes." He pulled his son to him and they embraced like Dancer was leaving for a lifetime.

A half hour later, Dancer had loaded his truck. As he backed out of the driveway, he debated with himself. He could head down Hill Street, and he'd be on US 60 headed for Little Rock in five minutes. Or he could go the other direction, up the hill, and cut over to 173 on Harris. That would take him right by Landis Park. Wouldn't hurt to stop for five minutes and just check out the game.

He headed up over the hill to Harris Street. He took the ramp on to 173, and from the overpass, he could see the softball diamond. It was like having a seat in the left field bleachers. He pulled the truck over, snug to the guardrail, and got out. The oldsters had just been retired and Alex Doyle was leading off. On the first pitch, he hit a weak line drive over the first basemen's head and loafed into first base. Now, just like when they were kids, Clayton was up. He swung viciously at the first pitch and almost corkscrewed himself into the ground.

Settle down, Clayton. Let the ball come to you.

Clayton stared out at left field and flexed his shoulders. The next pitch arced toward him. Clayton stepped into it and pasted a rocket shot over the left fielder's head.

Dancer leaned forward almost tumbling over the guardrail. The centerfielder raced across to cut off the ball before it reached the fence. Clayton had rounded second and was running, head down, going for the homerun. The outfielder scooped the ball on the run and fired it to the shortstop in shallow left field. He wheeled and threw a strike to the plate.

Clayton was barreling down the third base line, headed for home. The base coach held up his hands, and Clayton slammed on the brakes He retreated to third just as the catcher caught the throw from the shortstop.

Dancer got back in his truck. "Should have gone for it," he said. Gravel spit from his rear tires as he pulled off the shoulder on to the highway. He checked his mirror to see if anyone was coming up behind him, but all he could see was the trail of dust he had kicked up.

A Note from the Author

I want to thank Jon and Amana Katora of Hark! New Era Publishing for epublishing American Past Time. Working with them has been a wonderful experience.

In September 2003 I signed up for an introductory writing class at the University of Chicago's Graham School taught by Barbara Croft. Barbara was generous with her advice and offered me just enough encouragement to keep trying.

I have participated in writers workshops at the Iowa Festival, Tin House, Squaw Valley, Skidmore, Norman Mailer, Sewanee and Bread Loaf. These summer escapes provided me an opportunity to improve my craft, and even more importantly, a chance to make new friends.

The Zoetrope Virtual Studio has been my "workplace" since 2004. Through Zoetrope I met Ania Vesenny. Ania has read almost everything I have written. Her favorite word is "cut" which is why this novel is only 400 pages instead of a thousand.

I am very grateful for my Chicago-based novel workshop group who have read this novel through all its versions. Thank you Jill Svoboda, Anny Rusk and Ben Balskus.

Finally, I want to thank my family. My sisters Kendra, Carol and Christine who encouraged me, my children, Stephen, Nicole and Christie, who vastly expanded my understanding of how the world works and my wife Suzanne who allowed me to indulge this pursuit.